Midnight in Memphis

Midnight in Memphis

A Mystery

Thomas Dann

NEW YORK

Published in the United States by Crooked Lane Books, an imprint of The Quick Brown Fox & Company LLC.

Library of Congress Catalog-in-Publication data available upon request.

ISBN (hardcover): 979-8-89242-384-7
ISBN (paperback): 979-8-89242-385-4
ISBN (ebook): 979-8-89242-386-1

Cover design by Crooked Lane Books

Printed in the United States.

www.crookedlanebooks.com

Crooked Lane Books
34 West 27th St., 10th Floor
New York, NY 10001

First Edition: November 2025

The authorized representative in the EU for product safety and compliance is eucomply OÜPärnu mnt 139b-14, 11317 Tallinn, Estonia, hello@eucompliancepartner.com, +33757690241

10 9 8 7 6 5 4 3 2 1

To Melissa

Won't somebody tell me, answer if you can,
Won't somebody tell me, what is the soul of a man?
I'm going to ask the question, answer if you can,
If anybody here can tell me, what is the soul of a man?

—*Soul of a Man*, Blind Willie Johnson, 1930

Prologue

I'm standing in this water wishing that I had a boat,
I'm standing in this water wishing that I had a boat,
The only way I see is to take my clothes and float.

—*The Flood*, Sippie Wallace, 1927

Bad things happen when the Mississippi crests. The old Choctaws called it Misha Sipokni, the River Whose Age Is Beyond Knowing, and anyone standing with dry feet on high ground would agree it's a force beyond the reckoning of mere mortals. The river is elemental and takes whatever it wants, traces of the whole continent: mountains, glacial valleys, and endless plains, anything not nailed down, including the cluttered debris of humankind itself, swept down from all those cities and towns toward the Gulf of Mexico in a colossal cleansing absolution, a divine hand taking body and blood for the remission or concealment of sins.

It's docile enough during the quiet summer months, twisting out across the floodplain, a big brown cottonmouth sunning itself on drowsy afternoons, and up-close outsiders might even think it was just a muddy, mile-wide lake hemmed in by those far-off sandy shores, sleepy except for the gentle eddies that swirl and ripple endlessly south. But as with the rest of Creation, what is most real lies below the surface. Even at low water, the river runs a hundred feet deep, and they say the riverbed itself is a netherworld halfway between a dream and a nightmare. Back in the steamboat days a few crazy souls actually walked the bottom in diving bells trying to salvage riverboat wrecks. What they found was almost a figment of imagination, a yard-deep rush of moving sand where nothing was solid, and with each step what you thought was rock bottom was instantly spirited away underfoot, as if you were standing on nothing at all.

Come flood season the big river unmasks its true self, and on this question, there is no small disagreement among the God-fearing folk of the floodplain. What the moody Methodists see as a sure case of your cosmic insignificance, the fire and brimstone tent preachers declare is the vengeful hand of the Almighty Creator punishing your wicked ways. Either way, every spring the river's crest surges into a creeping, unstoppable inland tidal wave sweeping downstream. The channel overflows its banks across miles of bottomlands and cotton fields until it laps up against the levees where anxious townspeople wait for the crest, staring while their flood gauges disappear into dark waters inching toward the sandbagged levee tops.

Of course the truth is, this is a ritual as old as human habitation itself, going back thousands of years to those first peoples, the ancient Mississippians, who escaped the floods by clamoring onto the mammoth earthen mounds they built from the Minnesota headwaters to the Gulf, pyramids for whatever chiefs or gods held sway back then. And you can bet that just like today they watched those muddy waters rise and stretch to the horizon, leaving them marooned on their self-made islands in the middle of an endless brown sea.

But the real show is out in the channel where the raw power of the river makes the hand-wringing back on the levee tops look like child's play. The flow quickens from an unhurried glide to a churning torrent. Massive trees sweep downriver like battering rams, fierce hydraulics spawn vortexes that can swallow a rowboat whole or spit out logs like toothpicks, and violent upwellings billow to the surface in liquid brown cumulus clouds disgorging whatever secrets the river chooses to yield. They say if you work on the Mississippi, this is when life becomes much more interesting, and almighty dangerous.

Milo Tate, deckhand on the *Queen of Cairo*, was thinking just that, taking a last drag on his hand-rolled cigarette while the tugboat nudged a fully loaded coal barge downriver forty-five river miles north of Vicksburg. It was late March, and the river was at high flow from the northern snow melt and spring rains. The barge stretched out ahead of him, a charcoal gray football field that seemed to absorb all the light as the tug's powerful engines surged toward the center of the channel. This was Milo's ninth year on the river. Before that, fresh back from the war in Europe, he had worked a stint in a cotton gin in Indianola just outside of Greenville. Then he started drinking, lost a finger in the baling machine, got fired, and drank more. He hit rock bottom, feeling sorry for himself and his stub, and it was Captain Billy that saved him. Captain Billy's wife, Justine, was Tate's second cousin once removed on his daddy's side. She always liked Milo, God knows why, and Milo figured she must have pestered Captain Billy something fierce until he grudgingly hired Milo as his "third mate."

As Milo saw it, the *Queen* was ugly as sin, but not a complete rust bucket neither. Old tires lashed around her bow and gunwales combined with peeling paint and surface rust to make the boat look as if she belonged in the scrapyard, but looking closer she was always scrubbed clean and shipshape. And while at first glance the cluttered deck seemed to be a disaster, the piles of coiled hawsers were carefully arranged and ready when needed to manhandle the barges. In the cramped and dingy crew quarters the stench of cigarettes and diesel fuel had left a yellow patina on the faded centerfolds thumbtacked to the walls, but the galley was always stainless steel spotless and the food not half bad. And what mattered most, the engine room, was "Justine pristine," as Captain Billy liked to say. No dirt, no grime, just 2700 horsepower of well-oiled precision steel chugging away at 1000 rpms, sending comforting vibrations up through the *Queen*'s bones.

The *Queen* gave Milo a roof over his head and kept him mostly sober owing to Captain Billy's banning booze from the boat. In fact, as long as Milo's tobacco pouch and rolling papers held up, the quiet life of a boatman was A-OK. It suited a man with nine fingers and no ambitions. He never aspired to work his way up to river pilot, which appeared to be a sentiment universally shared by Captain Billy and the other two crew members Jamie and Jay. So Milo paid little attention to the sandbars, towheads, and cutbacks that kept Captain Billy and the JJs on alert in the wheelhouse, and they never sought his opinion. To Milo, one bend in the river looked pretty much the same as the next. The tedium was offset only by the happy truth that most times the work was brain-dead easy, he was actually earning good dough watching that boring scenery scroll by, and if he stayed away from the wheelhouse stud game, he'd have a nice fat bankroll to blow when they finally reached New Orleans again.

Plus, there was the music. Captain Billy and Jamie had jury-rigged a few scratchy old speakers inside the crew quarters and even outside the wheelhouse. You could hear the radio from most anywhere on the boat. And when it came to music, Milo was the river pilot and even Captain Billy had come to refer to him as their "Captain of the Airwaves." So instead of measuring the *Queen*'s progress on the river by charts and buoys, Milo had come to measure river miles by radio stations. St. Louis was

WMOX, which faded into KFVS near Cape Girardeau followed by WHBQ in Memphis, and so on. He knew the end of their journey was near at last when WWL in New Orleans crackled within range, booming its 50,000 watts of power across the whole lower Mississippi Valley.

During his time on the *Queen*, Milo had been riding a great confluence of American music, each tributary of the Mississippi bringing with it music carried down from its catch basin. Lonely high plains ballads floated in on the Missouri. Old-time country and bluegrass poured down the Cumberland and Ohio. Hillbilly tunes chimed in from the Arkansas River. Delta blues streamed in on the Yazoo, and western swing joined the beat from the Red River—and, of course, there was gospel raining down from everywhere—all flowing together down to the Great Conjoining of Good Times in New Orleans.

These days especially, there was a whole lot of mixing and matching going on. To Milo it was as if this year, 1955, was the year it all was finally coming together, with white bands singing "race music" dressed up as country and hillbilly, and colored singers showing up on the white stations. Milo's favorite disk jockeys up and down the river seemed to have their fingers on the pulse. Johnnie "Howlin'" Howell on KFVS, Dewey Taylor on "The Q" out of Memphis, and Bill "Hillbilly" Hall's Rockabilly Hour down in Vicksburg. These were toe-tapping times, and Milo took it as his solemn duty to navigate the shoals of sound for the *Queen*'s captain and crew. Jump blues and bebop, swing bands and rockabilly. Whatever was out there, it was all part of his Big Muddy Hit Parade.

Unfortunately, today this stretch of the river was an airwaves wasteland. The only radio station he could dial into was the scratchy sound of Delta blues from WROX in Clarksdale. Milo was guessing that it was only another oxbow or two before they could leave that race music behind and pick up the country station in Vicksburg, so he bided his time as the WROX disk jockey called out Tommy "Snake" Johnson's "Cool Drink of Water Blues":

> *I asked her for water, and she gave me gasoline.*
> *Man, that's the evilest woman that I ever seen.*

Ain't it the truth, Milo thought, remembering that acid-tongued Alice he had left behind in Natchez way back when. Life on shore sometimes felt like wrestling a porcupine. I'll take the simple life on this old river any time, he mused. Ain't no porcupines here.

Leaning on the tug's rusty gunwale, he watched a hundred-foot-long sycamore tree bucking in the barge's wake as if it was angry at the rumbling intruder that had invaded its realm, and he found himself thinking that it was—most definitely—good to be on a big boat. As he stared down absently at how the murky waters reflected the low-hanging gray March sky, he shivered off a chill. Even after these many years on the water, there still were times when the big river felt spooky fearsome. Then, as if summoned by his dark thoughts from the turbid depths below, the pale and bloated body of a woman ghosted to the surface. Quickly reaching for a boat hook, Milo managed to snag the swollen corpse at the last moment before the barge and its tender swept past. Barges on the Mississippi River stopped for almost nothing, and definitely not for the occasional floater.

Chapter 1

Storm Brewing

So, tell me who's that writin', John the Revelator,
Tell me who's that writin', John the Revelator,
Wrote the Book of the Seven Seals.

—*John the Revelator,* traditional

Burdett Vance leaned back, feet up on his desk, fingering the day's first Lucky Strike and wondering what the world was coming to. He was midway through his ritual perusal of Memphis's morning paper, the *Commerce Daily*, which he usually laid side by side with yesterday's edition of the *Memphis Press-Scimitar*, the competing evening newspaper. The *Daily*'s editors apparently believed their readers had not yet tired of headlines like "Commie Threat Keeps Citizens Alert" and "Memphis on Top 20 A-Bomb List," and on that Burdett agreed. People never stopped being afraid, and fear sold papers, no doubt about it.

As Burdett idly blew another smoke ring that spiraled upward into the shafts of pale sunlight streaming through the window blinds, he contemplated how mushroom clouds exuded a kind of terrible, mesmerizing beauty. The newsreels of A-bomb detonations held the same guilty fascination as a burning barn or a house disintegrating before the rush of flood waters; all were instinctively hypnotic, speaking to something buried millennia deep in the human brain. Burdett thought of it as just part of the cycle of Creation and Destruction that had been going on since time began, and from where he sat, it seemed as if Destruction held the edge. On the other hand, the whirling smoke ring rising in the shaft of sunlight before him seemed to be about the most peaceful, harmless, and delicate thing in Creation.

It brought to mind his very first smoke, him only nine years old out back in the shade of the corn crib with Eli, pretending that lit stubs of dried grapevines were cigars and blowing dueling smoke rings. But that was ages ago, and Eli was long dead. More than one lifetime had passed since then, he thought, casting his gaze around the room at the gray life he now lived.

The Memphis Homicide Division was on the fourth floor of Police Central, a neoclassical building in downtown Memphis that stood three blocks uphill from the Mississippi River, across Second Street from the Shelby County Courthouse. Burdett's window looked down on the courthouse steps flanked by the faux Grecian statues of "Wisdom" and "Justice," which to Burdett's mind were iffy propositions given the goings-on he had seen in that building. The squad room was crowded with a dozen battered and ink-stained oak desks that had been there since Central was built back in the twenties. Every desk was furnished with the standard-issue black telephone, oak swivel chair, mug full of pencils, and metal ashtray. Sometimes Burdett thought the butts that endlessly overflowed the ashtrays were standard issue too. The place smelled of old wood, stale cigarettes, and sweat.

Half of the desks were now occupied by other members of the squad who had been trailing in for the past hour. Jimbo

Stark was already thunderously working the phone, ham hands gripping the receiver and pounding his desk, while his partner Otis Bledsoe was studiously buried in his files, angular fingers nervously fiddling with his pencil. They made an odd pair but somehow it worked. Bobby Tyler and his partner Doug "Digger" Jones had been in and out already, getting started early to catch a witness before he left home for work. Digger's nickname was owing to an unfortunate case where he dug up a suspect's whole backyard vegetable garden looking for the body of the missing wife, only to find her home from a bender and standing quietly behind him on the back porch watching him go at it while smoking a cigarette with a smirk. As usual, the desks of Earl Ricketts and Chuck Renfro were empty. They came in late and left early because they could.

And then there was Harley Suggs, Burdett's partner. Burdett nodded as Harley plodded by, obliterating a perfectly good smoke ring as he tossed his hat onto the heap of papers that cluttered his desk. Harley was short and fireplug thick, with a large head and hands that oddly suited his stubble-cut red hair. He wore a nonstop hopeful grin of the ear-to-ear variety, expectant like he had just told a joke and was waiting for you to laugh. Harley wordlessly hooked a butt out of Burdett's pack and shambled back to his desk. It was their morning routine. They'd known each other since they were kids at Hume High, after Burdett moved up to Memphis for good to live with his uncle back in '27. They went separate ways after high school; Burdett ended up spending the last of his small inheritance to go to college at Memphis State while Harley hunkered down and became a beat cop.

But the war had level-set all that. It was Harley who had convinced Burdett to join the MPD after they mustered out. Some said Harley had done himself a big favor teaming up with

Burdett because Harley finally started to climb the ladder in the department. The two of them eventually made detective rank to work homicides together. Partners now for six years, they had settled into the unconscious habits of an old married couple. People around the department called them the Glance Brothers, owing to Harley's habit of constantly glancing at his partner to gauge his reaction, which Burdett had come to expect and reciprocate. Harley had a certain animal cunning, but at heart he was uncomplicated, which Burdett supposed was what he liked best about him. Sometimes Burdett saw Harley as his alter ego from a simpler parallel universe that could have been his, if life had played out differently. So Burdett chose to appreciate Harley's untroubled mind and ignore his shortcomings.

A quick glance at their desks told the story. Harley's was piled high with all the paperwork he never quite finished, and Burdett knew that eventually he would be the one who would have to do it. The only paperwork Burdett could pry out of Harley was to finish the reports on cleared cases, the fun part. Harley's ebullient personality presumed a certain entitlement to happiness, and everyone, including Burdett, instinctively wanted a piece of it. The flip side was a telltale obliviousness to the human misery around him. Maybe that made him a natural for homicide work. In any case, the combination of the two of them worked, and together they had the best close record in Homicide.

"Hey, Bird Dog, sports page." Without looking up, Burdett nudged that section of the paper in Harley's direction. Another part of their routine. "Thanks, bud." Creaking in his swivel chair, Harley stretched back sluggishly from his desk and was barely able to snag the newspaper without getting up. Then he propped up his feet on the only corner of his desk that was clear and kicked back. Burdett suspected that Harley kept the desk corner clear for precisely that purpose.

In ritual silence they buried themselves back in the papers. Burdett turned next to the previous evening's *Press-Scimitar*, generally considered the more progressive of the two newspapers, and below the fold he spotted another Winslow Hogue article about how, after forty-five years, the "compulsively corrupt Crump Machine" was finally on its last legs, what with Boss Crump now cold in his grave. Yeah, Winslow, maybe so, thought Burdett, but from where Burdett sat, it was more a question of whether they were putting a new name on the same old crony crew or putting a new passel of cronies in the mayor's office to take their turn feeding at the same old trough. Edward H. Crump was sworn in as mayor in '09, hand on the Bible, preaching reform just like this new crowd, but it wasn't long before he owned pretty much everything and everybody. He especially owned votes.

Familiar sights on Election Day were the busloads of "Crump's Crew," serial voters ferried from polling place to polling place. Courtesy of Boss Crump, they had poll-tax receipts in hand so they could vote at each stop—the receipts conveniently financed from payoffs to the Machine by saloon owners. And there was the promise of a big party after the polls closed, with a half pint of whisky for every man to take home at the end. Crump had a street-by-street card index of voters, and do not even think about a city job unless your name was in the right column in the voting records. The 98-percent winning election margins said it all; elections had the outcomes that Boss Crump chose, and nothing got done without his approval. All in the name of "e-fficient gub'ment," as he called it, his so-called "greater good," and even his naysayers had to agree that he had delivered. Streets got paved, parks were created, flood control happened, and the fire and police departments were expanded. After a while, the Boss did not even need to hold public office himself. So he happily ran things from his perch up on the top floor at E. H. C. Insurance Company, with a big picture window looking down on the steps of City Hall six floors below, watching the mortals' comings and goings. Zeus from up on Mount Olympus. And in the last ten years, Zeus's hand had been squeezing tighter and tighter at the necks of the mortals. Critics like Winslow Hogue called it a dictatorship. Every civic organization from the Shriners to the City Beautiful Commission was controlled by Crump people; his army of informers was everywhere.

As Boss Crump grew old and his power waned, he became more autocratic and abusive. Funny how that happens. If you worked for the city government, including the police—especially the police—you "volunteered" to work on the Machine's political campaigns for free or got reassigned to the graveyard shift. Citizens who failed to buy rat insurance from E. H. C. Insurance found predatory city inspectors at their doorsteps citing them for illegally harboring *ratus ratus*. Shop owners on Main Street who protested the lack of city services were suddenly provided those services in the form of construction crews tearing up the sidewalks in front of their stores to keep customers away. And somehow the tax assessments on property owned by dissenters were "updated" to be twice as high as their more cooperative neighbors. Accepting a Boss Crump favor was always a Faustian bargain, with an unknown price to be paid in an uncertain future. With informants in every corner, Boss Crump seemed omnipresent, and no transgression was too small to avoid his wrath. It was the principle of the thing.

Bottom line was, don't cross the Boss or you'll get burned. Burdett had flown dangerously close to that flame five years earlier when the Tennessee Children's Home Society scandal had shaken Memphis to its roots. The society was operated for decades by its proprietor Georgia Tann as a Catholic charity, but it actually was a front for her black-market baby adoption racket. They finagled thousands of white babies from poor mothers and sold them to wealthy families all over the country, including movie stars and even members of the Crump Machine—especially members of the Crump Machine. The million-dollar child trafficking scheme was eventually exposed, along with over 500 suspicious infant deaths, which is where Burdett came into the picture. He was new to Homicide at that point and was just starting to investigate the many unmarked graves clustered in a corner of Elmwood Cemetery and in the woods near the Home itself when the word came down not to go there. Tann was well insinuated into Memphis society, fashioning herself as a modern-day Florence Nightingale, and Machine friends were implicated in the tainted adoptions. But as Burdett saw it, too many "unmarketable" babies appeared to have died while the more marketable blue-eyed cherubs thrived and garnered premium prices. So he began gearing up the investigation anyway. After disinterring the first ten babies, all they had to show for the effort were ten piles of tiny bones and a baffled shrug from the medical examiner's office. Natural causes, by which they meant they couldn't tell. It still did not smell right, and Burdett readied himself to dig up the next ten. Then in a classic case of karmic justice, Tann died of uterine cancer—at least that was the official story. By that time, the state police had moved in and Burdett was pulled off the case, but his resistance was enough to brand him as no team player, which Burdett rightfully reckoned was a fair point.

Another brush with the Machine occurred almost back to back with the first one and ultimately proved to be a good thing—although Burdett avoided calamity only by being light-footed and lucky. He was chasing a theory that there was a killer working the black community, but he could not get anyone's attention in the department. The chief said it was a matter of "resources," but it was really a matter of "who gives a shit if another darkie goes down, just one less darkie," as one of his colleagues had put it. Burdett was told to stop riling the black community with scary rumors, and apparently that came all the way from the top, "from the Boss hisself." Turns out that with a tight election coming up, Boss Crump wanted to keep a lid on things rather than risk having the preachers up on their pulpits crying foul. But blacks were still dying.

Harley, being no martyr, stepped back from the investigation and kept his head down, but Burdett kept getting anonymous tips that pulled him further into the investigation, and when he stubbornly kept plugging away on his own, bad things started happening to him. Threatening calls, tires slashed, anonymous complaints filed. Things got tense. Then the son of one of Boss Crump's own house servants turned up dead. In a twisted way, that was Burdett's lucky break, and he suspected that Bessie Crump, also known as Miz Boss, had something to do with it when word came down from the Boss to let Burdett run with the investigation. In the end, Boss Crump was doubly grateful when Burdett managed to catch the culprit and close the case in time for the election, and Burdett gave all the credit to Crump, which the Boss accepted as tribute to the king. The press loved it. Boss Crump dubbed Burdett "my bird dog Burdett 'cause he don't never give up 'til he finds that ole bird," and the name stuck.

And indeed, the Boss was definitely one to take care of those who took care of him. Burdett still vividly recalled his one and only meeting with Crump. It was up in Crump's headquarters at the insurance company. He was surprised at how austere the office was. Strictly business, no pomp, four black phones on a massive desk, framed by that big window looking down on City Hall. And there was Boss Crump himself, all six-feet-five of him, unruly mane of white hair, big ears, cleft chin. And those clear blue eyes, amplified by ogled spectacles, peering out from under bushy white eyebrows and looking right through you. Then there was the large hand extended in warm greeting, followed by the other hand to wrap the handshake as if an unspoken pact had just been sealed, like it or not. In his surprisingly high, clipped voice, Boss Crump apologized for any "misunderstandin'" about the investigation and laid it off on an overzealous chief of police.

"Don't be mindin' him. That man's mind is as warped and out of shape with peevishment as a bale of cotton with three hoops off. He was just tryin' to make me happy, but you already done that. Just keep up the good work, Bird Dog."

With a wink of his eye, the Boss made Burdett his coconspirator, and Burdett had to admit to himself that once Crump turned on the charm, you could not help liking him. Leaving that meeting, he had finally understood how Crump had done it, beguiling the city while he squeezed it dry.

Boss Crump had been laid to rest in Elmwood Cemetery back in October, but like a ghost stubbornly lingering in its haunting ground, a specter of power, greed, and money still moved over the city. Now with the mayoral election approaching in the fall—the first after Crump's death—the scramble was on. It turned out that many of those GIs coming home from fighting the fascists in Europe did not take so kindly anymore to the home-grown, political boss variety that had reigned over Memphis for decades. Mussolini and Boss Crump had both made the trains and streetcars run on time, but so what? The entrenched Machine operatives who still ruled from the mayor's office and the County Commission were fighting hard to fend off the reformers while fighting each other for control of the Machine organization. Alliances were shifting as constantly as a kaleidoscope, where every edition of the *Commerce Daily* or the *Press-Scimitar* promised a new and multifaceted peek at the political landscape. It was a time ripe with opportunity, in a city rife with opportunists.

After a few minutes of silence, Burdett sensed that his partner was looking at him.

"What?"

"Bird Dog, didya ever think about takin' a break," Harley looked around the office, "from all this?"

"Why do that? After all, what's our motto here? 'Homicide's the place to be in Memphis friggin' Tennessee.' With this town being called the Murder Capital of the whole damn country, I'd say that's true. But why you askin'?" Harley started to answer when the phone rang on Burdett's desk.

"Howdy, Burdett, it's Frankie down in Vicksburg." That was Frank Babcock, his counterpart 250 miles south in the Vicksburg sheriff's office. "Looks like we got us another one of yours, my big city friend. Picked up yesterday north of here by one of the river tugs. We're bettin' two-to-one it got dumped off the Han-ra-han Bridge up there 'bout a week ago." Babcock had an annoying habit of drawing out certain words for emphasis. "Leastways, bein' found upriver, it sure don't come from Vicksburg. Now don't ya be tellin' me y'all cain't send one of yer fellas down here to pick it up too-day. It's really stinkin' up the place."

"Dumped off the bridge or jumped off the bridge, Frankie? Who says homicide? And how come you call me direct? You know we got a rotation up here. I'm busy."

"Bullet in the head makes me guess it might just possibly be un-na-tur-al causes, wise guy, and I reckon your higher-ups say this un's got your name on it, so that's the ro-tay-shun for ya." Burdett cursed silently. Assignment of cases in Homicide was supposed to rotate between the four detective teams, so this must be the chief dumping on them again to free up his stooges Rickets and Renfro for those "special projects."

"Okay, I'll get someone to make the run this morning. Just have it wrapped and ready. Any ID?"

"Nothin'. But get this. Stiff has a pair of silk stockin's knotted round her neck, and if you can believe it, stuffed inside is a beer bottle with a note corked up in it. That's a new one, dum-ditty. We didn't touch nothin', a course. Figured you'd wanna do that."

"You mean you figured you didn't want to dirty up your pretty fingers with the maggots."

"Hey, I done my share of rotters too, bozo." Yeah, yeah, Burdett thought as he rang off. He had no doubt that Frankie's curiosity had already gotten the better of him and he had taken a peek at the note. This one already sounded like yet another suicide bridge jumper, although the message in the bottle was an interesting touch. With any luck it was a suicide note that would close the case, bullet in the brain regardless. In any case, if the body washed down as far as Vicksburg, it could have been in the water for who knows how long. So it may have splashed in anywhere along the hundreds of miles of riverbank downstream or upstream from Memphis. Maybe it had nothing to do with Memphis at all. This could be a quick wrap either way. Without hanging up the receiver he dialed Jimmy Blake in the coroner's office to get a truck rolling. When he got off, Harley was just hanging up his phone too.

"Lieutenant Miller says the chief wants to see us," Harley said, and without another word he walked stiffly out the door toward the stairway. Already pondering next steps on the Vicksburg case, Burdett followed him upstairs to whatever awaited them in the grand offices of Chief Casper P. Donlough, where nothing good ever happened.

CHAPTER 2

Casper's Dictum

I'm going away, baby, take me seven long months to ride,
January, February, March, April, May, June, July,
Baby, when I marry, going to marry an Indian girl,
Big chief Lord be my daddy-in-law.

—*Big Chief Blues*, Furry Lewis, 1927

Harley once asked Burdett what a hog must be thinking as he is led to slaughter. At the time Burdett took it to be a fair question; the fact that Harley had even asked it showed he knew hogs up close, and this Burdett knew to be a fact. As long as Burdett could remember, Harley's family had kept a hog or two out back, even after they moved to town. And anyone who knows hogs understands that within the natural confines of their wallowing natures, hogs are smart and sentient souls. So Burdett was genuinely curious as to what metaphysical insight Harley might bring to the inner life of a doomed pig.

"A pig walkin' to the gallows," Harley began with authority, "is not thinkin' 'bout the gallows at all 'cause no pig never comes back from the slaughterhouse to tell about it. But pigs pick up stuff. They smell your thoughts sometimes, 'specially if they'd know'd you since they was piglets. So, I'm guessin' that this pig is likely strainin' his mind to understand that whiff of somethin' different in what *you're* thinkin' or feelin'. Always gives me the creeps."

Burdett had rolled his eyes at the time, thinking that if you're going to go down the road of personifying pigs, you might as well stop eating bacon. But now, making his way past the assembled petitioners waiting outside the chief's office, Burdett himself was catching a whiff in the air, in the way eyes synchronously averted, voices abruptly hushed, and scribbling pens paused for a beat. Lieutenant Marshall "Marshmallow" Miller was among the bootlicks. He was tall, thin, and melancholy as dust. The lines in his face trailed down from the corners of his mouth giving him a perpetual hangdog frown, and his flat voice droned so slowly that Burdett was forever tempted to finish his sentences for him. He was Burdett's nominal boss, but everyone knew that Donlough ran the show and Marshmallow was only a fawning factotum, presiding over the goings-on of the Homicide Division with the slightly bent eagerness of an overattentive undertaker. The hooded flicker in Miller's eyes when he saw Burdett said everything. Something was up, and everyone but Burdett and Harley seemed to know about it.

As they entered the chief's office, Donlough was standing framed in a window flanked by plush floor-to-ceiling drapes. The office air was thick with the reek of Donlough's cheap cologne, and the morning sunlight streamed in behind him as if it was stage lighting. Donlough's large corner office had a view of the river and was all dark wood and deep rugs, devoid of the battered regulation furniture and scuffed linoleum motif that graced every other office in Police Central. Buttoned up in his custom blue uniform with the extra braiding, Donlough was porcine, ruddy cheeked, and peculiarly animated. He had darting badger's eyes that missed nothing, and when his jaws worked, every bone in his face moved all at once, which was all the time because he was constantly popping Chiclets and chomping away, mouthing a silent "gotcha, gotcha, gotcha."

Donlough was one of Boss Crump's boys from way back. Buzz was that he was in play with both the old guard and the reformers in the quiet struggle for Machine control. Talking big about honest government and "ree-foam" but cutting crafty cotton broker deals that were good as gold until they weren't. Business as usual. He treated the whole department as his personal plantation: everyone was beholden to him, and naysayers were short-timers. It was his very own machine-within-the-Machine. The chief "knew things" about everyone, and that was the stick that he wielded to make him a player, regardless of who came out on top over at City Hall.

Being a player meant you got cut in. Which was how he always drove a new Lincoln and could buy that nice country spread down on Horseshoe Lake. And it was why the chief and Burdett never quite clicked. Burdett just wanted to do his job and mind his own business. He had painfully learned long ago that sometimes you simply needed to say no. However, the chief expected Burdett to do *his* jobs and mind *his* business. There had been a few run-ins, the worst being the debacle over those very same black murders when Boss Crump came down hard on Donlough for not controlling "his boy" Burdett, then suddenly reversed himself. The chief had overplayed his hand at first to please the Boss, then had had his head handed to him. He never forgave Burdett the embarrassment, which was only made worse by the protected status Burdett had received from the Boss after that. No more night shifts and no more forced work on the Crump election slate like the rest of the boys in the department. Donlough had not dared to retaliate, but now the Boss was dead. Revenge was in the air, and Burdett knew not to underestimate the chief. If Donlough had one well-developed talent, it was his uncanny ability to sniff out weakness in people—and poke it.

"Good morning, detectives. Have a seat." It was clear that Chief Donlough intended to remain standing, motioning Burdett and Harley toward the straight-backed guest chairs that were set out in front of him, just beyond the circle of sunlight. Marshmallow Miller hung back, his bent frame lit from below by the amber glow from sunlight illuminating the oriental carpet. As Burdett sank into his chair, he noticed once again how the chief's guest chairs were disconcertingly low, no doubt on purpose. Donlough's ever-present assistant Barb Bodine perched in the corner, spectacles on, poised to take notes. This was going to be another Donlough Show.

Burdett glanced at Harley to share a wink, but Harley was staring straight ahead, looking odd. The grin was still there but worn like a mask, his eyes unsmiling. Burdett caught another whiff. His instincts told him to beat a tactical retreat, and now. "Chief, I want to thank you for throwing us that Vicksburg case. I know it wasn't our turn, but I'm hoping we can make short work out of it." No sense in complaining about the rotation thing. It was a done deal anyway.

"Yer gonna know soon enough why I gave you that particular case, Mr. Grave Robber, but that's not why I brought ya here." Burdett bristled at the grave robber reference. Ever since Donlough had spotted the stone ax head that Burdett kept on his desk as a paperweight, he had mocked Burdett and his interest in collecting Native American artifacts. Just more ammunition for the chief's constant pokes. Donlough waved Burdett silent and continued with a nod toward pencil-ready Barb.

"I brought y'all here because these are times of great promise and great peril in our fine city. I believe that it's time that we, Memphis's finest, take the lead in welcomin' the change—and meetin' the threat. It's a new day in Memphis. Our colored citizens are showin' new interest in participatin' in our fine democratic process, and I welcome that." Donlough paused several beats for emphasis, measured by Chiclet chews, bones in his face all in motion, like the machinations inside his head.

"Which is why we need to make this department more responsive and representative of our constituency." The last sentence was directed almost entirely at scribbling Barb. He stretched out that last word and paused meaningfully, glancing over to make sure she got it all down.

"But our fine citizens expect more from us than that. They expect us to protect 'em against both threats from outside and threats from within. Y'all know what I'm talkin' 'bout. The God-hatin' communist threat is real, damn real. We gotta to do our part to fend off those reds, and that means ferretin' out their sympathizers—wherever and whoever they may be. Could be your neighbor. Could be little Casper's schoolteacher. Constant vigilance is what our citizens expect—no, demand—from us. Therefore, we're formin' a new unit within the department, the Special Investigations Unit"—raising his finger for emphasis—"as the vanguard of vigilance." So, that was the part intended for public consumption, Burdett was thinking. It looked to be practice for the chief's next press briefing.

Watching Donlough drone on, Burdett's translation went something like this: Donlough wants to get out ahead of the political power scuffle, maybe even run for mayor himself. Everyone knows that the potential Negro voters in the city outnumber the whites now, and white efforts to control the black vote are losing ground. What with the poll tax struck down and voting machines installed for the first time, the Machine can't buy elections like it used to by paying the poll taxes for blocks of friendly votes and diverting paper ballots. Donlough needs to garner support from the colored community to leverage his position. Meanwhile, how do you keep the whites distracted and in line? The Red Scare should do the trick.

You would think that here in the middle of the Bible Belt, miles from nowhere, would be the last place to find a commie spy, but for those Bible-thumping Baptists who already believed in the devil incarnate and Judgment Day, it was not a far leap of faith to believe in the unseen, godless Red Menace in their midst. Maybe it was even the same thing. If that was all there was to it, Burdett would have been thinking Donlough was clever enough, maneuvering like the big-time politician he was angling to be. But he sensed that Donlough had only finished with the windup; now Burdett readied himself for the pitch.

"So lemme cut to the chase, y'all. I need to know that I can count on each of ya to support the city and the department—to support me—on this. It's all hands on the bucket line, boys. I need the both'a ya to step up and take your places in the line. Lieutenant Miller here is gung ho. Are you with me too?" Burdett gave an obligatory but cautious nod. Harley's was more fervent.

"Good. So, here's the plan. Vance, you've done a passable job under Detective Suggs's leadership, and we think it's time to move you up in responsibility. I've directed Lieutenant Miller here to put you in charge of a very important department initiative of your very own. You're gonna lead our new Advanced Investigative Training Program. This is a big assignment, and I'm sure you're up to the challenge. And Suggs, in recognition of your mighty fine work and leadership, startin' today I'm reassignin' you to the new Special Investigations Unit. I'm confident that you'll do your best to hold back the commie barbarians at our gate. Watch out, you reds, here we come! Congratulations, men."

Burdett was stunned, and for a long moment he sat in paralyzed silence with his eyes lingering on an agitated dust mote dancing in the shaft of sunlight that stretched to his feet. Harley's leadership? This must be a joke.

"Uh, Chief, what training program? And what exactly is the Special Investigations Unit going to do?" Burdett asked, glancing at Harley questioningly. His partner would not look back, and then it struck Burdett that Harley had already known this was coming. Burdett felt a tightness in his chest as if all the air had been sucked from the room.

Not responding to Burdett's question, Chief Donlough punched his intercom.

"You can send him in now."

Burdett's eyes remained riveted on Harley and then shifted as everyone else turned to the sound of the door opening. A tall Negro police officer entered the room, dressed in sharply crisp blues with his hat under his arm. He was long and lanky with close-cropped, almost coppery hair. But most striking were his eyes, the amber eyes of a lion, and to Burdett they held a little of that fearlessness too. He moved cautiously but rolled with a cat-like grace as if ready to shift direction at any moment.

"Detective Vance, I wanna introduce you to Officer Eustace Johnson. Officer Johnson has over seven years' experience on the force and will be reportin' to you for the foreseeable future. Your job as head of the Advanced Investigative Training Program will be to train him to be a first-class homicide detective, so don't mess it up. He'll take over Detective Suggs's duties effective immediately. Men, I know y'all got a lotta work to do, so you may as well git to it. Suggs, I'll see you at our two o'clock team meetin' this afternoon. Thank you." The dirty work done, Chief Donlough perfunctorily shook their hands, his plump fingers as always eluding a firm grasp, then he punched his intercom again, the door opened, and Burdett, still stunned, followed Harley out into the hallway.

As soon as they were outside, Burdett grabbed Harley by the arm, "What's this bullshit, Harley? Special Investigative Training Program? You knew about this all along and didn't say a goddamn word."

Harley pulled his arm away, still not looking Burdett in the eye, "Cool off, Bird Dog. I knew you'd be upset, but at some point, you know I gotta take care of my own. If you had a family, you'd see it my way. This is my big break. I'm done with the stinkin' bodies and cryin' widows. Chasin' commies is the future. Sooner or later, you oughta get it into your head that you ain't goin' nowhere 'less you get close to the chief and stay there. You gotta stand on your own someday, and they said I can't carry you forever." He said the last bit louder, as if he thought someone might overhear.

"Carry *me*?" It hit Burdett like a brick. So this was how Harley had been playing things all along. "All I can say is now you've finally risen past the level of your own chickenshit incompetence. You deserve Ricketts and Renfro and the rest of Donlough's goons. Welcome to their club and to hell with you." Burdett expected that one to sting, knowing how often Harley had railed against what he called the "Downlow Toads," but he quickly realized that he was talking to a man whose loyalties had already shifted. His now ex-partner only shrugged, shook his head, and walked away without another word, and in that instant Burdett grasped the utter inevitability of what had just happened.

It is a curious thing when your view of the world around you suddenly gets flipped with the flick of a switch. Burdett sometimes felt he was a farsighted man who sees everything in the distance clear as a bell, but up close, in the inner circle where you trust people the most, everything is blurry. Now he had been given a new pair of glasses, and he was seeing things in painful 20/20. While Burdett had thought he was loyally covering for his partner, Harley had subtly positioned himself to Marshmallow Miller and the brass on the top floor as senior to Burdett and the one who was making it all happen, writing up the closed cases and rewriting history in the process.

Even now Burdett wanted to believe that maybe Harley had convinced himself of the lie, thinking that he was delegating work to Burdett instead of lazily ducking his job. And no doubt he had been bucking for promotion the whole time, while appeasing his conscience by telling himself that Burdett had him to thank for getting put on the force in the first place. Now Harley's recent kindly comments about the chief—uncharacteristic coming from such a diehard Donlough detractor—all made sense. Burdett's mind refused to give it a name, but in his heart, he knew that "betrayal" was the only word for it, and coming from your friend and partner it was an unforgivable sin.

Standing there in the silent hallway, as his mind reeled back over everything he had seen but not seen, Burdett became aware that he was not alone. Waiting calmly behind him stood the new trainee for the Advanced Investigative Training Program, the yoke they were tying around his neck.

"You shut up," Burdett said. The last thing he wanted was a wisecrack comment from a stranger and definitely not from that stranger. But Johnson took two quick steps forward, broad smile, outstretched hand.

"It's gonna be an honor and a pleasure working with you, Detective Vance. You can call me Eustace, though most everyone just calls me Eus. I was wondering if I could buy you lunch. Just to get acquainted."

"No, you can't buy me lunch, Officer Useless Johnson, but what you can do is go down and clean out the desk of that *son of a bitch*," he shouted the last phrase down the empty hallway. That ended the conversation, and Burdett left without shaking hands, taking the stairs back down to his desk, not caring whether his new trainee followed him. By the time Burdett walked into the squad room, Marshmallow had already faded back into his office and everyone else paused and watched silently as Burdett crossed the room trailed by Johnson. Word had traveled fast, and every detective there was wondering whether he would be the next to suffer Burdett's fate.

Back in 1948, the department had hired a dozen or so black policemen, a Boss Crump political stunt calculated to win back the black vote after the hotly contested '48 senate campaign against Estes Kefauver, but the new recruits had been restricted to foot patrols in the black areas of town and forbidden to arrest whites. Now, seven years later, only five remained on the five-hundred-man force, and they were relegated to obscurity as beat cops in black neighborhoods, not even rising to the level of second-class citizens in the otherwise lily-white police force. Maybe that was why Detective Burdett Vance had never met Officer Eustace Johnson.

Johnson was almost invisible outside of the Raines Station in South Memphis, and his arrival in the Homicide Division at Police Central was greeted as foul swamp gas blowing up from the Nonconnah Creek bottom down there—a bad omen, and nothing good could come of it. Burdett pointed Johnson to Harley's desk and sat down heavily at his own. After a while, it became clear that Harley had already boxed up his personal things the night before and left the chaotic mountain of paperwork on his desk for Burdett to sort out. Typical. So rather than continue to watch Johnson fidget, Burdett pointed to Harley's piles of files.

"You can start by clearing up that mess, and don't bother me 'til you're done."

Johnson quietly took the top file and opened it, but his eyes remained fixed on Burdett's with a look that to Burdett was a maddening amalgam of deference, sympathy—and knowing amusement.

★ ★ ★

Burdett buried himself in his own case files for a couple of hours, trying to shake it off, but he could not concentrate and decided that he had to get away and regroup. Putting on his hat, he walked over to Judy's Spot, a block down Jefferson Street from police headquarters. It was a cop breakfast, lunch, and dinner hangout, taking advantage of the round-the-clock shifts at Police Central. The place was empty except for a couple of traffic jockeys catching an early sandwich before the lunchtime rush. Burdett was glad because he needed time by himself to think.

The proprietress, Judy Carr, was alone at the front counter, surreptitiously stubbing out a cigarette in the small ashtray by the cash register and yelling something back to the kitchen in that scratchy voice of hers. Judy had become a local fixture. Back when Burdett was a kid first getting interested in girls, his uncle had told him that if you want to know how a girl will look when she gets older, check out her mother. For Judy, the opposite was true. She had a drop-dead gorgeous daughter, Jessie, who sometimes helped out at the restaurant, and if Judy was Jessie's future, then Jessie was Judy's past.

They shared the same velvety green eyes that closed halfway in a sleepy smile when they talked, and each displayed the same signature proud forehead and untamed red hair. Judy's red hair was out of a bottle now, and in her fifties, she had acquired a certain leathery look and smoker's voice that seemed to be payback for good times that may have been a little too good. Still, Judy tried hard and always looked put together, maybe even a touch dressed up for whatever it was she was doing, such as today's starched white blouse and gold earrings. People said she had been a hot number back in the twenties and thirties, and she still had the air of a woman who was really something in her day and knows it. Burdett often suspected that the name of Judy's restaurant was her way of keeping herself on the map. Judy's Spot. He liked her spirit.

"Hiya, hon. What can I do you for today?" Her universal greeting.

"Mornin', Judy. How's that daughter of yours? Still giving men the cold shoulder?"

"No, just men that are cops." Judy might be making her living off Memphis's Finest, but she made a point of telling every cop who gave Jessie the once over that if he touched the merchandise, he could get his meals elsewhere, and don't forget the loaded .38 she kept under the counter. But Burdett suspected that it wouldn't work out that way. He sometimes tried to imagine the futures of people he met. It had turned into a kind of game, a bet against himself that he could guess the outcomes of the lives he touched. He just had trouble imagining his own future.

In Jessie's case, the future seemed particularly foretold. Despite and perhaps because of Judy's fierce tenacity on the subject, Jessie indeed marries a cop—let's call him Johnny—settles down, has a couple of redheaded, green-eyed daughters with wild streaks, and then starts to worry that they might marry cops themselves. So she convinces Johnny to move out east near White Station so her girls can grow up and marry one of the lawyers or doctors that live out there. But that plan doesn't work out when Johnny takes a bullet executing a warrant on a junkie in a flophouse down on Trigg Avenue. So, streaming tears and hugging her little girls, Jessie suffers through the honor guard and funeral, dutifully accepts the folded flag, and pretty soon takes care of business by moving the schedule ahead a generation and marrying a rich doctor or lawyer herself that she meets at church while teaching Sunday school. Meanwhile, Judy retires, sells Judy's Spot, and moves into Jessie's extra bedroom out on Shady Grove Road where she can mother-hen the little girls while Jessie plays her weekly tennis game at the Hunt and Polo Club. It all works out. Burdett was already happy for both of them.

Judy was tapping her nails on the counter waiting for Burdett to order.

"I ate breakfast early, Judy, so I'm thinkin' lunch. Can you get Ernie to fix me up a grilled cheese and bacon sandwich the way I like it, hush puppies on the side and a Coke? I'll take it back here." Burdett pointed to the isolated booth in the back corner where he always ate, and for the next hour he sat there alone, chain-smoking Luckys, chasing down Cokes, and sorting through the morning's events.

Donlough appeared to be killing several birds with one stone. Filling the vacancy in Homicide with a colored officer would score points with the Negro voters while poking a stick in Burdett's eye. He had no doubt that it was personal because in the end the lasting impact would fall only on the two patsies, Burdett and Johnson. This public relations exercise would go nowhere. Inside of six months—after the ephemeral political benefits had been harvested for the election and the Advanced Investigative Training Program had faded from public consciousness—the hopeful Eustace Johnson would be back trudging the South Memphis beat. Nothing would have changed except that Johnson's nickname in the department now truly would be "Useless" Johnson. Then of course, Burdett would get tagged for the failure, which was likely what Donlough most wanted anyway.

And coddling and schooling Johnson would only slow Burdett down, making his work harder and his close rate worse. He could already envision the growing backlog of unclosed cases piling up while he was running in place "training" Johnson.

Again, more ammunition for Donlough to use against him. It was bad enough picking up the slack for Harley all those years, but they were supposed to be friends and he really did not mind it, at least not then. This Johnson thing was different; it was a charade targeted specifically and maliciously at Burdett. And no doubt Donlough already was planning his new nickname: Bird Dung. Shaking off his anger, Burdett forced his mind to focus on the other game that was being played. The Johnson stunt might be a bitter pill, but it was straightforward enough; what was harder to understand was Harley's new assignment.

Red Scare notwithstanding, the Special Investigations Unit obviously looked to be cover for Donlough's palace guard. Burdett guessed that Ricketts and Renfro were already charter members, and good riddance. It promised to be cushy work. All they had to do was periodically make headlines by busting some poor sap accused of being a "fellow traveler" pinko—who cared if no laws were broken—and Donlough would get all the credit for standing between the citizens and their worst fears while at the same time inflaming those fears.

Meanwhile, Donlough had a team of henchmen to do his bidding at taxpayer expense. It was perfect. It was the timing of Harley's reassignment that had Burdett puzzled. Looking back, it was now clear that Harley had been angling for this for years, but even with him stealing credit for their wins, apparently no one had thought he had the smarts for the big leagues—until now. Burdett knew firsthand that they were right. Harley may be cunning, but he lacked the finesse to be an effective political hatchet man. So why give him the nod now? Burdett suspected that everyone, including Chief Donlough, knew the truth about Harley, so maybe this was really another part of the chief's poke at Burdett, rewriting history, making it official that Harley was the real brains behind their successes, pegging Burdett as a loser.

Or did Donlough simply need more bodies on the street? If so, why? Lately, inside the department it had felt edgy, like the pressure drop just before the storm. More whispering, furtive looks, closed doors. Something was up, and the commie witch hunt angle looked more to be window dressing or distraction. There was nothing specific that Burdett could put his finger on; it was more of a feeling. Ever since Boss Crump had shed this mortal coil in October, there had been ever-increasing hints of something big at play just under the surface. It was not only about the well-publicized power struggles of a political machine in flux, but something darker, a hushed urgency. Like persistently percolating moonshine, odd things kept bubbling to the surface, and the whole department had developed that very distinct aroma, the ill-gotten, pungent smell of greed.

Burdett strolled into the squad room at a hair past two o'clock with nothing resolved in his mind and the phone ringing on his desk. It was Jimmy Blake.

"Hey, Bird Dog, come on over for dinner at around five. Should be tasty."

The body from Vicksburg was due to arrive by then, and the autopsy would already be underway. So, when the wall clock reached five o'clock, Burdett grabbed his hat and headed out the door, but then had a second thought. This was going to be especially messy, maybe the perfect way to welcome the new trainee to the mysteries and miseries of the Homicide Division.

"Johnson, come with me. Time for your first autopsy."

* * *

The Memphis Medical Examiner's Office was fondly referred to as Jimmy's Chop Shop. It was run by the city medical examiner, Dr. James Blake, who had developed a reputation for morbid humor but clear and thorough autopsy reports. The morgue itself was in the basement level of a nondescript cinder-block building on Poplar Avenue, with a below grade loading dock so ambulances and hearses could back up to disgorge the newly departed arrivals. Burdett and Johnson were handed lab coats and ushered into Autopsy Room #2 where Jimmy Blake, wearing a black rubber apron and gloves, was already toiling away. He was portly and wore heavy black plastic glasses with thick lenses. Today he was sporting a chef's hat tilted to one side to cover his bald head. During the holidays, he'd donned a Santa hat.

The body on the table was scarcely recognizable as a woman. Bloated and blackened, it oozed a constant stream of fluids into the gutters of the autopsy table. The smell was overpowering, and Burdett reflexively began breathing through his mouth rather than his nose. He was accustomed to the stench, but he was expecting his rookie companion to be mortified. A quick glance in Johnson's direction, however, revealed the opposite. As Johnson edged in for a closer look, his expression was cool, calm, even serene. Jimmy looked up from his labors inside the body cavity.

"Hiya, gents. Grab yourself a plate and step right up." Then he did a double take on Burdett and Eustace. "Now there's a pretty sight. What are you hangin' out with this guy for, Eus?"

Burdett did his own double take, "You two know each other?"

"Sure. Eus here's been workin' on colored cold cases the last few years. You didn't know that? He digs into the ones that get sloughed off by you guys," Jimmy said pointedly.

It was commonly acknowledged inside the department that, as far as Chief Donlough was concerned, Negro homicides were only the ordinary by-product of the booze, gambling, and vice culture of the colored end of town—part of the natural order of things, he said. The hard fact of life for midcentury Memphis was that Negro murders got short shrift by most of the detectives in Homicide who treated black victims almost as an annoyance. If the murderer was not immediately obvious, you tended to see check-the-box investigations of Negro murders that got back-burnered and cold-cased as quickly as possible. That was a game that Burdett refused to play, so he took umbrage at Jimmy's remark.

"Hold on, Jimmy, not so fast."

"Now, don't you go worryin', Bird Dog. I know you're okay," Jimmy said.

"Really, it's only something I do in my spare time, nothing official, no big deal." Johnson offered, then changed the subject, "Doc, got anything for us?" The three men stood for a long, awkward moment, looking silently at each other with their best poker faces. Then with a grunt Jimmy Blake turned to the autopsy table and its glaring bright lights.

"Okey-dokey. What we got here is a white female in her twenties. Cause of death a single gunshot wound to the left temple. She was dead before she hit the water."

"Self-inflicted? Where's the suicide note?" Burdett asked, looking around.

"That would be tidy, now, wouldn't it?" Blake scoffed. "No such luck, Bird Dog, as you'll soon see. Anyway, if you look at the hands, the fingers on the victim's right hand measure slightly thicker and have calluses from writing, indicating that she was right-handed, which is inconsistent with the bullet entry wound on the left side."

"So, it's front-right-back-left?" Eustace asked.

"Exactly, if the shooter was facing his victim, he's right-handed. A shot from behind makes him left-handed. Just a hunch, but the Chop Shop Doc thinks it was a left-handed shooter. You shoot someone point blank who's facing you, it's personal and you usually aim for the forehead."

"Can we tell from the angle of the entry wound?" Burdett asked, looking closely at the wound. He glanced at the other side of the head which was undamaged below where Jimmy had removed the top of the skull to examine the brain.

"It's a no-brainer, get it?" Blake chuckled. "Seriously, it's hard to tell so far. No exit wound. I recovered a .25 cal round from the cranial cavity, but it rattled around in there a bit. Ballistics won't be much help. There's fillings in the teeth in case you turn up dentals. Premortem contusions on the wrists suggest she was tied up, but hey, look at this. See the sharp edge on that bruise on the wrist? That looks to be handcuff marks to me. Anyway, the restraints were clearly removed before the body was dumped in the river. Clever. Less evidence left behind for us. No jewelry left either, so robbery might be a motive—or not. No indication of sexual intercourse or assault."

"How long has she been dead, Jimmy?" Burdett asked.

"The TOD is hard to say. This one reminds me of the case we had early last year, Eus. Remember the skinny guy they found washed up in the Wolf River? See here, the body's crawlin' with the typical midge larvae and water snails that you find on bodies that have been in the water, but so far, no sign of air bugs. Same as Slim."

"So, the killer probably shot her, took off her jewelry and whatever bound her wrists, and immediately dumped her into the river where the body stayed submerged until it was spotted yesterday," Johnson concluded, looking closely at the tiny moving specks on the body. He seemed unphased by the squirming mass that he was inspecting.

"Bingo, Eus. Only aquatic infestations, nothin' terrestrial. No time even for those pesky blowflies to lay their eggs, and they're usually quickest to sniff out a stiff."

"Wait a minute," Burdett interjected impatiently. "You say she didn't shoot herself, but so far the most I've heard to suggest that this isn't suicide are marks on the wrist that may or may not have been handcuffs. And maybe if she's planning suicide, she leaves her jewelry at home. The guys down in Vicksburg said there was a suicide note in a bottle. Where is it?" This was not going the way he had anticipated. And he had not expected Eustace Johnson to be such a morgue rat.

"Patience, my friend, we'll get to that." Jimmy replied. "You're the one who asked about time of death, so let me finish. Anyway, where was I, Eus? Right, the body had already reached the putrefaction stage when the tugboat snagged her. The bloating from gases released by bacteria in the body cavity caused it to bob to the surface. But check this out, Eus, no loosenin' of the skin yet. Exposed to air it'd normally reach this stage in four to ten days, and at this time of year probably on the longer side. But if we're right that the body was down deep in the Big Muddy all that time, it's more complicated. With all the levies confinin' the river, the Mississippi narrows at spots where it scours the bottom deep, over a hundred feet to the riverbed right out in front of town here. Believe it or not, 'fore you get to Vicksburg the bottom is actually below sea level. This time of year, the heavy cold water near the bottom just kinda hangs there, with the warmer and shallower water rollin' over it. That's why there's so many kooky currents. If this body was held at the bottom in that slow, cold current, everything would take longer. So I'd say multiply that four to ten days by at least—"

"Two," interjected Johnson, "Casper's Dictum."

"That's good, Eus, very good." Jimmy turns to Burdett, beaming with pride for his prize student. "Bird Dog, this guy's smart. That's a rule of thumb that this Kraut named Johann Casper noodled out a century ago to ballpark TOD: a body lyin' in open air for a week rots about twice as fast as a body that's been underwater, which rots twice as fast as a body in the ground. Although 'round here we got our own version of Casper's Dictum: for a Memphis cop, an honest day's pay is worth half of what you can get under the table, which is worth half of what you can get if you work Vice." Blake and Johnson both snickered and together looked expectantly to see Burdett's reaction to the joke, which left Burdett with the uneasy feeling that they had shared this particular humor before.

"Very funny, just don't let the chief hear that one," Burdett said, "Then what you're saying is that this body could've been in the water anywhere between eight and twenty days. Time is distance on the river, so how far upstream do we need to be looking?"

"When we worked on this same problem last year," Johnson volunteered, rubbing his large hands together and looking at the ceiling as he calculated, "we figured that the river current usually moves 'bout one and a half miles an hour, but in the spring flood season it runs faster, closer to three miles an hour or seventy-two miles a day. So, at that speed the outside distance in river miles from the point of recovery would be 1,440 miles and the inside would be 576 miles. Vicksburg is about 340 miles downriver from here, and St. Louis is about 400 miles upriver, which suggests that the body may have floated down from St. Louis or farther." Burdett was surprised to hear the figures spout so effortlessly from Johnson's mouth, but he liked the direction it was going. For a moment, he was hoping that maybe they had solved the case, at least as far as the Memphis police were concerned; this could become a St. Louis, Des Moines, or even Cincinnati homicide problem.

"But that's only if you assume that the body has been floatin' in midcurrent all along," Blake interjected. "Like I said, it could've been held down at the bottom or even hung up in an eddy."

"I need to see the note now," Burdett interrupted. He was beginning to think this was turning into a missing person scrape the whole way upriver to Cairo, maybe even further.

"It's over here," Blake responded. "It was stuffed in a beer bottle sealed with a cork of some kind, maybe from a whisky bottle. The bottle was inside a double layer of stockings tied around her neck, which I kinda thought was odd. We're still workin' on the dress. Tags on it are from Sears, which doesn't tell us much since there's a Sears store in every town in the country, plus the catalogue." He walked over to a side table on which there was a large, square stainless-steel pan usually used to weigh organs. In the pan was a mahogany-brown Goldcrest 51 beer bottle, and next to the bottle was a knot of damp nylons and wads of stained cloth that had once been a dress. Nestled among them was a small stainless-steel pan containing a single piece of paper.

"The bottle was crammed into one stocking and then shoved inside the other," Jimmy said. "Then the stockings were tied 'round the neck. My guess is that the stockings were the victim's."

"Prints on the bottle?" Burdett asked, looking at it closely. He did not like that it was a Goldcrest 51 bottle. That was a Memphis beer brewed by the Tennessee Brewery down on Front Street. So it might be a local girl after all.

"Nothin' we could use." Blake said. "The guys in Vicksburg had already pulled it out of the stockings to look at the note, and they weren't too careful." Cursing under his breath at Frankie Babcock, Burdett picked up the paper note with tweezers. It was thick brown paper that appeared have been torn from the six-pack carton that had contained the beer, and on the blank side of the paper in bold, black ink was written a simple, chilling message:

> *No more lynchings. Time for payback. By the time you done read this, next one will already be stone cold dead.*
>
> —The Mound Builder

Burdett now knew what Donlough had meant when he said this case had his name on it. For most of his life Burdett had spent his spare time exploring and excavating Indian mounds and collecting artifacts, the remnants of the long forgotten Mississippian civilization, a vast Stone Age empire dating back thousands of years and extending across the Mississippi River Valley from Minnesota to the Gulf of Mexico. Then they abruptly disappeared four hundred years ago, leaving behind hundreds of earthen mounds and pyramids up and down the Mississippi, many of which remained unexplored. Those lost peoples were called the Mound Builders.

Chapter 3

The Fourth Chickasaw Bluff

Now what makes Memphis women, baby, love a rounder so,
'cause he takes his time, doin' the work everywhere he goes.

—*Memphis Rounders Blues*, Frank Stokes, 1929

From the Chop Shop Burdett returned to his desk to write up his notes on the autopsy, digest the new information, and organize the first stages of the investigation. It all started with identifying Jane Doe, and he had a plan. He called it Shake the Tree.

At midcontinent in midcentury, Memphis was chafing to outgrow its river town reputation as a breeding ground for yellow fever, corruption, and violence. The city had prospered from its perch high above the floodplain on the fourth of the Chickasaw Bluffs that stretched south along the Tennessee side of the river from Kentucky all the way to the Mississippi state line. The Memphis merchant class had always shown a nimble talent for following the money, tainted or not. Memphis had been the one of the largest centers for trafficking slaves before the Civil War, and even during the war, the city got richer, trading with the Yankees while smuggling to the Rebels. Now the self-proclaimed King of the Mid-South aspired to be the global marketplace for the millions of bales of cotton wrung from the surrounding Delta plantations and the miles of board feet of hardwood lumber felled from the dense forests of Arkansas, Tennessee, and Mississippi.

As if they were arteries feeding the beating heart of a giant organism, the railroads and rural byways streamed toward Memphis in an unbroken flow of riches from the land that were headed out to the world's markets, and people from the land who were simply headed out. They hemorrhaged from the plantations and dusty farm towns, first to Memphis, then downriver to New Orleans or north to Chicago and beyond. But for some, the lingering gravitational pull of home or a simple lack of imagination halted their exodus in the first city they reached.

And so, like Burdett, most everyone in town had a close acquaintance with the snowy "cotton fall" that settled around small-town cotton gins and the earthy smell of lush Delta soil. Only one step removed from the countryside, they each had their own story of how they got there and what they left behind. And for the people still dug in back home, Memphis held the captivating aura of the big city, the promise of something newer or better for those with the courage or desperation to leave.

Burdett was counting on this "big city" cachet to help them identify the dead girl. It seemed that whenever he or Harley had dogged the local county sheriffs for information or help, the country constables would jump into line like buck privates in boot camp. So he put Johnson on the task of calling their rural brethren and running down any missing person reports from the river towns and county seats upriver from Vicksburg. That would be perfect filler for Johnson, easy but tedious. Meanwhile, he called his counterparts in Greenville, St. Louis, and Cairo, leaving messages for all of them. It was getting late, and it would probably take them until the next day to respond, but as Burdett listened to Johnson working the phone, he was already having doubts about his decision to have Johnson canvas the missing person reports. The calls were too short. You had to chat these guys up. Johnson was getting nowhere, almost hang-ups. Burdett thought he knew why.

"Okay, Johnson, it's getting too late to get anywhere with this. Let's pack it in and start fresh tomorrow."

"That's alright, Detective Vance, you go on. I'll make a few more calls and finish up these files," Johnson said studiously, not looking up.

"Suit yourself." Burdett said, thinking "eager beaver." He grabbed his hat and coat and headed for the door then paused. "By the way, now that you're in Homicide you don't need to wear a uniform. Tomorrow, you can come in a suit."

Johnson swiveled around in his chair and looked full on at Burdett.

"If you don't mind, Detective Vance, I'll wear my blues. Truth be told, I worked too hard to get 'em, and if I was to wear my Sunday clothes, I'd be only another darky in his Sunday suit to most people 'round here."

Their gaze locked for a long minute. Johnson's lion eyes glinted with that fearlessness again, his jaw twitched, and Burdett had the striking sensation of watching a large cat swishing its tail. Then the glare softened sideways into a sphinxlike smile, "Unless, boss, I was to keep flashin' my badge in folks' faces so's they can see their reflection in it."

"Very funny, Johnson. Suit yourself. And don't call me 'boss.'" Burdett said, stifling his own smile as he headed for the door while pattering through his head was that Lil Johnson song "If You Can Dish It, I Can Take It." Apparently, this new trainee could dish it and take it, just fine.

On his way out of the building, Burdett almost collided with Ricketts and Renfro running fast the other way.

"Whoa, boys! Haven't seen much of you today. What's the hurry so late at night? Can't be work. Way you're running, someone upstairs must've brought back free barbecue."

"Wouldn't ya like to know, Vance. Havin' fun yet with yer darkie?" Ricketts jeered. Typical from Ricketts, Burdett thought. Detective Earl Ricketts was no taller than a pool cue, and at a time when every able-bodied man had enlisted and shipped out to Europe or the Pacific, Ricketts had been too short for the army. That had left him an angry man with something unprovable to prove, and everything about him resonated from a deep-rooted fissure in his psyche. He carried an outsized Colt revolver and had taken to wearing broad-shouldered suits and elevator shoes, but there was no disguising that at heart he was a small man with a Napoleonic chip on his shoulder to match.

Burdett could have overlooked all that, but there was also a deeper darkness in Ricketts, a serpentine meanness coiled inside him waiting to strike. Rumors of handcuffed pistol whippings and blackmail had floated around the department, but nothing was ever proven. Burdett himself had even been called in once to investigate him as a murder suspect, and although he could have blamed that incident for the bad blood now between them, truth be told there had always been bad blood. The miracle was that Ricketts was on the force at all, but his father happened to be Deputy Chief Byron Ricketts, Donlough's number two up on the top floor. So, Daddy Ricketts swung him the job and kept him off the front lines. That and Ricketts's willingness to do anything to anybody to get ahead had guaranteed a virtual meteoric rise through the department. No walking the beat for that boy. Turns out he had genuine talent for ferreting out power and patronage, and he was fast making that his career. It was no surprise that he would be a charter member of Donlough's goon squad.

"Leastways my guy knows how to work an honest day instead of coasting on big daddy's coattails," Burdett shot back. Ricketts's face went dark, and Renfro closed quickly to block the conversation and keep the little man moving toward the elevator. That was Chuck Renfro's job. Big boned and rough cut, eyes like pieces of burnt-out cinder, he was more street smart than hard working and had hitched his wagon to Ricketts's pony, counting on the gratitude of Daddy Ricketts. As the elevator door opened and Renfro hurriedly steered his charge inside, Burdett caught a last glimpse of Ricketts, peeking around Renfro's shoulder with a look of smoldering hatred, leaving Burdett with the question as he watched the arrow climb to the top floor: What kind of emergency could be bringing these two slackers in at this time of night?

Outside in the police parking lot Burdett climbed into his dusty, bullet-nosed Studebaker Commander and turned east toward midtown where he lived alone in a peeling paint bungalow on Duvall near Overton Park. He bounced the Studey up the cracked concrete driveway and parked in back by a ramshackle garage topped by a corrugated tin roof green with moss. Crossing a backyard choked with rotting leaves left from the previous fall, he let himself in through the back door into the kitchen. With an economy of motion that comes from a well-worn routine, Burdett flicked the light switch, hung his hat and his .38 Special and shoulder holster on a hook just out of sight beside the back door, and tossed his coat over a kitchen chair.

On the kitchen table was a plate of food covered with foil and a note that said, "Hi, honey, had a hard day at the office? I'm waiting for you in the bedroom . . ."

That would be from Josie next door, and the joke was that they both knew there was no one in the bedroom. It was not an accident that Burdett was living in this house next door to Dewey and Josie Taylor. Dewey was Burdett's best friend. His family had lived next door to Burdett's uncle, and they had known each other since they were toddlers when Burdett and his father came into town for visits.

After Burdett moved in with his uncle for good, he and Dewey became tight, went to high school and Memphis State together, joined the army together, and survived the whole war in the same army unit. Dewey was half Choctaw Indian, which was a rarity around Memphis, or at least few Choctaws owned up to it. But Dewey was proud to be a member of the Mississippi band of Choctaws, the ones that dug in when the rest were driven out to Oklahoma in the Trail of Tears. That Choctaw connection was enough for Burdett to pull Dewey into his passion when they were teenagers, and whenever they could beg, borrow, or steal his uncle's pickup, they would set off to explore a new Indian mound, often camping out for days on the dig. Josephine Grant had come along for the ride sometimes. Even in high school Josie was hefty, but she had a nimbleness of body and spirit that belied her weight. Her eyes were always alive with mirth and matched by a deep and throaty laugh.

It was not long before they were a trio, which eventually became a duo with Burdett as the third wheel. Dewey and Josie tied the knot the day after he and Burdett enlisted, and when Dewey mustered out, they picked up exactly where they had left off. Burdett always envied Dewey being able to return from the war and fall right into home life like that. So they moved into their cozy bungalow on Duvall, tried and failed at having babies, and being people with lively minds and endless energy, they threw themselves into esoteric pursuits like collecting Confederate money, movie posters, and Indian artifacts. Their house was over-flowing with the stuff. To Burdett, they seemed to be filling it up so it would not feel so empty.

Josie had a studio out back where, blowtorch in hand, she welded iron sculptures, mostly quirky renditions of flowers and birds that seemed to be making their escape as they progressively spread out into the yard. For his part, Dewey had found a way to make a living from his booming voice, running one-liners, and uncanny imitations, as he manned the prime-time slot as a disc jockey at WHBQ. By Memphis standards, they were quite the bohemian couple. Burdett sometimes suspected that their biggest project was The Life of Burdett Vance. Josie was a mother hen rounding up her chick, so she cooked up the idea of him moving into the house next door. And she was always setting him up with any eligible girl she stumbled across, although her taste ran to the kooky type. The note she had left him was clearly intended to remind him of what he was missing, and it did.

Burdett peeled off the aluminum foil to reveal a plate of fried chicken, mashed potatoes, and cornbread, still warm. Pouring a glass of Old Yannissee whiskey, he grabbed a knife and fork and moved into a living room lined with shelves of dusty books, old records, and a wall of dark, glass-fronted display cases filled with the fruits of his expeditions with Dewey. He switched on a low lamp on the table next to his weathered leather easy chair and edged aside the previous night's debris to make way for Josie's offering. Then he dropped *The Definitive Blind Willie McTell* onto the spindle of his record player and picked up his old six-string steel guitar to pick along.

In his pensive moments, Burdett always gravitated to the calming comfort of the blues, music of his youth. It recalled happier times down on the family farm, before everything changed, when summer evenings passed contentedly with mules baying in the pasture, Maxie humming in the kitchen, and him and his best buddy, her son Eli, trading chords picked up that day from some old bluesman down by the mill or the general store. Most whites in Memphis considered the blues to be colored music—they called it race music, as if that said it all. But he made no apologies; that was simply part of who he was and where he had come from, something he kept mostly to himself. Now, alone in his living room, Burdett settled in to drink and think, pondering his own dimly lit image reflected in the glass-fronted cases.

Working his way through a chord progression, Burdett's mind drifted again to the autopsy and flashes of the girl on the cold stainless-steel table. He sensed something about the case did not fit. *No more lynchings. Time for payback. By the time you done read this, next one will be stone cold dead.* Even though the body had been dumped into the churning river, the note in the bottle was meant to be found and read. But then why ditch the body in the river where it was liable to wash down into the Gulf and be lost forever? Maybe the body had been deposited in a place where it would not be swept away, where it would be found when it floated to the surface—where it would be found after someone else was already "stone cold dead." That thought gave new urgency to the case.

And what was the reference to lynchings about? There was no doubt that Memphis had an ugly and violent history of racism going back to its inception. It was always there, a dark undercurrent of low-level violence and white-on-black intimidation that sometimes roiled explosively to the surface. But now the tables had been turned; violence and revenge seemed to be flowing the other way, and coldly targeted at the sacred heart of racial supremacy: lily-white Southern womanhood.

Burdett shook off the thought and refocused on the threshold question: Where did the murder occur? If it was not in Memphis, then perhaps it was not his problem. Upstream from

Vicksburg there were literally scores of backwater cutoffs, bayous, and chutes stretching all the way to Minnesota. Setting his guitar aside and rummaging through the topographical maps he used for exploring Indian sites along the river, Burdett plotted out the spots with road access where a body was not likely to be washed out into the current. He then noted the names of the towns nearby to add to Johnson's list. But near Memphis there were only two likely spots: McKeller Lake at the downriver end of the city and the Wolf River cutoff that lay at the base of downtown itself. And then there was the question of the "next one." *By the time you done read this, next one will be stone cold dead.* Brooding over that question while he listened to the comforting and familiar sound of the blues crackling off his record player, Burdett felt a chill go through him as Blind Willie sang,

> *Tombstones is my pillow, cold grounds is my bed,*
> *The blue skies is my blanket, and the moonlight*
> *is my spread.*

He eventually ate his dinner and went to bed, but in his mind a billowing black cloud was blocking out the moon. He had a very bad feeling that something evil and dark was beginning to move across his river city. As he tried to sleep, he wrestled with everything he knew about Donlough's schemes, about Harley, Ricketts, and Renfro, and about the Vicksburg Jane Doe, searching for an elusive—or illusory—connection. As his mind drifted toward sleep, he imagined that he was frenetically working a jigsaw puzzle blindfolded, trying every piece, then turning it to a different angle and trying again. Nothing quite fit, but in his dream state he felt an uncanny certainty that, as with all jigsaw puzzles, every piece eventually would fall into place and then the obscure puzzle picture would be satisfyingly complete and crystal clear. But for now, the answer was hiding just out of view. If he could only take off the blindfold. Finally, a hazy notion formed and morphed into a soft cotton cushion that at last brought sleep: Tomorrow he would know more.

Chapter 4

But Liking It

If you be my kid, I'll be your teddy bear,
I'll get in your pocket and follow you everywhere.
When you see me coming, heist your window high,
And when you see me leaving, hang your head and cry.

—*Be My Kid Blues*, Elizabeth Johnson, 1928

By 7 a.m. the next morning, Burdett's Studebaker was parked in the lot at Gannon's Diner, and Burdett was in his usual window booth buttering a steaming biscuit before a plateful of eggs, biscuits, and grits, bacon on the side. Breakfast was his favorite meal, and Gannon's was his favorite place to eat it. Both were simple and straightforward, as guileless and truthful as white tile and scrubbed Formica. The coffee was hot, and the air was richly suffused with the warm aroma of sizzling bacon, "food of the gods" as he liked to say. He looked up, startled as a once familiar face slid into the booth.

"Howdy, Burdett. I said to myself, look at that poor boy sittin' over there all alone. Mind if I stop by for a visit?"

"Hi, Emme, it's been a while." And that was the most he could utter. Emmeline Bryce was tall and gracefully angular, with milky skin and the palest blue eyes Burdett had ever known.

She had a friendly smile and a clear voice that modulated with the acquired casual confidence of someone completely at ease in her own skin, at least on the surface. Her strawberry blonde hair was tied back in a ponytail, and she was wearing a powder blue sweater with a single strand of pearls and white gloves. Nothing fancy, but she looked stunning.

"It's so good to see you, Burdett."

"You're looking well." Burdett replied, studying her up close for the first time in years. Time had started to show in a way that brought her soft youthfulness into clearer focus. It suited her. He was glad to see smile lines beginning to show instead of frown lines of unhappiness, and he hoped that was a sign of how her life had been. He wondered idly how she would look in another ten years. Maybe trending more to brittle. But for now, he marveled that she looked more beautiful than ever as his eyes traced a stray lock of blonde hair down her cheek. And she even sounded different; from her years of living in town, her flat country accent had softened in an elegant way. She seemed more . . . sophisticated.

Their lives had overlapped intensely right after the war, when Emme was new in town and Burdett had just mustered out. In those days she inhabited that stratum of Memphis society populated by country girls trying to become city girls. They came from the hundreds of farms and farm towns throughout the South, drawn to Memphis by the lure of jobs during the war and husbands after V-J Day, and they stayed either because they found them or because there was no going back.

Burdett had returned from the war at loose ends. Like a lot of other GIs, he had changed in an indefinable way, while everything back home had stayed the same. Emme was the one thing about Memphis that was definitely different. She was a fast learner, and there was a fiery ambition and fresh sharpness in her that was real and immediate next to the syrupy Southern politeness of so many Memphis belles he knew. She was a keeper, and he fell for her hard and fast. But while he was making plans for their life together, she was making her own plans.

One day she ended it. In retrospect, Burdett should not have been surprised. She was nice enough about it, but the message was loud and clear: Emme saw no future in a man with so few prospects and so many demons—and she didn't even know the half of them. He kept telling himself that Emme was Emme, a free spirit who could not be tamed. But he knew it went deeper. She grew up dirt poor up north of the Hatchie River west of Covington, and like many rural children of the Depression that Burdett had known who had brushed up against starvation, there was a grasping hunger—or fear of hunger—that never left her. It gave her an earthiness that was appealing, but also a restlessness lurking just below the charm. She was a bluebird forever looking for the next berry—pretty to look at, but pretty preoccupied too.

Truth was, Emme had been looking for better prospects, had found one, and was honest enough to tell him so to his face. That was fair, but it still hit him like a sucker punch, and for a while it left him unraveled and even more adrift. Without a doubt, she had been the best thing that had ever happened to him. The loss was numbing at first, and Burdett still winced when he thought back on it. Hers had become a future that he refused to imagine.

Not long afterwards he had joined the police force, to get a grip as much as anything else. They still ran into each other now and then, and it was always friendly. But she kept her distance, so he could never get anything going. And in any case, for the most part they traveled in very different circles. Burdett had heard that she married the scion of a wealthy cotton broker. That ended scandalously when he ran off with his secretary and took all the money, which made Emme damaged goods in Memphis society. Since then she had been on her own, doing what she had to do to survive, and a luminous looker like Emme stayed radiantly visible as she traded her way up from one richer and more powerful man to the next, until at last she was rumored to have reached the top, the secret squeeze of the late great Boss Crump himself. For these reasons and a few more that Burdett dared not admit even to himself, she was—in the profoundest sense—untouchable.

"How have you been, Burdett? How's Harley? Do people still call you Bird Dog?" Her voice sounded musical. Hearing it thrilled him and hurt him all at once.

"I used to think my friends called me that, but now I'm not so sure. I mean I'm not so sure they're my friends anymore. Otherwise, it's just the same old same old. Good to see you, Emme. Life's good for you, I hope?" Burdett felt like he was repeating himself, and truth be told, he was near speechless and all he could do was mouth trite niceties. She ordered a cup of coffee, slipped off her gloves and grabbed a biscuit off his plate with a casual, friendly intimacy, bringing back old times. And just like that, they picked up their conversation as if it had been only yesterday. Everything about Emme was as easy and familiar as the confection of relief and joy that comes when you wake up from a troubled dream to the comfort of your own bed.

Burdett winced through the ten-minute version of his last few years: joining the police force, moving into the Duvall Street bungalow next to Dewey and Josie, nothing much to speak of. He tried to avoid the nitty-gritty of his daily diet of homicidal humanity but was surprised to see that she actually seemed interested in the details of his work. He figured that after growing up on a farm she was probably used to getting blood on her hands, but in his experience not many girls—not even country girls—had the fortitude to delve into the gruesome particulars of crime scenes and autopsies. Or maybe they simply thought it was just too unseemly. Either way, his work had always been a conversation stopper with women. But Emme was different. Her sharpness and curiosity reminded Burdett of why he had been drawn to her in the first place. She sugarcoated nothing, and she even had a few helpful suggestions on the Vicksburg case—such as, could you tell if the girl had had a ring on her finger, or had she had her nails and eyebrows done—things that he had not thought of but that might be clues to the girl's background.

So, they talked on as Gannon's emptied out after the breakfast rush. By the time the waitress came around with yet another pot of coffee, they had covered a lot of ground regarding his life, but she never asked the one question that he was waiting for: whether he was married or involved. Either she didn't care or she already knew the answer. He hoped that perhaps he was not the only one keeping tabs from afar.

Emme's own story was mostly what he had heard over the grapevine, but a few things were news to him. She owned up to having a thing with Boss Crump and how his sudden death had hit her hard. She allowed as how he had been larger than life to her; even in the end he had had a vigor and force of will that she revered or needed or loved or whatever it is that a twenty-eight-year-old woman felt for an eighty-year-old man.

"It was not what you think," Emme said, "Ed Crump was more like a teacher to me. We would while away the hours with his stories of the Memphis that he found the day he arrived from Holly Springs sixty years ago. It was just a rowdy river town then, a lot crazier than it is now."

He had told her how Memphis society then had just the thinnest veneer of gentility, where parasoled Sunday strolls in Overton Park passed almost side by side with sheriff-sanctioned lynchings out in the county. Emme cringed as she recounted Crump's description of some of the worst lynchings in years past, which the Boss regarded as a particularly personal affront to the orderly society that he envisioned. As Emme saw it, Boss Crump saw his life's work as harnessing and controlling the pervasive chaos and inefficiency within his dominion, and the anarchy of the lynching posse was anathema to that world order. Besides, the "Negro polity" as he called it was foundational to his power base; he had to protect them—as long as they maintained their fealty and did what they were told. So lynchings in Memphis and its environs were officially banned, and when they happened, justice was always speedy and absolute, at least until all-white juries had their way.

"This is gonna sound funny, but I wish you could have known the man."

"I did meet him once, you know. He's the one gave me that nickname."

"I know, he told me." They both let that sink in for a minute. "And now things have gone to Hell in a handbasket."

With Boss Crump in the ground, Emme said it was everyone out for himself, and real friends were getting scarce as fifty-dollar gold pieces. Everyone jumped to the meanest judgments about her, and she lamented how in unison the good womenfolk of the city had turned their backs on her. Burdett took this to be expected. After all, as he knew from personal experience, Miz Boss Crump was a force to be reckoned with. It always seemed peculiar to him how, when a husband was alive—especially a rich and powerful husband—a wife could tolerate all manner of dalliances and look the other way to stay cozily cocooned in her exalted position, but as soon as he kicked, she acted surprised and discovered a newfound outrage at the cheating. History is written by the victors, and a rich widow is certainly the kind of victor who can be counted on to do what it takes to write her piece of history the way she likes it. Especially Bessie Crump.

"The worst part of it has been my own friends," she said. "They've turned against me with a spitefulness that's just dog-gone hateful. And some of us even go to the same church! But thinking back, I'm guessin' they've always felt that way but didn't feel free to say it. Girls can be so mean, especially when they're jealous."

Emme's anguish was real, but Burdett also suspected that her torment came mainly from the male side of the equation. You find yourself with no protector for the first time since you stepped down off the Covington bus. Maybe you made some enemies on the way up, when you were riding high. No doubt Emme had cause to worry. It grated on Burdett that he had been only the first to fill those protector shoes; maybe Boss Crump was the last, maybe not. Meanwhile, Emme was as radioactive as Hiroshima, and her painful isolation was only the fallout. In the parlors where tea was being served over the latest gossip, she was fair game as the righteous matrons clucked and shook their heads, but in the back rooms where cigars were being chewed and deals were being cut over the Crump Machine spoils, no one would want to make a move on Emme. It might look to be premature pretensions to the throne and invite untimely blow-back from the other pretenders. To Burdett that made Emme herself simply part of the spoils.

"Believe me," Emme continued, "It's as if *all* my friends have turned on me, and sometimes I really, *really* hate them." A dark cloud moved over her face. Then she seemed to catch herself and forced a brave smile. "Burdett, I've got big dreams and sometimes I just want to leave this old town and be done with it, but honestly, I can't imagine where else I'd go. Daddy and Mama passed a while back. Just that empty farmhouse up there in Fulton is all that's left. And anyway, I'm not the same person I was then. I can't ever go home. Not now, not ever." Burdett saw a tear welling in her eye but resisted reaching out to her.

"Come on, Emme, you gotta be patient, and I'm sure in good time you'll find yourself another daddy." He couldn't resist saying what was on his mind but instantly regretted it. "Sorry, that was out of line."

"That's alright, sugar. Comin' from you, I deserve it. But to tell you the truth, what I need most right now, right this minute, is not a boyfriend but a real friend, Bird Dog." Emme reached across the table and softly placed her hand on his, and it was like slipping on a kid glove. Then those palest of blue eyes fixed onto his with that indescribably open, vulnerable, and loving look that had always melted him.

"All of this has made me think a lot about my life and the choices I've made. I think of those days when we were together, and they were some of the happiest days of my life. I don't know what I was thinking when I left you, Burdett, and I want to say something that I should've said a long time ago. I'm really, really sorry that I hurt you." Burdett did not know what to say and sensed that he was tearing up too. Then Emme seemed to gather herself back together and let out a long sigh. "Well, enough of that. Bird Dog, it's been wonderful to see you. I mean it. Thanks for listening, and this time let's really try to stay in touch. Have you got a pen?"

And without another word, Emme wrote down her phone number on the corner of his newspaper, gave him a soft kiss on the cheek and walked out of the diner. As he paid his sixty-cents breakfast check and savored the lingering smell of her perfume, Burdett watched her through the diner window until she turned the corner out of sight, leaving him wondering what that was all about, but liking it.

Chapter 5

Swarming Mosquitoes

Now, I'm sittin' in my kitchen, mosquitoes all around
my screen,
Now, I'm sittin' in my kitchen, mosquitoes all around
my screen,
If I don't arrange to get a mosquito bomb, I'll be seldom
seen.

—*Mosquito Moan*, Blind Lemon Jefferson, 1929

Fifteen minutes later Burdett walked into Police Central, and the place was buzzing. In the hallway near the fourth-floor elevator Ricketts, Renfro, and Harley were walking together toward the new office space down the hall from Homicide that lately had been assigned to the so-called Special Investigations Unit. They hushed as soon as they saw him. Burdett made a point of ignoring them, especially Harley. Eustace Johnson was already on the job, and Burdett could not tell whether Johnson had been there toiling at his desk the whole night: same blue uniform, same pile of case files, still on the phone. Burdett settled in at his desk, lit a Lucky, and made himself look busy, but the conspiratorial whispering of the Stooges had left him irritated and uneasy. After a minute, Johnson quietly stepped over and handed him a note.

"Your phone's been ringing all morning. Mister Winslow Hogue over at the *Press-Scimitar* called me, thinking he'd reached Detective Suggs's desk, but it's you he wants to talk to." Winslow Hogue, venerated and self-proclaimed muckraking reporter for the *Press-Scimitar,* spearheaded the newspaper's long campaign against corruption and the Crump Machine. He had a bloodhound's nose for whatever caused controversy and sold papers.

"Thanks, but I try to stay away from reporters," Burdett said loudly for the room to hear. He then turned back to his work, but Johnson kept standing there next to him.

"You got something else to say?"

"Funny thing 'bout bein' a person of my persuasion. You're invisible. People sometimes don't even reconnize you're there," Johnson said, glancing in the direction of the now empty hallway. "I make a point of stayin' outa sight and outa trouble, but you may not have that choice."

"Oh, yeah?"

Johnson sat down in the chair next to Burdett's desk and leaning forward, continued in a low voice. "A lot was goin' on last night. Ricketts, Renfro, and Suggs was talkin' 'bout how someone ransacked Commissioner Boyle's office and even Boss Crump's old digs up at E.H.C. Insurance. The Chief assigned both cases to them, and they must be keepin' it on the QT 'cause they're all actin' like they's hidin' somethin'." Finance Commissioner Robert Boyle was the Crump Machine's money man, in charge of the city's finances and Crump's largess, and the invasion of the Boss's own office at E.H.C. Insurance Company was a virtual declaration of war. Question was, who was declaring war on whom and why was it being kept so quiet? "Those boys was also talkin' 'bout how they're investigatin' burglaries out East in Chickasaw Gardens, which seems a might peculiar since they're sayin' nothin' was taken. Just so's you know, that's probably what this Mister Hogue wants to talk about."

"That much I figured out already, but thanks for the tip. Got any word yet on our missing person?"

"Nothin' yet. Those good old boy county sheriffs ain't much on cooperatin'." No surprise, Burdett thought. As he had feared, Johnson did not sound white enough on the telephone.

"Detective Vance, I hate to say this, but I wonder whether these sheriffs just don't want to talk to a colored officer on the phone. That's a fact that I can't change. I'll keep callin', but don't expect much." Well, at least he's not delusional, Burdett acknowledged to himself, but since he had nothing else at that point to keep Johnson busy, he pulled out the list of additional towns he had prepared the previous night.

"Don't worry about it. If those boys are missing someone and they know we have a body, they'll call us eventually. We're just shaking the tree. I cobbled together a list of more towns to check. They're near spots along the river where the body may have gone in." He handed Johnson the list, and as Johnson made his way back to his desk, Burdett looked at the note from Hogue: "Call asap. Important." Burdett idly thumbed through papers for an appropriate interval, casting glances around the squad room, then surreptitiously dialed Hogue's number.

"Hi, it's me. My place in fifteen minutes." Burdett said quietly, then hung up and casually picked up his fedora. Heading for the door, he told Johnson loudly for the whole room to hear, "I got errands to do. Back in an hour." Johnson nodded meaningfully.

* * *

Burdett Vance and Winslow Hogue had a complicated but long-standing relationship that they preferred to keep on the down-low. They had worked out their own peculiar set of ground rules for bartering their stock-in-trade: off-the-record information. Burdett called it what it was—trading tips on the sly—but Hogue characteristically had managed to elevate their sessions to something loftier that he dubbed "Socratic dueling." Facts were seldom stated outright, and questions were only answered with questions, suggesting where to look or whom to ask, which after all, was half the battle. That satisfied Burdett's instinctive desire to keep a low-profile deniability, and from the sounds of it, Hogue had his own reasons, maybe simply keeping his editors at bay. In any case, Burdett genuinely liked and respected Hogue, and knew that Hogue reckoned the same.

Hogue was a droll raconteur with a penchant for the better class of bourbon and the choicer cut of steak. His was a carefully contrived slovenliness: shoes scuffed and suit rumpled but always a crisp shirt and matching tie and handkerchief. And he had a way of looking far off and talking away from you, but then his sharp eyes would suddenly turn on you sideways through his heavy horn-rimmed glasses, as if he already knew what you were hiding, and you could not hold his gaze and lie at the same time. It was a bona fide talent, no doubt about it. But Burdett respected him most of all because his aim was true. Hogue genuinely wanted to goad and cajole Memphis into modernity by crimping the corruption and making the city a place where *all* Memphians could live in peace and where investors from outside wanted to risk their dough to build the city's economy.

Instead, the city had a reputation as a place where if you could not play the insider game, you did not play. Like a third-world country, outsiders were required to have "local partners," which to Hogue meant Memphis would sadly continue to muddle along as the oversized, hardscrabble river town that it had been for the last century. Burdett himself was not much for spouting such lofty civic aims, preferring instead to focus on catching criminals and avoiding politics, but Hogue managed to make even that resonate like a higher calling, waxing eloquent over whiskey on how the truly righteous man is one who speaks the truth and wants nothing. Sometimes Burdett suspected Hogue was trying to keep him on the straight and narrow by daring him to do different.

Burdett rolled the Studebaker into his driveway right on time, noting Hogue's Hudson was already parked in front. Hogue was ensconced in his usual rocker up on the front porch, brown fedora pushed back on his head and rumpled suit seeming to expand his bulk. As Burdett approached, he was drawing on a long cigar.

"Well, if it isn't the newly anointed impresario of the so-called Advanced Investigative Training Program," Hogue said in greeting as Burdett eased into the opposite chair, tapped out a cigarette, and surveyed the deserted streetscape below. The morning had warmed with the sun, the daffodils were blooming, and the trees around the house were showing the budding green signs of early spring. One of Josie's whimsical iron sculptures, a three-foot-tall dancing rooster with an oversized cocked hat and a cigarette hanging from its beak, was the centerpiece of his front yard. She called it "The Great Crested Birdett."

The air was filled with the fresh smell of spring, and Burdett was grateful for the break from the stifled gloominess of the squad room. He made a note to himself to do this more often. Hogue blew out a stream of cigar smoke that he targeted at an imaginary point in space, and they both gazed silently for a moment at the billowing cloud as if it contained Hogue's thoughts.

"Although I suspect that condolences are more in order, may I nevertheless be the first to congratulate you on your new assignment? Please do not trouble yourself to respond, my good fellow, my question is purely rhetorical, which might also be said of our illustrious police chief's new Special Investigations Unit. But enough pleasantries. I have time for only one cigar, so shall we get down to business?"

"It's too early in the day for anything else," Burdett responded with a smile. So Donlough had already gone to the press with his black-and-red strategy, and from the sounds of it, Hogue had pegged it for exactly what it was.

"Yes, Chief Donlough managed once again to bloviate on his own perspicacity—*ad nauseum infinitum*—but me being the consummate professional, it was my solemn duty as a leading member of the Fourth Estate to hear him out and to scribe an appropriate item to appear above the fold in this evening's paper." Winslow paused to blow another billowing thought into the air. "And speaking of papers, have you read our much lauded, if somewhat overrated, morning paper today? Would it surprise you that the most interesting and tantalizing thing about today's edition is what's *not* in it?"

"Why is that different from any other day?"

"Would it surprise you if late yesterday Judge Coffey signed search warrants for a veritable plethora of safe deposit boxes at United Planters Bank?" That got Burdett's attention.

"Hmm. Yes, nosy minds might indeed want to know—present company excepted of course—but that's none of my business and search warrants get issued every day. So, if this is so unusual, isn't the real question whether it would also surprise Ella Mae Burns over in the bailiff's office across the hall from the judge's chambers?" Burdett asked. He was thinking that prying eyes like Ella Mae's always mind the comings and goings and will cough it up if you make them feel important enough.

"Precisely. If I had your sagacious insight, perhaps I would have thought of that myself. Well, if you happen to talk to this Ella Mae personage anytime soon, don't you think it might be interesting to see just how surprised she is?" Burdett knew enough of Hogue's trade craft to guess that Hogue had already queried Ella Mae and gotten nowhere, and he was hoping Detective Burdett Vance could get a better result. Badges can work wonders. He nodded his silent assent.

Then it was Burdett's turn, "And there was nothing in the morning paper reporting any break-ins in Chickasaw Gardens either?" Hogue stopped rocking in his chair and his brow knitted as he grew momentarily silent. So this was news to him.

"Now what in God's creation would a low-down burglar want to steal from the decent denizens of Chickasaw Gardens?"

"Beats me, but what would you think if nothing was taken, at least nothing anyone was willing to cotton to? Have you considered asking the officers in charge, our friends Ricketts, Renfro, and Harley Suggs in the Special Investigations Unit?" Burdett smiled, knowing that this was just what Hogue needed to make him take the bit and run with it. If Donlough's crew was on a case, it raised any garden variety break-in to a different, political level, and now they would be dodging Hogue's calls for a week. Then, in for a penny, in for a pound, Burdett continued, "And while you're at it, have you considered asking 'em who was rummaging through Boyle's office last night or who picked the lock on Crump's insurance company office in the wee hours?" More silence, wheels turning.

"Okay, Burdett my good man, it's been nice talking to you, but apparently, I have a surfeit of work to do before the paper's witching hour, so regrettably I must finish my cigar en route. Let us continue our exchange later, perhaps closer to cocktail hour."

"Not so fast, Win. You've got three inches left on that cigar, and I get at least one more question. How come you didn't ask me nothin' about the girl that turned up downriver near Vicksburg? Not a word in the paper about her either. We could sure use a missing person story on her." That was it, the quid pro quo, and Hogue honored it.

"Duly noted, my friend. No doubt some ardent soul at our paper is dutifully composing it this very minute, but perhaps it might hasten their endeavors if you could jot down a few of the salient facts so that we get it right—as we always seek to do." Meaning, you write it, and we'll print it, which was exactly what Burdett wanted. Even a short blurb in the paper might be enough to shake a few leads out of the tree.

"Okay, I'll get you something later today. One o'clock soon enough for this evening's paper?"

"Please make it short and to the point. I'll have them save three inches for you below the fold. If you get it to me late, it'll be buried inside on page four or kicked to tomorrow." Fair enough.

They ended the meeting with Burdett harboring a guilty pleasure that now Hogue would throw a wrench into the works for Donlough's people. When Burdett arrived back at Police Central, he skipped across the street to the courthouse, where a quick badge flash for Ella Mae at the bailiff's office confirmed what Burdett already suspected: Ricketts and Harley had walked into Judge Coffey's chambers with a pile of documents and left in less than five minutes. Five minutes to get a "slew" of search warrants signed? That was hardly enough time for the judge to fan through the papers, much less read them. So, even old Judge Coffey was in on it, whatever "it" was. And as he connected the dots from Coffey to Ricketts to Renfro to Harley, the jigsaw pieces were slowly beginning to come together and the picture of a web emerged, with Chief Casper P. Donlough the spider perched at the center of it. Burglaries, break-ins, ransacked offices, searches of bank boxes. Donlough and probably others were methodically hunting for something, and judging by the whispers in the hallway that morning, they had not found it. Meanwhile, Burdett had to get back to his own search, to identify Jane Doe and the man who killed her before he killed again, if he had not already.

CHAPTER 6

Watch What You Pray For

Backwater rising, Southern peoples can't make no time,
I said, backwater rising, Southern peoples can't make no time,
And I can't get no hearing from that Memphis girl of mine.

—*Rising High Water Blues,*
Blind Lemon Jefferson, 1927

Burdett always thought that faith in human nature is a fickle thing. People may think that they know you through and through, but it turns out that there was a deep dark part of you that they did not know at all. And maybe that is the part of your flawed self that makes you truly human. You spend your life with your family and friends. You share your thoughts, your feelings, your love. You reveal yourself to the whole world in so many ways, but in the end, you hold back that last dark piece of who you are. It is the voice that only you can hear because it is actually your own voice inside your head, your secret soul, and you save it for no one but yourself. That is part of you that no one really knows.

Meanwhile, your true believers ignore those little signs of where that deep dark place is, while it just sits there, a black hole in space. For some souls that black hole slowly sucks in whatever is nearby until it devours everything and everybody. That was a part of human nature that Burdett had come to know all too well. He wondered sometimes what shock and surprise a victim must feel in his last dying thoughts, because no one who dies at the hand of someone they know really thought the other person had it in him to pull the trigger or plunge the knife. And as their dying eyes close inward, the last thing they see is that big black hole pulling them into nothingness, and them thinking it was some horrible joke how unpredictable human nature turned out to be.

But every now and then something happens that gives hope that human nature might be predictable after all. And because you want to believe, it gives life to your fading hopes that living is not just a matter of waiting for the next random, capricious calamity. That was how Burdett Vance's morning started when he returned from his down-low meeting with Winslow Hogue.

He had been hoping that curiosity would get the best of some small-town sheriff, and after slamming down the phone and ignoring the call from that "Negro policeman" up in Memphis ("What could they be thinkin' up there, givin' badges to those people, and him callin' 'bout a white girl too?"), he would go home and lie in his bed in the dark listening to the wind and wondering if maybe that runaway Smith or Jones or Murphy girl had turned up in the city after all.

Then he would realize that it would only get worse the longer he put off returning the call. He would start to worry about what the police in Memphis would say when he admitted that there was indeed a missing girl from his small town and he had not told them when they had first called, him knowing how city cops liked to put down their unschooled rural brethren, sometimes doing it in the newspapers that circulated back home. Then his worry would sour into bile gurgling up from his stomach as he agonized over how this might find its way back to the good people in his hamlet and what with the election coming up this fall. His mind churning, he would figure out a way to blame it on someone else or even lie that he had only now learned the girl was missing. Or maybe he would simply lay it on "the colored boy that called me 'cause, I tell ya, I couldna understand a damn word he said."

And sure enough, there was a note on Burdett's desk from Sheriff Bobby Sturgis down in Clarksdale, Mississippi. The message had been for Burdett, of course, and not for Johnson, which told Burdett something already. Burdett phoned Sturgis, who hemmed and hawed and made friendly, and then offhandedly mentioned getting a "garbled" phone call talkin' 'bout them lookin' for a missin' girl, and come to think of it, there was this runaway that had, uh, slipped his mind last night when he got the call from, uh, Burdett's office.

The facts took a while to tease out, what with all the backpedaling and obfuscation by Sturgis, but once the picture filled in, Burdett understood why Sturgis was so nervous, almost pleading for Burdett to go easy on him. This was not just any girl. The missing girl was Cece Quaid, daughter of Palmer Quaid who owned a massive spread outside of Clarksdale and who undoubtedly swung a big riding crop down in Coahoma County. She had left home ten days earlier saying she was driving down to Jackson to stay overnight with a girlfriend and go shopping, but she had never shown up there, and the girlfriend claimed she knew nothing of the visit.

According to Sturgis, Cece Quaid was a wild un, and most everone had 'spected her to show up in a day or two, rode hard and put to bed wet, but she ain't turned up. They had mostly searched down around Jackson and Greenville and points south, but Burdett suspected that they were only chasing her intended misdirection. If she was in the wind and wanted to be, she might have headed the other way, north toward Memphis. Burdett got the rest of the details on the girl, make and model of her car, what she was last wearing, what clothes she might have taken with her, then asked Sturgis to get her dental records and send them up asap.

"So, ya'll really got a body up there?" Burdett could almost hear Sturgis grimacing. There was a long silence on the other end of the line as Sturgis no doubt was running quick calculations on the implications for his already perilous situation if whoever they had in the morgue up in Memphis turned out to be the Quaid girl. Sturgis rung off saying he was gonna git on it right 'way, then rang back two beats later to say the girl's tooth doctor was right there in Memphis and was awready 'spectin' Burdett's call, and let's pray that it ain't that poor child y'all got up there. Burdett hated to admit it, but he was praying that it was. It had to be someone's poor child, so it might as well be this one.

Burdett then briefed Johnson, who had been sitting quietly at his desk listening to the conversation. Having overheard the particulars on Cece Quaid's car, Johnson had already phoned in for a citywide alert. Daddy's little girl had driven off in a powder pink Nash Metropolitan, which in Memphis would be as easy to spot as a white barn owl in a tree full of crows. And it was. They hardly had time to pick up the dental X-rays and run them over to Jimmy Blake's for comparison before a report came in that a patrol car had sighted the Nash downtown two blocks east of the Peabody Hotel. Right under their noses. Burdett sensed that the pace of the case was picking up as he and Johnson drove the few blocks from the Chop Shop to the girl's car. The uniformed patrolman who was waiting at the car was a familiar face, Tommy "T-Bone" Thibodeaux. He was leaning up against his black-and-white, eating the last of a Krystal hamburger.

"Hey, T-Bone, how ya been? Good work spotting this little honey so fast. Have you touched it?"

"No way, Bird Dog, you taught me my lesson on that, and I only needed one kick in the head to remember it." Thibodeaux was grinning with pride, the last bite of the burger tucked into one cheek like a wad of tobacco. The lesson that he had painfully learned was back when he was a rookie and stumbled on an old pickup with the driver leaning dead over the wheel, big head wound, and blood spattered on the opposite window. It was his first murder scene, and he panicked, opening the door and letting the body fall out. When Burdett got there, it was quite a sight to see, what with the dead guy hanging upside down out of the truck, T-Bone still desperately wiping the blood off his hands, and the medics and crime scene crew all shaking their heads in disbelief.

But Burdett respected the way Thibodeaux owned up to his stupidity and made a point of improving his craft in the years that followed. T-Bone was always asking for pointers, and over time they had gotten to be friends. If he kept it up, Burdett thought, he might have a real future in the department.

"Truth is, I've been watchin' this car the last few days," said Thibodeaux, simultaneously giving Johnson the once-over. "It's a fancy little thing, and it didn't make no sense it bein' parked here. But it's parked legal, so there weren't much to do 'til I heard y'all was lookin' for it."

Burdett pulled a slim jim out of his trunk and, wearing gloves, he jimmied the Nash's door lock and popped the trunk. There was no obvious sign of foul play in the front of the car, only the usual girl clutter of bobby pins, sunglasses, and empty pop bottles. Different flavors of pop maybe meant different people in the car. Burdett made a note to have the techs dust the bottles for prints. Johnson called him from the rear, and inside the trunk was a more interesting tableau. Nestled among shopping bags from Lowenstein's Department Store was a tidy suitcase, same powder pink as the car, initials CLQ embossed on it. Cecelia Lucy Quaid was not coming back.

Lifting the suitcase as though it contained her last remains, Burdett carefully wrapped it in plastic, put it in the crime scene truck along with the shopping bags, and instructed Thibodeaux to have the car dusted for fingerprints and then towed to the police impound lot. Then he stood for a moment and looked around to size up where they were. Two blocks west loomed the grand Peabody Hotel, with its fabled ducks swimming in the lobby fountain. He remembered the Skyway Ballroom on the top floor, and on the roof above, an outdoor dance floor with a backdrop made up to look to like the big house on a Delta plantation. He had taken Emme there a few times back in the days before air conditioning, when you could see the big bands and dance away summer nights high above the city heat, cooled by the evening breezes off the river. He had a flashback of standing there with Emme as the summer sun set over Arkansas and the breeze wisped strands of hair across her face.

Focusing back on the present, Cece Quaid's story seemed to unfold before his eyes because it was not an unusual one. High-spirited country girl sneaks into town on the sly to meet some guy at the Peabody, parks away from the hotel to cover her tracks, and probably takes the rear stairs once she gets there. Quick fling and home to daddy's plantation before the dinner bell rings. Only this time it did not turn out as planned.

Burdett turned to share his thoughts with Johnson, but found Johnson looking the other way, two blocks south toward Beale Street, with his head held high, almost sniffing the wind. Even in its waning days, Beale Street remained a hotbed of music, gambling, drugs, and general mayhem, almost exclusively for the enjoyment of colored Memphis, the one exception being the Midnight Rambles on Thursday nights, the only time when whites were welcome.

Following Johnson's gaze, Burdett could imagine another scenario that Daddy Quaid would like even less. Proper white women avoided Beale Street, very few ventured there alone, and none went there for any reason they would want their family to know. Johnson turned and caught Burdett watching him.

"Are you thinkin' what I'm thinkin'?" Johnson asked.

"No, I'm definitely not." Burdett responded pointedly, turning back to face the Peabody.

"Well, I'm thinkin' there's too many places to park between here and the hotel, so why park this far away and so close to this low-down part of town, unless there was a reason."

"Let's start with the obvious and check the hotel, Johnson. Last thing we need is a rumor about some murdered white girl runnin' around on Beale." Burdett cut the conversation short by sliding into their squad car. He started the engine and waited for Johnson to follow. In silence they wheeled over to the Peabody, leaving the car in front and badging the bell captain away as they entered the hotel.

The grand lobby was cool and dark, echoing sounds of the splashing fountain and an occasional chortle from the ducks. Those ducks had been there as long as Burdett could remember. They said it all started with some hunters returning from duck hunting in the flooded woods over in Arkansas and leaving their decoys in the fountain, but now they had real ducks and a bona fide tourist attraction when the ducks were paraded into the elevator every night for the ride up to their rooftop coop.

No one at the front desk remembered any woman of Cece Quaid's description, so Burdett and Eustace split up to canvass the staff. Burdett came up dry with the bellhops, hotel store clerks, and the sole waitress on duty in the dining room. While he waited for Johnson, he took the waitress up on her offer of a cup of coffee and ruminated over his breakfast encounter with Emme. There seemed to be a raw vulnerability eating at her, and although every bone in his body told him to stand back, he still caught himself fingering his shirt pocket where he had put her phone number, unconsciously knowing that he would call her as soon as he got the chance.

Emme was like that, as precious and fleeting as a bird of paradise soaring through the forest canopy. She must know that about herself, he thought, how she could make you feel thrilled and excited believing that you were the one, imagining that with her you would never be lonely again. Such power, so . . . irresistible.

Then, snapping out of his reverie with an almost involuntary jerk, he willed himself back to pondering the fate of Cece Quaid as Johnson crossed the lobby and headed in his direction. The excited look on Johnson's face as he approached Burdett's table said it all.

"I think maybe we got us somethin'," he said. "I circled out back with the housekeepin' ladies who remember seein' someone like Miss Quaid a week or two back. Recently the woman's been what they call a secret regular. The maids chuckled 'cause she'd always be sneakin' 'round, not actin' like she owns the place like most whites do. You know what I mean."

Johnson remained standing and appeared reluctant to sit down, glancing toward the restaurant manager who was peeking out from the kitchen door.

"Let's go someplace where we can eat lunch and talk," he said. Then Burdett got it. Jim Crow was alive and well in Memphis. There were places for whites and places for blacks, and that was that. Even the city's parks had been Jim Crow'd to the point where most of the "public" parks were whites only. And although the almighty U.S. Supreme Court had shaken that world last year by trying to integrate the public schools, a lot of people said that would never happen, that nothing would ever change. Burdett drained the last of his coffee and heaved himself up in weary resignation to the way things were.

Moving through the lobby, Johnson insisted that they stop at the front desk again before leaving. "Here's the best part. The maids say some days they see this woman with a man who didn't appear to be the husband—a Mr. Aiken. Most times when he's here he stays in Room 650 with a Do Not Disturb sign out day and night, takes his room service tray at the door, and always leaves a nice tip on the dresser and the smell of perfume on the pillows. Last time he was here, they saw her sneak out of his room late, a couple of hours after him and way past checkout time, carryin' her own suitcase instead of callin' for the bellhop. The maids remembered 'cause they finished late on account of it."

Checking the hotel register at the front desk, they found that a Mr. and Mrs. Robert Aiken had stayed there a week and a half before. Robert Aiken from Aiken Farms, Aiken, Arkansas. Another one of those moneyed planters with company towns named after and owned by their families. And two bits said the real Mrs. Aiken had not left the Aiken family seat in a month.

"Good work, Eustace," Burdett said as they pulled away from the hotel. "I don't expect I'd ever be able to pull that out of the hotel maids. Hear no evil, see no evil, speak no evil is all I ever get."

"Detective Vance, there's people that'll talk to me, and there's those that'll talk to you. That's just somethin' you and me got to remember—and use." Driving down Union Avenue looking for a dive, any dive, that would serve a meal to Burdett and Johnson together, Jim Crow be damned, Burdett had to admit that Johnson might be right. Maybe a knack for probing behind the impenetrable face that black Memphis chose to show white Memphis would come in handy. Eustace Johnson might prove to be useful after all. Interesting that Johnson saw it that way too.

Eustace steered them to Payne's Bar-B-Q, a fluorescent-and-Formica ribs joint off Central Avenue, where they settled into pulled pork sandwiches and coleslaw on paper plates with Dr. Pepper chasers, all for 30 cents apiece. The excitement of the hunt had sparked their appetites, and they wolfed down their sandwiches while exchanging thoughts on the case. At least they had a suspect now, although neither of them was particularly happy that the suspect was Aiken. He would not be just any old hick from Hicksville, and the planter class in the Delta was well insinuated into the Memphis power structure. Given the way the city had functioned for the last forty years under Boss Crump's control, it was likely to get very complicated if they pursued Aiken, and complications were never good.

Then there were a few unexplained facts. The maids said Quaid left with her suitcase a couple of hours after Aiken, and her suitcase was in the car along with her purchases from Lowenstein's. So she must have made it to her car, then gone shopping, then come back there. Something happened to her after she left Lowenstein's and returned to her car, but why come back to the hotel? Was she supposed to meet up with Aiken again, or with someone else?

And from that moment, as if some sort of invisible tripwire had been crossed, the case seemed to fall apart. When they got back to the car, crackling over the radio was a cryptic message passed on from Jimmy Blake: "No match, different girl." So, they were back at square one. Jane Doe was still slabbed out unidentified in the morgue, and for all they knew Cece Quaid was still trysting with this Aiken guy, someplace where she didn't need her clothes but where she was most certifiably alive.

Burdett shook his head at what happened when all of your guessing and scheming and machinations collided with facts in the real world. It was a bad feeling only made worse by the unpleasant prospect that he would be no better off in the next world, given that the good Lord had apparently answered the prayers of the bumbling and dissembling Sheriff Bobby Sturgis, instead of his. No surprise there; his prayers had never been answered.

Back in the squad room Burdett and Eustace sat at their desks in silence for a long time. To Burdett, the frustrations of the previous two days were a wave that had finally broken over him, and all he could do was submit to it until the wave had spent its power. So he said nothing because whatever he said would come out wrong. He was still frustrated that Donlough had saddled him with Johnson—alright, Johnson wasn't so bad—but now even cops in his own department were turning their backs on him. Just one more handicap. Regardless of what happened in the Jane Doe case, where was the future in this entire situation? He was frustrated that these boondock, redneck sheriffs were blowing off Johnson just because he sounded colored on the phone, even when a girl in their own community might be in danger or dead. He was frustrated that there was such a swirl of feverishly secretive activity all around him and he did not know what or why. He was discouraged that Donlough was so clearly and cleverly out to get him now that Boss Crump was gone, and he knew in his heart that Donlough held all the cards and eventually would succeed. So, instead of doing the right thing and turning to Johnson to say something encouraging to the poor guy, Burdett just closed his eyes, took a long pull on his cigarette, and let the wave sweep over him.

Chapter 7

The Dish Best Served Stone Cold

Rollin' down this country road, sun at my back,
Got my baby beside me and a suitcase packed.
The wheels are spinnin', got a fire in my soul,
This jalopy's a-rockin', it's ready to roll.

—*Highway 78*, The Rockin' Sixtets, 1951

Eustace sat at his desk and sensed the tension from across the room where Detective Vance sat brooding. An electrical charge was vibrating in the air. It was wonderful. This was right where he wanted to be, in the middle of a homicide investigation that was happening right now, not years ago. His years of work and planning were finally paying off, he thought, and maybe, just maybe, he would finally get the chance to finish what he started a decade before. He smiled as he pondered events of the previous day.

The scowl on Vance's face when the Chief told him they were being paired up was routine to Eustace, seeing as how down at the Raines Station he had gotten that look every single day for the last six years from whichever white sergeant was on duty. But even for his being so smart, Vance had not seen it coming at all. Eustace did not hold it against him that he had been so rude and unfriendly, as he had never expected anything else. It did not matter. All he wanted was the chance at last to take down the killer he had been stalking these many years. Everything else was simply the means to that end.

It had never been his original plan to be a cop. Freezing in the air over Germany, he had promised himself that when he got home, he would do something big, something good, something powerful. Then that day as the war was winding down and he lay on his bunk at the airbase in Rametelli contemplating going home at last, they delivered a one-sentence telegram that derailed everything. His little brother Caleb was dead, murdered back in Memphis where everyone was supposed to be safe. Only fifteen years old, Caleb had been his right arm. They were not merely brothers; they were best friends, joined at the hip, together for life. Now it was just Eustace, by himself, forever. The sense of loneliness and loss left a tomb in his heart.

Returning from the war, he stepped down from the train in Memphis with no more grand plans left, only a singular purpose, to avenge his beloved brother. From talk in the neighborhood, he learned that Caleb had been killed as he walked home alone from a friend's house, beaten senseless and stabbed, a stray dog put down. He remembered the night when he finally had the killers' names, sitting at the kitchen table, fists clenched, his service automatic on the table in front of him, plotting revenge, imagining the bastards' last pleas for mercy before he pulled the trigger. His wife, Maggie, could see the darkness in him, and he imagined that it nearly killed her to think about losing him twice.

"Eus, honey, forget the past," she said. "Don't waste yourself on what can never be changed. You're a fine man. Be a teacher like your daddy, become a doctor. Help people. Think about the future. Don't be low-down." He would never forget her face, streaming tears, his guardian angel pleading to his better self.

"I don't know, Maggie. I miss Caleb every day. It's an ache in my head and my stomach and my heart all at once. It just hurts too much." Hot tears welled in his eyes, and he had to push down the lump in his throat to continue. "It's hard to describe the feeling. A buddy in my unit got burned real bad when his plane caught fire. His whole right arm was charred, and the pain was so terrible, he wanted to cut it off. That's how it is, baby. I've just got to find a way to cut it off."

They had talked on into the night, but in the end, what saved him was the simple, soothing truth of a lover's touch. Wise Maggie had held him in her arms until the fetid air of hate that he had been struggling to hold inside exhaled from his body and he was able to gratefully breathe the sweet perfume of her unconditional love. She saved him that night, but that did not mean he could walk away from it either. The pain was still there; he could not ignore it, and he knew that someday it would have to be excised. It actually had not taken long to learn who had killed Caleb. Out in the neighborhood the names of the killers were on everyone's lips. Witnesses had seen them beat Caleb senseless and then finish him off in cold blood. The problem was that they were white, and one of them was the worst kind of white, the invulnerable kind. Justice required a more elegant solution.

Which was why he had jumped at the chance to join the Memphis Metropolitan Police. Everyone knew it was merely Crump's nod to black voters back in '48, but Maggie encouraged him to go for it anyway, hoping that the challenge would give him a loftier sense of purpose. As usual, she was right, but maybe it was not the sense of purpose she meant. With Jim Crow as the written and unwritten law of the land, he had no illusions about being a token black on a hostile, all-white police force, but he did it anyway because that was the cross that he had pledged to bear in order to find justice for Caleb. He had been willing to pay the price for revenge with the coinage of voluntary servitude. One side of that coin was deeply demeaning, what with the finger-wagging sergeants telling him hands-off those insolent, race-baiting whites and keep your Negras in line, boy. The flip side was unexpectedly inspirational as his own people treated him with a respect and admiration that he had never experienced before, like they knew all about that coin and his cross. So, when his fellow recruits quit one by one in exhaustion, humiliation, or dismay, he soldiered on, keeping his nose clean and his eyes fixed patiently on the prize. Each step was one step closer.

He had promised Maggie he was moving on, but what no one, including Maggie, knew was what really kept him going: from the beginning he was moonlighting, stalking the two racist killers who had executed Caleb just for kicks. People like that would kill again, it was only a matter of time, and so he split his time between the two of them. Watching and waiting. Maggie had no idea how many nights he had claimed he was doing overtime while he quietly staked out that double-wide on Summer Avenue or the little house on Tutwiler. Or that he had followed a certain black Buick and rusty pickup as they made the rounds of bars and honky-tonks in Frasier and Whitehaven or the whorehouses down over State Line in Southaven. He was sure that someday those lowlife scum would make a slip, and when they did, Eustace Johnson would be there to shine a light on it.

Three years ago, it had paid off with one of them. A loud fight in the double-wide, crashes, then pin-drop silence. A body wrapped in a rug, thrown in the back of the pickup, and dumped in an alley downtown. Question was, what to do about it? Eustace could not arrest this white man. No one would believe a black man's word against a white's. So he made an anonymous call to the one person whom he thought might do something. There was a police investigation, the killer miraculously confessed, and off he went to prison for life. That one was easy and satisfying. He had played by the rules, bided his time, and justice was done. The killer had been careless, easy prey for the diligent.

That killer's partner in crime presented a more elusive target, just as violent and cold-blooded, but more calculating and cautious. Eustace knew that the man had continued to do terrible things, but he covered his tracks, and Eustace could never find an opening. Plus, the man had protected status, so for Eustace there could be no mistakes.

He came close once. The killer pistol-whipped a drunk in a dark alley in Midtown. So Eustace made another anonymous call to that same police detective. The police arrived with the medics in minutes, but the victim had been so drunk he could not identify his assailant, and he died from his injuries the next day. Just another unsolved Negro murder like Caleb's. Revenge would have to wait.

This new Donlough publicity stunt promised to be Eustace's next best chance. When word came down that the Chief was looking for Negro volunteers for a training program, everyone else shook their heads, knowing it would come to no good. But he raised his hand straightaway, and the next thing he knew, he was up at Police Central standing before the Chief himself. That was the worst and the best moment, Eustace thought. He felt as if he was waiting on the auction block while the Chief silently looked him over, checking muscle and bone. He remembered how hard it was to hold it in, eyes forward, fist clenched. At last, the Chief seemed satisfied and nodded his head to the rest of the assembled brass.

"This one'll do. Cuts a nice figure for a darkie. Perfect poster boy for our friends at the *Commerce Daily*," Donlough said to no one in particular, then turned back to Eustace, nose to nose, the smell of Chiclets on his breath. "Okay, boy, we gonna give you the opportunity of a lifetime. This is your big chance to make a mark for yourself, ya hear? We got a spot picked out for ya on the robbery detail, and you'll be the first nig—Negro to ever do that, you got me?" Chief Donlough stood there smacking his Chiclets, waiting for the only acceptable response, but Eustace swallowed hard and took his shot.

"I'm mighty grateful, Chief, but with all due respect I think I could make more of a contribution in Homicide."

He remembered how the Chief snorted in disbelief, "Oh ya do, do ya?" He glanced at the other brass as if Eustace had made some kind of uppity joke. "So, Officer, uh, Johnson, now how could ya know that? All you been doin' since ya got that fancy uniform is puttin' shoe leather to pavement in the colored section. You don't know nothin' 'bout homicide, or robbery neither for that matter."

"Actually, Chief, on my own I been workin' old colored murder cases. You can ask Dr. Blake down at the coroner's office."

"You gettin' smart with me, boy?" Somewhere Eustace had heard that when the Chief stops chewing, look out. The Chief's face had frozen into a scowling frown, a motionless ticking time bomb. Eustace knew he was in the danger zone, but it was too late to back out.

"And I hear that Detective Vance in Homicide is good. I could work with him."

That halted the Chief dead in his tracks. A light bulb had just gone off in his head, and his chewing started up again as a crooked smile slowly spread across his jowled face.

"Vance, you say. Now that's a interestin' proposition. Okay, Johnson, we'll think about it. Now you get on outta here, boy. Dis-missed."

Eustace smiled to himself in satisfaction. Any means to an end he told himself, and that was pretty much how it had played out. Now here he was, assigned to the one person whom he believed could and would actually help him. He knew he did not have much time. The election was only seven months away, and once that was over, no doubt this whole charade about training black officers for real police work would be over too, and he would be down at Raines again where he had started, never to be heard from again. If they could just close out this Mound Builder business and free up their time, he thought, maybe he could convince Vance to pick up the ten-year-old case of a teenage colored boy beaten and knifed in the neck by ruthless white men.

Glancing over at Vance, Eustace saw that he was on his fourth Lucky, still sullenly silent. He certainly is a moody one, Eustace thought. Up close, Vance was wirier and more muscular than he had remembered him at a distance. Dark hair, heavy eyebrows and a lean, drawn face. Vance was intense but there also was something immensely sad about him, and now he just sat there with his eyes closed, thumb tapping the ash off his cigarette several times for every drag he took. Best to keep your head down for now, Eustace told himself. Let him get over it. Be patient.

That was when the telephone rang and Eustace's hopes of quickly wrapping up the Jane Doe murder came to a crashing end. Another woman's body had been found floating, this time in the backwaters of McKeller Lake—and there was something inside the stockings tied around her neck.

* * *

There was nothing pretty about McKeller Lake. It was formed when the city fathers managed to convince the U.S. Army Corps of Engineers to fill in a land bridge out to President's Island. Until then the island had been home only to prisoners, moonshiners, squatters, and white-tailed deer. The land bridge transformed the slackwater side of President's Island into prime industrial waterfront real estate, and a cash bonanza naturally was had by its lucky owners who not surprisingly were the city fathers and their kin, better known as the Crump Machine. They even had named the newly created lake after an old Boss Crump crony, Senator Kenneth McKeller. So McKeller Lake was not really even a lake at all, but rather a closed off loop of the Mississippi River whose swift channel swept past the lake's outlet at the downstream end of the island. Consequently, the waters of McKeller Lake displayed the same impenetrable brown murkiness as the Big Muddy itself, and the inky, low hanging clouds that had blown in that morning made it darker still, as if nightfall had arrived hours early.

The island side of McKeller Lake was now a concrete bulkheaded industrial port, but parts of the shallower mainland side were still wild and undeveloped. Vine covered trees crowded overgrown banks, and the surface of McKeller's murky backwater was covered with a raft of flotsam and jetsam that had bobbed in from the main river channel. That was where the police perimeter had been set up.

Bright lights powered by a portable generator illuminated a body visible near the water's edge as Eustace followed Vance past the police tape and they got the basics from the officer in charge of the crime scene. A passing work boat had spotted the body floating among the rest of the debris shortly after noon. Judging from the smell, Eustace's guess was that it had been the workmen's noses that had led them to the body. Inquiries were being made around the lakeside establishments, but so far no one had reported seeing or hearing anything unusual.

Eustace leaned over the body for a closer look and saw the same signs of decay as the Vicksburg Jane Doe, and from the looks of it, there was another gunshot wound to the head, this one in the center forehead. She may have once been a beautiful girl, but now it was hard to tell. Her dress matched the description of what the maids at the Peabody had told him Cece Quaid was wearing when she left the hotel. The stockings wrapped around her neck contained another bottle.

Eustace watched as Vance carefully untied the stockings and with gloved hands removed a beer bottle, holding it up to the light. It was a carbon copy of the Jane Doe setup: double layer of stockings, probably off the girl herself, knotted around the neck, Gold Crest 51 bottle, note inside. The bottle was sealed with a liquor bottle cork, and it took another minute before Vance was able to extract the paper from inside, which looked identical to the scrap of beer carton paper they had found on Jane Doe. Vance took tweezers from his jacket pocket and carefully unfolded the paper. Looking over his shoulder, Eustace could see the now familiar handwriting and shivered off a chill:

You can consider this one payback
for what they done to George Brooks.

–The Mound Builder

Burdett looked puzzled, "Who the hell is George Brooks?"

To Eustace the name felt like an electric shock, and he could only shake his head and mutter so that Burdett alone could hear, "This is bad, very, very bad."

"What do you mean?"

"Don't you remember George Brooks? Back in '38 he was seen goin' with a white woman, and the police set him up and filled him full of bullets. They say it was someone down in Vice that was behind it. The police covered it up, and coloreds in the city almost went berserk."

"Yeah, come to think of it, I do remember something about it, but didn't the cops fire because Brooks shot first?"

"That's what you whites were told. That ain't what really happened."

"Well, anyway, it's ancient history now. That was almost twenty years ago." Eustace shook his head, thinking Vance just didn't get it.

"But what I'm sayin' is, it don't matter. That first Mound Builder note was already talkin' about payback for lynchin's in this town. That was only one, but if word gets out that there's more dead girls, people are gonna think that there's a Negro out there lookin' for revenge and killin' white girls. And what do you think is gonna happen then?" For what seemed to be an eternity, the two of them stared at each other, their eyes locked, both imagining in their darkest thoughts just what was going to happen.

CHAPTER 8

Crump's Stash

Dead presidents, yeah, they're gettin' me down,
Chasin' after paper, but it never can be found.
Thought they'd set me free, thought they'd ease my mind,
But these dead presidents are just leavin' me behind.

—*These Dead Presidents* by Little Willie, 1952

Burdett was hoping for time alone to organize his thoughts and plan the next steps, but the frying pan in the kitchen had already sparked into flames, and within hours the situation escalated from a simmering investigation into a fiery crisis. Once the body was delivered to the morgue, it took Jimmy Blake about two minutes to match the dental records of Cece Quaid. The news spread at light speed to the top floor at Police Central, then out the front door to the street.

Chief Donlough waded in immediately to make sure that he personally would be the one to call the girl's father. Turns out that, along with many Delta planters who had houses in town, old man Quaid was a longtime Crump supporter. So Donlough took this as an occasion to ingratiate himself, even though the next of kin call was normally a job for the lead officer on the case, namely Burdett Vance. It chafed a bit, but the truth was,

Burdett was glad to let the Chief do it. How many times had he stood there looking into the fragile faces of a family that was about to fall apart into grief or hearing their choked silence on the phone as their worst nightmare came true? This was one call he was happy to miss. Only Donlough would think that being the purveyor of such bottomless sorrow would open doors with Quaid; if experience were any guide, Donlough would be the last person on earth that Palmer Quaid would ever want to hear from again.

Donlough had hardly rung off with Quaid when the story hit the news. And by this time, it was not only reporting on Cece Quaid's death. Now every article was about the Mound Builder, his quest for revenge for the George Brooks killing and who knows how many other lynchings, and the other still unnamed body down in Jimmy's Chop Shop. This kind of sensational news was too hard to contain, and the department's notorious leaks were more like a sieve that had become a gusher. Every radio station was blasting an ever more salacious version, promising updates on the hour. The story had hit late in the news cycle, but even *the Press-Scimitar* managed to splash it across the front page of its late edition, adding information about the seventeen-year-old Brooks killing.

By then Burdett had a stack of messages as thick as a phone book including calls from Winslow Hoguc and every other reporter in town, and a panicky message from Emme saying she needed to see him right away. Before he could answer any of them, he and Johnson received a summons to come to Donlough's office immediately. When they arrived, Ricketts, Renfro and Harley were already there, along with Vinnie Dugan, which was no surprise since Burdett had heard that Harley had been paired up with Dugan who himself had been transferred out of Vice to the Special Investigations Unit.

Vinnie's real name was Walter, but everyone called him Vinnie, short for Vino, on account of the port wine stain birthmark across his left jaw. Vinnie had a whining voice that always made Burdett cringe and an established reputation for being an errand boy for the Crump people. Burdett had never had much use for him, and the feeling appeared to be mutual. So now it was the Four Stooges, and they were all arrayed behind Donlough, dark suits, hands in pockets and shoulders hunched, vultures perched in a tree eying fresh roadkill. Donlough's Chiclet-chewing was in overdrive, and he wasted no time getting to the point.

"We got us a situation on our hands now, fellas. This Mound Builder foolishness is gonna cause a panic if'n we don't get it under control a-sap. This is bigger than you can even imagine. Don't ya know that the Cotton Carnival gets going in just two months? That's what puts this city on the map for the whole damn world. King Cotton! How's that gonna go down if the whole city's a-feared of goin' out to party like they always done. And this year's king is Eddy Creegman, a personal friend of mine and a big supporter—of law and order, a course."

Donlough was pounding his fist on his desk, but Burdett was doing his own calculus. Whereas down in New Orleans Mardi Gras had its roots in religious austerity what with its Bacchanalian excesses being billed as the purging of sin before getting down to the serious business of Lenten deprivation, the Cotton Carnival was more in keeping with Memphis's mercantile mindset. It had been cooked up back in the Depression by the boys down at the Cotton Exchange after cotton prices bottomed out, as part of a campaign to boost the demand for cotton. The message was, "Use more cotton." Cotton clothes, cotton sheets, cotton curtains, even cotton candy, sort of.

The Cotton Carnival had now grown into the biggest social event of the mid-South, with a king, queen, royal court, secret societies, parades, the works. But it was mainly a weeklong series of boozy private parties held by the white Memphis elite in the country clubs and hotels across the city. It was also the biggest spend of the whole year, which made it a must for the merchants, restauranteurs, hoteliers, and just about everyone else who needed to earn a buck. With the Mound Builder on the loose, the fear was that would-be revelers would hunker down and take a pass on the festivities, which would shut down the Carnival as bad as the blackouts during the war years.

So as Burdett saw it, the pressure on the Chief now came from the whole power structure of Memphis—and their wives. There was an eight-week fuse burning itself down toward Coronation Day in late May, and if Donlough did not put down the Mound Builder in time, he could forget his political aspirations, because disappointed wives have long memories.

"Just let me get my hands on the bastard that leaked this story!" Donlough hissed. "I want this case closed lickety split. Vance, I'm puttin' the full resources of the department on this investigation, so don't screw it up. Catch this damn killer fast or start thinkin' about the traffic beat. And to make sure," Donlough paused and turned his gaze to the lurking vultures, "I've decided to get our Special Investigations Unit involved." As Donlough gestured toward the quartet behind him, Harley fidgeted, Dugan squinted, Ricketts smirked, and Renfro's mouth crooked a smile. "They know how to manage investigations the way I like. Meanwhile, I will personally handle ALL external communications. No one talks to the press, is that clear?"

In that moment, Burdett saw the case starting to slip away from him, as if Donlough had thrown him a slider fading low and away while he swung his bat to reach for it. The Chief wanted the Stooges to manage *him*, not the other way around. But sometimes the world slows down for a batter who is in the zone, and the ball grows large and sluggish as it hurls toward an inescapable collision with the bat. Donlough's pitch suddenly seemed unexpectedly easy to hit. In his muscle memory, at an instinctive level Burdett had already played through the possibilities of this conversation and was now only repeating what his mind had unconsciously rehearsed. So he made his play, "Chief, now that we have *all* hands on the bucket line and the boys here have so kindly volunteered to help us in *any way* that's needed, I promise to make sure that they're put to their highest and best use. As you said, we have a tricky situation here, and I'm sure you'd agree that, having just announced Officer Johnson's appointment to the Advanced Investigative Training Program, we should keep him in a prominent role in the case?"

Donlough's face clouded as he worked his Chiclets furiously, straining to fathom Burdett's angle. Burdett knew he had him boxed in. The Stooges would refuse to work directly with Johnson, so Donlough could not take Burdett off the case without doing the same with Johnson, which would not go down well in this racially charged atmosphere. Headlines came to mind like "Sole Negro Officer Pulled from Lynching Revenge Case." The whole world would think the fix was on again, George Brooks style. At last, Donlough muttered an expletive under his breath and conceded.

"Okay, Vance, keep Johnson out front, and use the boys here where you need 'em—but keep them *and me* informed of everthing, and I mean everthing." So that was the bargain. Burdett stayed in control of the investigation with Eustace as insurance. In any case, Donlough mainly wanted the Stooges involved as his eyes and ears; he could not care less what kind of busy work they were forced to do. And Burdett had just the right kind of busy work in mind for them.

Burdett scheduled a team meeting with Harley, Dugan, Renfro, and Ricketts for that next morning and then eased out of Donlough's office with Eustace in tow. He was in the usual state of annoyance that followed his interactions with Donlough, but he was philosophical regarding the situation. After all, he thought, it was beyond obvious that the race angle of the case had implications for Donlough's political strategy to cultivate the black vote. The real question was whether that was going to start driving the investigation. Clearly this was important enough for Donlough to take his crew off whatever it was that they were feverishly hunting. But eventually Donlough would demand results to still the political turmoil, a sacrificial lamb, some hapless and innocent citizen whose name happened to surface as a suspect, and whose face was not white.

"Hey, boss, thanks for sticking up for me back there." Eustace had caught up. "And I think you were right."

"I said don't call me 'boss,' and it's obvious that you had to stay on the case," Burdett responded. "I need you to dig into this George Brooks thing and any other lynchings that have happened in recent years."

"Sure, no question 'bout that, but I mean you were right to use me to keep 'em from takin' over the case," Eustace smiled knowingly. He doesn't miss much, Burdett thought. "And what were you thinkin' of havin' those boys do, maybe work the phones on Jane Doe?"

"Eustace, you surprise me sometimes, maybe even all the time. But since you mention it, yeah, that's exactly what I was thinking. Meanwhile, check the department files on Brooks and any lynchings that have happened in the last twenty years, and then I want you to track down everyone who was close to George Brooks. Every friend, every relative. See what you can find from the press reports from those days. Somehow, I just don't buy this revenge thing, not yet, but we've got to check it out."

"You don't know how that Brooks killin' hit the coloreds in this town. I was only a teenager then, but the white-washin' of the whole thing left an open wound. People remember the last of anything. Memphis has a long history of lynching; almost forty have happened in the city and out in the county since Memphis was founded. My people remember Brooks as Memphis's last public lynching. And to make it worse, it was by the police themselves who was supposed to be protectin' us. It was nothin' to you whites, but it was big to us."

"Sure, and let's assume the killer knew all that. Then why not seek revenge seventeen years ago, and why not go after the people that actually did it? No, it's the timing that's the key. Why would this guy do it now, so many years later?"

"Maybe he's been locked up. I was thinkin' of callin' up to Henning to see if anyone's been released recently that was locked up longer than fifteen years." Henning, Tennessee, was home to the Fort Pillow State Prison, named after the Civil War fort where Confederate General Nathan Bedford Forrest executed over three hundred Negro Union soldiers for the crime of fighting against slavery. "May as well be checkin' the prisons in Mississippi and Arkansas too."

"Good idea, let's put our friends on that task too, but I still don't get it. What if it's something else? Maybe we should be asking who would stand to benefit if the colored community turned against the police and Donlough and took their votes elsewhere—even back to the Republicans like they used to. Everything's up for grabs these days, and the stakes are high. Maybe high enough to kill for it. Look at Chief Donlough. He knows his whole plan hinges on making this go away. This is important enough to pull his crew off whatever he's had 'em looking for. And I sure wish I knew what *that* was."

"Oh, that. Ask my opinion, it ain't much of a secret. I heard all 'bout it from the coloreds that's cleanin' the offices and houses. It's the whites' pot of gold at the end of the rainbow.

Crump's Stash. Just a fairytale been floatin' 'round the city since the Boss died, real quiet-like, so's only a few is supposed to know about it. But 'course *we* know all about it, leastwise what there is to know—which is none of my business."

"Crump's Stash? What the hell is that?"

"Rumor's that after forty-five years of takin' his percent off the bootleggers, saloon keepers, policy runners, and the rest, Crump had built up this big stash of cold cash, maybe even gold. But when he died, no one could find it. 'Course no one knew whether it even existed in the first place, and the papers said there was plenty of cash that he had in banks all 'round Memphis, so it's not like he ever really needed it. I think it's just another Boss Crump legend that someone cooked up, but there's sure a lotta dreamers sneakin' 'round lookin' for it now."

"With all the odd break-ins, how come you never said nothin' about this before?" Burdett asked, wondering what else Johnson might be holding out on him.

"That's whites' business, and I plan to stay as far away from it as I can. If someone came in here this minute and put a satchel on my desk sayin' it was Crump's Stash and I could have it, I wouldn't touch it with a fifty-foot cane pole. No doubt they'd treat it almost like I'd touched a white woman. I wouldn't last long enough to enjoy it. Be another George Brooks, without the fun." His hazel eyes twinkled.

"How much money is it supposed to be?"

"They say millions."

Chapter 9

You Don't Know What You Don't Know

So high the water was risin' our men sinkin' down,
Man, the water was risin' at places all around,
It was fifty men and children come to sink and drown.

—*High Water Everywhere—Part II,*
Charlie Patton, 1929

Returning to the office, Burdett followed up on Emme's note, but it was early evening before he could reach her. He found her almost in hysterics.

"Burdett, my God, thank heavens. Cece Quaid was my friend! I can't believe she's dead, and like this. It's awful! I saw her only a couple of weeks ago shoppin' downtown. Now they say that's around the time when she disappeared, so it might even have been the same day! I can't believe this is happening. I'm really frightened!"

"Okay, Emme, calm down," he soothed her. The shrillness of fear and anguish in her voice was almost earsplitting. "Can you meet me for dinner at Mario's in an hour? We can go over everything then."

"Oh, thank you, thank you, Burdett," she gushed. "I'll be there, and please, please don't be late." As she hung up, he thought he could hear a muted sob. Burdett sat for a moment, pondering Emme's angst, and feeling a little shaken himself. He had been expecting similar panicky calls to come rolling in but not from Emme. It was human nature to fear most what could not be seen. Mankind's blessing and curse was the mind's fertile imagination. Man or woman, it made no difference. Give them that toxic cocktail of the usual fears spiked with even a thimbleful of unseen menace, and they became thirsty drunks draining the poisoned glass to the last drop as their imaginations ran amok.

It had become routine for the crew in Homicide. Whenever there was a report of a killer on the loose, the fright calls flooded in. This time it undoubtedly would be worse. Burdett was sure that calls would swamp their office the whole week, powered by the near certain hysteria over the Mound Builder. And someone would have to field them. He made a mental note to assign a Stooge to the task. But what unsettled him now was that this call hit so close to home, and Emme did not impress him as the flighty, high anxiety type. It was the last thing that she needed as her life teetered. Now he felt a ripple of that fear himself. This time—maybe for the first time—it was personal.

Swinging by his bungalow to change before dinner, Burdett returned the call from Hogue.

"No surprise to hear from you, Win. Did you get my message about those search warrants? And may I assume that you no longer need the write-up on our Jane Doe?"

"My, my, my. Aren't these interesting times we live in, my constabulary friend? Am I correct that ten years ago it was the Yellow Menace, yesterday it was the Red Menace, and today it is the Black Menace? Won't it be interesting to see how our brocaded Chief deals with the shifting sands of fate? And, yes, you are quite right. No need now to tax your creative energies on the story of the unfortunate Miss Doe. That has been taken care of, although there are certain salient details still wanting, such as, what efforts have been made so far to identify the poor soul? But fear not, good fellow, I know your meticulous methods, and so unless you object, may I take the liberty of sketching out the usual procedures?"

"Does a mule have a tail?" Burdett responded cryptically.

"Thank you, I will take your quaint if somewhat obtuse response as a yes." Hogue appeared to have done most of his homework already. Burdett proceeded immediately to his purpose in making the call.

"So, tell me, Winslow, what is the likelihood that the *Press-Scimitar*'s archives contain anything about a killing that happened around seventeen years ago?"

"Would it surprise you if by wild coincidence I have just such a file on my desk at this very moment, a file on a certain ill-fated man of color with the given name of Brooks?" Burdett smiled silently. Hogue was definitely ahead of the curve on this one. "But wouldn't one think that your own police files would be a better source of such information?"

"Imagine that," Burdett responded. He took that as a dig. Eustace was checking the official files as well, but if he was right and there indeed had been a cover-up on Brooks, the police files would be just history reinvented—maybe the last place to find reliable information. "But wouldn't the newspaper clippings at least tell me what the gullible public was led to believe happened to Brooks?" Burdett did not say that he was also hoping that the paper had interviewed Brooks's family and friends, possibly even the Mound Builder himself.

"Positively Sherlockian of you, my good man, and perhaps especially important if the instant terror gripping our fair city is indeed a Brooksian vendetta. And what else of interest appeared on the notes found on the bodies?" Now Hogue was fishing. If at that moment Hogue had been there in person instead of on the phone, Burdett had no doubt that Winslow would be giving him that quick sideways tell-the-truth look. Burdett sensed that Hogue might only know what was already in the news. He decided to sidestep it.

"Mind if I send over Johnson in the morning to take a look at what you have?"

"Very good, have it your way. And speaking of Officer Johnson, how goes it with your Abyssinian charge?"

Burdett had to pause to construct his answer; come to think of it, he had to admit to himself that so far Eustace Johnson was actually proving more useful on this case than Harley would have been.

"Between me and you, Win, better than expected, and pretty handy for this Mound Builder mess."

"Ah, yes, the Mound Builder. Now that you touch on the nom de meurtrier, what do you make of it?" Burdett had been pondering what might lie behind the Mound Builder's name ever since he had seen the first note. He was at a loss as to the connection between the name and the murders, other than the obvious one.

"Spooky, huh? But isn't that what he wants us to think? Would it make any difference if he called himself the Grave Digger?"

"Yes, but he didn't, did he? No matter, it's catchy, which I am not ashamed to admit works for yours truly. In fact, despite my prodigious literary powers, I couldn't have named him better myself. Certainly sells papers, my boy, and after all, isn't that the point? Of the newspaper business, of course, not of the murders."

"Yeah, right, Winslow. Listen, I gotta run, so that's all for now. And needless to say, this conversation didn't happen, if you know what I mean. Donlough is waging a total clampdown after the leak this afternoon. Any idea who inside spilled the beans?"

"Now you are treading on very thin ice, my friend, very thin. Of course, I would never, ever reveal a source. But since this time I have no source other than yourself, I feel free to speculate that it was a very small source. Very small." It had to be Ricketts, Burdett thought. Come to think of it, he was always cozying up to the radio guys who broke the story. Son of a bitch. Probably screwing up the case just to harass Burdett.

"Interesting theory, Win. And we know that small, rickety sources can have big mouths." He could hear Hogue chuckle on the other end. "Oh, and wait a minute, one last question before I go. Out of curiosity, have you heard any gossip about this so-called Crump's Stash?"

"Ah, yes, glad you mentioned it. I've been picking up snippets here and there for months but nothing concrete. Unless you've heard something new, my personal opinion is that this supposed Crump's Stash is merely a recent invention, a ruinous rumor directed at the chitchat class, perhaps even emanating from one of our craftier Crump men determined to divert the dim-witted from the real treasure—our illustrious late leader's prodigious Tennessee empire and gravy train. No doubt it will lure a legion of hapless lesser souls into a fruitless quest for El Dorado. Our eminent police chief is perhaps one notable example."

Hogue paused as he usually did when hoping to get a response. "However, in my humble opinion, it's just Blackbeard's Treasure or the Lost Dutchman's Gold Mine revisited, merely an illusion, a figment, a chimera. Indeed, the only gold to be found will be on the front page of our *Press-Scimitar* if I can ever cobble together enough of these spicy morsels to satisfy the appetites of my punctilious editors. It's a pity sometimes that we can't print bald rumors. My job would be so much easier—as would my reputation, I suppose. Needless to say, anything of substance on this subject would be of interest . . . but in the meantime, my friend, don't be tempted to join the flock of fools by chasing this fantasy. One's time and money would be better spent playing the hounds across the river."

Outside of cotton futures, the greyhound races across the bridge in West Memphis, Arkansas, were Memphians' only legal gambling. Burdett still remembered the best advice he ever got at the track: bet on the hound that pisses just before the race. Simple physics: lighter equals faster. Dog racing aside, Hogue's mention of Donlough revealed that he had already made the connection to the recent furtive activities of Donlough and company, but Burdett opted not to fan the rumors. So he ended the call and headed out the door, thinking he would rather bet his time and money on a quiet dinner with Emmeline Bryce.

★ ★ ★

Burdett arrived early at Mario's Ristorante, one of his favorite Midtown haunts. The place had a dark, warm, and cozy feel, suffused with the steamy smell of Italian spices that offset the evening's early spring chill outside. He hoped it would have the same effect on Emme. Scanning the restaurant, he spotted her already waiting, wedged into a high-backed red leather banquette in the rear, visible only in quarter profile. He shrugged off the notion that perhaps she wanted to avoid being seen with him twice in one day. More likely she simply wanted to avoid being seen at all, which was a shame because she was worth seeing. She smiled weakly as he eased into the banquette across from her, but she still looked radiant. She had let her strawberry blonde hair down, and she was wearing a pastel pink dress that gave her a glow despite the distressed look on her face.

Burdett ordered two glasses of ice with a pitcher of water on the side and pulled a pint of Old Yannissee out of his coat pocket. Liquor flowed freely at scores of less savory dives scattered across the city that were willing to pay the toll to the Machine, but with the teetotalling Baptists and their Blue Laws still in sway, no law-abiding restaurant sold liquor by the drink. So Burdett routinely brown-bagged his own and paid the setup fee. The glasses arrived, and in silence Burdett poured whiskey for both of them, waiting patiently for Emme to begin. As she added a splash of water to her drink, Burdett could see that her hand was shaking. She was the picture of pent-up anxiety, summoning the courage to keep her voice steady but without success.

"I don't know what to say," she stammered. "Poor Cece! And her family! Burdett, I'm afraid, really afraid. I may have been with her the day she disappeared. Maybe I was even the last person to see her alive! What if I saw something and didn't even know it? What if I even saw her killer? And what if he saw *me* and doesn't want to take a chance. He could kill me too!" Emme's voice was shrill with fear and felt to Burdett like the ear-piercing screech of brakes grinding in his head.

"Calm down, Emme. Let's order dinner, and then why don't you start at the beginning and tell me everything you know?" Now it was Burdett's hand on hers, but breakfast seemed a lifetime ago. "Getting it all out will make you feel a lot better. Let's go through every detail, and then if you don't mind, we'll go through it again and I'll take a few notes." The waiter came, and Burdett ordered the veal Parmesan and asparagus special for both of them. Then Emme walked him through what she knew.

She and Cece Quaid had been casual acquaintances. They occasionally traveled in the same social circles when Cece was in town. Ten days ago, they ran into each other downtown shopping at Lowenstein's. They stopped for coffee in the department store's coffee shop and then left the store together at around four o'clock. It all tied to when Quaid was last seen at the Peabody, and the bags in the Nash's trunk were from Lowenstein's. But Burdett was still struggling to put it all together in the right sequence. If Quaid left the hotel to go shopping over at Lowenstein's, it was only four blocks away on Main Street, so she could have walked there. There must be witnesses who saw her at the store or walking there and back to her car. But where had she gone after four o'clock?

"Burdett, are you listenin' to me?" He snapped out of his thoughts and focused again on Emme. "I said that the last few days I'm sure someone's been watching me. Don't ask me how I know, it's just a feelin'. At first, I wrote it off to how I feel about my whole miserable life these days, the way people now always seem to be staring and whispering." Burdett was straining to hear anything that could be evidence to warrant the hysteria. "But that's not all. I hadn't connected it together until today, but last week someone also tried to break into my apartment."

"Tried? How do you know that?"

"When I got home last Thursday night, there were crowbar marks on my door."

"But they never got in?"

"No, maybe someone scared 'em away. Burdett, I don't know what to do. I don't feel safe there!"

Burdett considered the situation for a moment. She could be right, but he needed to know more. "Emme, you need protection. I have an extra pistol at home that I want you to have." Emme's eyes widened with alarm, then she shook her head.

"I can't do that, but if it would make you feel better, I've got a little one that—someone—gave me a while ago because I live alone. I promise I'll dig it out and keep it with me. And don't worry, I know how to use it. You grow up in the country around here, it's second nature." Burdett did not want to ask Emme which sugar daddy had given her the gun.

"Okay. Second, do you have a friend that you can stay with, at least for a little while until we can find this guy?"

Emme only shook her head sadly, "Like I said this morning, no friends. They all seem to hate me now."

Then an idea came to Burdett. An all-night vigil at Emme's apartment was a perfect job for the Stooges. From the house phone he quickly called headquarters and set it up. There was a lot of grumbling, but it was too easy to justify: protection of a potential key witness who might be the last one to have seen the victim alive and even may have seen the killer, a witness who also fits the victim profile. And there was tangible evidence that she may be in imminent danger. As Burdett returned to the table, Emme searched his face for signs of hope.

"It's okay, Emme, tonight I'll have a couple of our guys posted outside your place. Someone should be on duty there by the time you get home from dinner."

Emme's relief was palpable, and it seemed to have revived her appetite just as the food arrived. They spent the next two hours going over everything again while Burdett took notes, and then simply enjoying each other's company as Burdett saw her slowly unwind. To get her to relax he asked her what her happiest memory was, and without hesitation she told him that, "besides the time we were datin' years ago, of course," it was fishing trips with her dad when she was a kid. She described how in the summertime they would trailer their skiff down to a landing on the Mississippi near their farm in Fulton, motor across to the bayous on the Arkansas side, and fish for bass and catfish or hunt squirrels, or explore the cypress swamps, usually camping overnight.

"Those were some of the happiest times, bein' with my daddy, so far away from everything." Emme had a wistful look in her eyes, but she seemed calm, precisely as Burdett had hoped.

"Right, I remember you used to talk about those fishing and hunting trips before, in just the same way. I had a few good times like that myself with my pop when I was a kid," Burdett said. Then he shuddered quietly inside. "But I lost my appetite for being out on the river ages ago. It's like climbing ladders, I guess; the older you get, the wobblier they feel, and it's been a long time since that river felt like a place to be in a tippy boat."

"It's not like that at all, silly. You just have to know what you're doin'." He listened on as she explained how to make sure your motor was reliable and how to climb upriver in the calmer shallows near the riverbank so that your course across the river angled down with the current to where you wanted to land on the other side. He was fascinated by her sense of mastery of it all. It was a world that he had avoided, and definitely not one that anyone would associate with the beautiful woman sitting across the table from him.

When they finally left Mario's, Burdett followed Emme's coupe to her place to make sure there was already a Stooge on stakeout. Ten years earlier when they were together, she had shared a bungalow with girlfriends out east off Union Avenue, but now Emme lived alone in Midtown on the ground level of a tidy four-plex just off East Parkway. Carefully trimmed hedges and walkways told of regular gardening help, but the daffodils and crocuses in bloom suggested a more feminine touch. As he walked Emme to her door, Burdett spotted Ricketts's and Renfro's silhouettes in the unmarked car parked across the street. He signaled Renfro that he would clear the apartment.

"Emme, I don't mean anything by this, but I need to check your apartment to make sure it's safe, okay?"

A wry smile crossed her face. "Darlin', you can peek anywhere you like."

Clutching her purse tensely in her right hand, Emme cautiously unlocked the door and stepped aside as Burdett proceeded awkwardly into her apartment. Sure enough, there were crowbar marks on the door. He started by checking the closets and then securing the locks on the windows and doors. Being inside a person's home can be a window into their personality, especially if they live by themselves. They may change their clothes and hair to present a different person to the world every day, but their home remains a constant. Emme's place had an orderly compactness to it, everything was just right, feminine but not overdone: galley kitchen with a row of spice bottles on the windowsill and a slightly crusty stove suggesting she liked to cook; bedroom with a home-stitched quilt on the double bed; bathroom crowded with cosmetics; dining table piled with papers; and a tidy living room with family photos framed on a side table. As he gave Emme the all-clear to come inside, Burdett spotted among the photos a black-and-white picture that he remembered from years before. It was taken on a sunny day, and Emme looked to be fifteen, long and leggy, posing with her parents in front of a tidy farmhouse, hydrangeas in bloom around its foundations.

"I remember this photo," Burdett said, picking up the picture. "So, you're still holding on to the family place?"

"Yeah, I've got a neighbor tillin' it now. I used to go up there every now and then to spend a night or two, but with Mama and Daddy gone it started to feel a little creepy to be there by myself. Fulton's in the middle of nowhere, and I always hated drivin' by the prison to get there."

Burdette did not blame her. He had motored up to Fulton once with Emme to meet her parents. Lauderdale County was bleak, and Fulton was its most dismal and remote outpost, located on the densely vine-covered bluffs where the Hatchie River flowed into an oxbow of the Mississippi, bounded by floodplains and swamps on either side. Good place to farm the rich bottomlands but also a good place to put a prison, which was exactly what they did when they built the Fort Pillow State

Prison and Penal Farm a few miles up the road outside Henning. With the Mississippi and Hatchie rivers west and south and Cold Creek to the north, escapees had only one way to flee: east. The Lauderdale County sheriff and Fort Pillow prison guards were quite handy at sealing off those escape routes, but the occasional escape warning siren at the prison had become a fixture for the surrounding countryside, same as the civil defense air raid siren tests in Memphis at noon every Saturday, a weekly reminder to be afraid.

Yes, creepy was a good word for it, and Fulton was certainly no place for a single woman to be living alone. But even while her parents were alive, there had been a desolate sadness to the place. When he and Emme rolled up in front of the old farmhouse that day, her parents stood waiting on the front porch, squinting through crow-footed eyes, furrowed brows, and tight lips, dry as the sparrows taking dust baths in the driveway. Burdett immediately cottoned to the fact that they must view him as the city slicker who was about to take their little girl away forever. They no doubt would prefer some local farm boy, maybe a member of their little Baptist church, congregation of fifty, who would stick around and take over the farm. Mama Bryce didn't mince words; she just turned her back on him and headed into the house with Emme in her wake. So Daddy Bryce invited him to take a look around the place.

The farm had a scruffy but familiar feel to it. Chickens and guinea fowl plucked ticks among the weeds around the house, swallows swooped in and out of the barn, and a creaking windmill rotated slowly in the light breeze pulling a trickle of water up from the well and into the horse trough. Burdett breathed deeply of the smells of hay and manure, and they transported him instantly to the past. So it came naturally that to be polite, he talked up his early days on the mule farm down in Mississippi. That lit up the old man, and he proceeded to give Burdett a proud tour of the barn and mule corral. No tractor yet, just a weathered aluminum skiff sporting a 15-horse outboard trailered up in the barn. So they hung by the corral and talked mules, hines, and burrows, which Burdett knew he could do till the cows came home.

But the truth was, there were no cows, Daddy Bryce's four mules were just sad swaybacks on their last legs, and the whole place displayed the end-of-the-line signs of a hundred rundown farms that Burdett had visited with his dad selling mules during his early days down in the Delta. The old farmhouse was the tell. Its last coat of paint was thirty years old, and the house was fast on its way to weathered bare wood, a tacit admission by Daddy Bryce that the endgame was near, and it would never receive another coat. The last stop on the tour was the family graveyard, situated high on a hill set back from the house. The old man first proudly pointed out the headstones of his forebearers, then quietly showed Burdett a row of smaller markers in shorter graves, where he counted on his fingers Emme's little sisters and brothers, all lost in childhood, as if making the point that Emme too was the end of the line.

"We had us some hard times here, I don't mind sayin'," Daddy Bryce shared, staring sadly down at those tiny graves. "We knowed hunger, we knowed sickness, and we sure as rain knowed death. But what don't kill ya can make ya tougher. That's our Emme. Tough as any man I ever knowed, tough as any of my sons woulda been."

"You must be right proud of her, Mr. Bryce," Burdett said, grasping for words.

"That I am," the old man replied curtly, as he turned back toward the house.

Walking down from that hill, Burdett could hear raised voices below coming through the open kitchen window, then sudden silence when the old man tactfully called out to one of the porch hounds as they approached. Over supper Mama Bryce kept a stiff upper lip and served up a decent enough table, but there was a strain between her and Emme that was thick in the air, echoes of harsh words exchanged while the men were doing rounds on the farm. Maybe that was why Emme laid down her napkin as soon as dessert was done and announced that they had to get back to town.

Rolling out of the gravel farm lane and onto the tarmac of the county road, she had said, "And that's that." Then silence all the way back to Memphis, and that was indeed that. When he asked her later why she had taken him there in the first place, Emme just looked away, saying that she had wanted to see life back on the farm through his fresh eyes, but truth was, she had only seen it again through her own eyes, and that was enough.

"So, am I safe?" Burdett jerked back to the present. Emme was standing expectantly in the middle of her living room where she had been waiting for his next instruction.

"Safe as Fort Knox," he said, putting down the photograph. "If you need help, for any reason, just call out to the car posted across the street. You're in good hands. I guess I should go. Good night, Emme."

Burdett moved to the door, but as he started to open it, he felt a tug on his sleeve and there was Emme, standing so close he could feel her warmth, smell her perfume. She kissed him gently on the lips, lingering there for a moment, and then pulled away to let him go.

"Thanks, Bird Dog, you're one in a million."

Outside her door Burdett paused for a moment, the feel of her lips still tingling on his, the distant echo of a faded memory. Then he walked over to check on Ricketts and Renfro, and whatever spell Emme had cast was broken as soon as Ricketts opened his mouth and started to grouse.

"Well, here comes our lover boy." Burdett knew they could have seen nothing, so he threw it right back.

"Poor little Ricketts, are you jealous? Don't worry, she won't come out here to bother you. Yours is too small to interest a real woman."

"Screw you, Vance."

"Yeah, screw you too." Even in the dark Burdett could see with satisfaction that Ricketts was getting agitated. He always got that jumpy look about him.

"You better be gettin' somethin,' Vance, 'cause this is pure bullshit." Renfro grumbled. "I had to get outa bed to be here, so don't expect me to show up for no meetin' tomorrow mornin'."

"Stop your bitchin', Renfro, you'll get your beauty sleep. Harley and Vinnie will relieve you soon enough—right? So don't worry that your poor little eyes'll look puffy in the morning, and don't even think about no-showin' unless you want to explain it to the Chief in person. That goes for you too, shorty." Ricketts jumped at that and started to open his door, but Renfro pulled him back.

"Okay, Vance, just get the fuck outa here and let us get this over with." Renfro growled. Burdett took it as his cue to leave. He was not sure whether Renfro was angrier about the lousy assignment that Burdett had given him or the fact that he was constantly having to reel in that hothead Ricketts. Burdett actually was a little sorry for him but only a little. Renfro had made his choice when he signed on to nursemaid Daddy Ricketts's little boy.

Driving home to get some shut-eye himself, Burdett had to chuckle at how Donlough's effort to micro-monitor the case had turned out to be a positive, giving him the bodies that he needed to keep Emme safe and get the tedious busy work done. But now he was back at the jigsaw puzzle again, working blindfolded, only this time Emme was there blindfolded with him. What was it that Emme had seen that day? Could she actually have laid eyes on the killer? Was there a way to revive those memories? Would they have time before the killer struck again?

Pulling into his driveway a few minutes later, Burdett noticed that the light was still on over at Dewey and Josie's, and sure enough, he hardly had a chance to unlock the rear door and take off his hat and coat before there was a tap on the front door. Dewey was standing there, a cigarette hanging from his mouth and a beer in each hand. Burdett was tired but waved him in, taking one of the beers as he passed by.

"Thanks for the brew, Dewey, but I'm warnin' you, this boy is bushed," Burdett said as he turned on a few lights, picked up his guitar, and settled into his beat-up leather easy chair.

"No problem, daddy-o, I'll just stay a few. I'm headed down to the station soon anyways." Burdett chuckled to himself at how Dewey had been picking up the lingo down at WHBQ; hanging out with those kids was rubbing off on him. Dewey was still in his thirties, but Burdett wondered if they called him "the old man" or "gramps" behind his back anyway. Dewey had already made himself at home in "his" chair, an overstuffed affair that shared the side table with Burdett's. The table was still littered with empty plates and glasses, layered sticky rings from the bottles and glasses of times past, and an ashtray burgeoning with butts.

"Man, you gotta clean this pad up. It's gettin' skanky. You'll never get a babe to come back to this dump—unless she's a skanky babe, of course," he said, brushing away a few stray ashes before putting his bottle down, then in a dead-on imitation of Burdett's voice, he answered himself, "But I like that crusty look, reminds me of my favorite blues joint." They both laughed and then grew quiet while they downed their beers and Burdett waited to see what was on Dewey's mind. Studying Dewey's troubled Choctaw face, jet black hair, high cheekbones, and pocked cheeks, he knew this was not simply a casual fly-by.

"Crazy about this Mound Builder thing, huh?" So that was it. "Whole city's wigged out over it, man. Me and Josie are worried about you." Now Dewey was deadly serious.

"Worried about me? I thought you were gonna to say worried about Josie."

"No, man, she don't exactly fit the profile," Dewey said, hefting his belly suggestively, and Burdett had to admit that it had not even occurred to him that Josie could be in danger. "Bird Dog, did ya ever think why, of all people, it's you on this case?"

"Pretty obvious. They're homicides, and, ugh, hello, I'm a homicide detective. But if you can believe it, Chief Donlough himself tagged me with it because of our little hobby. Like I told you before, he's always ridin' me about our digs. Killer callin' himself the Mound Builder? Call in the Grave Robber! He actually called me that yesterday. Now he's holdin' my feet to the fire to get the case closed overnight, when it could take years. Anyway, I get where you're goin' with this, but I'm on the case because the killer chose that moniker, not the other way around."

"That's actually what's worryin' me. They say that it's a race thing, a colored guy killin' white girls. But why would he choose a name like that? This Indian stuff is not somethin' that I see a lot of Negroes payin' attention to. They've got bigger problems to deal with. You and I know most of the guys workin' the digs between Cairo and the Gulf, and they're all white. Except me, of course. There's a million names to choose, so why that one?" Burdett shrugged, but that seemed to agitate Dewey even more.

"Maybe it's only a coincidence, but what if it's not? What if this guy chose that name on purpose? You say it's not a surprise that you were put on this case because Donlough and everyone else in the department knows you're interested in exploring Indian mounds. That's exactly the point. What if this Mound Builder guy chose the name for the same reason? Maybe this killer wanted you on the case, have you considered that? Maybe it's someone who knows you. Have you asked yourself who else in the department knows about your hobby?"

Burdett knew Dewey and Josie to be amateur conspiracy theorists, and this was starting to sound like their newest obsession. He shook his head.

"You and Josie shouldn't get so wound up about this. You can run down rabbit holes like that until all you're left with is your own paranoia. Sure, I been tryin' to figure out what's the connection between this guy and the history of your people around here, and I keep comin' back to the conclusion that there is no connection. He's just tryin' to scare everyone. And I'm sure that other than the Chief's poke at me, it has nothin' to do with me. Look, I've worked on hundreds of cases, and not a single one had a thing to do with me personally. There is nothin' in this case so far that's any different," Burdett declared, although he immediately realized that now with Emme popping up in the middle of the case as a potential witness—or victim—that was not exactly true.

"And that ain't all. Josie says it just ain't natural for these things to be happenin' to you all at once. You bop along all this time with nothin' happenin' in your life—sorry, but it's true—and suddenly everything is comin' at you. And the Chief is out to get you with that colored cop scheme—how is Harley, anyway?"

"I don't want to talk about him."

"And from what you're sayin', you seem to be bumpin' up against some powerful players hereabouts. Then out of the blue after all these years Emme surfaces. Yeah, Willie over at

Gannon's told me he saw you two together at breakfast the other day. Small world, brother, too small."

"There wasn't nothin' to it, Dewey. We just ran into each other there."

"Okay, but be careful. She may be a sweet girl and all, but she always had a nose for power, and I have to ask myself, why now? Josie has her hackles up on this one. She don't want you to get hurt again."

Burdett sat for a long minute pondering what Dewey was saying. He could not discount the fact that Dewey and Josie were the only people in his life who saw him in 20/20 clarity for who he really was, and they were absolutely positively in his corner, but this only seemed to be more of their usual hairbrained conspiracy talk. Still, maybe there was a kernel of truth in it. Burdett had spent his life learning one thing: almost always the most obvious explanation was the right one. Nine times out of ten it was the violent thief, abusive boyfriend, jealous husband, or angry wife. No mystery to it. His job was mainly to gather enough evidence to put them in jail. So in this case, Burdett was going with the obvious: the reverberations of Boss Crump's demise permeated everything these days, and this race thing was as old as Memphis itself.

"Buddy, I think you may have a point, but most of this is more likely tied to the plain fact that a lot of things and people got put in motion when Crump died last fall, including Emme. Sure, Chief Donlough is lookin' to fill the void by maneuverin' to get support from the Negro voters. I already figured that one out. And it looks as though Emme got cut loose and shunned after the Boss's passing, which is what happens. So, yeah, they're related, but right now she just seems to be alone and afraid of what the future holds. Don't worry, man, I was burned once, I'll be careful."

"We don't mean to talk her down, Bird Dog, we're only tryin' to protect you. That's all I wanted to say. But be careful with this one. Josie told me I had to make you promise you would. Promise?"

"Sure. Listen, I appreciate you and Josie worryin', and I'm really okay, but I promise," Burdett said, and they clinked their bottles to seal the deal.

Dewey downed his beer, gave Burdett a hug, and left the way he came. Casting his gaze around the trashed-out room, Burdett decided that maybe he would get his place cleaned up like Dewey suggested. It had gotten disgusting, even for him. He opened a couple of windows to let in the spring night air and gathered the empty bottles and full ashtrays. An hour later he had the place more or less swept clean and everything wiped down and straightened up. The whole time, he was making good on his promise to Dewey and Josie, taking a fresh look at the case as if the whole Mound Builder thing was somehow connected to him, until he satisfied himself that there was nothing there. He was sure that in the end the obvious explanation was the right one. It had nothing to do with Indian mounds; the real Mound Builder was just imagining himself standing over the mound of a fresh grave—or a row of fresh graves. That was scary enough.

Chapter 10

High Ground

Then I went and I stood up on a high, high old lonesome hill,
Lord, and all I could do was look down on the house, baby, where I used to live.

—*Back Water Blues*, Bessie Smith, 1927

Burdett was at his desk the next morning before sunrise, getting himself organized for the eight o'clock meeting with Eustace and the Four Stooges. He had spent half the night lying awake, mentally mapping out the evidence and trying to get his head around the case. Gulping his second cup of coffee, he shook his head to clear his mind. He had to decide exactly where to focus the team's efforts for the coming day. A picture of what had happened to those two girls was beginning to emerge but only in its broadest outline.

The autopsy results would not be out until later, but he already suspected what they would find. Single gunshot wound, .25 caliber round. He now suspected that Jane Doe had been dumped into McKellar Lake as well, with the killer thinking that the body would be discovered there when it floated to the top, which is exactly what happened to Cece Quaid.

The killer had murdered Quaid while Jane Doe was still in the water, maybe even at the same time, planning that one of the bodies would float to the surface and then the other body would emerge in the same place a few days later. Now that he thought about it, the notes were interchangeable, so it did not matter which body surfaced first. But the killer had not counted on the tricky currents in the lake which had carried Doe's body out into the river channel and from there south toward Vicksburg.

Since they knew when Quaid had disappeared and hence the approximate time of her death—ten days earlier—then the first murder had probably occurred around the same time, a clever calculation that after so many days, any evidence left at the lake's edge would have long since washed away with the spring rains. Then of course there were the stockings taken off the girls and messages on paper torn from the same beer carton and stuffed into identical beer bottles. There was a kind of spontaneous, improvised quality to it all, as if the killer was using whatever materials were handy, and it was all the same materials, coming from the same source, in a single location that they would have to find.

By eight o'clock Burdett had his game plan ready. It had dawned on him that melding the Stooges into a working unit was going to be like harness-training a team of mules. Back on the farm, old Jake had been his wise man where mules and life in general were concerned. He was small and wiry, but he was a bona fide mule whisperer and could muscle those massive animals any which way. And his lessons on mules had stuck with Burdett his whole life. "Little Burd, now don't you be thinkin' mules is stubborn. No, they's right smart, and just like smart people, they wants to know what they doin' before they do it . . . No, no, Little Burd, don't let no mule lean into your space, or he gonna think it's *his* space . . . You lookin' at a mule's ass is gonna get you a hoof in the face." But the main lesson Jake had taught Little Burd was that if you understand mules, you pretty much understand people too. Which was definitely the case where the Stooges were concerned.

The whole lot of them were stubborn, cunning, and always ready to kick or bite. Jake's words came back to him, don't let them lean into your space or they'll never stop trying to dominate. The trick was to establish who was the leader from the start. Eustace arrived on the dot, so far, so good. Burdett told him to finish checking out the department's official records on Brooks first, then to stop off at the Chop Shop to follow up on the Quaid autopsy before heading over to the *Press-Scimitar* to research Hogue's files on Brooks. Eustace was gone by the time the others straggled in late, bristling with attitude as if they were being pressed onto a chain gang out east at the Shelby County Penal Farm. Ricketts arrived last looking particularly sour, and Burdett wondered whether that was the first time he had ever endured a late-night stakeout.

"Thanks for nothin', Vance," Ricketts sneered. "A whole night spent watchin' that slut's house, and for what? Probably just so's you could play the big man and score with her." Ricketts grinned at the other three as if he had scored himself.

"Shut your fuckin' mouth, Ricketts. Must be a frightening experience for daddy's little boy, doin' real police work after his bedtime. And, ooh, in the dark too. Well, you can bitch all you want. You're mine today, and since you arrived last, I've got a few things in mind, special just for you." Burdett then proceeded to detail to Dugan, Harley, Renfro, and Ricketts the list of grunt work that he needed done.

Burdett put Harley on the missing person calls to all of the county sheriffs on the list, including callbacks to the ones that had blown off Eustace. They still needed to identify Jane Doe, and Burdett knew from experience that Harley was good at yukking it up with his country cousins. For the same reason, he told Harley to canvass the prisons in the tristate area to get a list of all recent inmate releases. Renfro and Dugan had more smarts, so Burdett sent them downtown to spread out and canvass for witnesses around the Peabody, Lowenstein's, and the rest of the stores on Main Street; if Emme saw something, maybe someone else did too and could remember. They seemed satisfied with their assignments and said nothing. Lastly, he put Ricketts on fielding the fright calls. With any luck Ricketts would drive some tortured soul so far over the edge that they would complain to the papers and invite Donlough's ire.

"Oh, that's just great," Ricketts railed. "Talkin' to lunatics for the next ten hours is gonna turn me into a lunatic my own self by the end. And it'll be those last two hours that the real freaks come out. Come on, any numbskull could do that."

"My thoughts precisely," Burdett responded, stifling a smile. "But look at it this way, Ricketts. You never know when you'll find a diamond in the pigsty. Every now and then one of these crazies may know somethin', and you can be the one to hear it first. Not just any numbskull can do that." Ricketts scowled as the others snickered.

Everyone was to report back to the squad room at six o'clock, when they would regroup before starting the next night's rotation at Emme's. This time they would rotate among three four-hour shifts in pairs, starting with Harley and Dugan from eight to midnight, Ricketts and Renfro next from midnight to four, and then Burdett and Eustace taking the last shift from four to daylight.

"Bird Dog," Harley finally spoke up. "I get what you're doin' with givin' us this dumb-ass busy work, but where's Johnson?

Why don't you have him doin' some of this crap? Hopefully, you got him workin' on some suitable colored work."

Burdett's eyes narrowed. "It's none of your business, but since my deal with the Chief is that I keep you bozos informed, I've got Johnson workin' the colored community on the George Brooks angle, something that you would be utterly unqualified to do."

"And what are *you* doin'?" Harley challenged him.

"Me?" Burdett smiled inscrutably, "I'm going to kick back and take a drive in the country."

⋆ ⋆ ⋆

And a drive in the country was just what Burdett had in mind. Since they now had a positive ID on Cece Quaid, he needed to talk to her family down near Clarksdale. He put in a call to the Quaids to set up an interview, grabbed a biscuit and coffee reload from Judy's Spot, and hit the road. By nine o'clock he had already slipped over the Mississippi state line south into Desoto County headed down Highway 61, the Great River Road, for the ninety-minute drive to Clarksdale.

The Great River Road hugged the Mississippi River for three thousand miles from Minnesota to the Gulf of Mexico, hopping back and forth across river bridges as it made its way south. Descending steeply from the bluff country at Memphis, the highway straightened out, and Burdett entered the empty flatness of the deep Delta. Far off to the east was a low ridge that marked the beginning of Mississippi hill country, while in the middle distance to the west the endless, straight levee stretched south ahead of Burdett as far as the eye could see. Gray cloud cover had already dimmed the morning sky, mud season had not yet yielded to spring, and the vast dark fields were like earthbound night oddly brightening the concrete highway that spanned the floodplain into the distance. A receding line of off-kilter telephone poles marked the highway, and the rhythmic tap of the car's tires striking the asphalt seams of the roadway marked the time.

It was a familiar sound, and with time on his hands as he headed south, Burdett thought of the hundreds of times in his youth he had traveled up and down this same stretch of Highway 61. But for decades now, not so much. As he drove deeper into the drabness of the Delta, closer to what used to be home, a familiar feeling of loss and foreboding returned. And springtime, the flood season, was always the worst; there was not even the white fluff of cotton in the fields to brighten his spirits, only gray skies and black earth. If spring was supposed to be the season of rebirth, it did not feel that way to Burdett.

Burdett wrenched his thoughts away from the aching past, trying to think about something else. Donlough's antics were always an entertaining diversion. Burdett had no doubt that the wild goose chase for Boss Crump's pot of gold would draw Donlough and his crew like bluebottle flies to a cow pie. If you believed Crump's Stash existed, you could see why Donlough might think he had the inside track to get to it first, what with his animal cunning at work and the whole police force at his disposal. Let in a trusted few for a cut and keep the rest ignorant while they unwittingly did his dirty work. Made sense.

Now it looked as though Donlough even had a judge on the payroll. Burdett pictured Donlough sitting in his cavernous office happily chomping Chiclets and daydreaming of how Boss Crump's secret war chest would make him unstoppable, powerful enough to take over the whole shebang. Boss Donlough. The Donlough Machine. Burdett was sure the Chief would like the sound of that. And all those break-ins? Maybe it was even the cops doing the breaking and entering. Ricketts was not above that. Then who better to put in charge of the investigation? Yes, it all fit together.

The Mound Builder had sidetracked all that. What had been a straight-up murder investigation had now become political dynamite. If that was what the Mound Builder wanted, he had succeeded, and they were playing right into his hands. White girls were popping up in the waters around the city, and Donlough's focus was on damage control to avoid a colored—or white—backlash. But if Burdett could keep the Stooges busy enough to leave maneuvering room for him and Eustace, maybe he could get the job done after all. Maybe there was time. As the miles clicked by on the road to Clarksdale, Burdett's foot unconsciously pressed harder and harder on the accelerator.

Soon enough he was braking for the entrance to Mount Magnolia, the Quaid plantation. Given the flatness of the Delta, the name Mount Magnolia seemed an anomaly. A separate, utilitarian service road of sandy clay and river gravel evidenced a no-frills farming operation, but the approach to the main house suggested a loftier sensibility. Clusters of daffodils framed the entrance, and the half-mile long pea gravel lane was flanked by a manicured alley of budding honey locusts alternating with well-trimmed holly bushes. The drive ended in a circle before a white antebellum mansion with Greek revival touches. It was built on a slightly higher elevation and surrounded by enormous magnolias that were dark green thunder clouds climbing to the sky, punctuated with splotches of enormous white flowers. As Burdett's car crunched to a stop at the front door, he was thinking how welcoming the cool shade of those trees must be on stifling Delta summer days, but today they only prolonged the gloomy morning chill.

Looking up at the house, he noticed a curtain on the second floor move slightly. He grabbed his notebook and steeled himself for the difficult conversations that were soon to follow. A columned portico framed the front door, which featured a massive brass knocker that Burdett took to be a long-dead artisan's rendition of a magnolia flower. Burdett was slightly disappointed when, before he had a chance to try the knocker, the door opened and he was greeted by a maid in white uniform. She nodded as he introduced himself, and he saw that her face was drawn in grief, tears still on her cheeks.

"Miz Quaid cain't see no visitors just now. She's awful broke up. Miss Cece was her onliest child." That brought a welling of tears that said Cece Quaid was not only one woman's child. "Mr. Quaid be out back, this way." Burdett followed her through a dark house filled with antiques, oriental rugs, and dim portraits in gilded frames, figures in gray uniforms with swords and sashes. Echoes of a bygone world. They emerged through French doors onto a spacious flagstone patio shaded by a massive twisting wisteria vine that stretched across a heavy wooden pergola with clusters of flower buds barely starting to show lavender blue. But the patio was empty.

The maid directed him to a brick walkway that led toward another towering bank of magnolias footed by massive, impenetrable azaleas, but as he neared the end of the walkway, Burdett could see an opening with mossy brick steps leading upward and disappearing into the vegetation. The maid motioned him toward the stairs and, shoulders slumping, she turned wordlessly toward the house, moving slowly, each step agonizingly painful as if she carried an invisible but unbearable weight.

As Burdett climbed the first steps, he looked upward and saw that the stairway ascended steeply through a tunnel of vegetation for at least fifty feet, and as if it was a telescope pointed at the heavens, it ended in a circumscribed view of the low, slow-moving clouds in the sky above. He climbed until he emerged at the top, where the scene caught him up short. He stood amidst a circular cathedral of elms that were still starkly bare from the winter, beyond which was a stunning view of the surrounding countryside. The panorama was obstructed only by the billowing tops of the magnolias behind him, which now appeared at eye level. Burdett then realized that he was standing on the top of a massive Indian mound. Of course, Mount Magnolia. And in the middle of that fairy ring of elms, centered on the half-acre flat top of the mound, was a swimming pool.

"Nice view from up here, isn't it, Detective Vance?" Burdett turned toward the voice as an elegant, gray-haired man rose from a poolside chaise. Palmer Quaid extended a hand, fleetingly nodding a courtesy bow to Burdett's before looking away into the distance. His patrician blue rheumy eyes were teary, but he was trying to put on a brave face. "This is an Indian mound, you know. Maybe a thousand years old. Those old Indians weren't stupid. They didn't build these things just for their pagan gods or to bury their dead. Seems to me, living 'round here all my life as I have, that they just needed to make sure there was high ground when the river rose. We're only a stone's throw from the levee, and you can see the Mississippi over yonder, only a mile away." Burdett peered out to see a muddy gray ribbon in the far distance beyond the levee, partially obscured by leafless trees as it snaked its way through the flat alluvial plain.

Quaid turned to Burdett and gave him a careful assessment.

"So, you say your name is Burdett Vance. That name is familiar. I seem to recall a certain Burdett Vance that used to be a mule dealer in these parts. Any relation?"

"Good memory. That was my father. He died a long time ago."

"That's too bad. Sorry to hear it."

"Thanks. We had a place down in Bolivar County north of Greenville. I imagine back in the day he must've sold quite a few mules up this way," Burdett looked down into the swimming pool, still full of the previous winter's murky water and rotting leaves. "Helluva spot for a swimming pool."

"No place better to catch the breezes, but everything is not as it appears, Detective Vance. See that pool house over there? It'll sleep the whole family, and it's stocked with food for a week and sealed up to keep the snakes out. Over there behind it is a five-thousand-gallon water tank so we have fresh water when the river floods. And thanks to this mound, we don't need a water tower on the plantation." The cinder block structure on the other side of the pool was dolled up with white paint, shutters, and climbing roses, but it reminded Burdett more of the bomb shelters that were fast becoming the rage in Memphis. These days, at the county fair there were sales booths with model bomb shelters stocked with tidy stacks of canned food and air vents fluttering with gaily colored ribbons meant to assure fearful purchasers that they would not suffocate before the radioactive fallout had passed. Of course, that fear was what they were really selling.

"Snakes are the real problem, you know," Quaid continued, "When the waters rise, old Mr. Snake heads for the hills just like us. Can't blame him. He lies up on high ground like this. You'll see 'em stretched out on the raised roadbeds, gettin' whipped up onto your axle if you run 'em over. I heard that down by the Yazoo last year the fellas workin' at the ESSO in Starkey stopped pumpin' gas because there were too many cottonmouths hidin' up under the trucks that came through after the high water. Anyway, we aim to be real snake-proof up here on this mound if and when the time comes."

As Palmer Quaid talked about his Indian mound, Burdett was suppressing his excitement that maybe he had found the connection between Cece Quaid and the Mound Builder. But exactly what that connection might be continued to elude his grasp.

"Mr. Quaid, who else knows about this Indian mound?"

"I imagine everyone in the county knows. It's no secret."

"Did you ever hear your daughter Cece bragging about the mound and the swimming pool on top?"

Quaid's eyes began to tear as he heard her name. "All the time. Cecelia was very proud of it. After all, it's the centerpiece of the whole plantation, hence the name. Is there a connection between that and this Mound Builder?"

"Not sure, but it's a right powerful coincidence," Burdett said. What he was thinking was that if Mount Magnolia was such a source of pride for old man Quaid, someone who wanted to get at him could be sending a message by killing his daughter and naming himself the Mound Builder.

"Have you or your daughter received any threats?"

Quaid waived off the question as if trying to swat a fly. "Cecelia? No. Me, all the time, but that's the nature of doing business, isn't it? Been that way all my life, but I'm a hard man and nothing ever comes of it." Burdett made a note to himself to look into Quaid's business dealings. With more information in hand, he could circle back to Quaid later for more questioning. Until then, there was no point in upsetting him by suggesting that his daughter's death could have been his fault. Looking back at the pool and pool house, Burdett nodded with admiration.

"In any case, Mr. Quaid, it's a very impressive setup you got here. And how long has it been since you needed this refuge?"

"I was here in the great flood of '27 and again in '38. In those days, the Army Corps of Engineers said they had the river licked, but it knocked down the levees just the same. The Corps says the same thing now, but fool me thrice, shame on me." Quaid pointed down toward the steps. "You might have noticed that our house down there is built on an Indian mound too, smaller than this one, but when the water starts to rise, every foot counts. You can plan for the future, but sometimes the future doesn't work out as you planned." With that, Quaid grew silent, eyes focused again on the horizon.

"And sometimes even high ground doesn't save you from the flood, Mr. Quaid."

Quaid turned and looked hard at Burdett. A host of emotions seemed to be churning just under the surface. "I suspect you may know what you're talking about, Detective Vance. Or are you referring to Cecelia?"

"Both."

"Okay, Detective, so you came all the way down here from the city for a purpose. I know you've got business to take care of and we're grieving, so let's get on with it. First, here is the photo of Cecelia that you asked for on the phone." Quaid stepped over to a table next to the chaise and picked up a photograph, handing it to Burdett. The photo was a headshot of a brunette beauty with the kind of winning smile that probably got her anything she wanted from Daddy.

"So, there you have it. Now what do you want to know?"

Burdett pulled out his notebook and tried to keep it businesslike, working through the standard checklist of questions about Quaid's daughter, her friends, any boyfriends. Then he asked Quaid whether there was any reason why she decided to go to Memphis after telling her family she was headed for Jackson.

"I think you know the reason, Detective, and his name is Aiken." This was the door that Burdett had been waiting to open, and they spent the next few minutes covering everything that Quaid knew about his daughter's relationship with Robert Aiken, and when he knew it. Quaid showed increasing irritation about the whole sordid affair until at last he exploded.

"If Bobby Aiken did this, he's a dead man!" The blue eyes were steely now.

"With all due respect, Mr. Quaid, please don't forget that you're talkin' to a police officer, and words like that could land you in a heap of trouble if someone—Aiken, for instance—happens to turn up dead."

"I don't care. In fact, I'm telling you right now that I am offering a twenty-five-thousand-dollar reward to whoever finds my daughter's killer, dead or alive." The patrician veneer was slipping, and Burdett could tell that Palmer Quaid was a man used to getting what he wanted even if toes got stepped on—or broken.

"You should leave this to the police, Mr. Quaid. Twenty-five thousand dollars is a scary amount of money that can make people do crazy things."

"Then I'll make it fifty thousand." Burdett could see that the conversation was headed in the wrong direction and steered it elsewhere.

"Did Cece know anyone involved in the Crump organization up in Memphis?" Quaid seemed to be caught off guard.

"What's that supposed to mean?"

"It's supposed to mean exactly what I said. Did she know anyone involved in the Crump organization? I'm not trying to be cute."

"Of course she did. She went to school at Miss Henderson's in Memphis and half of her friends were the daughters or sons of people active in the government in one way or another."

The phrase "active in government" seemed to Burdett to be a very polite way of describing the pervasive corruption of the Crump Machine. "Anyone in particular that she spent time with?"

"I already gave you a list of her friends. That's all I know. And what does this have to do with Cecelia's murder?" Quaid was beginning to show exasperation. Burdett honestly did not know the answer to that question, so he dropped the subject. He was nearing the end of the interview with Quaid, and the time was approaching to ask The Question. In any witness interview when you were coaxing information from someone who did not have to talk to you, there was usually one question that you knew could be the showstopper, the one where you pushed a little too far and the chatty witness abruptly gulped and shut up. But you still had to ask it and measure the reaction, and so you always waited until the very last.

"Did Cece know any colored men in Memphis?"

"What do you mean by 'know'?"

"You tell me. As you must know, there are racial implications here."

"I don't appreciate your suggestions or your tone, Detective Vance. How dare you make such insinuations about my family! How dare you sully my poor daughter's name! I think we have reached the end of this conversation. And now you will please show yourself out." With that, he walked over to a bell mounted on a post near the stairway and rang it. Rather than have the maid trudge up the steps to see him out, Burdett apologized for any unintended offense, thanked Quaid for his time, and headed down the mossy steps on his own. As he descended, his feet fell into a rhythm on the steps while the words of Ma Rainey came beating into his head:

The blues done wrapped around me, tighter than that
big snake's grip,
I can't shake this misery, no matter how I dip and slip.

Burdett knew from experience that the snakes of grief crawling inside Quaid's head were there to stay, Mount Magnolia be damned.

Burdett had noticed from the top of the mound that sound carried up, and while talking to Quaid he had heard the sound of another car crunching on the pea gravel in front of the house. When he emerged onto the front portico, however, there was no other car to be seen. Acting on a hunch, Burdett stepped around behind the garage. There, parked just out of sight, was a familiar car, a standard unmarked Buick Special police cruiser with Tennessee government plates. Looking inside on the front seat he could see an open notebook with the directions to Quaid's plantation scrawled in handwriting that he recognized in a heartbeat. It was the messy scrawl of his ex-partner, Harley Suggs.

CHAPTER 11

Stones in My Passway

Hey, Mr. Mailman, did you bring me any news,
Because if you didn't, it will give me those special
delivery blues.

—*Special Delivery Blues*, Sippie Wallace, 1926

Burdett waited at the plantation entrance for Harley to emerge. It was not a long wait. Ten minutes later the Buick Special came roaring out, grinding pea gravel as it bounced onto the county road, but Burdett's car blocked the way. Burdett walked up to the car and tapped on the window until Harley rolled it down.

"What the hell are you doing here, Harley? Aren't you supposed to be making the missing person calls like I told you? I thought by now you'd have worked your way up to Jonesboro at least. Or surprise me. By some stroke of luck, you ID'd the girl on the first call and came down here just to tell me?" Burdett was letting his anger do a slow burn, and Harley looked caught.

"Come on, Bird Dog, the Chief just told me to tail you and report back on your progress. He's pretty nervous about this colored angle."

"Bullshit, Harley, if you were only followin' me, you wouldn't have needed the directions that you wrote in your notebook and you wouldn't have stayed there after I left. In fact, you would have waited right here the way I waited for you. You came down here to meet with Quaid, only I got here first. What did you discuss with Quaid?"

"It's none of your business, Burdett. This is way the hell over your pay grade, and if I was you, I'd back off and stick to my own job."

Burdett grunted skeptically. "Let me guess. Quaid already knew what his daughter was doin' in Memphis. He told me so. No doubt the Chief has promised him that nothin' will come out to sully her reputation—or his. Family pride can be worth a king's ransom. So, what's in that envelope over there? He just now offered a $50,000 reward to find the killer, so it must be a fortune." Harley's face turned red as he involuntarily glanced at the fat envelope on the seat next to him. Burdett had hit a bull's eye.

"Come on, Burdett, as your friend I'm pleadin' with you, back off on this one. Some colored guy in South Memphis whacked these girls and you know it. So nail that guy before all hell breaks loose or he kills someone else; everyone, especially the Chief, will be whoppin' grateful, if you know what I mean. You'd be out of Donlough's doghouse for good."

"It doesn't work that way, Harley. You know that. It never did."

"No, Bird Dog, it just never did for you."

The two former partners stared each other down as Harley silently pulled away in the direction of Memphis. Burdett followed at a distance, and to put even more space between them, he stopped for an early lunch at the Blue & White Restaurant on Highway 61 in Tunica. The diner was a local fixture, a converted gas station where Burdett could still see the oil patches beside the islands that used to hold gas pumps. It had been years since he had eaten there, but their catfish and deep-fried pickles had an almost narcotic effect. Sliding into a booth, Burdett downshifted into Delta time where minutes became molasses, and a syrupy force was slowing down the present to pull him again into the past.

Palmer Quaid's reference to his old man had been lurking in the back of his brain ever since he had descended those stone steps from Quaid's snake refuge. Now, smelling the familiar aromas of the Blue & White, it all tumbled back to him. Mule dealer. Sounded quaint these days, but it meant something different back in the twenties. Those were happy days for a boy on the Delta whose father was a big-time mule dealer, in an era when mule dealers were envied and prosperous, just like car dealers now.

At a time when the whole Delta economy ran off the backs and hinds of mules, Burdett Vance Sr. and his little boy were living high on the hog by Mississippi lowland standards. The first tractors had only just arrived, and most everyone still needed at least one mule every four years. Do the math, his daddy used to tell him: five thousand farms in the Delta times one mule every four years, plus rich planters like Quaid had gang teams of them. So, in Burdett Sr.'s barns, corrals, and pastures they had hundreds, as well as the herds of donkeys and mares that were needed to breed them.

Burdett imagined how his old man might have been on a first-name basis with Palmer Quaid or granddaddy Quaid. He could still summon the earthy smell of manure and hay and the sounds of braying mules wafting through his open window on summer mornings. By the time Burdett was twelve, he knew everything there was to know about mules, mule breeding, mule training, and mule selling. The future seemed certain. Everything came to a sudden end, but now in hindsight Burdett could see that even then it was only a fragile illusion; the days of the fat and happy mule merchant were already numbered once tractors got cheap, and the lives of everyone you know can be swept away any day, in a heartbeat. Still, for a while, life was pretty good. Burdett Vance Sr. and his boy Little Burdett were a team, as tight as a father and motherless son could be.

Burdett's pondering of the past was abruptly brought back to the present as the door of the Blue & White opened. Harley stepped into the restaurant, looked around, and beelined toward Burdett's booth.

"Hi, Bird Dog, I knowed you couldn't resist stoppin' here, so I doubled back."

"That's right, Harley, you do know me pretty well, so you must know that right now I feel like eatin' alone. You got somethin' else to say?"

"Yeah, I do," Harley said as he slid into the booth seat across from Burdett. The waitress immediately approached, but Burdett waived her off.

"He's not staying, darlin'."

"Bird Dog, first off, I wanna to say that I'm real sorry 'bout how all this came down. You and me go way back, and I always want to count you as a friend."

"Friend? This is how you treat friends?"

"I know I done wrong by you. I shoulda talked to you before 'bout how I was needin' to get away from all the murder stuff. Honestly, I couldn't take it no more, and Loralei told me she'd leave if I came home smellin' like formaldehyde again. I didn't know how to tell you, and then everything happened all at once."

"What do you mean by 'all at once'?"

"I mean I never asked for this new job of huntin' commies. They just come to me t'other day and told me I was gettin' transferred."

"Who is 'they'"?

"The Chief and Marshmallow. But now I'm not so sure what this is really about. Not much talk about commies, but a lot about that pile of Boss Crump's cash that's up for grabs. I don't like the feel of it, and I definitely don't like workin' with Ricketts. He gives me the heebie-jeebies."

"Harley, I won't sugarcoat how I feel about this. Yeah, we go way back, which is why what you did was such a kick in the gut. But I welcome the apology, so let's start fresh from here and see where it goes." Burdett stretched out his hand and they shook on it.

"Thanks, Bird Dog, that means a lot to me. Do what you have to do to even the score. I deserve it, and I ain't gonna complain. But there's somethin' else you gotta know. It's about that Emme Bryce." Burdett felt a spike of anger, fear, and guilt run up his spine. "Word's goin' 'round that you two are gettin' together again. Be careful there, brother. She's made enemies, and one of them is the Chief hisself. Seems like he made a run at her a few months ago, more of a power grab if ya ask me. She not only told him to go to Hell—actually laughed in his face—but told his wife about it too. The wife threw him out, at least for now, and he's been havin' to bunk out at his weekend place on Horseshoe Lake, drivin' into town for work every day. He's still pissed 'bout it. So if you're really back with her, ya got two targets on you. And if she's really a material witness, it could cost you your job."

"Sounds like the Chief got what he deserved, but why do I have to keep telling everyone that there is nothing goin' on with me and Emme? That's all in the past, and there's really nothing to it, Harley, so maybe you could try spreadin' that rumor instead."

"Whatever ya say, man. Like I said, I got yer back. Now you go on and enjoy yer lunch." And with that, Harley rose, shook Burdett's hand again, and shambled out of the restaurant, but not before snagging a deep-fried pickle from Burdett's plate with a wink.

Burdett took his time cleaning his plate, draining another cup of coffee to chase a piece of lemon meringue pie, and thinking. The conversation with Harley had not been their first kiss-and-make-up over their years of friendship and partnering, and probably would not be their last. He had to admit to himself that he was glad to get it behind him. He was already missing his lifelong friend, but mostly he was missing the years of friendship ahead of them that now might never happen. Harley's confirmation that the so-called Special Investigations Unit was about chasing cash instead of commies only confirmed Burdett's suspicions about it. And the comment about his reassignment made Burdett wonder if Harley was being moved aside mainly to make room for Johnson. If so, whose idea was that? Out of the scores of experienced detectives on the force, why assign Johnson to Burdett? Simple answer: Donlough's ire. But it was the bit about Emme that came out of nowhere. It was laughable that the portly police chief would think that he himself had a play with Emme, and, God love her, Emme apparently thought so too. But she had played a perilous game by outing him to his wife. Calling the bluff of the chief of police was not a winning hand. Maybe Emme was right. Maybe it was time she left Memphis after all.

★ ★ ★

It was after two o'clock by the time Burdett's car revved its way up the steep incline on the southern edge of the bluff near the state line. His ascent from the grayness of the Delta lowlands had brought him back to the naked present and the nagging urgency of the task at hand. There were too many moving parts in this case. More than ever, they needed to ID Jane Doe to crack this. If they knew who she was and where she had been, maybe they could see the pattern. Harley should stop messing around and make the missing person calls like he was told.

Meanwhile, Burdett could feel the case rapidly constricting around him. Donlough was turning it into a cash cow opportunity to fund his political ambitions, but with that came the resulting downstream pressure from powerful people who only paid for results that they liked. Either because of the usual corrupting influences of money and politics, or perhaps for reasons less obvious but more ominous, he was being told where to look and where not to look. It brought back memories of that Georgia Tann black-market baby-selling case years back when the powers that be just wanted it to go away. Burdett had to move quickly before more avenues of the investigation were closed off. He suspected that when he returned, there would be yet another decree from the Chief sitting on his desk. He needed more dots before he could begin connecting them.

As Burdett crossed the Mississippi state line into Memphis, he knew what he had to do. He turned west on E. H. Crump Boulevard and swung onto the Tennessee-Arkansas Bridge that spanned the massive, muddy Mississippi River. Then he descended on the Arkansas side past the levee and into the low country, driving as fast he could toward the drab Delta town of Aiken, Arkansas, the seat of the Aiken family. It was a town he knew well, located in the shadow of Crowley's Ridge between the St. Francis and Tyronza Rivers in the midst of the remains of the ancient Mississippian metropolis of Casqui. Casqui's palisaded and moated city had been chronicled by the Spanish explorer Hernando de Soto in 1547. Hundreds of huts, each built on its own mound. After that first European contact, disease wiped out almost the entire population. Casqui was abandoned. It was now only a scattering of overgrown mounds that Burdett and Dewey had explored extensively.

This time Burdett did not call ahead; he simply showed up at Bobby Aiken's doorstep. Unlike Palmer Quaid's genteel style of old-time landed aristocracy, the Aiken empire evidenced a more hardscrabble commercial mentality. The town of Aiken was dominated by the Aiken Grain & Feed Company's massive grain elevator positioned alongside the railroad siding, and the entire town seemed to have grown up around the elevator and rail connection.

It was clear that some canny Aiken ancestor had decreed that all town business be Aiken business under the constant and watchful eye of an Aiken. Although the Aiken land holdings sprawled east and south from the town for thousands of acres, the Aiken "big house" was snugged in tight, artfully positioned with a view of the Grain & Feed, the Aiken General Store, and the Aiken Tractor & Machinery Company. Almost as a belated effort to rise above the bleak commercialism that surrounded it, the family residence was set off by a wrought iron fence and high shrubbery enclosing gardens and grounds that showed the same signs of meticulous toil that characterized many homes of the Delta's chosen few. Living in that land where labor was cheap and jobs were few, servants were many.

Burdett was greeted by yet another maid in uniform and shown to a sitting room where a pear-shaped woman who had to be the real Mrs. Aiken welcomed him with all the graciousness of the lady of the manor. Mrs. Aiken clearly had no understanding of the purpose of Burdett's visit, and so she showed him unannounced into a sunroom where Bobby Aiken lounged next to a silver coffee service, reading the *Commercial Daily* and wearing penny loafers without socks. He looked to be in his early forties, but his receding hairline, flushed complexion, and emerging double chin suggested that his hard partying days were beginning to take their toll.

The room was verdant with potted plants and had floor-to-ceiling windows facing south, away from the noises of the bustling farm town, a quiet haven of lazy tranquility with a ceiling fan ticking slowly overhead and a couple of flies buzzing on the sunny windowsill. Burdett noted that the languorous Bobby seemed to show little inclination to keep a watchful Aiken eye on the family business. While Aiken's wife was clueless as to why Burdett was there, Aiken himself was not, and as soon as she was out of earshot, he came out of his corner swinging.

"I don't have to talk to you, officer whoever the fuck you are. That wasn't the deal. So you can just show yourself out and don't forget to shut the door behind you," he said, turning back to his paper which he snapped with an air of dismissal. So someone had already gotten to him.

"Don't waste my time me comin' all the way out here, Aiken. Sure, we called you. Didn't he tell you I was comin'?" Burdett was bluffing, but he sensed that Aiken was just bluster himself.

"Sure, 'course he did," Aiken responded, now with a hint of uncertainty. "Anyways, I got nothin' to hide, and your boy Ricketts told me I was not a suspect and not to worry about no publicity. He said I don't have to talk to no one." So it had been Ricketts.

"Exactly. Only I'm not just anyone. I'm here to pick up the money."

"But he told me he'd be comin' by for it tomorrow." Aiken frowned while Burdett smiled to himself, thinking that at least Ricketts appeared to be sticking to the phones for the day like he had been told. Maybe Ricketts actually believed that bullshit about him being the one who could field the tip that broke the case.

"Have it your way, Aiken, I'll tell the boss you refused to pay up, and we can read all about you in both the *Commerce Daily* and the *Press-Scimitar* tomorrow. They're lappin' this stuff up," Burdett said, thumping Aiken's newspaper for emphasis. Maybe it was a built-in reflex to hearing the word "boss," but Aiken reacted as if he had been poked with a cattle prod, jumping out of his easy chair and waving his hands as if to ward off an imagined demon.

"Hold on, don't get so damn hot. I got it right here. Jeez, y'all need to communicate better." Aiken stepped into the next room, leaving Burdett there wondering how a guy like this could lead such a reckless life, spending his afternoons screwing around with the daughter of a man like Palmer Quaid, and now ready to hand over a pile of cash to a complete stranger.

At that moment Burdett was absolutely certain in his gut that Bobby Aiken was such a lightweight that he could never have cooked up something as bizarrely cruel as this Mound Builder thing. They could check his alibi if he had one, but it would only be a waste of time. Burdett suspected that if there was any justice to be found for Aiken, it would be rendered someday, somewhere by a Quaid. Aiken returned in a moment with a fat envelope that he handed to Burdett, "There, you got what you came for, so get out—please."

"Not so fast. Just so we can conclude this, Bobby, when was the last time you saw Miss Quaid?"

"Can you keep your voice down?" he hissed, glancing toward the closed door. "It was when I left our room at the Peabody 'bout ten days ago. You can check with the hotel. She said she was fixin' to go shoppin', then back home to Clarksdale. Listen, we was only havin' fun, and it was no big deal for neither of us. In any case, I can prove where I was after that. I was at the City Club playin' cards all afternoon, and I have half a dozen witnesses to back me up."

Burdett tested Aiken's story from a few different angles, asking for the names of his afternoon companions, even asking how Aiken could simply walk out the door of the Peabody and never have a second thought about Cece until she was found dead ten days later, but Aiken could not be budged. He insisted that sometimes they did not talk for weeks, and he never called her at home. She was always the one who called him when she could sneak away to Memphis, and even then, she always called his office over at the Grain & Feed.

"Listen. Cece—God rest her soul—was a big girl and knew what she was doin'. And I can tell you for a goddamn fact that I wasn't the only one."

"You mean there were others?" The suspect list had just expanded tenfold.

"Sure, man. That girl was crazy. I'm not namin' names, but she must've done half the guys at the country club." Great, Burdett thought, his suspects now included half the men of Memphis's country club set, who coincidentally were also Aiken's alibi witnesses. That was not what he needed.

Burdett finally opened the envelope and counted the money. A thousand dollars in crisp twenties. He handed it back to Aiken.

"Forget it," he said in disgust, "Let Ricketts pick it up himself. Wouldn't want him to shake you down twice. And by the way, you got off cheap."

Chapter 12

Beat 'em at Their Own Game

Now you're seein' the seeds you planted and they're startin'
to grow,
When the pain hits hard, and you feel the blow,
You'll remember what you said, and maybe then
you'll know,
That Judgment Day comes, you're gonna reap just
what you sow.

—*Reap Just What You Sow*, Jackie Jones, 1955

Meanwhile, Eustace had had a busy day. After making a quick call at the coroner's office to get Jimmy Blake's report on the second body, he had exited the squad room that morning before Vance's meeting with the so-called Four Stooges. He was glad to get away. He could not stand being in the same room with them for fear that he would show his hatred and tip his hand. So he headed down to police archives in the sub-basement of Police Central to see what he could ferret out regarding the department's investigation of the Brooks killing. Luckily, Vance had phoned ahead to tell them Eustace was coming. Otherwise, he doubted that the archives clerk would have given him the time of day. Stepping off the elevator in the basement, he approached a balding clerk sporting a triple chin and a name tag that said "Bucky."

"Hello, I'm Officer Eustace Johnson from Homicide." Lord, that felt good, but by the way that Bucky stiffened, Eustace could tell that this Bucky fellow had no use for colored cops. To make his point, the clerk wordlessly waved Eustace to a seat by the door and ponderously proceeded to clear the other work off his desk before he looked up with a self-satisfied smile that said he had somehow put Eustace in his place.

"So, whatcha want, boy?"

"I'd like to see the files on a case from 'bout seventeen years ago. George Brooks was the victim's name. It was so far back; you may not remember it."

"I ain't that old, boy, but anyways I don't have to remember it. That file ain't here no more. It was picked up not ten minutes ago by that Detective Ricketts. Little guy in a hurry. See, here's where he done signed for it." Bucky shoved the sign-out book across the desk so that Eustace could read the signature. It was Ricketts alright. Son of a bitch. Why did he need those files? And if he didn't, then who did? Eustace thanked the clerk who only grunted in response and returned to his newspaper as if Eustace was already gone. Leaving empty handed, all Eustace could think was that Ricketts was trying to make him look bad while scoring points by delivering the files up to Homicide himself. They were probably already on Vance's desk—or maybe on Donlough's.

With no squad car assigned to him and doubting he would ever get one anyway—blacks on the force didn't get cars—Eustace walked the nine blocks over to the offices of the *Press-Scimitar.* The newspaper was a lean operation. There was a small reception area opening onto the street, and everyone seemed to be in a hurry no matter which way they were going, in or out.

A quirky receptionist named Lulu with cat's eye glasses and bright red lipstick appeared to reign supreme over the chaos, calling out to everyone as they streamed by with messages, reminders, and wisecracks. The passersby all looked surprised to see a Negro in police uniform; glancing at each other, the message was the same: this was new.

"Don't worry, y'all," Lulu announced to the throng. "He's not here to arrest no one, are you Mr. Nice Police Officer?" Eustace was unsure whether she was making fun of him or only being friendly.

"I'm here to see Mr. Hogue. Tell him it's Johnson from Homicide. Workin' with Detective Vance."

"Okay, now you have a seat over there and he'll be right out." Eustace looked around for a chair and there was none. "Oh, come on now, that was a joke, Officer Johnson."

It was hard for Eustace to take offense as he saw that she joked with everyone in a nonstop monologue. The bustle and the questioning glances made Eustace want to hug the wall to stay out of the way. Lulu rang upstairs, and in a few minutes the rumpled figure of Winslow Hogue squeezed out of the small elevator. His white hair had a wild waviness that accentuated his dishevelment as he warmly shook Eustace's hand with an enthusiasm that Eustace had seldom encountered with whites.

"Well, Officer Johnson, I am most definitely pleased to make your august acquaintance. Please come up to my humble office." Eustace followed as Hogue chattered his way up the elevator, down a hallway lined with file cabinets, and into a cluttered office that smelled of cigars and seemed to be the perfect reflection of the rumpled man that occupied it. Clearing papers off a chair, Hogue beckoned him to sit.

"Well, well, well. First, let me congratulate you on your new assignment and good fortune," Hogue began, as he eased himself into his own squeaky desk chair and reached for the cigar that still burned in the ashtray on his desk. Hogue took a few long pulls to get it going again, but his eyes were locked on Eustace's, seemingly using the opportunity to make a careful appraisal of his visitor. "Detective Vance called me, and I know you came here on specific business, but before we get started, I thought it might be nice to, shall we say, get acquainted."

Through his thick horn-rims Hogue's eyes glinted, and Eustace was instantly on guard. Never trust whites, he reminded himself, and this one seemed especially dangerous because he was coming on so nice.

"May I get you a cup of coffee?"

"No, sir. I'm fine." Too nice.

"May I call you Eustace?"

"I 'spect you'll call me whatever you want, but I answer best to Officer Johnson."

Hogue gave a sly smile and waived his cigar dismissively. "Touché. Then Officer Johnson it is." Hogue paused for a long moment taking another pull on his cigar as he seemed to be contemplating what to say next. "Officer Johnson, may I speak frankly?" Eustace shrugged; he was just going to listen.

"You find yourself in an uncommonly tricky situation, uncommonly tricky. On the one hand, your ascendency to this so-called Advanced Investigative Training Program is a rare opportunity to work with one of the best men that you will find on the force. How that happened is a complete mystery for which I can only imagine there is quite a tale to tell . . ." Hogue gave Eustace a quick sideways glance, looking for an answer, but Eustace returned it with his best inscrutable smile. He had a lifetime of practice at that. Hogue knowingly smiled, patient as a schoolteacher, as if he had seen right through it. What did he already know?

"I s'pose you'll have to ask Chief Donlough what he was thinkin', Mr. Hogue. It came as a complete surprise to me," Eustace lied with a shrug and an innocent look. The knowing smile again.

"Of course, all in good time, my man, all in good time. But no doubt a bright young man with a future would be asking himself these same questions. And I'm sure that you are good at asking questions or else they wouldn't have assigned you to work homicides with our friend Detective Vance. Or so they'd say. Pardon my bluntness, but I suspect they don't give a Wolf River rat's ass whether you know how to ask good questions or do anything else besides pound pavement down in the colored section. In fact, the more incompetent you prove to be, the better." Eustace could feel his neck burning at the insult, and Hogue must have sensed it, holding up his hand to stem the anger.

"And that is why we have to beat them at their own game. Let me speak plainly, son. Burdett Vance is a close friend. Chief Donlough and his crowd have no good intentions here. If I know their methods—and I do—your usefulness will fade with the newspaper headlines, and the plan will be for you to fail stupendously and to take my friend down with you. I'm sure you know the sharp edge of the history between whites and blacks in this town better than I, but there is much personal history here that you don't know and don't need to know. Believe me when I say that the ill will between Donlough and Vance runs deeply, both ways."

Eustace took it all in, but there was nothing surprising in what Hogue had to say. He was used to being a hot potato on the police force, and from what he had seen, whites were always arguing among themselves anyway and stabbing each other in the back. That was their business. He had no plans to be working with Vance any longer than it took him to do what he had to do. Still, it was interesting that Hogue was talking as if he was some kind of coconspirator. It made him curious to see what was behind it.

"Much obliged for the warnin', Mr. Hogue, but my expectations are simple and humble. I've learned that patience is a virtue, and as they say, history is filled with the sound of silk slippers goin' downstairs and wooden shoes comin' up."

Hogue's bushy eyebrows lifted in surprise. "My, my, quoting Voltaire, are we? Perhaps I underestimate you, Officer Johnson."

Eustace smiled and his eyes slipped sideways as he gave his most amiable shrug. It was the most nonthreatening look he could muster. "My mama was a schoolteacher, is all. So, back to what you was sayin', how do you think we beat 'em at their own game?" Hogue stared at Eustace for a few moments as if digesting their conversation and measuring the man anew, then he leaned forward in his chair with a glance at the open door and down the hallway.

"It starts with me telling you that I will do whatever I can to help you succeed. I ask nothing in return, although any news tidbits that you might see fit to contribute when I pass the collection plate would be much appreciated by the uninformed masses attending the Church of Knowledge." Hogue paused as his eyes twinkled again.

"And for now, Detective Vance would not have sent you over here unless he trusted you and believed you had a head on your shoulders. So shall we begin with the current assignment?" Hogue picked up a thick file and tossed it across his desk. "This is the *Press-Scimitar's* George Brooks file. Not much there, but you can read it and make notes of what's in it, only please don't take it out of the building. And as a bonus, I can also get you into the archives of both our paper and the *Commerce Daily*, as both papers have the same parsimonious owner and share the same archive facilities down in the basement. Here is a note authorizing you to look at whatever you want, and I've made a call down to Mr. Phipps in the archives who can show you where to look."

Eustace stood and took the file. "Thank you, Mr. Hogue. And thank you for offerin' to help in general." He leaned over the desk and firmly shook Hogue's hand, looking him steadily in the eye. "Now, where do I go?"

"I'll ring downstairs to Lulu at reception and she'll tell you. And let me be clear. I'm helping you because of my friend Detective Vance. You do right by him, y'hear?"

Eustace left Hogue's office and headed for the newspaper archives, mulling over what Hogue had said about Vance. There was no reason to doubt that their friendship was real, and that Hogue was dead set to protect it. But Eustace himself had been reading Hogue's articles in the *Press-Scimitar* for years, and he suspected that Hogue had a larger agenda at work. So be it. If he could count on Hogue's support to "beat them at their own game," did it really matter what Hogue's game actually was? Besides, with a little cultivation, Eustace suspected that Hogue could be very useful when the time came to get his own story in the evening paper.

* * *

Otis Phipps was not much more helpful than Bucky had been over at the MPD archives, but at least he kept it to himself. From the looks of his cubbyhole office, he did double duty as keeper of the archives and building superintendent, and his thick fingers and string of keys said he spent more time on the latter. With a snort, Phipps took Eustace directly into a large, low-ceilinged room with rows of floor-to-ceiling shelves filled with boxes organized by year. Near the back, he showed Eustace where the yellowed archives from 1938 were located and then directed him to a large, well-lit oak table where he could spread out his work. Phipps hurried on to other tasks, and Eustace found himself alone in a silence broken only by the hum of the overhead fluorescent lights. He got right down to business.

The Brooks file that Hogue had given him contained only articles that the *Press-Scimitar* had published at the time and a few letters that appeared to be from white readers applauding the supposedly decisive action by the police. The articles at least allowed him to pinpoint the dates of the Brooks killing and the subsequent investigation, and from there he went to the 1938 archives and started pulling down boxes. Eustace managed to get through most of the boxes relatively quickly and turned up nothing. The last few crates were on a high shelf, so he went to look for a ladder. Phipps was gone, his office locked, but down the hallway Eustace spied a janitor rounding the corner with a pushcart.

"Excuse me, sir, where can I find a ladder?" The janitor turned around and blinked his eyes.

"Eustace Johnson? Is that you?" Eustace looked closer and smiled with recognition.

"Mr. Coakley, I didn't know you worked here!" Kingsley Coakley was better known as "the King" at their church, United Methodist. He had made the church his life and seemed to be everywhere: on the vestry, usher at services, and teacher in Sunday school where he had taught both of Eustace's boys. And come Christmas time, he enjoyed lifetime tenure as one of the three wise men in the Christmas pageant. That's how his nickname "the King" had stuck, but almost as a counterpoint to his truly humble nature. He did not talk much about himself. Maggie always said about the King that she suspected there was more there than met the eye.

"Work here? Shoot, I been here twenty-five years now, but this job ain't much to talk 'bout, so's I don't. It's good to see you, boy, and you lookin' mighty fine in that uniform! We all be right proud of you, Eustace." The King gave Eustace a two-handed shake and squeezed his shoulder. His close-cropped hair was white, but his grip was strong. "What brings ya'll here today, son?"

Eustace told the King about his research on the Brooks affair, indicating that it might be connected to the killings that were now making headlines. The King seemed to shudder at the mention of the Mound Builder murders. He unlocked the building super's office with a key from his own massive key ring and shortly produced a stepladder, following Eustace to help bring down the remaining file boxes.

"I tell ya, son, these killin's have everone jumpy, whites and coloreds both. So, you needs anything else, you ask the King. You may as well know it's me organized most of this stuff down here by my own self, startin' in the thirties. Back in the Depression days we was lookin' for any ways to keep our jobs, so's I come up with this idea to reorganize the basement archives, which back then was piled high like pack rats lived here. Lord be praised, kept me bringin' home a paycheck for years. So you just give me a holler, ya hear?"

The King left, and soon Eustace was plowing through boxes and hitting pay dirt. As it turned out, the *Press-Scimitar* was only following the *Commerce Daily*'s lead on the Brooks story. The *Commerce Daily*'s files were much more complete, with reporters' notes and lists of witnesses. Even a few black-and-white photographs.

The first was a photograph of the scene of the incident. Brooks's body was already gone, but the photographer had caught a shot of his bullet-riddled car with blood on the seats. That one never made the papers. The police investigation wrapped up within days, and the second photo was a standard press conference scene with Boss Crump himself captioned announcing the conclusion of the investigation: "Our police force has conducted an investigation like y'all never seen before. I tell ya, folks are sayin' this was the best investigation ever. And all the evidence shows that this man fired down on the police in cold blood." As if his say-so would put an end to the controversy. That one appeared on the front page of the *Commerce Daily*.

Boss Crump, hair snowy white even then, towered over the uniformed brass that clustered around him. There was the old chief of police Floyd Dobbins, now dead, standing slightly behind the Boss, and just behind him a younger and thinner Casper Donlough, wearing standard issue blues then and hat pulled down tight. They looked to be circling the wagons on this one, Eustace thought, as he turned to the third photo. It captured an angry crowd scene down on South Belleview near where the shooting had happened. Blacks protesting the killing and police whitewashing it. Eustace remembered that time well. His parents would not let him and his brother Caleb set foot outside the house until the unrest was over.

Eustace spent the next couple of hours systematically reviewing every document and making a list of every name that appeared in the files and why. The paper had put a couple of reporters on the story, and their interviews with witnesses and police were cursory at best. But the interesting thing was that the interviews with police who were on the scene were almost identical, regardless of which reporter conducted the interview. Each officer said exactly the same thing, using almost the same words, and each one was quoted as saying "Brooks shot first." Meanwhile, the notes of interviews of the colored eyewitnesses were more varied, everyone having seen something a little different. Some were not sure where the shots came from, but most seemed certain that only the police had fired. At last, he turned again to the three photos. Flipping through them once more, the obvious question to Eustace was, is this all there is in the file? At that moment, the King checked in to see how he was doing.

"Thanks, Mr. Coakley, I do have a question for you. These files contain lots of notes and all the articles that were published around that time, but only three photos. Do you know if any others were saved?" The King's face beamed as if Eustace had just switched on a light.

"Now you be talkin' 'bout my baby. Follow me, son." The King led Eustace back to a locked door that the King jangled open with another key from his massive ring. Inside was a small, cool room lined with deep gray metal file cabinets, each drawer labeled with a separate year.

"We spent us years pullin' together photos and negatives from everwhere, as far back as we could. Earliestmost ones go way back to 1891, the year I was born. I predicts that someday what's in this room is gonna be more valuable 'n everthing out there. So let's see, 1938. Here it is. Hep ya self." The King pulled out a drawer marked "1938" and stepped back proudly. It took Eustace only a few minutes to locate a sheaf of 8 by 10 photos in a file marked "Brooks," and he returned with them to the table for closer examination under bright lights. As if the King had read Eustace's mind, he showed up at Eustace's elbow with a large magnifying glass.

"Mister Otis won't be missin' this anytime soon."

Shuffling quickly through the photos, Eustace separated them into stacks for the scene of the shooting, the press conference, and the protest. The uncurated collection of shots of the shooting provided a more complete tableau; the photographer had reached the scene much sooner than the photo in the *Commerce Daily* file had suggested. He found multiple shots of Brooks's bullet-riddled body, hunched in the driver's seat, pistol prominently visible near his bloodied hand, every window shattered by gunfire, and blood everywhere. In the black-and-white photos, the blood was black ink smeared across the whole scene. Eustace shook his head, remembering the photographs of Chicago gangland killings from the same period. They were not nearly as bloody. Someone wanted Brooks to be very, very dead. The kind of dead that is a warning to others.

Turning to the photos of the protest, they were mostly crowd shots of angry dark faces. Many of the pictures were blurred, as if the photographer had been running with the crowd. The same faces kept showing up, and Eustace could tell that although the crowd was probably not that large, the photographer had managed to catch enough shots at different angles to make it seem larger. Around the fringes of the photos were the trailing spectators waiting for something to happen, a few carrying liquor bottles, ready to party. Eustace wondered if somewhere in those photos he was looking right at the Mound Builder himself, but he saw only one familiar face, the sore thumb sticking out of the crowd as a youthful Byron Hogue, the lone white man among the throng, no doubt covering the story for the *Press-Scimitar.* But something did not make sense. A quick check confirmed that Hogue's byline was not on any of the articles in the evening paper. He made a mental note to ask Hogue why.

Lastly, Eustace spread out the shots of Crump's press conference. The photographer had taken pictures from many angles, and he could tell that the one selected for the front page of the

Commerce Daily was taken from a low angle, so Boss Crump looked even more imposing than usual in his double-breasted wide-lapeled suit, handkerchief in the pocket and signature wide-brimmed fedora with the brim tilted to one side. A familiar site to any Memphian. On closer examination of the crowd of officials and police arrayed behind Crump, it was clear that the Boss had pulled out all the stops to demonstrate to the simmering black citizens of Memphis that the entirety of Memphis officialdom was arrayed against them. And except for Boss Crump and the late Chief Dobbins, it appeared that much of that 1938 officialdom was still firmly in place in 1955. They all seemed to want to bask in the glow of the Boss's limelight, Eustace thought as he examined the faces more closely with the magnifying glass.

That was when he noticed that even Deputy Chief Byron Ricketts had gotten into the act, although back then he was only beginning to climb the ranks. And then Eustace's eyes riveted on the figure next to him; half obscured by his father was the diminutive figure of little Earl Ricketts, already a teenager but still looking childlike, tagging along with dad for the day. Eustace's eyes narrowed as he considered his nemesis's younger incarnation, a monster in the making. And hanging from the younger Ricketts's belt loop Eustace spied the harbinger of the young man's future career, a pair of police-issue handcuffs.

As if struck by a bolt of lightning, Eustace suddenly made the connection. Jimmy Blake had said one of the dead girls' wrists showed that she had been bound, possibly with handcuffs. Who else carries handcuffs but a cop? Did that mean that the murderer they sought might be one of their own, and not a nameless Negro man looking for vengeance as they had been led to believe? And Ricketts clearly knew all about George Brooks.

Eustace knew what he wanted the answer to be, but he was in no position to pursue that line of investigation openly. It would be his ruin if he even suggested it. That idea had to come from someone else, someone white, and they had to believe the idea was their own.

Chapter 13

Bread Crumbs

You ain't nothin' but a no-good man,
Always messin' up my plan.
You ain't nothin' but a no-good man,
And I'm done holdin' your hand.

—*No-Good Man*, Big Mama Reeves, 1953

Eustace was waiting quietly at his desk in the corner of the squad room when Burdett returned to Police Central a half hour before the scheduled six o'clock meeting with the rest of the team. Everyone else on the Homicide squad had been coldly ignoring Eustace, but nevertheless he felt a sensation of serene contentment, as though he would rather be there than any place else in the world.

As Burdett tossed his notebook on his desk, Eustace looked up and checked his watch, "Back just in time. Everybody, and I mean everybody, been wonderin' where you went," he said, gesturing his head upstairs. Eustace gathered his notes and a couple of files and loped over to the chair next to Burdett's desk, handing Burdett a message from Donlough directing him to come to his office as soon as he returned. Burdett pocketed the message and turned to Eustace.

"I had to drop out of sight for a while, down to Clarksdale then over to Aiken," Burdett said in a lowered voice, looking around the room. "Turns out I was not the only one who had that idea. Seems our boys are out passin' the hat for Donlough with promises to keep their names out of the papers." Eustace nodded knowingly; that would explain why Donlough had imposed a press embargo. "Whatcha got for me, Eustace?"

Consulting his notes, Eustace gave a quick update on what had turned up during the day, leading off with the autopsy report. Quaid's autopsy came back with one significant new finding. Quaid's panties were missing, and she also had had sexual intercourse shortly before she was killed. That corroborated what they already knew from the hotel staff and Aiken, so no news there, but it definitely pegged the likely time of death to that afternoon. Eustace shared that he hoped that none of this leaked out, because the press would go wild over any suggestion of white girls being violated by the Mound Builder. Burdett nodded agreement, indicating that he was sure now that Donlough would never let the real story about Aiken see the light of day. Fortunately, a potential big break in the case had come from the note and bottle found with her body. The bottle was sealed well, which kept the paper completely dry, and as expected this one appeared to have been torn from a six-pack carton like the first note.

"So, there's a rough side and a smooth side of the paper, and on the smooth side, they picked up a latent print, which appears to match a partial that they lifted off the bottle itself. Looks as though whoever did this must have been eatin' fried chicken or some other greasy food before handlin' the note and bottle, 'cause the print was real clear."

"Surprisingly careless, but a lucky break for us. Greasy prints hold up pretty well underwater, for a while anyway. Got a match yet?" To Eustace, Burdett seemed to be getting excited, like he thought maybe the case was coming together faster than they had expected.

"They're still workin' on it. And one more thing. You remember how Jane Doe had been handcuffed? You ever stop to think who is it that carries handcuffs?" Eustace held his breath and watched carefully as Burdett stopped and thought for a moment.

"I'll have to think on that one. Are you sure Jimmy said she was handcuffed? I only seem to remember him saying those marks *might* be from handcuffs."

"Like you say, it's somethin' to think on—and who might be walkin' 'round with cuffs." Having planted the seed, Eustace shrugged nonchalantly, turning to the pile of papers on his desk. "Meanwhile, I made some progress over at the newspaper." Eustace showed Burdett the long list of names he had turned up in his search of newspaper archives of both the *Press-Scimitar* and the *Commerce Daily*, plus a stack of photos. He pointed out the picture of Boss Crump and his crew, including Earl Ricketts.

"Look at that, even then little Ricketts was literally riding his old man's coattails. Nice work, Eustace, getting into the archives of both papers so fast. And photos too. How'd you pull that off?" Burdett no doubt had expected cooperation from Hogue but apparently he was surprised that anyone else at either paper would allow a Negro police officer to take anything as evidence. Eustace gave a quick rundown on how the King had given him the run of the place and showed him the film archives.

"That was the good Lord smilin' on us. Makes me glad I'm a churchgoer." Eustace winked, and continued, "Once I got the files and pictures pulled together in a heap down there, I got Mr. Hogue to make it all official-like, so's I could take 'em with me. But speakin' of Mr. Hogue, I got a question. You'll see he shows up in those photos and he was already workin' at the *Press-Scimitar* then, so why isn't his name on any of the articles that the paper published about Brooks?" Burdett paused for a long moment, and Eustace was beginning to think that he would not or could not answer, then he seemed to set aside his doubts.

"Winslow Hogue did write about the whole terrible affair, but the hammer came down from the Machine, and his articles never saw the light of day. He had ferreted out that the police officers' stories didn't match other witnesses, but they were already dug in and committed to the lie. It was the beginning of Hogue's lifelong campaign against the Machine." Eustace nodded; now the conversation in Hogue's office made sense. Burdett shook his head appreciatively as he flipped through the pile of photographs from the aftermath of the George Brooks killing.

"As I said, good work, Eustace. Maybe you could spend more time going over the photos to see if you recognize anyone. And how about the list of people to interview? Anything pop up there?"

"Mostly the usual names that everyone knows, like Robert Church and Lieutenant Lee. I expect most of these others are dead."

"That's okay. Just means we can cross them off the suspect list. Why don't you plan to get on it first thing tomorrow."

"If'n I can keep my eyes open tomorrow after our stakeout tonight," Eustace joked.

"Don't worry, I got us on the four-to-eight dawn rotation, so that just means we start our day early and wrap up the stakeout in time to reward ourselves with a good breakfast."

"Uh, there's one more thing, and I 'spect I've saved the best for last," Eustace said. This was the big break that had come only later that afternoon. "After I finished up at the paper, I kept wonderin' why Miss Quaid's car ended up where it did. She'd already left the Peabody and gone shoppin', right? But for some reason she returned to that spot, and with all due respect I'm still thinkin' that it had more to do with Beale Street than the Peabody, since why would she be sneakin' back to the hotel? So on a hunch, I swung by the impoundment lot an hour ago to take a closer look at the girl's Nash." Eustace got up and walked back to his desk to pick up a small plain envelope. "The print boys was done, so I went over every nook and cranny of that car, and this is what I found way down under the driver's seat." Eustace then leaned forward and opened the envelope so that Burdett could see inside. There was a small glass vial containing white powder.

"Well, well, well," Burdett said, shaking his head again in amazement. "This case is just full of surprises. So daddy's little girl was doing some shopping alright, and not only at Lowenstein's."

Chapter 14

Justifiable

We done told you, our God's done warned you, Jesus comin' soon.
Well, God is warning the nation, He's a-warnin' them every way
To turn away from evil and seek the Lord and pray.

—*Jesus Is Coming*, Blind Willie Johnson, 1928

Burdett had a few minutes before the team meeting, so he headed up to Chief Donlough's office to get that over with. Barb Bledsoe showed him in immediately, but Donlough let him stand silently while he sat at his desk and finished what he was reading. Then he leaned back in his chair, popped a Chiclet, and took a long look at Burdett while he chewed.

"Detective Vance, why you are devotin' so much of your damn time and my good men as bodyguards for Emmeline Bryce instead of havin' 'em work on solvin' these murders like I told you?" Burdett was not surprised that Ricketts and Renfro had already complained to the Chief, and based on what Harley had told him, he was even less surprised that Donlough had taken the bait.

"Simple, Chief, she appears to be a material witness in the case. She was with the Quaid woman the day Quaid disappeared, possibly the last person to see her alive, and she may have actually seen the murderer."

"But you don't know that for a fact, now, do ya? You're only takin' her word for it."

"I'm not taking her word at all. In fact, she says she doesn't remember anything besides having coffee with Quaid shortly before the girl disappeared. But she appears to be at risk, and she fits the victim profile."

"And that is why you two are eatin' all of your meals together?"

"What are you talking about?" Burdett was stunned. Did Donlough have someone following him?

"You know damn well what I'm talkin' 'bout. You were seen yesterday mornin' at breakfast with her at Gannon's, and later you had dinner and drinks and spent practically the entire evenin' with her. That sounds like you were doin' more than only interviewin' a witness. I seem to recall that you have past history with this woman, correct?"

Every now and then you find yourself simply whiting out. Something happens to trigger it, your mind goes completely blank, and you can't think of a single thing to say. There is just nothing there. That was where Burdett found himself, and it took him a few heartbeats too long to get back on track, even knowing he had done absolutely nothing wrong. But by then the Chief was already talking.

"Detective Vance, let me make somethin' clear. You are treadin' on matters that are far beyond your understandin'. Don't you be contrivin' to tie this Bryce woman into this case. If I find that you've diverted my men for your personal escapades—to pursue some ridiculous fantasy with that woman—you are history. Understand? And believe me, it would give me great pleasure to throw you out on the street." Harley's warning at the

Blue & White now made perfect sense. The Chief's litany of reasons for disliking Burdett was long and as far as Burdett was concerned, reciprocated.

"Chief, I don't know enough at this point to even respond to you. And with all respect, neither do you. This isn't personal. Miss Bryce has given us reason to believe that she may be a material witness, and there's hard evidence of an attempted break-in at her home after the murders began. We don't know for sure, but there is more than enough reason to suspect that she may be in danger.

"So you say, Vance, but that's not what my men are seein'."

"What neither of us wants to see is a newspaper headline claimin' that we let this killer get to our only material witness—who also happened to have been Boss Crump's mistress. And I suspect it's *other men* that are having ridiculous fantasies about Miss Bryce." There was a pregnant pause as Donlough stopped dead in his tracks, his face turning red with bottled-up anger. "And as soon as we can determine what Miss Bryce knows, we'll take steps to either terminate the protection—or increase it."

"That's not the way it looks to me, Detective. I don't buy any of her crap. The damage to her door was only a garden variety burglar, and he didn't even get in. You don't know this woman like I do. She's nuthin' but a cold, connivin' gold digger. All you have is her word for it, and frankly with her history I have a hard time believin' anything she has to say. If I were you, I'd cut her loose now, and the fact that you won't do that tells me all I need to know. You have twenty-four hours to either nail down her story or pull my men. Now get the hell outta here."

Burdett exited the Chief's office without another word, but he was thinking that Donlough must have known about his meetings with Emme because he was having her followed, and it was odd that Donlough was so sure that the attempted break-in at Emme's was only a garden variety burglary and that the burglar never got inside.

★ ★ ★

By the time Burdett made it down to the squad room, everyone was there. Over in his corner Eustace seemed to be engaged in an intense hushed phone conversation, but Burdett paid him no mind. He was still reeling from Donlough's onslaught, and even worse from his complete inability at first to respond. Clearly Ricketts and Renfro and maybe even Harley had been feeding Donlough a tangle of lies, starting with the lewd insinuations they had made directly to his face and ending with who knows what. Whatever they had said, Donlough again chose to believe the worst about Burdett and Emme because he wanted to, especially given her recent history with the Chief.

Burdett's sense of outrage was tempered by another truth, however. He had to admit to himself that they might not be that far off the mark regarding how he really felt about Emme, even though they could not know that. He had told no one, not even Emme, what was really going on inside his head and heart, and he was convinced that his decisions so far regarding the case had been justifiable. Totally justifiable.

The six o'clock team meeting started with the expected grumbling from Ricketts and Renfro. Dugan was merely biding his time, but Harley was noticeably silent. The four of them had turned up exactly nothing, and Burdett sensed that they were quietly seething over the obvious fact that during the same time period, Eustace had struck gold. Before the meeting, Burdett had sent Eustace down to the lab with the vial of white powder for testing and fingerprints, but they had little doubt that it would test positive for cocaine.

The coke scene in Memphis was thought to reside mostly on the colored side of town, but just like the crossover music that Burdett was hearing so much about recently from Dewey, there was an increasing crossover of the white powdery stuff as well, especially in the fast circles frequented by the likes of Cece Quaid. Since there was no match yet on prints from the beer bottle and note, Burdett decided to focus on the cocaine connection. Ricketts and Dugan had done rotations in Vice, so Burdett told them to head there first thing the next morning to see what they could find on coke dealers who sold to whites, especially if they operated down near Beale Street or the Peabody.

"And, Ricketts, you report back to me *before* you head over to Arkansas, got it?"

"Arkansas? I don't know what the hell yer talkin' 'bout, Vance." Ricketts was shifting in his seat and avoiding eye contact.

"Yeah, right. As I said, report to me first. And Renfro, tomorrow I want you to track down every friend of Cece Quaid that you can find here in town. I got a list here from her family and from Aiken, and I'll see if I can come up with more names from Miss Bryce. See what you can sniff out about any possible drug use, but try to be subtle for a change. We don't want their daddies calling in favors from their poker buddies over at City Hall." With Eustace working the Brooks angle and Ricketts, Renfro, and Dugan chasing the coke trail, Burdett turned to Harley.

"Well, Harley, after your frolic today, you've still got a ton of work to do on the missing person calls, so you stay here tomorrow and work the phones. And since our boy Ricketts is going to be out and about passing the collection plate for the Chief tomorrow, you can handle the fright calls too, until he gets back."

"Alright, Bird Dog, I had this comin', so I'll do my penance. But I'll have my ear stuck to the phone for hours. Can't you cut me a break?" Harley gave Burdett his best winning grin, like old times, almost.

Burdett then stood up and leaned over Harley until they were almost nose to nose, "But, Harley, don't you know that this is what you signed up for, now that you're part of the Chief's goon squad? You step 'n' fetch it for the Chief, doing whatever he asks you to do, no questions, no whinin'. If he says lean over, you lean over, and if he says do what Burdett says, you do what Burdett says. You're mine until he says different or we catch this killer. You got that? Anyway, just for old times' sake, I *am* givin' you a break. I'm not havin' you go with the good Officer Johnson here to pound on doors down in South Memphis. We know there's not many commies down that way, now, don't we?"

With that, Burdett handed out the night's rotation assignment for the stakeout at Emme's and then ended the meeting. Everyone else cleared out, but Eustace lingered. At last he spoke up, "Detective Vance, we don't have to be at the stakeout 'til four AM. We'll need to get some shuteye 'fore that, but in the meantime how would you like to come to my house this evenin' for a fine home-cooked meal? I was just talkin' to Maggie on the phone, and she would be pleased to meet you in person and share our table."

Chapter 15

The Colored Side of Town

I'm walkin' through the valley and the sun sinkin' down,
Got the shadow on my shoulder and my face has a frown.
The preacher say it's time and the devil say it's death,
Lord, just give me one more sunrise, and I'll be in
your debt.

—*Sunrise Blues*, Jimmy Johnson, 1947

Fifteen minutes later Burdett was cruising south on Lamar Avenue and headed for the home and hearth of Eustace and Maggie Johnson. It had taken Burdett about two seconds to accept Eustace's offer as he contemplated the bleak dinner he had planned—a stack of saltines and the rest of that lonely block of cheddar molding in his ice box. Plus, he was curious. Now he was following Eustace's dusty Dodge coupe, which presently turned down a side street of carbon-copy, nondescript clapboard houses, some with porches and others with only bare stoops.

A few black residents were in evidence on the stoops and porches. Heads raised in unison as they all watched him pass by. Stranger in a strange land. Eustace directed him to stop in front of a house that was identical to the rest but different. There was the same lockstep row house architecture, but even in the fading light, the profusion of shrubs and flowers in the yard and the riotous climbing rose trellis across the front porch made it stand out like a school bus in a funeral procession: forsythia, daffodils, and hyacinth exploded with color, tulips were just coming up, and azaleas were on the way, all framing a perfectly trimmed patch of green lawn.

"Nice garden, Eustace. Who's got the green thumb?"

"My Maggie has a green thumb for sure, but like most things in this life, that thumb full of inspiration begs a whole backload of perspiration. That's where I come in," Eustace said, chuckling as he climbed the porch steps and opened the front door. Stepping into a cramped foyer, Burdett could only stop and stare. In the hallway and in every room as far as he could see, the walls were crowded floor to ceiling with sagging bookshelves.

"Jeez, Eustace, I'd say you got yourself a whole library here," he said as he looked around at the thousands of volumes. The place even had that musty library smell. And a quick glance confirmed that it was not trashy stuff.

"Yeah, my mom and pop were schoolteachers and were big readers, and I guess I got the bug. Maggie too. Here, let me show you somethin' that you'll especially appreciate." Eustace guided him into the small living room and to a bookshelf next to what looked to be the most comfortable and well-lit reading chair in the room. "These are all books on forensics. Everything you'll ever find about the science of crime and the criminal mind. I'm hoping that it'll come in mighty handy now." Eustace was beaming like a proud father. Burdett had a feeling that this might be why Eustace wanted him to come to his home in the first place, and he found it hard to meet the man's gaze. Eustace was so hopeful, and so naïve. It made Burdett feel even worse when he considered how badly it eventually had to end.

"Impressive, Eustace, very impressive."

At that moment Burdett heard footsteps clacking down the hallway, and into the room burst a woman whose kinetic energy was a force of nature. Smooth skinned and curvaceously compact, she had intelligent eyes that met Burdett's gaze directly, with a confident smile and a voice that was firmly husky.

"And you must be the famous Detective Burdett Vance. Hi, I'm Margaret, also called Maggie by certain low-down husbands." She gave Eustace a quick kiss. "Shame on the both of you for sneaking into this house without announcing yourselves properly!" Eustace sheepishly fumbled with an introduction which Maggie brushed off with a wave of her hand as she headed toward the kitchen.

"Enough of that. Come on back, dinner's almost done." Burdett followed her down the hallway and was met halfway by a stampede of children headed the other direction.

"Hold on, boys, I want you to meet Detective Vance. He's a real-life detective, and he's here for dinner, so no fighting or I'll have him investigating *you*." Burdett smiled down at two little hazel eyed boys, a couple of lion cubs squirming out of their father's grasp and running off. "That's Little Caleb and Eustace Junior, revved up as usual."

Maggie was good as her word and had dinner on the table in a heartbeat, "I know you two have a lot more work ahead of you tonight, so no sense standin' 'round jawin' when we could be chewin'."

"Don't worry, Maggie, you got no complaints from me," Burdett said as he pulled out his chair, "I'm starving." It was indeed the deliciously old-fashioned, home-cooked meal that Eustace had promised: meatloaf, mashed potatoes and gravy, turnip greens, and sweet potato casserole topped with a melted marshmallow crust, a real feast which he and Eustace proceeded to dispatch as if they had not eaten in a week. Burdett made nice, asking all the polite questions such as how Eustace and

Maggie had met and when. Turns out they were college sweethearts at the Tuskegee Institute, and similar to Burdett's friends Dewey and Josie, they tied the knot shortly before Eustace shipped off to the war in Europe. It was an enjoyable conversation, but soon enough it became clear that Maggie had her own agenda for inviting him to dinner.

Having dispensed with the pleasantries, the conversation turned serious as she raised the specter of the Mound Builder murders. In hushed voices, they discussed the tensions in the city and their fears of where it might lead. It was clear that Maggie knew pretty much all there was to know about the case, which made Burdett wonder what other goings-on at Police Central were discussed in the Johnson household. Maggie had strong but carefully circumscribed opinions, and in some undefined way she seemed to be testing Burdett.

"Honestly, it's a tragedy for those girls and their families, but the whole Mound Builder scare may just be something that someone cooked up for the election this fall. Don't you wonder if this is only another way to divide the whites and blacks again to keep us down?"

Burdett weighed his words carefully, "Maggie, I've got nothin' but questions myself where this case is concerned, but there is one thing about which I have no doubt. Someone has murdered two young women who deserved to live their lives, and I plan to follow this case wherever it takes me to find the killer. Every possibility has to be considered, includin' what you just described, although a killing spree like this would be wildly extreme for that. The challenge for me and Eustace both is to follow the evidence where it leads us and let go of any notions that might only blind us to the truth."

"Amen to that!" Eustace volunteered, trying to lighten the mood. Maggie rose from the table to clear off the dishes, but as soon as Eustace left the room to check on the boys upstairs, she was back at Burdett's side, speaking with singular intensity.

"Sure, I trust you to follow the truth, Detective Vance. I know people, and I trust you. But I also have to trust you to do the right thing by Eustace. If you knew how hard that man has labored just so he could work with you. This isn't only a job to him, it's his life. It's like he's trying to set things right for his whole race, one case at a time. He's got to succeed at this. You have to give him the chance he deserves."

Burdett looked hard at Maggie, understanding with newfound respect that she was not asking, she was telling. Not a threat, more of a righteous challenge. You're a man who can do the right thing, so do it. As he cast his gaze around that chockablock house filled with books, love, and life, it all became very clear. Turning back to her as the sound of Eustace's steps could be heard coming downstairs, he responded in a low voice, "Don't worry, Maggie, I will."

"Alright then, it's settled," she smiled. "So, shall we move to the parlor for pie?" Maggie had pulled together a tray with two pies, a tall stack of plates and handful of forks which Burdett was eyeing curiously when the doorbell rang as if on cue.

"I hope you don't mind, but we've invited a few friends to join us for dessert."

As they moved to the parlor, Eustace was already opening the front door, and in came a procession of distinguished men in dark suits, starched white shirts, and ties. Burdett vaguely recognized a few of them. They were all preachers; there must have been a dozen of them.

"Detective Vance," Eustace began, "Let me introduce you to Reverend Walter Raymond, pastor of Mount Zion Baptist Church, Dr. Jerry Tyler from Antioch Missionary Baptist Church, Reverend John Taylor from Mount Bethel AME Church,

Reverend Martin Young, pastor of the New Abyssinian Baptist Church . . ." He continued the introductions around the room with Burdett shaking the hand of each one until he reached the last, most distinguished member of the group, Dr. Henry Stevens, pastor of South-Central Baptist Church, which Burdett knew to be the largest of the black churches in Memphis.

Dr. Stevens was a tall gray-haired man with a deep voice that could, and did, fill the biggest church sanctuary in the city. Burdett never paid much attention to what went on in churches, black or white, but he recalled that Dr. Stevens had a reputation as one of the key leaders of the Memphis black community, which was no small thing. Much of the political power structure of black Memphis resided in the many Negro congregations of the city, and these were the men who ruled from the pulpits, swaying souls and votes with their sermons. Burdett had to chuckle to himself, imagining what Donlough would do to be standing in the room and glad-handing at that minute.

Maggie had been distributing plates of pie, and for the next few minutes the room devolved into a din of animated conversation and clinking silverware. Burdett was still wondering what was up when Eustace applied fork to glass and hushed the room as Dr. Stevens stepped forward and raised his voice a decibel, subtly signaling to the room and to Burdett that he was now speaking to and for the group.

"Detective Vance, we are honored that you have taken time from your urgent work to meet with us. The tragedies that have befallen our city in recent days speak to a very dark time in our history, one which every person in this room prays with all his might will be left to the past and never again visited upon our people." The room echoed with murmurs of "Amen."

"Today, even as we speak, we witness a terrible hysteria gripping this city, opening old wounds, and creating many new ones. The newspapers don't report it, but out on the street our people are seeing an ugliness that chills the soul. Scuffles, beatings, cursings—a spreading wildfire. Our congregations have reported over a hundred incidents in only the last twenty-four hours. It's as though someone has given permission to every white racist in the city to be as bigoted and oppressive as he wants.

"We have no doubt that these people have always been there. Every society has its element of small-minded and fearful souls, but something has been triggered by these terrible Mound Builder threats of revenge. Dark forces have been unleashed to do as they please. Unfortunately, the police—present company excepted—do not appear to be able or willing to do much about it. History has not forgotten the terrible massacre of our people in 1866 when a white mob raped, robbed, and killed scores of blacks in this city while the police stood aside. It can happen again."

This prompted another round of murmurs from the assembled clergy. Burdett was starting to suspect where the preacher was going with this, but he was also surprised to hear about what was happening across the city. He had not paid much attention to anything but the investigation over the past few days. The room silenced as Dr. Stevens raised his finger and continued.

"But what we are really talking about here, what lies at the core of our dismay, is fear. Fear is the surest fuel for hatred, and fear of the unknown is inexhaustible. We perpetuate it within ourselves like Satan's temptation and enthrone it at the very heart of our solitude. Our community—white and black alike—is tapping into a wellspring of fear that has been there ever since one of our peoples enslaved the other centuries ago. It comes from the certain knowledge of how any of us would feel, colored or white, if we were the victims or the perpetrators. Fear, resentment, revenge, and what next? But fear is only a quagmire of the mind. We are nearing midnight in Memphis, but as the Bible says, 'Yea, though I walk through the valley of the shadow of death, I will fear no evil: for thou art with me; thy rod and thy staff they comfort me.'" Amens again around the room, but the good Dr. Stevens was only gathering steam.

"Like it or not, we must face our fear. God helps those who help themselves. That's in the Bible too, isn't it? No, it's not. The Bible says God helps the helpless—and thank the Lord for that. But it's Benjamin Franklin who said God helps those who help themselves, and if that's the spirit that founded this great country, then that's what we need to do.

"Now, if you asked me to help you move a pile of bricks, but then you only watched me as I moved the bricks for you, then I was not actually helping you. I was working for you. Many righteous Christians fall into the snare of passivity. We will not. Our congregations stand ready to do anything they can to help put an end to the terror that this so-called Mound Builder is casting upon this city. However, we are humble enough to know that we cannot do it alone.

"You may be asking yourself, Detective Vance, why do we reach out to you in particular? Well, experience teaches us that things in this world happen on two levels, with the higher ups and with the lower downs, the talkers and the doers. We fear that in this time of political upheaval the higher ups may have other things on their minds. They may be too distracted to appreciate the true impact on the colored citizens of Memphis. The ugliness that this Mound Builder has let loose will wipe out all of the good works of people like my brothers here." Nods and amens around the room, and Burdett noticed that Eustace and Maggie were among the most fervent.

"However it may be that these murders are solved, it is important to whites and coloreds alike that they believe that the *real* murderer has been found. No more cover-ups and scapegoats. We must put an end to this terrible, corrosive fear. They have to trust that when you say that you've caught this sinner, you have put away the real murderer and not just some unlucky colored man who fits the bill, which unfortunately is the sad legacy of this city. The man who can best assure that this happens is the man in charge of the case, and that is you." Burdett's heart thudded. No, not me.

"You may not know us, but we know you. Officer Johnson here has vouched for you, which counts mightily. He says that you are a man of integrity, a man to be trusted, and that your sense of justice is color-blind." Stevens stopped for a beat, looking Burdett levelly in the eye. "We know your history and we believe him, and so we say to you, find out the truth and please, please settle for nothing but the truth. We can't ask for anything more than that, and we won't ask for anything less. We wish you Godspeed.

"Now let us pray. Dear Lord, please deliver us through this valley of the shadow of death. Help us to cast away the legacy of fear of our fellow man and to embrace strength in unity against all evil. Allow us to find in our hearts the will to trust those who help us, not because they must, but because they have the will to do what is right, no matter what. Please inspire us to reward their trust, and to exercise wisdom, grace, and patience as we help ourselves in this time of great challenge, in God's name. Amen." Amens murmured throughout the room.

Burdett was speechless, but knowing that he had to say something, he struggled to summon words of comfort for the ministers. This world of preachers was not one that he knew well. Harley once wondered how a man growing up in a Bible

Belt river town like Memphis with more churches than gas stations could know so little about either the river or the religions, but as far as Burdett was concerned, he knew enough about both and wanted nothing to do with either. Still, here he was, standing in a room full of preachers who all looked at him with eager expressions of a hope that he knew was completely unfounded.

The truth was that he did not know if the Mound Builder would ever be caught. So far, they had no real suspects, and he knew from experience that this type of case could take months or even years to solve—if ever. It might even take a few more murders to generate enough evidence to identify the killer. He suspected that this was not the message that his audience wanted to hear, but he gave it his best shot.

"Dr. Stevens, thank you for your kind words of confidence. Please rest assured that Officer Johnson and I and the rest of our team are doing everything we can to find the killer. And let me also add that Chief Donlough is equally committed to bringing the Mound Builder to justice." Burdett was careful to add the last comment on the off chance that news of this meeting ever made its way back to Donlough. "I can't honestly know if we will be successful. What I can tell you is that we will do everything we can to pursue the evidence and to find the real killer, whoever he may be. As God is my witness, I promise you that."

There was not much more that could be said, and the assembled clergy soon headed for the door. When the last of the surprise guests had left, Eustace and Burdett helped gather the dishes and take them to the kitchen, where the two of them and Maggie all stood silent for a moment, waiting for someone to say something. At last Burdett jumped in.

"Well played, you two. And I imagine that the good brethren were just sitting outside in their cars waiting for the signal to come on in. What was it, a window shade pulled down? A wave out the front door?"

"It was the light on the front porch," Eustace said. "I hope you're not angry. We thought it was important for you to know how much they're all—we're all—depending on you. There could be a lot of lives at stake here, and not only the ones that the Mound Builder gets."

Burdett wanted to tell them that he did feel ambushed. The posse of ministers had left him with a heavy sense of obligation that was yet another burden being foisted upon him, one more source of pressure telling him to solve the case and get it done fast. None of it was making his job a bit easier; none of it was leading him even one step closer to finding the killer. But at the same time, Burdett could not help but feel himself strangely uplifted and inspired by the trust these people were putting in him. This was new. Why him? Why not Donlough or someone else with real power to make things happen? It felt good, but Burdett also knew that he was falling for their flattery and feeling inspired in spite of himself, and he was certain that this was precisely what the virtuous colored clergy of Memphis had intended.

"No, it's okay. I guess I don't mind. It's best to know how this is playin' out on the colored side of town."

Chapter 16

Midnight Ramblers

You'll see pretty browns in beautiful gowns,
You'll see tailor-mades and hand-me-downs,
You'll meet honest men, and pick-pockets skilled,
You'll find that business never ceases 'til somebody's killed!

—*Beale Street Blues,* W. C Handy, 1909

Burdett said his goodbye to Maggie, and as he walked out to his car with Eustace, he could not help but smile. True to herself to the last, Maggie had bid him farewell with a steady gaze and firm handshake that lingered just long enough to say they had a pact. She was definitely a lioness, a match for her mate.

He turned to Eustace as they reached the car, "Thanks for the dinner, Eustace. It was great to meet Maggie. She's pretty special."

"You're tellin' me," Eustace proudly. "So, I guess I'll see you at four o'clock sharp. Where do you want to meet?"

"Actually, I was thinkin' that maybe we'd meet a couple of hours early. Go for a midnight ramble before we settle in for the stakeout. I'll explain later. Meet me at one-thirty at my house.

I'm at 465 Duvall just off Poplar, can you find it? We'll take my car from there."

Traffic was light and it took a mere ten minutes for Burdett to get across town to his bungalow. It was only nine o'clock, still early, and he knew that he needed to catch what little sleep time was left. But first he had to call Emme. She picked up on the first ring.

"Hello?" Her voice sounded velvety.

"Hi, Emme, it's me. Just thought I'd check in before going down myself. There should already be a car outside. Could you go take a look?"

"Hi, Burdett. Yes, Mr. Renfro and his partner are out there now. I just gave them some coffee and cookies."

"That's great," Burdett said. At least the Stooges were doing one thing he told them to do. And Emme was smart to sugar-coat it with food and drink. "Officer Johnson and I have the dawn rotation, so I'll be outside starting at four."

"Thank you so much for all this, Burdett. I don't know what I'd do without you. Could I ask you just one more a favor? When you get here tonight, could you check in on me?"

Burdett thought on it for a moment and then decided it would be a bad idea, "I don't think so, Emme. I'll have my partner with me and . . ."

"Sure, I understand, but could you at least knock on the door to let me know when you leave? You'd do that with anyone, right?" She had a point.

"Okay, I'll let you know in the morning before we go. It'll be around eight. In the meantime, I want you to think about a couple of things. First, think of everyone you know who was a friend of Cece's. Make a list. Second, tomorrow I want to take you back to Lowenstein's to walk you through the entire time you were with Cece. If you did see anything, maybe being there will jog your memory."

"I'd love that. And we can go to the café there in the store too. I'll order the same thing and you can order what Cece had. I still can't imagine what I might have seen, but it might work."

"Alright, Emme, see you in the morning."

"Good night, Bird Dog, and God bless."

Burdett hung up the phone smiling. That Emme sure had a way about her. Almost intoxicating.

Burdett's alarm clock jolted him awake at one o'clock, and he rose from a restless sleep, shaking off the vestigial threads of a recurring nightmare. In the dream he was forever plunging toward the sound of a thundering torrent obscured in the darkness below, and as the sound became a deafening roar it hit him that this was not darkness at all, but he was blind, and he must be falling fast on his way to Hell. Burdett switched on the light to banish the last of the dream and sat for a moment on the edge of his bed, clearing his mind and gathering his strength for the long night and day that lay ahead. A feeling in his bones told him that something big was going to happen today; he just did not know what it was. He felt a surge of excitement that woke him up even more than a shot of strong black coffee.

Twenty minutes later he was already showered and dressed, catching his first cigarette while sitting in the rocking chair on his front porch, gazing down on the streetscape below. It actually was nice to be up and out in the wee hours. The fresh night air had that enveloping coolness of early spring, and the waxing gibbous moon was shining brightly in the western sky as if it were a floating streetlight that had somehow slipped its moorings. It was a satisfyingly solitary moment as his thoughts drifted along with that moon. The previous day had left a lot to digest. Then, in the pin-drop silence of the night, Burdett could hear the sound of a car approaching two blocks away. Presently headlights swept the street, and Eustace's Dodge pulled up behind Burdett's Studebaker. Skipping down his front steps, Burdett gave a passing bang on the roof of Eustace's Dodge and headed for the driver's side of the Studey. Eustace slid wordlessly into the passenger seat, holding a thermos of coffee with two tall mugs and a brown bag containing something that infused the air with the aroma of fresh baked bread.

"Hey, thanks," Burdett said, taking his first sip of the coffee. It was piping hot. "What's in that bag? The smell is killin' me."

"Maggie sends her greetings. Sweet woman kept herself up past midnight just to make sure we had hot buttermilk biscuits to keep us goin'. She must like you," Eustace said, grinning.

"Somehow, I suspect it's her husband she's really looking out for, but I gratefully accept." Burdett and Eustace paused for a few bites, savoring their treat. At last Burdett spoke, "So, I'm sure you're wonderin' why I dragged you out so early. Well, Eustace, I'm thinkin' that maybe you were right. Cece Quaid parked her car close enough to the Peabody to avoid suspicion, but nearer to Beale, close enough to walk there in two minutes. The coke in her car cinched it. So that's where we're goin' now. If a pretty white girl like Cece Quaid was hanging around down there on Beale, day or night, alone or with a crowd, somebody would've noticed."

"Now you're talkin'!" Eustace slapped his knee as if he was ready to dance.

It took them less than fifteen minutes to get to famous Beale Street, home of the blues and reputed den of thieves, pickpockets, junkies, and prostitutes. Most of Memphis by that time of night was locked up and bedded down, but it was Friday night and Beale Street was wide awake and hopping. With spring in the air and that bright moon, the night had an exciting tingle to it, and the crowds moved with giddy exuberance.

Even at two o'clock there was a carnival atmosphere; Beale was still abuzz with the serious late-night partiers, boozers, and hang-abouts, and not a white face to be seen. Neon signs flashed on the marquees above the doors of the Palace and the New Daisy. Sandwiched in between them, business at the One Minute Café was going strong, dishing out big hot dogs to the hungry throngs, topped with chili and mounds of onions, all for twenty-five cents a plate. Steamy smells mingled with a mish-mash of music that came from every direction.

Burdett could hear a horn section blaring from an upstairs open window of Club Handy on the corner of Hernando and Beale Street over the Pantaze Drug Store. And a few doors down Hernando the sound of blues wafted from the Flamingo Room, formerly the Hotel Men's Improvement Club, where a troupe of waiters from the hotels around town had pooled their money to start their own place. Then there was the rest of the high life and low life, the many saloons, some nameless and signless, speak-easies that seemed to come and go with the change of seasons or the latest crackdown.

Burdett was hoping to catch the Beale Street establishment at just the right time, when everyone was still working but business was slowing down for the night. When talkers would have time to talk. With Eustace in tow, he bee-lined first for Big Mama's, his favorite blues spot. At the door he greeted Jimmy the maître d'. Jimmy wore a dapper suit and splashy tie, which didn't disguise his thick neck and muscular shoulders. Burdett gave him a slap on the back, and it felt rock hard.

"Hey, Jimmy, it's been a while."

"Whoa, is that you, Bird Dog? Long time, no see. I was beginnin' to think you'd given up the guit box. And who's this righteous brother in blue?" Jimmy said as he cocked his head toward Eustace.

"Jimmy, meet Officer Eustace Johnson, now assigned to work with me," Burdett said as Eustace and Jimmy shook hands. "Is Fast Willie around?"

"Sure, Bird Dog, he's backstage. You know the way." They entered the smoky club, and it took a few moments for Burdett's eyes to adjust. The place looked to be between acts, so the stage lights were off, and the large room was lit only by dim votive candles on the tables, the low light from neon beer signs behind the bar, and the eerie glow from a massive jukebox. The jukebox set the mood with a Lonnie Clark tune Burdett knew well, "Broke Down Engine."

If you ever been down, mama, you know just how I feel,
Just like a broke down engine, ain't got no driving wheel.

As they weaved their way through the half-empty tables, dark faces illuminated by the candlelight looked up from their drinks and watched them pass. Entering the side door that led backstage, Burdett cast a glance backwards and saw every face in the room still silently watching them, a few already edging their way nervously toward the street entrance. Burdett had no doubt that in a place like this, he and Eustace must have been an odd sight indeed. Everyone smelled trouble. Burdett was looking for Fast Willie Brown, the proprietor of Big Mama's and maybe the one person on Beale Street that would tell him if there was anything to be known about Cece Quaid's antics around Beale.

"You certainly seem to know your way around this place." Eustace observed as they waited in a corner and watched the next act hustle onstage.

"Me and Willie go way back."

In a few minutes, a backstage door opened, and a massive man dressed in a shiny black tux as big as a tent emerged from the bright dressing room light, squinting into the backstage darkness. Spotting Burdett and Eustace, he heaved toward them in a slow rolling gait.

"Fast Willie, good to see you, man." Burdett and Fast Willie shook hands warmly as Willie's hooded eyes popped wide open like a frog that had spotted a fly, a toothy grin spreading across his wide face.

"Now if it ain't Bluesman Burdett hisself, po-lice by day, artiste by night." Fast Willie's hair was worn slightly long and pomade-plastered onto his head in tight wavy curls, diamond stickpin in his tie. "I judge by the uniform on your colored friend here that this time it's po-lice by night."

"Willie, meet Eustace Johnson. We're workin' together on that Mound Builder murder case."

"No shit. Well, nice to meet you, Officer Eustace. It's good to see that they've finally wised up over at Po-lice Central and put one of our own on the job." He shook Eustace's hand with a paw as big as a baseball mitt, "You're welcome in my place anytime if you be a friend of my man Burdett here. So, Burdett, what can I do for you boys? That Mound Builder thing is some scary shit."

"You might've heard that one of the murder victims is a Clarksdale girl by the name of Cece Quaid. Here's her picture. We got reason to think that maybe she was showin' up 'round this neighborhood, maybe lookin' to make a buy." Burdett thumbed his nose and Fast Willie nodded, taking a long look at the photo provided by Palmer Quaid.

"Yeah, I seen her 'round sometimes, travelin' with a pack of young white punks here for the Midnight Rambles on Thursdays. They'd get drunk, throw 'round a lot of money and leave. Stone-cold tippers. That's all I know. I 'spect most of the spots on the Street knows 'em same as me."

"Did you ever see her or anyone from that crowd making any purchases around here?"

Fast Willie's face immediately clouded over. "I'll forgive you that one, my friend. You know I cain't be rattin' out my people here on the Street. It'd be bad for my business and worse for my health. I may be Fast Willie, but I ain't that fast," he chuckled. "Leastwise, I can tell you this, 'cause I see'd it with my own eyes. Those white kids was gittin' powder from somewheres. You could tell by how they acted." Willie rubbed his nose and sniffed meaningfully.

"Okay, Willie, you've been mighty helpful. Stay healthy, wealthy, and wise."

"And you go catch that Mound Builder motherfucker, so's you can come back and sit in again. The boys is missin' their white bluesman, although things is changin'. Folks is still comin' in to catch the blues, but the musicians theyselves would rather play jazz. So it's blues for the people and jazz to keep the players on they toes."

"Got it, Willie, and I'll see you around." Burdett said as they headed for the door.

* * *

Moments later Burdett and Eustace were again on the street, and Eustace was chuckling to himself about what he had just heard.

"Looks like you and Willie definitely go way back. White bluesman?" Eustace commented with a grunt.

"I can pick a few chords of some of the old blues songs, and some nights I'd sit in with a few of his boys. We had some fun, but it never came to nothin'. What?" Eustace was smiling in amusement.

"You don't need to explain yourself to me. If you want to be hangin' out down here incognito, posin' as whatever kinda bluesman you want, that's your business."

"Look, you don't really know me yet, Johnson. I wasn't posin' at all. Growin' up down in Mississippi, the only people I ever played with were colored. If you like to play, you want to play with someone that's good, that's all. Look at you. You want to be a homicide detective, to get really good at it. So, what you should be doing is working with the best homicide detective you can find, not that I'm it, but that's what you should want. Now, are you posin' or are you simply bein' you?"

Eustace had to think about that for a while and grew silent as they continued to hit the other blues joints on Beale and its side alleys. He did not really believe that Burdett's approach to canvassing Beale Street was going to produce much. With him in full uniform and traveling with a white man who could only be another cop, the shadows moving in the alleys receded into the darkness, tendrils of pitch smoke leaving behind acrid whiffs of cigarettes, booze, and reefer. The few who would talk told pretty much the same story as Fast Willie. Definite sightings of the girl and her crowd, but not much else to share except that indeed they were lousy tippers. Creak Hopkins at the Daisy remembered them as troublemakers when they got drunk. No one would breathe a word about their coke buys, but the body language told Eustace that they were on the right track.

After a while, Eustace tugged at Burdett's sleeve and eased him into the shadow of an alley.

"I see how you're partial to the blues joints." Eustace said, "But I 'spect we may be lookin' in the wrong places. You're talkin' 'bout a passel of edgy white kids, and their type are not so much into that old blues stuff. Let's check out the backstreet jitterbug and R&B rooms that're playin' that new music. That's what the whites hangin' around the Stroll are lookin' for. Follow me—but hang back a few steps." With that, Eustace slipped off his uniform jacket, buried his hat, loosened his tie, and strode out into the brightly lit street with a newfound swagger in his step. Almost immediately he was getting small nods from passersby and the occasional murmured "Hey, Eus." As he glanced over his shoulder at the trailing Burdett, he could see the dawning realization on Burdett's face that Eustace Johnson was no stranger to Beale Street either.

Eustace was targeting the dimly lit backstreet clubs of the Chitlin' Circuit that were a shock of electricity after the subdued blues joints they had visited. Their first stop was the High Cotton Lounge. It had started out as an old shotgun shack, but someone had built a big party room out back and turned it into a dance club. From the street the music inside was rattling the windows and walls, saying come in, come in. Inside it was steamy, crowded, and alive with dancers as they boogied across the dance floor to the driving rhythm of an animated band, hopping to their own blend of jazz, blues, and something else entirely new, all wrapped together.

Looking at Burdett's face, Eustace wondered whether Burdett was thinking that a whole different kind of music had arrived on the scene since he had last carried his guitar case down Beale. And he would be right. But to Eustace, it was a homecoming for a home he had never left. As he threaded through the crowd, he turned back to make sure Burdett was following and had to smile as Burdett looked agape at the scene. Now if he'll just keep that mouth shut, Eustace thought, and let me do the talking instead of bigfooting the conversation. Eustace shouldered his way up to the crowded bar and signaled the bartender.

"Hey, Eus, my man," said Doogie Brown as he pulled down a fifth of whiskey from the overhead rack. "Where you been hidin' out, brother? Just cuz you's one of the po-lice now don't mean you cain't be out havin' fun. What can I getcha?"

"I'm not funnin' tonight," Eustace said, nodding in Burdett's direction. "I'm workin' a murder case."

"Diggin' up more of those old dead colored cases, huh?" Doogie said as he nodded his head and acknowledged Burdett sidling up to the bar.

"Not quite," Eustace said. "This is my partner, Detective Vance. We're lookin' into those white girl murders."

"You mean those Mound Builder killin's? White girls? They let you do that?" Doogie asked incredulously.

"Yes, they do," Burdett interjected as he pulled out Quaid's picture. "Here's one of 'em. Name's Cece Quaid. You seen her 'round?" Doogie reacted with a nervous shake of his head.

"N-no, I don't know nothin' 'bout no white woman. Excuse me, I'm workin'." With that, his face closed down, and he moved on to other customers down the bar.

Eustace waited a few beats before speaking, "With all due respect, boss, why don't you lend me that photo and go see if you can pick up a few licks from the band while I talk to my friend here."

* * *

Burdett suppressed his irritation but faded back and observed from a distance as Eustace followed Doogie to the other end of the bar. The pulsing sound of the R&B music drowned out all others, but Burdett could see that Eustace and Doogie were having an animated conversation. Finally, Eustace shook Doogie's hand and made his way back to Burdett.

"As I 'spected, he knows all about Miss Quaid. She was a regular, and a regular pain in the butt. Drunk and high-handed most times. And always askin' if Doogie could make a connection. Brought along a whole crowd with her, so the owners didn't want to chase away their money. And boy, did she know it. Acted like she owned the place, although he said that's typical for whites. He didn't see her with any coloreds, but I 'spect she did her business out in the parkin' lot."

The story at High Cotton was a pattern that repeated itself as they canvassed the other Chitlin Circuit joints. They did manage to find a waitress who recently had seen Quaid with a colored man, but she did not know him and had not seen him since. By 3:30 AM, the nightlife on Beale had petered out, so they decided to pack it in and head for the stakeout at Emme's.

"Well, I guess one thing is clear enough," Eustace said. "Cece Quaid and her crowd were circling the Beale Street dives lookin' for action like luna moths 'round a streetlight."

"Yep. And that means we gotta approach this from a different direction. Find out who was their supplier, and we may find the killer. Let's see what Ricketts and Dugan turned up from Vice. After all, trackin' the powder trade is right up their alley."

Burdett and Eustace grabbed nickel cups of steaming coffee from the One Minute before leaving the bright lights of Beale. Once they were back in the Studey, Burdett paused before starting the car.

"Eustace, I'd appreciate it if you could keep that white bluesman stuff to yourself. That's a private part of my life and has nothin' to do with my job. I don't want it spread around. I can only imagine the field day Ricketts or Donlough would have with it. I can almost hear it now: grave robbin' white bluesman."

"Oh, you don't have to worry 'bout me. If I wanted to spread that stuff around, I'd a done it a long time ago. You didn't think that white bluesman thing ever fooled anybody, did you? We've known about your midnight rambles for a long time."

* * *

As they walked back to the car, Eustace prepared himself for a sustained grilling by Burdett. They had to spend the next few hours together with nothing to do but sit in painful silence or talk, and he knew that Vance must still have a ton of questions, starting with his and Maggie's little escapade back at their house. Maggie had warned him right after Burdett had left the house.

"You best be careful what you say to that man, Eus. Do you really think that show with the preachers worked? He seems more God forlorn than God fearin'."

"I hear ya, Mama. Never trust a white man, just make him think you do."

"Leastways don't trust him to police one of his own." Eustace did a double take, but Maggie just shook her head. "Now why are you looking at me like that? Eustace Johnson, you don't fool me for a second. You know what I'm talkin' about, what with you working late nights always around payday. You're still after that policeman that killed Caleb, aren't you? And after you promised me." Eustace had felt caught but not sorry.

"Okay, Maggie, you're right. But he's in my sights now, and I'm gonna get him no matter what you say."

"Even if it gets you killed just like your brother? What about us?"

And it just got worse from there. In fact, they had argued the rest of the evening until it was almost time for him to leave. Then, in true Maggie style, to make up she baked that bag of biscuits for him. Delivered them with a thermos and a kiss too, as he headed out the door.

But Maggie was right that Vance most likely already had cottoned to the fact that the surprise clergy visit had been her idea. It was obvious enough. With the Mound Builder investigation keeping Eustace going at full speed, how would he have had the time to pull together that clutch of clergy on such short notice? Plus, he had to admit to himself that he had been so absorbed with the case that it was like being shut in a windowless room while a thunderstorm rumbled closer outside. He had missed the reports of the flashpoint encounters that were happening across the entire city, flickers of sheet lightning before the approaching gail. It had taken Maggie to wake him up to what was going on around him. She was the one who came up with a plan to put Vance on the spot and make him see what was coming unless he did things right. And the way Vance had rolled with it said something. It made Eustace hopeful that maybe his instincts regarding Vance had been right all along. White man or not, maybe he was the one who could help him do right by Caleb, regardless of what Maggie thought.

Chapter 17

Peeling Onions

I'll fly away, oh, glory, I'll fly away,
When I die, hallelujah, by and by I'll fly away,
Just a few more weary days and then I'll fly away,
To a land where joy shall never end, I'll fly away.

—*I'll Fly Away*, Alan Jackson, 1929

Burdett and Eustace arrived outside Emme's in time to relieve Harley and Vinnie Dugan fifteen minutes early. Burdett knew that he did not really need to spend this time posted up outside of Emme's apartment; it would have been easy to find a couple of beat cops to do the job. Sure, he needed to set an example for the Stooges, but he also had to admit to himself that he wanted Emme to know that he was there himself watching over her, at least for part of the night. A few hours of lost sleep was a small price to pay. And there was another reason that centered on his new charge, Eustace Johnson. Johnson was one of the jigsaw pieces that had been tumbling around loose in his head, and Burdett still did not know where he fit into the puzzle. There was no better place to ferret out the answers than sitting elbow to elbow waiting out the dawn in front of Emme Bryce's place. So he dove right in.

"Okay, Eustace Johnson, tell me how this whole preacher surprise happened. Whose idea was it and how long have you been plannin' it?"

Eustace sat for a long pause in the darkness, then spoke. "Alright, boss, I'll come clean. It was my idea, but Maggie ran with it. She's real worried about this whole Mound Builder thing, but she's also worried about me. And it's not as simple as Dr. Stevens made it out to be."

"What do you mean?"

"Permission to speak freely?"

"We're not in the army anymore, Johnson. Say whatcha gotta say."

"*You* look at a room full of colored preachers and they all look the same to you. I mean no disrespect, but that's just the way it is. The men in that room were some of the most powerful and influential men in Memphis. And although they all believe in God and seem to speak with one voice on the Mound Builder situation, it stops there when it comes to how this city is run. I was amazed myself that Maggie could get all of them in the same room."

"How so?"

"Half of 'em is longtime Crump men, Dr. Stevens bein' an example. They been deliverin' the colored vote for the Machine for decades. And for doin' that, Boss Crump would give 'em crumbs, like post office jobs for their people, maybe pave a street or two, and like that Douglass Park that Crump put out by the Wolf River swamp just for Negroes and mosquitos. Meanwhile, the Machine has been dead against real integration. All the other city parks—the nicer ones—are just for whites. And forget school desegregation, regardless of what the Supreme Court says. Separate but equal all the way, and don't be talkin' 'bout havin' any Negro hold public office. Like I say, these Crump preachers are satisfied with the crumbs, thinkin' that's progress."

"Yeah, I'd say that about sums up Memphis politics for the last lifetime. So what of it?" Burdett had a feeling he was about to hear what of it.

"Well, the other half of those preachers—and their congregations—don't see it that way. They're angry. We've been givin' the colored vote to Crump all these years, but the truth is that it's black votes that decide elections now. These new preachers say it's our time to start pickin' the winners. All that's in play now that Crump's gone, but this Mound Builder thing could set us back years."

"Us? Are you part of this?"

"Naw, I'm just watchin' it all from the pews," Eustace said. In the dim light Burdett could see Eustace dissembling with that sideways smile, but he was seeing through that now and not buying it. It would be one more turn of the kaleidoscope, and he decided to change the subject.

"Okay, Eustace, you're just a bystander and it's only a coincidence that Maggie knows all these preachers well enough to get 'em to your house on short notice. So what's your own story? How'd you come to be a cop in Memphis?"

"Now that's a million-dollar question. Lookin' back, it was more fate than choice, but I guess you could say that 'bout most anyone's life."

"That you can," Burdett replied, thinking how his own life felt so much that way. At times it seemed that he was just playing out a story that had been written for him by an invisible hand before he was even born, a story where there was no such thing as accident, coincidence, good luck or bad. Just fate. Burdett settled into his seat, coffee in hand. "Take it from the beginning. We got all the time in the world."

"Not much to tell early on. Born down in Holly Springs, but my family moved up to Memphis when I was ten. What with so many blacks movin' off the land and into town in those days, they needed schoolteachers in Memphis, and that's what my folks did."

"Holly Springs? Isn't that where Crump grew up? Did you ever run into the Boss or any of his kin down there?"

"It's probably not a far cry to say that down Holly Springs' way everyone knew everybody even if they wasn't cousins, but that's beside the point. What I'm sayin' is that outside of Tuskegee and the war, I've lived in Memphis pretty much the whole time since we moved here almost thirty years ago. My roots go deep here. Seems like half the preachers in town were my parents' students in high school."

"So why not become a teacher or a preacher yourself? Isn't that why you went to Tuskegee? Isn't Maggie a teacher?"

"How'd you know that?"

Burdett shrugged, "She runs your house like a teacher runs a classroom, that's why. Never lose control of the classroom, stick to the schedule, make sure they know who's boss." They both chuckled. "So, what happened? Why not carry on the family tradition?"

"Guess you could say it started with the war. Me and my buddies at Tuskegee enlisted in the army right after Pearl Harbor. Us bein' colored, the army didn't know what to do with us, so we got stationed nearby at the Tuskegee Army Airfield. We were all colored in that unit except the white commanding officers. Not including the white officers there was about five hundred of us, you know, pilots, ground crew, support. It takes a heap of folks to keep planes in the air."

"Yeah, I heard of those guys. So, you must have gotten to know some of the pilots?"

"You could say that. It was a flying formation kinda relationship."

"No shit, you were a flyboy?" Burdett shook his head in disbelief. Eustace was a surprise a minute. "Always loved and hated those guys. I was only a grunt dodging Kraut 75s and freezing my ass in the snow and mud, praying for the air cover to show and cursing 'em as they flew back to base in time to meet pretty girls at a pub. And to think you were one of 'em."

"Well, ain't that funny? Sometimes I was up there freezin' *my* ass off in that thin air and wonderin' how nice it'd be down on firm ground where you could actually light a fire to get warm and not worry whether you was gonna get blown to pieces the next second. They gave us parachutes, but nobody took much comfort from 'em. Think about it. Your plane goes down, and even if you make it out of the cockpit and avoid gettin' hit by the spinnin' tail, you're over enemy ground and those are the people that've been catchin' our bombs for who knows how long. They surely gotta hate you. So, even if you're lucky and your 'chute opens, they shoot you as soon as you touch down, or worse." Burdett could see Eustace getting agitated just imagining it.

"So what happened?"

"It was January '45, just a few months before the surrender, and we was flyin' our P-47 Thunderbolts for bomber escort on a run over Stuttgart to soften 'em up before the final push. Used to be those Messies were like swarming bees when they would fall out of the sky, but by then there was not much of 'em left. It was the flak from below that would get you, black puffs of death, and on this run we were flyin' through a solid black cloud of it. The bombers had dropped their loads and we'd turned toward our base at Termoli down the Italian coast when I could feel my engine start to give out. Sometimes you couldn't tell if you'd been hit 'til you got back to base and counted the holes, but this time it sounded like the hole was in the engine."

Eustace was talking faster and faster, and now paused to take a deep breath as if he was still at altitude and gasping for air. Burdett had not known Eustace could get so animated, experiencing the fear and excitement all over again.

"There was two hundred miles to go, and those Alps ahead were a towerin' wall 'tween me and the coast. I knew I'd never make it, so I headed for Switzerland where you could see the mountains pokin' up through the clouds. Those mountains came at me like they was a magnet drawin' me in. I aimed for the lowest pass I could spot and must have slipped over the lip with not more'n a hundred feet to spare. The ground fell out below me on the other side like the breath of God, and that gave me enough air to sputter down through an icy valley.

"I remember seein' this village way down the valley with its church steeples, pretty as a postcard. I was droppin' like a stone by then, but everything seemed to go into slow motion. As I was fixin' to clip the treetops, a frozen lake appeared out of nowhere below me. I dropped down and skidded across that ice like I was slidin' into home plate, spinning to a stop a hair before I reached the rocky shore. It was a God-given miracle." Eustace paused for a few seconds, and in the darkness, Burdett could swear his lips were moving in silent prayer. Probably did it every time he told the story, and no wonder.

"Amazin' tale, Eustace. Hard to believe you survived."

"It wasn't over yet. I was hopin' there were friendlies on this side of the mountains, but it turns out I was only in the foothills of the Alps, still in Germany. Lucky for me it was a Sunday mornin'. Whoever lived 'round there must've been at church down in the village, and I'd come in so low and quiet that no one heard me skid across that lake. So, God saved me again, gatherin' his flock down in the village to let me live, when by rights I shoulda had a pitchfork in the chest. Then I torched the plane, guessin' that it'd be a while before they figured if I was burned up in it, and I cleared out fast, which turned out to be a good call.

"It wasn't thirty minutes 'fore I heard the sound of a half-track workin' its way up the valley. It was too easy to track me through the snow so I circled back behind 'em to the road and ran as fast as I could, followin' the tread track until I heard the half-track comin' back and slipped away into the forest again. That day and into the night it was cat 'n' mouse with the sound of dogs echoin' through the forest, but lucky for me it started snowin' hard by late afternoon, coverin' my tracks and my scent. Then it was only a matter of not bein' seen or freezin' solid." Eustace shivered at the memory and took another sip of coffee to warm himself.

"I made it to the border and sashayed into Switzerland 'fore dawn the next day. I remember how great it felt, makin' it to safety, not havin' to worry 'bout how much noise I made stompin' 'cross that crunchy frozen ground."

"Jeez, what a tale. How long did it take to make it back to base?"

"I was thinkin' I was scot-free, but those damn Swiss throwed me into one of their own POW camps anyway. It was chock-full of shot-down fliers and crew, and those Swiss army guards weren't much different than the Krauts. Spoke the same language too. Turns out their dander was up 'cause of the stray bombs that kept landin' on 'em on cloudy days. Anyway, that's where I stayed for the next five months 'til we got liberated."

"Helluva way to end the war, but at least you survived it," Burdett said, thinking on his own last days before the fighting ended, which he spent wondering if, after surviving everything he had gone through, he would end up catching a random bullet pot-shotted by some retreating German.

"That wasn't the worst of it. The worst was when I finally got back to my unit where they told me my little brother Caleb was dead. Only fifteen years old when he was beaten and had his throat cut back here in Memphis. Killers got away clean. I swore I'd get 'em." There was a long pause while Burdett absorbed that information.

"So, that's it. You returned to Memphis to do right by your brother?"

"That's right, at least at the start. It was a cold case by the time I came home. Took another few years 'fore they let any of us on the force, and I jumped at it. And it took me three years after that, but I eventually put one of Caleb's killers away for good."

"White or colored?" Burdett asked, although he already suspected the answer.

"White."

"And how did you pull that off? How come I never heard about it?"

"Oh, you did. It didn't take me all those years to find out who done it. I knew that almost as soon as I came home. It took me three years after I joined to get that one convicted of somethin' else. Man's name was DeWitt."

"DeWitt? Del DeWitt? But I put that redneck away for life four years ago for killin' a girl from Murphreesboro."

"Exactly. He'd never go to jail for killin' a colored man, and in any case, they wouldn't let me arrest no white man. You know that and I know that." Eustace then told him how he had watched and waited, mostly on paydays when DeWitt often would get ugly drunk. He knew that sooner or later DeWitt would slip up, and Eustace planned to be there when it happened. Meanwhile Maggie thought he was only pulling the night shift too often, or at least that's what he assumed. It took years, but then one night DeWitt and a girl he had picked up in a hole-in-the-wall backroom bar on Jackson Avenue had stumbled back to DeWitt's double-wide in Bartlett. Eustace was parked outside and readying to pack it in when he heard a fight break out.

"It was nasty and loud, then everything went dead silent. The kind of silent that gives your soul a chill. Sure enough, 'fore long he comes slinkin' out the side door, lookin' this way and that, carryin' somethin' big and heavy wrapped up in a carpet. He tossed it in the bay of his pickup, and I followed him downtown to where he dumped the body in an alley. Then I tipped the police."

"That was you? Never saw a man tumble so fast when me and Harley came bangin' on his door that night. We got there so quick his truck was still warm. That's why the bozo thought we already knew everything. He spilled his guts right then and there." Burdett paused as he quietly recalled the scene. "Small world. It was actually me that got your call that night. Imagine that."

"I know'd it was you," Eustace said carefully, "'Cause it was you that I called."

A long silence reigned in the car. Burdett knew that Eustace was waiting for him to process the information and respond, but Burdett had already moved several steps down that path and this new piece of information confirmed what he had begun to suspect.

"Well now, ain't that nice and tidy? A week ago, I didn't know you from Adam, and in the last few days I seem to be meetin' you comin' and goin', Eustace. Ain't that funny? Somethin' tells me that, just as it was no coincidence that you called me that night, it's no accident that you got assigned to me in Homicide and that every colored preacher in town is claimin' they know all about me when I never set foot in a church if I can help it. Even Maggie knows more about me than she should after you and me workin' together for only a few days. And her sayin' you'd worked so hard to be able to work with me? So why don't you tell me why you called me that night, and what does everyone else know that I don't?"

Eustace sipped his now cold coffee, staring off into the darkness for a few moments and then laid it out for Burdett, how it all started early on with Jimmy Blake saying Burdett was the only cop in Homicide who gave a damn about Negro murders. Eustace had been keeping tabs on him ever since, and then there was the press that Burdett had gotten four years ago after he caught the serial killer who had been terrorizing the black community. Not the stories in the *Commerce Daily* and the *Press-Scimitar* that had focused on Boss Crump's crowing when the case was solved, but the stories in Memphis's Negro-owned newspaper, the *Tri-State Guardian*, which had focused on the man who had pushed forward with the investigation, Detective Burdett Vance. To the colored community Vance was an anomaly. A hero. He was the real news.

"After generations of havin' the police givin' lip service to protectin' us, there was you workin' away on your own time to save us from that beast. That was almost as big a story for us as you catchin' that man. Boss Crump got our votes in that election, but everyone holds you in a special place, 'cause you got our trust. It was natural that I'd call you 'bout DeWitt."

Burdett shook his head over the irony. They trusted him because they believed he was driven by a sense of justice. Maybe that was part of it, but in his mind, he was only a bird dog following a scent.

"What about the other guy? Do you know his name? And how was it that Donlough saw fit to assign you to me? Was that you too?"

"The other killer's still in the wind, and that's why I wanted to be in Homicide. I want to be there if he ever resurfaces," Eustace said evasively. "And how did I get here? Ask Jimmy Blake. They called for volunteers for their trumped-up train-ing' program—we both know that's a joke, don't we?—and at his urging I stepped right up. Jimmy told me all about your run-ins with the Chief. All it took was me droppin' your name to the Chief, and I saw that light bulb blinkin' on in his head. He came up with the idea all by himself, or at least that's how he sees it." Burdett could see Eustace's white teeth, smiling in the darkness.

"Yeah, right," Burdett said sarcastically. He could picture Donlough now, rubbing his hands together and chuckling between Chiclet chews. Everything finally made sense, but he came away from the conversation with a queasy feeling, like he had been played for years. Not played bad, just played.

"So, what tricks have you got up your sleeve next, Eustace? What are you really after?"

"That's pretty much all there is to tell. I'm just lookin' for-ward to workin' with you and catchin' this Mound Builder guy. So that's my story, what's yours?" Eustace asked, changing the subject. Burdett wasn't satisfied with that answer, but he decided to give it a rest.

"My story? Not much to say. Grew up on a farm down near Mound City, half a mile from the levee. My old man had a big livestock operation, raisin' mules for the cotton plantations and sharecroppers. Back then the whole cotton economy seemed to run on mule power. We had hundreds of those ornery animals. Of course that didn't last. Times were changin' fast once tractors came in. Then in '27 my old man died, the mules all died, we lost the farm, and I moved to Memphis to live with my uncle. Simple." Real simple.

"The mules *all* died? Just like that? Seems like everything happened at once."

"Yeah, you could say that."

"What about your mama and the rest of your family?"

"She died from the Spanish flu in '18. Never even knew her. I got no other kin but my uncle and his family up here. There really ain't much else to tell," Burdett summarized with a finality that ended the conversation. "Listen, I'm gonna catch some shuteye. Wake me up in two hours or if you see anything."

Burdett sank down in the driver's seat, pulled his hat over his eyes, and for the next few minutes pretended to be sleeping while Eustace fidgeted next to him. Pretty soon his exhaustion caught up with him, and he faded into a dream with cascading images of mule corrals, the smell of hay, cotton fields, his father laughing, Eli playing his guitar, and the great flood.

★ ★ ★

While Vance dozed, Eustace indeed fidgeted. Tonight, had he revealed too much? He had walked Vance right up to the edge of sharing his whole plan, and then stepped back. But more than anything he had revealed to Vance how his mind really worked, and a lifetime spent dealing with whites told him that no good could come from that. Now Vance knew for sure how Eustace operated by patiently dissembling, getting his way by letting whites see what they wanted to see. So why had he done it? Eustace had not only revealed himself to Burdett but also, surprisingly, had revealed to himself some inner desire. Eustace spent the following hours listening to Vance's breathing and trying to understand what that inner desire really was.

Of course, he had not told Vance everything. The second killer was firmly in his sights; he would get only one shot, and he did not plan to miss. Now it was only a matter of time.

And as for the story about the preachers' disagreements over Negro power, he could not even begin to reveal to Burdett the depth of his anger at how white racism lay at the heart of what had happened to Caleb and was at the core of the whole Crump Machine. The Machine allowed tragedies like Caleb's to be repeated over and over again, and he hated them for it. Boss Crump and his cronies had an unrepentant plantation mentality; they knew what was best for everyone, especially those ignorant darkies, and they ran the city to keep them unwitting and mollified. Which pretty much described Dr. Stephens and his cohort of appeasing gradualists. Eustace was done with that. He hadn't survived the war for nothing, and he was determined to find justice for his people, starting with one cold-blooded killer.

Chapter 18

Mary Had a Little Lamb

I love my whiskey, and I love my gin,
But the way I love my coke is a doggone sin.
Hey, hey, honey, take a whiff on me,
It takes a little coke to give me ease.

—*Cocaine Habit Blues*, Memphis Jug Band, 1930

Come daylight, they packed it in and Burdett knocked on Emme's door to tell her they were leaving. The curtain in the front window moved, then she opened the door a crack dressed only in her nightgown, the flimsy type given to her by who knows who. Even with no makeup and sleep in her eyes, she looked dreamy and glad to see him. She allowed as how she had slept like a baby, just knowing he was there.

As Burdett got back into the patrol car, Eustace gave a grunt.

"What?"

"I saw that," Eustace said. "You best be careful." Burdett bristled with anger.

"No, *you* best be careful, real careful what you say, Johnson. Not one more word outta your mouth."

"I know what I saw, her half-dressed at the door. It don't look right. Either you got somethin' goin' on there, or she's playin' you. Best wait 'til this case is over, don't ya think?"

"You got balls tellin' me what to do. Know your place, Johnson." Eustace had said his peace, so he went quiet while Burdett brooded over the truth of what he had just heard. He had to admit, Eustace was right. It didn't look right. He just didn't like hearing it.

"Listen, Johnson, let me tell you what I've been tellin' everybody else. I knew that woman years ago, but there is nothin' goin' on now. Let's just leave it at that. We're both tired and hungry. Let's get some chow."

So before heading back to Police Central, Burdett and Eustace bee-lined to Judy's Spot for breakfast. She shushed them to a booth in the rear where Eustace would not be seen. Judy had an open-door policy race-wise but was not looking for trouble either. Then, for the first time ever, Judy sat down with them in the booth. Burdett could tell from the distraught look on her face that something was wrong, and he suspected he knew what it was.

"Burdett, tell me, is it true? Is somebody really tryin' to kill our daughters for somethin' that happened before they were even born? Is my Jessie in danger?" These questions must be on the minds of every parent in Memphis, and Judy's red haired and green-eyed daughter certainly fit the victim profile.

"Judy, at this point we don't know what's true and what isn't, but you best tell Jessie to lay low and avoid goin' out alone for a while. Travel with a pack and she'll be safe, but if she ever thinks she's in danger, have her call the police, or better yet, call me direct. Here's my number." Burdett wrote down his home and office numbers on a napkin.

"Oh, thank you, Burdett! And you too, officer . . . ?

"Johnson. Eustace Johnson, and you're most welcome," Eustace said with a nod of his head.

"Judy, while I've got you here, maybe you could answer a question for us. Did Jessie know Cece Quaid?" Burdett was trying to get a feel for exactly how much danger Jessie might be in.

"That girl? Certainly not! I overheard Jessie and her girlfriends talkin' down Cece Quaid a couple of months ago. In fact, believe it or not they were sittin' right here in this very same booth. The gist was that they thought she was—alright, I'll say it—a real bitch. They wanted nothin' to do with her."

"Well, looks like that was a good call, Judy. You shouldn't get too worried. Jessie'll be safe as long as she's careful. And hopefully it won't take us too long to catch this guy." Burdett was trying to be reassuring, but he did not really believe it himself.

"You're a peach, Burdett. Y'all go on and enjoy your breakfast now, and this one's on me!"

As Judy walked away, heels clicking and bracelets jingling, Burdett caught Eustace's eye and knew they both were thinking the same thing. They had almost nothing. No suspect, no murder weapon, no real motive. But within a few minutes they did have something very real and concrete: steaming coffee with plates of eggs, country ham, grits with redeye gravy, and dipping biscuits, all courtesy of Judy. So they settled hungrily into their meal and planned out the rest of the day.

The first order of business was to identify everyone from Cece's and Emme's circles of girlfriends who might be at risk. The calculus there was simple. If they did not bother to contact a woman who later turned up dead, they would be blamed for the pointless death. Next, they worked up a task list for the Stooges, which they were guaranteed to hate.

But all those plans went out the window minutes later when they walked into the squad room to learn that a third female body had been found floating, this time in Audubon Lake, and Burdett found himself reflexively hoping that this body did not have red hair and green eyes.

* * *

Audubon Lake was the centerpiece of Audubon Park, which lay in the heart of East Memphis—white Memphis. And that seemed to be the point. A kid down at the lake had been throwing rocks at the ducks and looking for tadpoles when he spotted the girl's body in the shallows. By the time Burdett and Eustace arrived at the scene, the press was already there pushing against the police tape and trying to get a better shot of the crime scene. Burdett surveyed the area, noting that Audubon Lake shared many of the same convenient features as McKeller Lake. If you wanted to dump a body without being seen, it was easy. There were no houses near the lake, and streetlights were few. On cool and rainy nights in late March no one would be hanging out in the park. All the killer needed to do was drive down to the parking lot by the pavilion, do the dirty deed, and drive away, with no one the wiser.

Like the others, the latest body had a head wound, stockings tied around the neck, and a note in a bottle signed by the Mound Builder. The message was written in the same black ink, same scrawled scrip, same brown paper:

> *It's time whites pay. This one be for Ell Persons.*
>
> —*The Mound Builder*

"What the hell is that about?" Burdett asked. He looked questioningly at Eustace, who just shook his head in worry and beckoned Burdett over to where no one could hear them.

"Ell Persons was one of the worst lynchin's ever 'round here. Awful rape and killin' of a white girl back in '17, and the police tagged Persons for it, based on a newfangled forensic test where they claimed photographs could capture in the dead girl's eyes the last image that she had seen—even though her head was cut off. That was a numbskull theory by a Frenchman named Bertillon. I read all about it. So they dug up the girl—or more like they dug up her head—and said they could see Persons in her pupils with a horrible, twisted expression on his face."

Burdett shook his head, "That's right out of some stupid horror movie. It's hard to imagine that the MPD actually bought that garbage. How many dead bodies have you seen, Eustace? Probably a lot if what Jimmy Blake tells me is true. I've looked into the eyes of more stiffs than I can count, and I can tell you for a fact that there ain't nothin' there. Less than nothin'."

"You know how it is," Eustace said, "People may think they believe what they know, but they only truly believe what they feel. It was crazy alright, but with a gruesome killin' of a little white girl, it was all that was needed to set off a lynchin'. The *Commerce Daily* even carried the time and place of the lynchin' in advance, as though it was a Sousa band concert. People was actually there sellin' refreshments. Can you believe that? Five thousand people showed up to tear that poor man's body to shreds. Then they scattered pieces all over the colored parts of town, as a warning. Even threw Person's head at a crowd of us. It's been a long time, but coloreds still remember that one too. This ain't only 'bout George Brooks no more."

"Unfortunately, it looks like you may be right about that," Burdett said. "If someone wants revenge for the years of evil done to the colored people of this town, no tellin' how many white girls are gonna have to die to make that right."

"I've got a pretty good idea of how many that might be," Eustace said. "A colored lady named Ida Wells who was from Holly Springs like me started trackin' lynchin's here sixty years ago, and people have been keepin' count ever since. In the last hundred years there's been thirty-nine men lynched here, plus George Brooks and who knows how many others that just got put down like Caleb. So that's two lynchin's avenged, and at least thirty-eight more white girls to go. Wait 'til that hits the papers." The thought stunned both of them, and they knew that this was a reign of terror that could last not months but years if they did not find the killer. Burdett imagined the fears of four hundred thousand souls, the entire white and colored population of Memphis combined, entwining into a vortex of hysteria and that would devour the whole city. For both of them the sense of fear and urgency was overwhelming. All they could do was to focus on the case in front of them and not be consumed by murders that had not yet occurred.

This time the girl was not so hard to identify. There was already a matching missing person report from Whitehaven, a suburb down near the Mississippi state line. A woman named Mary Lou Warren had disappeared without a trace approximately eleven days earlier, although the report was not made until after the first two murders hit the papers. She had shown up early on the list of possibles for Jane Doe, but like Quaid she was ruled out when her dental records did not match. However, Jimmy Blake still had her dentals down at the Chop Shop, and the match was made as soon as the body arrived in the morgue later that morning.

Warren had been reported missing by her live-in boyfriend, so while Blake dove into the autopsy, Burdett and Eustace ran down to Whitehaven. Whitehaven was a place where good old country boys lived, while Memphis was where they worked. A pickup truck parked in every driveway, and no blacks in sight. The boyfriend, Johnny Willet, was waiting for them at the house he rented with Warren, a barren little mobile home occupying a weedy lot on a street crying with neglect. Willet was crying too. All he could tell them was that she had run up to Midtown for errands and never returned. He claimed that they had had a row, and at first he thought she was only staying over with her folks or with a friend. But since the Mound Builder scare started, he had been sick with worry over her and complained that those damn cops didn't do nothin' once they cottoned that she was not the Jane Doe they already had. Willet had worked himself up into a lather and did not seem to know anything useful, when Burdett finally took a stab in the dark.

"Mr. Willet, thank you for your cooperation. Oh, and one last thing," Burdett paused as he looked pointedly around the room, "We understand that Miss Warren was into coke. Isn't that really why she went up to Memphis?"

Willet froze and his eyes involuntarily flickered toward a small chest of drawers that supported a dusty television. Eustace picked up on it and moved quickly to put his hand on the top drawer and then paused, waiting for Burdett's next move.

"Hold on, Officer Johnson," Burdett said. "Mr. Willet hasn't answered my question." Then he leaned into Willet's face, "Listen, buddy, we're not looking to nab losers like you, we're looking for a man who has murdered three women, including your dear friend Miss Warren who you're making such a fuss over. So, I can wait while Officer Johnson here gets a search warrant for that drawer and the rest of this house, or you can tell us what we want to know now. Who knows, maybe we'll even find the murder weapon somewhere around this dump."

Willet writhed in his seat as if he wanted to slither out of his own skin. His eyes showed sheer panic, but then his shoulders slumped in defeat, "Okay, yeah, that's where she gone to. She had a friend what could find us some snow, so I gave her twenty bucks to get it. Honest, this weren't the first time she done run off. I only thought she was on a bender somewheres with my money, but not dead! I swear I didn't do it!"

"Who was this friend?"

"I don't know, man. Some bimbo named Cece. Never met the bitch."

CHAPTER 19

Down on the Farm

Early one morning, on my way to the penal farm,
Baby, all locked up, and ain't done nothin' wrong,
Loaded in the dog wagon, and down the road we go,
Ah, baby, oh, baby, you don't know.

—*Penal Farm Blues*, Scrapper Blackwell, 1929

Heading back north toward downtown, Burdett was getting a tingle of excitement, feeling that they were closing in on the Mound Builder at last. All of a sudden there seemed to be an abundance of promising leads. It reminded him of lazy summer days fishing in a lake for hours without a single bite and suddenly the fish are rising to the top all around you. Lots of lines out, time to reel in a few catfish and fry 'em up in the pan.

They had prints on the bottle and note found on Cece Quaid and more from Quaid's car. Eustace volunteered to check with the print guys and see if any of the latent prints found so far matched Warren's. And they could do the comparison on Jane Doe too, in case they had not already. Meanwhile, Burdett decided to call the Stooges together for an impromptu meeting and to regroup. He buttonholed Renfro and Ricketts as they lounged at their desks in the Special Investigations squad room and grabbed Harley and Dugan as they stepped off the elevator. Burdett started the meeting with a recap of what they knew about the Warren murder.

"So, we've now got three Mound Builder murders and counting, and him claimin' each one as revenge for lynchings. Johnson here says there's been thirty-nine lynchings over the years in the city and county, so that gives you an idea of what we're looking at here." Ricketts grunted and cast a look at Renfro as if to say of course it would be Johnson who would know that. Burdett ignored him, "Now this guy is workin' his way into East Memphis and really scarin' the shit outta everyone out there. Once the *Press-Scimitar* hits the stands this evening, all of white Memphis will be in a panic. Harley and Dugan, here's a list of Warren's known associates, at least the ones that her boyfriend would name. Run 'em down and find out if they knew Quaid or anything about who this coke dealer might be." That was when he noticed Ricketts puffing out his chest, a grinning Cheshire cat.

"You got somethin' to say, Ricketts?"

"Damn right I do, cuz I just solved the case, Vance. I know who that coke dealing, mound building Negra son of a bitch is."

Ricketts's cockiness made Burdett cringe. "And?" he asked.

"I sat on that damn tipster phone for hours, and guess what? I got two hot tips on coloreds who make a business of sellin' coke to whites, and one has got to be our guy. The first is Sticky Munro, who you'll be pleased to know was delivered only yesterday to the penal farm to serve out six months for reefer possession. Likes to rough up his bitches. But my bet's on the other one, Slider Sykes. Y'all know him? Small-time coke dealer holed up in a shack over to Orange Mound right across the tracks from the country club, sells to whites on accounta he delivers. Actually collared him once when I was in Vice. Watch out for Slider. He's one angry mother. Always got a gun or a knife. Picked up his nickname pitchin' in the Negro league and never got over being turned down for the majors when the league collapsed after integration. Went straight downhill from there. Word is, he disappeared a week or two ago, so he must be runnin'. My money says he's our boy." Ricketts pumped out his chest again triumphantly. "Like I said, boys, case closed!"

"Okay, Ricketts, good work. We finally have a couple of names. But let's hold off makin' Munro or Sykes for the killer, at least not yet. You and Renfro put out an alert for Sykes. And Ricketts, check with your buddies in Vice to see what they've got on this guy. They must have a snitch who's made a buy there in the past few weeks—it has to be something recent to support probable cause for a search warrant if we can't match the prints—and take it to Wilson in the DA's office to walk it through with the judge. Radio me as soon as you have the warrant, but don't be goin' to his house 'til we can all do it together, you hear? Do you hear me, Ricketts? Say it."

"Fuck you, Vance, I hear ya."

"Good. Meanwhile, I'll grab Johnson and hit the penal farm to check out Munro."

As if on cue, Eustace arrived with the latest news on the latents. Prints of all three victims were found in Quaid's car. They were still looking for a match for the prints on the bottle and note. Burdett told Eustace to call them back and tell them to run prints on Munro and Sykes, then he called over to Judy's Spot to order a couple of fifty-cent club sandwiches to go. She had them ready when Burdett and Eustace swung by on their way out east of the city to visit the newest resident of the Shelby County Penal Farm.

* * *

Eustace never had a good feeling about the Shelby County Penal Farm. It was a low-security prison facility located out in the county, snugged up against the swampy bottomlands of the Wolf River, which with its cottonmouth inhabitants formed a natural barrier to any wandering thoughts of the prisoners. It had been established on the site of the old Nashoba community where, before the Civil War, blacks had been allowed to earn their freedom by working on the farm. To Eustace, that involuntary servitude seemed to have continued at the modern-day penal facility, where mostly black prisoners worked the same ground, hoping to earn their freedom too. But the city was growing out that way, and it seemed to Eustace to be only a matter of time before the good citizens of Shelby County would start asking themselves why there was a penal colony in their midst.

Eustace and Burdett checked in at the front office and settled down in an interview room to eat their lunches while they waited for Sticky Munro. They had only eaten half their sandwiches when Munro ambled into the room. Given Munro's history with women, Eustace had thought that he looked to be a good candidate for a suspect, but seeing him in the flesh he thought, maybe not. Munro was ponderously overweight, sweating profusely even though it was a cool spring day. He was not a tall man, but when he sat down, he was sitting on so much lard that he looked tall in his chair. His baggy cheeks sagged with fat, but so did his eyebrows, which gave him the perpetual hangdog look of an obese bloodhound. Eustace figured that six months of work on the Farm were likely to shed a few of those pounds off him unless he was able to bribe his way out of it. His thick fingers fidgeted in a dainty movement that seemed out of place with his bulk.

"I ain't done nothin'," Munro said before they could even make introductions. Burdett nodded to Eustace to take the lead.

"If that was the case, Sticky, then why are you here?" Eustace shot back.

"I mean ain't done nothin' but that. So why you here?"

"I'm Officer Johnson and this is Detective Burdett Vance. Memphis Police. We want to talk to you about those white girls found floatin' around town."

Munro giggled, almost gleefully, "Oh, yeah, ain't that a stitch. We finally gotta brother out there payin' those fuckers back after all these years? I hope he kills 'em all."

"Those are dangerous words, Sticky, since the way we see it, you're the one's been doin' the killin'," Burdett said. "Officer Johnson, did you get that down? Sticky here just admitted his motive for the killings. And come to think of it, the timing looks about right, with you dumping those girls in the water just before you checked in here. Very clever." Munro went quiet, knowing it could take a lot less than that to convict a black man in this town.

"Where were you two weeks ago?" Eustace asked. Munro's face brightened.

"Naw, in the hospital on accounta my diabetes." He lifted one pants leg to reveal a bandage. "Had me laid up for more 'n a week 'fore I came here. That's how come I didn't start my vacation here on the Farm last month like the sentencin' judge done said. You can check it out."

"We will," said Burdett.

Eustace figured that would make it easy to cross Munro off the list since he did not look as if he could physically pull off the murders anyway.

"Mr. Munro, we appreciate your time and cooperation," Eustace said. "Could I ask you a few more questions?"

"Sure. Ain't never been questioned before by a brother with a badge." Eustace gave his warmest smile.

"Thank you. And would you like the other half of my sandwich?" Eustace had noticed Munro eyeing their lunch and imagined that prison fare must leave a man of Munro's appetites wanting. After a pause to allow Munro to get down his first bite, Eustace continued.

"What do you know about Slider Sykes?"

Munro gulped. "That mothafucka? You don't be turnin' your back on him. He'd slit his own mother's throat if she stood between him and a loose twenty. I heard he's movin' some stuff south of Midtown," Munro said with raised eyebrow, flicking his nose. "He been workin' that young white crowd. Don't know how he gets away with it. Must have friends like you two."

Eustace ignored the jab. "And by any chance do you know a police detective named Earl Ricketts?"

Burdett immediately cast a questioning look at Eustace.

"I don't want no trouble, now. I didn't mean what I just said," Munro said, shifting uneasily in his seat.

"Don't worry, it'll stay between us," Eustace said, flashing that benign smile and exchanging nods with Burdett.

"He's mean like no po-lice I ever see'd. Pistol-whips you just for the pleasure of showin' off that big gun of his. He didn't like that I couldn't cough up the usual cash. Put me outta business just for that. If he sent you here, tell him I'm flat broke. I can't afford no more."

"No, he didn't send us, Mr. Munro," Eustace said, looking at Burdett with satisfaction. "Thank you for your time."

Chapter 20

To the Devil's Lair

Just give me one more sniffle, another sniffle of that dope,
I'll catch a cow like a cowboy, and throw a bull without a rope.

—*Dope Head Blues*, Victoria Spivey, 1927

Alone again in the car, Burdett and Eustace were quiet for a while, and Burdett's mind seemed to be at work as he absentmindedly fingered a pack of matches, a cigarette poised in his other hand.

"Okay, Eustace, I get the point," Burdett said at last, lighting the cigarette. "Munro didn't get fingered by an anonymous caller. Ricketts set us up to go after him as payback for Munro stiffing him. So, we probably should expect the same with Sykes. I didn't think to follow that thread with Munro. Glad you did. Exactly what made you ask about Ricketts?"

"No reason, really. It just popped into my head when I asked about Sykes." What Eustace did not say was that he had been watching Ricketts's activities for a very long time and knew Ricketts too well to take at face value anything he said. From the beginning he had doubted whether any anonymous caller had fingered those two suspects. This was all Ricketts's idea, using the Mound Builder investigation to settle old scores, and if things went sideways, it would be Vance who got the whipping. At that moment, the radio crackled from dispatch with a message to proceed immediately to an address on Simms Street in Orange Mound. Prints on the bottle and note matched Sykes. Ricketts and Renfro already had the warrant for Sykes's place, and they were on their way with Harley and Vinny, followed by a deuce of black-and-whites as backups. It was showtime.

* * *

By the time Burdett and Eustace eased into Orange Mound, the police cars were positioned two blocks away from Sykes's lair, where a huddle of uniformed officers waited quietly for them to arrive, T-Bone Thibodeaux among them. Ricketts, Renfro, Harley, and Vinny had already circled around through the alley to cover the rear. Burdett took a few minutes to survey the layout. The Orange Mound section of Memphis was the first community in the country built by Negroes for Negroes. Located on the former grounds of the Deadrick Plantation, it was mostly shotgun shacks dating to the turn of the century. Sykes's place was a crumble-down affair strategically positioned on Simms Street across the Southern Railroad tracks from the River City Country Club, but it may as well have been a world away. The country club was built on the site of the old Buntyn mansion, which before the advent of cars had its own whistle stop on the railroad, Buntyn Station. From the club, whites could conveniently slip across the tracks unnoticed and do their business. The front of the shack was almost entirely obscured by a massive, run-riot privet hedge, better to keep nosey neighbors from seeing comings and goings. With blinds drawn, multiple locks on the front door, and bars on the windows, it looked as fortified as a flimsy shotgun shack could be.

"Bars on windows are good at keeping people out," Eustace observed, "But they keep 'em in too. There's only two ways out, front and back doors. My guess is that they'll be pilin' out the back."

Burdett nodded and quietly sent two of the uniforms around back to reinforce the others while he directed Thibodeaux and his partner to the front. Eustace watched as Burdett opened his car trunk and grabbed his handy tools of the trade: a pump scattergun, a pocketful of shells and a sledgehammer. Eustace checked his own gun, and on Burdett's signal they crab-walked across the front porch, ducking below the windows, to either side of the front door. Burdett silently finger-counted to three, and Thibodeaux smashed the locks with the sledge, kicking in the door. In the dim light inside shapes moved in all directions, rats scrambling from the light.

"Freeze, police!" Burdett yelled, coming in low and fast. Eustace was right behind him, adrenaline pumping as they moved into the dim interior. Then Eustace heard gunshots out back. The house was so dim inside that every dark corner seemed to be hiding another gunman. It was a series of walk-through common rooms with bedrooms off each room. Eustace moved toward a dark bedroom, cautiously reaching around the edge of the door for the light switch.

"Sykes, are you in there?" Then he heard a metallic click as a gun loomed in front of his face.

"Don't move, mothafucka." Beyond the barrel of the gun was a face with drug-fueled eyes, wild as a trapped animal. Time slowed to cold molasses at midnight as Eustace froze, his entire being focused on that single finger tightening on a trigger six inches from his face. Then the blast. The last thing he would ever hear. But it wasn't. He heard a second blast. In disbelief he realized that he was still standing there, ears ringing but miraculously alive and untouched, time speeding up again. He slowly became aware of the splintered, inch-wide holes in the wall behind which the junkie had been standing, and him now fully visible lying on the floor with matching holes in his chest. A pool of blood slowly expanded around the body. Turning, he saw Burdett standing close behind him pumping his shotgun to chamber the next shell, digging into his pockets to load two more into the magazine then moving to the next room. He had shot the shooter through the wall. Eustace could only stand there, still frozen, trying to climb out of his shock and catch up to the living present.

* * *

Burdett cleared the rest of the house, and out back he found two more dead men, guns at their sides. They had come out ready to fight but had no chance. While Renfro checked the bodies for IDs, Ricketts looked elated.

"We got 'em both! It was a fuckin' turkey shoot! Goddamn, I love it!" He was almost dancing in place.

Burdett sidled over to Renfro and asked him quietly, "Okay, Renfro, how did it go down? Was Ricketts trigger happy or is this clean?"

"Oh, he's trigger happy alright but can't hit shit with that big cannon of his," Renfro said under his breath. "It was clean. They came out waving their guns. I nailed 'em both," he added with a toothy grin. Burdett looked over at Ricketts who was acting out the shootout for Harley, Vinny, Thibodeaux and the other uniformed cop who had been inside with Burdett.

"Ricketts, get over here and tell me one of these bodies is Sykes." Ricketts took a look and shook his head but seemed not to care; he was having too much fun.

"No? Okay, Renfro, get on the radio and get a crime scene crew over here." Then Burdett turned to Ricketts and just shook his head.

"Wh-what are you lookin' at, Vance?"

"Absolutely nothin'," Burdett said, "and that's the point."

Burdett left Ricketts fuming and went back inside thinking how Ricketts was such a menace, ready to go off at any second. Always dangerously overcompensating, deeply cold-blooded, and based on what Renfro had said, just as incompetent. Eustace was checking the third body. No identification, but the dead man clearly was not Sykes. Too young.

"Are you alright, Eustace?" Burdett asked, noticing that Eustace was quiet. "Sorry I had to fire so close, but all I could see was that gun at your head. I could tell he was right there on the other side of that wall, so I took him out." Burdett heard himself making excuses for doing what he knew he had to do, maybe because he was not sure how his black partner would take his shoot-first-ask-questions-later approach.

"Sorry?" Eustace asked incredulously. His face seemed overwhelmed with relief. "Don't you be feelin' sorry. A lifetime passed through my mind in those few seconds. I'd never see Maggie and the kids again. Never see 'em grow up. Never even see the next minute. You gave all that back to me. I owe you." Eustace held out his hand.

"I hope you'd do the same for me," Burdett said, shaking that large hand, feeling that firm grip.

"For your sake I hope I never have to."

Then they heard a strange shuffling sound from the closet in the bedroom. Guns drawn, they closed in on the closet. Then they heard a gravelly voice.

"Don't shoot! Don't shoot! I ain't got no gun. I'm comin' out, fellas!" The closet door cracked open, and two hands came out waving. The hands belonged to a skinny thirty-something woman with a dusty pallor and a fifty-something face pleading for mercy. Then she perked up when she saw Eustace and directed her comments to him, saying her name was Shirley Pearl, but you can call me the Pearl. From the way she said it, Burdett doubted that it was her real name. More of a stripper's stage name. The Pearl said she did not live there but she "sorta" knew Slider, not saying how. She had heard that he had left suddenly a couple of weeks before. No one had seen him since. Word had spread on the street that the house was empty and unlocked, so she had come there to party with her friends. She clearly traveled with a rough crowd but did not seem to care much that all three were dead, so she was pretty rough herself. A survivor. Already sashaying up to Eustace and giving him the once over.

"You should stick around, sugar, 'cause Slider's comin' back," the Pearl said. "I know that for sure."

"How come, sister?" Eustace asked, inching away.

"Look at where you found me," she said, pointing to the closet. "His suitcase may be gone, but those is fine shoes and look at that suit. And I do love the smell of his cologne. No, baby, he may have lit out in a hurry, but he's comin' back for those. I never leave my good stuff behind when I run."

That left Burdett thinking, building a vision of the future as he imagined how Sykes's plan was playing out. Sykes had not been seen for two weeks. So he had gone to ground right around the time the victims were killed. Now that the place had been shot up by cops looking for him, he would never return, but that may not have been his original plan. With those fine clothes waiting for him, he may have left thinking he would sneak back for other things. That meant he was still around, lying low. It made Burdett wonder what else Sykes might have planned to retrieve. While Eustace continued to interview the Pearl and the forensics team arrived to begin their work, he began a quiet, methodical search of the house.

The Pearl had been right about the clothes in the closet, but the rest of the bedroom told tales too; Slider appeared to be into rough sex, with handcuffs on the bedposts and sex toys on the bedside table. Maybe that explained the handcuff marks on the dead girls. The kitchen was a mess. Dishes piled high in the sink and food in the rusty icebox that had not been touched in weeks: sour milk, molding bread, everything rotting. Empty liquor bottles were everywhere, and Burdett noted that a few lacked their cork caps. Burdett poked through the trash can and stopped cold. Inside were empty Gold Crest 51 bottles and the torn-up pieces of a six-pack carton. Taking a handkerchief from his pocket, he carefully removed two bottles and the torn paper and laid them out on the kitchen table. At that moment, the entire case clicked together with crystal clarity. There were four bottles missing, and he already knew where three of them were. The remaining torn pieces of the six-pack carton were clearly drafts of the notes found on the three bodies, a few even signed "The Mound Builder."

They had found the killer. Then he noticed there was one scrap with only a few scribbled words in the same handwriting that did not match the three known notes. Scrawled in black ink were the words "My revenge continues. This one has her own moun—." Over Burdett's shoulder Eustace made a low whispering whistle sound.

"I'd say we found him, and it ain't over."

Burdett immediately ordered an all-points lookout for Slider Sykes and cleared the house to protect the scene and make room for the forensics team. As the Stooges, Thibodeaux, and the other uniformed officers spread out to canvass the neighborhood for witnesses, Burdett paused for a moment to watch the techs unpack their equipment. That was when he noticed a carpet in the living room that seemed out of place. Carefully lifting it, he found a dark blackish red stain on the floor. It was dried blood, and a lot of it. He was certain that the techs would match it to at least one of the victims.

This house was the mother lode, a happy hunting ground for evidence that hopefully would connect all the dots at last. Sykes, the Mound Builder, had fled in a hurry, and there had been no attempt to sanitize it. Who knows whose prints might show up here? If there was a fourth victim in danger, her prints might be here too.

Leaving the techs to their work, Burdett walked outside and started a careful examination of the exterior. The yard was a small city dump: trash was piled everywhere and last year's weeds were hip high. A breeding ground for rats—human and animal. There was no garage, but around the side of the house, Burdett spotted an exterior slant-topped cellar door secured with a shiny new padlock. Retrieving his sledgehammer, he pounded off the lock, opened the double doors, and stepped down into the fetid darkness of the cellar.

It reeked of rats and snakes. He spied a pull-string for the overhead light, and a single bare bulb flickered on to illuminate a clutter of assorted debris plus the occasional scatter of rat droppings. Burdett stood in place for a long time absorbing the scene and letting his eyes adjust to the dimness. No snakes that he could see but enough visible snake skins to make him cautious. Then, as his eyes acclimated, footprints appeared in the dust on the floor as if they were invisible ink revealed by candle heat. Someone had recently been going back and forth into the recesses of the cellar. He followed the track, but it came to a dead end at a stone foundation wall. Burdett again stood still and patiently tried to absorb what was in front of him, peering up among the cobwebbed rafters, scrutinizing the grimy floor, trying to think what might be within reach of where he stood.

Finally, the wall itself came into focus right in front of him as he noticed that the mortar around one stone was off color. It crumbled away at his touch, just moist dirt from the floor that had been wedged into the cracks. He brushed away the dirt and jimmied the stone loose, revealing a cavity containing a dark metal box. Bingo. Using his handkerchief, he carefully extracted the box and carried it gingerly upstairs to the kitchen table where the fingerprint techs immediately dusted it and recovered what prints were still there. Finally, with a crowd now gathered around him, Burdett unlatched the metal catch and opened the box to reveal a bag of white powder and neat packs of twenty-dollar bills topped off by a fully loaded Smith & Wesson 38 Special.

"There must be ten thousand dollars here," Eustace said. "That's a lot of money. Enough to buy this house and the one next door. His business with whites must have been good. But why did Sykes leave it?"

"Maybe he didn't mean to, at least not for good." Burdett answered. "Like your lady friend said, he was probably planning to sneak back for it. Bet he thought this was the safest place to keep it, and he was probably right. Side entrance to the cellar. Wouldn't even have to go inside the house to get it."

Eustace carefully examined Sykes's pistol without touching it. "This is a .38, so he still has the .25 with him if he hasn't already tossed it into the river."

"A fourth bottle, a fourth unfinished note; he's not done with that .25. We've got to find the fourth victim before he does." Burdett had a look of alarm on his face.

"Don't worry, I'll take care of it," Eustace said to Burdett and asked one of the patrolmen to send a cruiser to Emme Bryce's house.

Then Ricketts and Renfro came back from canvassing the block and recounted what they had learned from the neighbors.

"No surprise how everyone backed off'n their porches soon as they saw us fannin' out to ask questions," Renfro said. "Typical. But once you get 'em talkin', it's clear that everyone's pretty happy we've rooted out this drug den. Lucky for us the old lady across the street was the biggest snoop. Name's Ida Miller. If you can believe it, she has a chair set up in her front window just to spy. Lives alone, so that's her entertainment, I guess. She says the shack was round-the-clock commotion. Lights on all night, people comin' and goin' at all hours. And all types: low-down coloreds, white men in hats and suits, even society dames wearin' white gloves. Go figure. She don't remember the last time she saw Sykes. Kept to himself, the shifty type. Drives a shiny two-tone Chevy Bel Air, but he was always parked in back, so she wouldn't know anyway what his comin's and goin's were. She says the place had been dark the last two weeks or so, until last night."

Burdett nodded. That all squared with what Shirley Pearl had told them. He wondered how many upstanding society types from the country club across the tracks would turn up in the fingerprint report, although he didn't like it that the white women were wearing their fancy gloves. That was standard attire for proper ladies venturing out on the town, and he doubted they would take them off in a filthy pigsty like Sykes's place. Not unless they stayed to party. Free samples of blow could have that effect.

"Did you ask her whether she had seen the pink Nash parked at the house?" Burdett asked. Given Sykes's possible connection to Cece Quaid, that was the most obvious question, but Renfro and Ricketts only looked at each other in embarrassment.

"Come on, Vance, she's just a senile old coot who don't know nothin'." Ricketts interjected, trying to cover. "Thanks to me, we know who the Mound Builder is now, so who cares what that old biddy has to say?"

"Guess I need to talk to old Miz Miller myself. So why don't you make yourself useful and tape off the premises before folks trash the place," Burdett said, suppressing his irritation. "It's the house right across the street, right?" Without another word Burdett walked out of Sykes's shack, brushing past Eustace.

* * *

Eustace followed Burdett as he marched purposefully across the street toward a tidy clapboard where they could see a gray head with glasses bobbing in the parlor window. The front door opened as they climbed the porch steps, and they were confronted by a wizened octogenarian shaking her cane at them.

"Now don't you be makin' no more threats, ya hear. I may be old, but I ain't stupid. I got my rights." Eustace could see that she was no fool and was a force to be reckoned with.

"Miz Miller, I'm Officer Eustace Johnson and this is Detective Burdett Vance. Don't worry, we're not here to threaten you. We just want to ask a few more questions, things those other officers forgot to ask."

"I already told 'em alls I know. Now git." She started to swing her door shut, but Eustace gently held it open.

"Hold on now, mama. We don't mean no harm. We're only here to help you jog that fine memory of yours." He flashed his most winning grin and could see her resistance wavering. "Could we just sit a spell with you out here on your lovely porch? You certainly have a fine view from up here. Reminds me of my own porch at home." The faint suggestion of a smile crept into her face as her eyes glanced over to what must be her favorite porch chair, then focused on Eustace with a sharp look of appraisal, as if seeing him for the first time.

"Well, look at you, son, struttin' so grand in that uniform. I always liked a handsome man in uniform."

And with that she hobbled over, plopped into her chair, and readied herself for a chat. Burdett and Eustace nodded at each other, then they started from the beginning, taking turns encouraging her to tell all she knew about the goings-on in the mysterious house across the street. When Burdett asked her if she had ever seen a pink car out front, she lit up.

"Oh, yes, my yes, that was the cutest little car. I seen it there ever now and then. For bein' so small, I could not believe how many of those white girls could fit inside."

"What do you mean?" Eustace asked, feeling his pulse quicken.

"Time before last, it pulls up and this whole posse of cute little white girls piles out, four or five of 'em gigglin' like they was goin' to a tea party, only I knows they was up to no good. Went into that wicked house, and that's the last I saw of the whole bunch."

"Do you think you could identify them if we showed you pictures?" Eustace asked.

"Now, son, I'm stone stupefied you ask that question," she said with a knowing smile. "You of all people should know that all white folks looks alike."

Undeterred, the detectives spent the next fifteen minutes extracting every last detail out of Ida Miller's quirky memory: when the girls came ("the day after Tilly May's baby was born"), what the girls were wearing ("oh, fancy dresses, lady gloves, and those silly little white-girl hats, not real hats like I wear to church"), the color of their hair ("mostly blondes, sugar, right from the bottle"), who answered the door ("who do you think?"), and when they left ("can't say, that pink car just kinda disappeared like Cindrella's pumpkin and I didn't pay it no mind"). Eventually she started repeating herself, so they thanked her and took their leave, both thinking that the Mound Builder's trail had finally and definitively led to Slider Sykes.

At that point, everything went into motion. The dragnet search for Sykes was in high gear. They posted an all-points lookout for Sykes's Chevy Bel Air, and copies of his mugshot photo were sent to all four television stations and the papers with a request to the public to report if he or his Bel Air had been sighted. Burdett made arrangements to have rotating uniformed pairs stake out the house in case Sykes returned, but he didn't think that was likely.

The whole case was falling into place. The lab found a match with the pool of dried blood under Sykes's rug: Cece Quaid. So that was where she had died. A report came back on fingerprints in Sykes's house: matches for Quaid, Warren, Doe, Sykes, and the four squatting partiers. There were numerous other prints from fingertips not yet identified. One other thing, the unidentified prints in Quaid's car matched Warren and Jane Doe. Now they just needed to land Sykes, then it truly would be "case closed." Burdett could not wait to tell Emme the good news, and he planned to do it in person.

CHAPTER 21

Hinge of History

Lord, it thunderin' and it lightnin', and the wind begin to blow,
Lord, there was thousands of poor people didn't have no place to go.

—*Backwater Blues*, Bessie Smith, 1927

Breaking the good news to Emme in person proved to be more difficult than Burdett expected. She didn't answer her phone and was nowhere to be found. He swung by her house and knocked on the door, but there was no answer. The patrol car that Eustace had requested was parked dutifully in front of her place, but the officer on duty had not seen her. This was alarming. With Sykes still on the loose, she remained in danger, so Burdett radioed in a lookout alert and then drove around aimlessly looking for her, just to be doing something.

Eventually, dusk settled over the city, and after checking in at Central and picking up a few Mound Builder case files that he wanted to study, he headed back to his Duvall Street bungalow, exhausted. What a day. Burdett poured himself three fingers of Old Yannissee and cued up a Bessie Smith record on his turntable, but he was still knotted with nervous energy and worried over Emme. He needed to do something to keep his mind occupied, so he carried his box of Mound Builder files to his dining room table. Not that he had a real dining room. It was only an alcove off the living room and he never used it for eating. Instead, he had moved a couple of standing lamps over to the table and suspended a lamp from the ceiling with a dark green metal shade and a 150-watt bulb that cast light onto the table much brighter than the pale fluorescents in the squad room.

From the box he spread out files on Slider Sykes and the three Mound Builder murders, each murder with its own stack. His plan was to put together a timeline with every fact known about each murder to see if any new connections appeared or if there were any clues as to where Sykes might be hiding or who his next victim might be. Burdett was just opening the first file when he heard a tap on his front door. His only visitors were Dewey and Josie who constantly floated in and out, sharing his whiskey, beer, and blues records. Much as he loved them, Burdett also knew they were snoopy types, so he hurriedly packed away the files before he answered the door.

His heart skipped a beat as Emme breezed by him and into the house. She had her blonde hair in a wavy soft bob, and she was wearing a blue flowered dress that seemed to perfectly match her eyes.

"Jeez, Emme, where have you been? I've been lookin' for you everywhere. I have great news!" Burdett wanted to grab her and hold her tight, but he resisted the impulse. Then he paused. "Wait, why are you here?"

"I was in the neighborhood, and since you said you lived here on Duvall, I thought I'd drive by. Your car was in the driveway—I hope you don't mind. What's happened?"

"It's all over the news. Didn't you hear? We identified the Mound Builder! He's a drug dealer named Slider Sykes. We raided his shack over in Orange Mound, and it was full of evidence. Mound Builder notes, beer bottles like the ones we found on the dead girls, and even Cece's blood all over the floor."

"Oh, my God! Cece's blood!" Emme choked with emotion, "Then it's all over!" But Burdett could only shake his head.

"No, and that's why I was so worried. Sykes is still on the loose. You're still in danger." Emme collapsed onto a chair and buried her face in her hands, shaking her head.

"I can't stand this. It'll never end for me until one of us is dead!" Burdett laid his hand on her shoulder to comfort her.

"Nonsense, it won't be long now before we get him. The whole police department is on the case." She was still trembling. He had to do something. "Listen, I just poured myself a whiskey, would you . . . ?"

She nodded and knitted her hands together nervously. He poured her a drink, knocked a handful of ice cubes from the tray in his freezer, and handed her the glass before settling into his own chair. Emme seemed nervous, perched on the edge of her chair as though there was something else on her mind, and it did not take long for her to get to it.

"Burdett, I thought we were gonna have lunch today at Lowenstein's and retrace when I last saw Cece. I was really looking forward to it."

"Oh, Emme, I'm sorry. It plumb slipped my mind. We obviously had a lot goin' on today."

"That's okay. I figured you must have had a good reason, and it turns out you did. Anyway, I decided to go over there by myself to see if I could jog my memory. That's where I was this afternoon." That explains why she disappeared, Burdett thought.

"Did anything come back to you?"

"Nothin' really, just a funny feeling. Cece seemed distracted that day. When we were in the department store café, she kept looking at the entrance as if she was expecting someone. Then a colored man in a fancy suit came in, and suddenly she had to go to the ladies' room. It seemed like nothin' then, and there was nothin' else that I saw to connect them, but thinkin' back on it now, I'm not so sure."

"That's good information, Emme," Burdett said as he got up and stepped over to the boxes of case files. "Come take a look at these photos."

Burdett spread out photos on the table of ten black men whom they had identified as potential suspects, including Sticky Munroe and Slider Sykes. Without hesitation Emme fingered Sykes.

"That was him, I'm sure of it." Another nail in Sykes's coffin, thought Burdett. Definitely their man. At last, everything tied together.

"And, Burdett, I have a confession, so I may as well say it right now. I wasn't just in the neighborhood. I really needed to talk to you, to be with you. I couldn't stay in that apartment one more second knowin' that someone might be lurkin' out there waitin' for the chance to get at me."

"That's why we're keeping our men outside your door all night. They're there now." Burdett sensed that he was entering dangerous territory. He flashed on his conversation with Chief Donlough earlier that day. Donlough was watching them. If Donlough had someone following her, they could have trailed her to his place already.

"How can you be sure that this stalker didn't follow you here just now?"

"Don't worry about that. I slipped out the back and made sure I wasn't followed. I've been doin' that ever since the break-in." As always, Emme seemed pretty confident of herself, although Burdett knew that in fact she had been followed the previous day—or he had. "I appreciate the protection, but havin' police outside all the time makes me feel like I'm in prison. I've got no one I can talk to."

"Sure you do, Emme. You've got tons of friends around town."

Emme put her hand on his arm and squeezed. "I wish that was so, but like I told you the other day at Gannon's, things have changed. You probably wouldn't care if it was you, but you're different, Burdett. You don't want to talk to other people anyway. You only want to be left alone listenin' to your old records. I don't want that, and for me these days, Memphis is pretty lonely. Turns out that everyone hated me all along. And now, God help me, I really hate them too. I hate this whole town. I don't know how much longer I can stand it. I feel like I have enemies everywhere, and I don't even know who they are. You don't know what it's like to be a stranger in your own town."

"I think I do," Burdett said, as he admitted to himself the lonely truth about how she had just described him. He felt himself instinctively retreating inwards. So he decided simply to let her do the talking while she sipped her whiskey, with him chiming in now and then to keep her going, until she started to calm down.

She was wandering curiously around the room now while he watched her—more like he could not keep his eyes off her—and he had no doubt that she knew it. Her voice was mesmerizing as she chattered away. He could sit there and listen to her for hours. Moving slowly as though she was breathing in his private self, she picked up a few blues records, cocked her head to see what else was in the stack, fingered her way across the spines of books on his bookcases, and strolled over to the glass-fronted wooden cases that lined the opposite wall.

"So, this is your collection of Indian stuff. You finally got it out of the boxes. People talk about it, you know."

"Really, who? What have you heard?"

"Oh, everyone knows about it, with you diggin' up these things all over the Delta," she said. "It's kinda mysterious 'cause you never show this to anyone—not even to me back when we were together. I guess that's part of why we all talked about you. If you make people curious, they certainly will gossip. They go on about you sittin' in this old house by yourself, playin' your scratchy blues records, and lookin' at all this dusty stuff."

"Sounds kinda weird when you say it like that," Burdett admitted, thinking she must have always thought that. "But then I guess it's good that I don't care what anybody else thinks because it's none of their business."

"Touchy, aren't we?" Before he could say anything else, she had opened the glass front of the center cabinet for a better look. He restrained the urge to ease the cabinet shut again and stood behind her, looking over her shoulder to see what she found interesting. The shelves of the cabinet were covered with a careful array of arrowheads, figurines, pots, ax heads, beads, and pipes. Each shelf he had laid out in a mosaic of the forgotten past, with rows of arrowheads or beads forming concentric circles of white quartz, gray flint, and black granite radiating out from clusters of figurines in the center. Each item was numbered on the bottom, which tied to his journal where he had described where and when he found it. Each artifact had its own story, and there were boxes and boxes of others out in the garage.

"This is beautiful," Emme whispered, almost to herself. "It's a real work of art, Burdy." They stood there silently for a long moment as she took in the contents of each shelf. He was so close to her now that he could smell her hair and almost feel her body heat, but an invisible force, like two magnets repelling each other, kept him hovering back. Then he almost gasped as she casually picked up a small stone figurine lying at the center of the shelf at eye level.

"What's this?"

"I can't believe that you'd choose that one." It was as if she had passed a hidden test that even he did not know existed. "That's a pipe, the very first piece I ever found. It's what got me started on all this in the first place." He gently took the pipe from her hand and placed it under the light. It was a deeply polished brown stone figure, about six inches long, an odd animal with short hind legs and tall front legs and shoulders, and a head with huge flat ears that housed the pipe's bowl. From its head extended a long nose that curled back between its forelegs.

"You never told me about this. What is it? Where'd you find it? It must be very old."

"It is, and like I said, it's what got me started on all this. What do you remember about the Great Flood of '27?" Then, seeing her blank expression he felt stupid for asking. "Of course, you weren't even alive then, and Fulton was on high ground behind the bluffs anyway so nothin' there got flooded, but it was a bad time for most people around here, especially on low ground. I was living down close to Greenville where the flooding was the worst, lost my dad and a lot of friends that spring." He waved off her gesture of sympathy, "It's okay, it was a long time ago. I moved up here to Memphis to live with my uncle, Danny Doyle. You might have known him; he was a career cop and a Crump man through and through. I called him Uncle Deedy. He was married to my mother's sister Amy, and they had a couple of boys already, so everyone thought it would be good for me to be up here with them.

"Sounds like a hard time, Burdett. I always thought you were born in Memphis."

"No, I just haven't liked to talk about it." He then went on to describe how, after the flood waters subsided and the finger-pointing began, everybody was pretty jumpy. Lots of people had died, lots more had their homes washed down to the Gulf, and Memphis was having another flood, only this time it was people, droves of them, a rising human tide flowing upriver from Sharkey, Pissaquena, Greenville, and all the rest of those low-lying Mississippi and Arkansas towns that were under the worst water after the levees breached. That unhappy wave, mostly dirt-poor sharecroppers off the plantations, spooked Memphis folks—whites and blacks both. Through that whole summer the town had that edgy feeling as if the city was getting more of those New Madrid earthquake tremors that no one consciously feels but that keep the dogs barking. Everyone was nervous and knew things were changing but didn't know how.

"Yeah, that was before I was born, but I remember hearin' about it," Emme said. "Everyone was tellin' Daddy that it was best to stay away from Memphis 'til Boss Crump got it sorted out. Daddy told me he wouldn't let Momma go there to shop for that whole year."

"Exactly. Uncle Deedy was thinkin' the same thing, and he must have heard somethin' was gonna happen, because one mornin' in October he announced out of the blue that he was takin' me and my cousins Billy and DJ outta school to go campin' down on a stretch of bottomland that he knew south of Horseshoe Lake on the Arkansas side. He said there was great huntin' and fishin', and of course we were jumpin' for joy because we were gettin' out of school to do it. Funny thing was, these huntin' trips were usually only us boys and men, but this time he brought Aunt Amy too." Burdett described how they had loaded up the Ford truck with gear, guns, and dogs, and enough food to last half a week, longer if they also hooked some fish or shot enough squirrels and rabbits.

"Uncle Deedy said we could probably stay fat roastin' water moccasin meat on a stick, but Aunt Amy rolled her eyes, so I suppose he was just sayin' we were gonna have to stay motivated to eat enough."

"Snake meat's actually pretty good if you fix it up right," Emme said. "On our fishin' trips Daddy used to shoot a couple and grill 'em up just to show me how Indians lived."

Burdett shook his head in wonderment and then described how they had crossed the bridge over into Arkansas with Burdett, Billy, and DJ stretched out in the truck bed with their blue tick hounds Purdy and Blush. By noon it was as if they were on another planet. As far as they could see in every direction, the great flood had scoured the ground or covered it in a deep layer of muddy sand with the slate gray pallor of a week-old corpse's skin. Trees twisted and uprooted, debris washed up into piles the size of houses, and every now and then there was the rotted carcass of a cow or mule. Hardly a human soul to be seen. Burdett described how he could not look at it, after what all had happened that spring during the flood. So he had buried his head in a blanket, hugged Purdy and waited for them to get to their destination.

"After a long time on that bumpy, washed-out road, we made it up to higher ground, jouncin' along a rough track in a forest that looked like it hadn't been flooded at all. Later we figured out we were at the southern end of Crowley's Ridge, where it peters out just as it reaches the Mississippi down near Helena. Anyway, Uncle Deedy stopped the truck and yelled, "We're here!" wherever that was. Tell me if this is borin' you."

"Oh, no, I love hearin' about this stuff. Keep goin'." Emme sipped her drink and seemed riveted, so he forged ahead with the story.

"We set up camp in a hurry, and us boys we went out explorin' with the dogs. Turns out our campsite was the only high ground around, a flat area the size of a Piggly Wiggly parking lot that sloped down steep on every side except where we had come up in the truck. The country that stretched out around us was washed out in every direction but one; a quarter mile east toward the river was a vast canebrake, a fifty-foot-tall wall of bamboo that stretched north and south 'til it disappeared in the mist."

"Uh-oh," Emme said, "This is startin' to sound ominous."

"Wait, I'm gettin' to that. Billy was already jumpin' with excitement about us huntin' in that canebrake, but Uncle Deedy just shook his head and said we'd only be huntin' along the edge of it. He said that the canebrake stretched for miles, all the way to the river, and he told us if we went pokin' around in there, we might never find our way back. I remember him sayin', 'There's things in there that eat boys like you—and yer dogs too.' I went to sleep that night listenin' to the sounds outside and wonderin' what kinds of animals might be lurkin' just out of sight in that canebrake that might want to eat me. I was thinkin' maybe I should ask Uncle Deedy if I could keep my .22 in the tent, just in case, but he stayed up so late stokin' the fire and cleanin' guns that I fell asleep."

Burdett described how the next morning and every morning after that they were up before daylight, stoking down hot biscuits and coffee, arguing over who got what gun, and by nine o'clock they would sashay back into camp toting rabbits, raccoons, opossums, and whatever else was foolish enough to be moving around after dawn. Then Aunt Amy would give them a proper breakfast of her special grits and pan-fried mystery meat, which was generally what they had shot the day before. In the afternoons they poked around the campsite or explored or drove the truck over to fish for bass and catfish on a nearby cutoff lake that was once a loop of the big river. To Burdett, it was heaven.

"I know how you feel," said Emme. "Sounds just like those trips with Daddy, my happiest times."

"Yeah, it was just like that. On the fifth mornin' I'm with DJ and Purdy huntin' rabbits down the south edge of that canebrake when Purdy takes off through the mist into this big gap in the brake. Thinkin' that he'll get himself eaten like Uncle Deedy said, we take off after him, but DJ's carryin' the heavy 12 gauge and I'm runnin' fast with the light .22, so pretty soon we lose sight of each other. With Purdy bayin' in the distance, I keep goin'. Then it comes to me that this twisty corridor through the brake is more like a canyon, cut through the brake by raging currents from the Great Flood that spring, and I know for sure that it's gotta go clear through to the river, which means Purdy could be runnin' for miles.

"Weren't you scared?" Emme seemed to hang on to his every word.

"I was, maybe a little. Finally, I come around a bend in the canebrake and there in front of me is Purdy, waggin' his tail with a rabbit in his mouth."

But what stopped Burdett dead in his tracks was what he saw behind the dog. The river's current had scoured its course through the canebrake but had glanced off a hill rising from nowhere above the morning mist. An Indian mound. It was covered with massive oaks, trunks six feet across, gnarled and interlocking, that must have been at least five hundred years old. No one had ever logged these trees like other scrub-covered Indian mounds that Burdett had seen poking up in the middle of cotton fields around the Delta country. It had been hidden there for centuries inside the labyrinth of that canebrake.

"Scramblin' up and over the massive tree roots, I climb to the top of the mound. Here and there I catch glimpses through the trees of an endless sea of cane leaves stretchin' in all directions and ripplin' like wheat in the wind, and far off in the distance to the east, catchin' the rays of the rising sun, is a sparklin' silver strip of water—the Mississippi River itself. I must have been the first person in centuries to have seen this. It was a magical place. Near the center of the mound top, one of those huge oaks had toppled over recently, maybe during the flood. The upheaval of its roots left a crater. I'm lookin' around the edge for arrowheads and snakes when I see this gaping hole at the bottom of the crater. It was some kind of cave inside, but leanin' my head into the opening, I can see that it's only about six feet deep with a flat raised stone area directly below me."

"Jeez, Burdett, a cave like that must have been squirmin' with snakes. Tell me you didn't go in there!" Emme said with a shiver.

"Snakes? Maybe, but Purdy's pokin' around and not seemin' particularly interested so I figure nothin's livin' down there and I drop down onto the raised area. Lookin' around me in the dim light, I can't see much at first besides chards of broken pottery, but as my eyes adjust, way back in the shadows I see it. A human skeleton. This skeleton is actually sittin' upright, held up by wooden braces, its legs crossed Indian style, and arms stretched out on either side as almost a welcoming gesture. It seems to be lookin' right through me with those empty eye sockets."

"Jeez!" Emme gasped.

"I almost die right there. Lookin' down I can see that I must be standin' on what was an altar. It's gotta be this guy's tomb. I get this very bad feelin' that I need to get out of there in a hurry when I spot somethin' in the skeleton's right hand, like he was reachin' out to give it to me. I stretch down as far as I can without gettin' off the platform, snag it, and scramble out of that tomb like my life depended on it.

"And it was this pipe. Like I said, the very first thing I ever found—and maybe the most important. But it's what inspired me to keep lookin'." Burdett gazed down at the small stone pipe in his hands, his fingers wrapped around the bowl.

"I get the feelin' that you hold it like that often," Emme said. "Did you ever go back to explore that tomb again?"

"I tried to. Purdy and I made it back to camp by lunchtime, and there was a group of men there talkin' to Uncle Deedy. I thought they were there to look for me, but they weren't. Uncle Deedy only turned to me and said, 'Good, you're back. Pack your stuff. We're goin' back to town.' It was Boss Crump's men, come to tell him he was wanted back in town, pronto. We left, and Uncle Deedy never took us there again, no matter how we begged. It wasn't 'til I could drive a few years later that me and the boys went back down that way. I tried to find the tomb again, but by then the canebrake had grown back, closed up as if that breach was never there. To tell the truth, it was almost like a dream, and I wouldn't be so sure that it had even happened, if I didn't have this." He held the pipe up in the light for a moment, and then carefully placed it in her outstretched hands. "It's the most precious thing I own."

Watching his eyes still, she held the stone figure and stroked the polished smooth surface.

"What makes this pipe so valuable to you?"

"Because of what it stands for. See that curved nose? It's a trunk, like an elephant. It's a mastodon, really. They've been extinct for thousands of years. The person who made this pipe, whether it was the guy in the tomb or someone else generations before him, had been here when there were still mastodons roaming these parts. That man actually had seen one himself. It's really a missing link, connecting the earliest humans with an earlier world without people, where animals ruled." Burdett explained how people study history to make sense of humanity. But if you go all the way back, past recorded history and before even fragments like this, you eventually reach a time before the idea of history even existed, before there were things like love, power, cruelty, or deceit. The mastodon pipe was like the hinge between all that came before, and all that came after. "Mastodons were giants, but they were true innocents. They weren't afraid of humans, which doomed them."

"Sounds like you're on the side of the mastodons," Emme said, moving almost imperceptibly closer to him. "I think that's really sweet. These days, you don't meet many true innocents, but I suspect there's a bit of the true innocent in you, Burdett. It's part of what attracted me to you way back when."

"How can you say that when my entire life is a steady diet of evil?"

"Aren't innocence and righteousness the same thing? That's what Ed Crump told me. And you strike me as a very righteous man. I think it's sexy." Burdett immediately bridled at the thought of her with the Boss.

"So was the righteous Boss Crump sexy?" he asked.

"Not at all! That old man was miles from righteous, and he sure as heck wasn't sexy. It was never like that between us. But he told me *you* just *exuded* righteousness, and that he was keepin' his eye on his Bird Dog."

"You two talked about *me*?"

"We talked about everything. But let me say it again, that's all we ever did."

"So let me get this straight. All you two did was talk, you talked about me being so righteous, and you think that's sexy?"

Emme returned the pipe to its spot in the cabinet, gently closed the glass doors and turned back toward Burdett to find him already standing close. Looking steadily into his eyes, she whispered, "Well, Mr. Burdett Vance, I liked your little tale about the mastodons. You're so good at tellin' stories, so what's *our* story? What's really happenin' here?"

Cupping her face in his hands, he gave her a long, soft kiss on the lips, "This is what's really happening here."

Burdett felt Emme melt into him like a dream, returning his kiss with an urgency that surprised him as if, like him, she had been holding herself back all this time. The feeling of being desired like that was intoxicating, and Burdett surrendered completely to an impulse that had been building in him from the moment he had met Emme over a decade before. In his wildest dreams he had never thought this moment would ever come.

"Oh, Burdett," Emme murmured, "I'm so glad you're in my life again."

"Shh, don't say a word, Emme. Just feel it."

They took their time, savoring each moment as, with each kiss, another article of clothing fell to the floor. In Burdett's arms, Emme felt like an unbearably fragile treasure that could vaporize into a figment of his imagination at any instant. He gently moved his hands over her naked body, trying to memorize every soft curve as if he might never experience this moment with her again. The insistence in her lips and hands told him that she must feel the same, as they tumbled into the marvel of the present, where there was no fear or dread, no past or future, just an all-consuming now.

CHAPTER 22

After the Deluge

If it keeps on rainin', levee's goin' to break,
And the water gonna come, and we'll have no place to stay.

—*When the Levee Breaks*, Memphis Minnie, 1929

At dawn Burdett awoke to the sight of blonde hair flowing in waves across his field of vision. He wanted to touch it to assure himself that it was real, that Emme was actually there with him, that it was not a dream. She was asleep, her naked body curled up against his, but as he stirred, she turned over and faced him with a sleepy smile.

"Mmm," she purred as she burrowed into the crook of his arm.

"Sleep well?" he asked, stroking the curve of her hip.

"Mmm," she said, bringing her leg across his body. He kissed her on the mouth and as she responded they slid again into a rhythmic embrace, making love with the morning sunlight streaming through the window. Burdett felt himself again falling hard for Emme, and he remembered how from the beginning, years ago, she had struck a deep chord in him with her magnetic combination of natural earthiness and resilience but also vulnerability. With her it was as if he had found his natural state, and he wanted to hold her like that forever.

Although Burdett felt the persistent tug of the Mound Builder case, he was also thinking that it was Sunday morning, most folks were still at church, and no one would miss him, for a few hours anyway. So he let himself enjoy the guilty pleasure of lounging in bed with Emme, talking, making love, and talking more. With painful honesty she shared with him what her life had really been like and how much she wanted to escape from herself and start over, and she had a plan. The final chapter with Boss Crump had been her chance to make the break.

"Burdett, I know talkin' about this is gonna be weird for you, but let me say my piece because otherwise you'll always be wonderin'. My time with Ed Crump was not at all what people think."

"That's okay, Emme, you don't have to explain yourself." Burdett was not sure that he wanted to hear what she was about to say.

"Like I keep sayin', there was nothin' physical. He just liked spendin' time with me because I listened without judgin'—unlike his wife, I have to say—and I liked spendin' time with him because he was truly the most fascinatin' person I ever knew. To see him play this city like the organ master at Calvary Church was a wonder. All the ins and outs, schemes and personalities, backstabbin' and paybacks. He was a wizard at it. And when we were together, he'd tell me all about it. I think it helped him to vent, and I just loved soakin' it up. It made me wish I'd been born a man so I could pull those strings of power too." Burdett was thinking that she was good at pulling strings herself, but he wasn't saying it.

"So you had a front row seat, huh?"

"And he was so smart. He made Memphis grow into a modern city and made himself a fortune along with it 'cause he knew his people. Here's one for you. Every day he read the Negro newspapers and *Ebony* magazine just so's he could keep his finger on the pulse of colored Memphis."

"Finger on their pulse, or did he just want 'em under his thumb?"

"Now, don't be mean! He said he just wanted to keep up with the Negro mind, and what's wrong with that? Sure, he pushed back on integratin' just like everybody else, but he hated violence. Ed once told me that a white mob was just a passel of scared children lookin' for their daddy to tell 'em everything would be alright. So that's what he did, he kept the peace." That's what Emme wanted too, Burdett thought, someone to tell her everything would be alright. But who wouldn't want that? Boss Crump had been good at it, gaslighting the whole city, black and white alike.

"I'd say he was keepin' *his* version of the peace, but it looks like you became a true believer in him, Emme. Do you miss him?" At that he could see her tear up.

"Miss him? Yeah, we got to be pretty close. He was a great teacher. He made me laugh. He showed me how to have a vision of what I wanted to do and make it happen. The city seems empty without him. A little piece of its soul is gone. We were goin' into business together, did you know that?"

"Business, what kind of business?"

"We were plannin' Memphis's first riverboat casino. Worked on it for the last couple of years. We had it all lined up, even optioned a sidewheeler down in New Orleans to be our first casino."

"Wow, Emme, amazing." Burdett was genuinely impressed with her gumption.

"That was going to be my way out of all this. I'm tired of havin' to rely on men to get things done, to survive. My plan is to be my own boss, beholden to no one once I paid back the money Ed was going to lend me to get started. That was what that pile of papers on my dining room table was about. He liked the idea because it would bring more tourists to Memphis. Always lookin' for ways to improve the city. That was Ed for you."

"So what's happening with the project now that the Boss is dead?"

"Oh, I haven't given up on it. Too much blood, sweat, and tears invested to do that. I'm looking for new backers, but I don't think I'll find 'em in Memphis. That's why I need to get outta here." With that she closed the subject and turned the conversation to Burdett's least favorite topic.

"How about you, Burdett? Tell me what's it been like for you, really."

Burdett had heard enough about the inner workings of Boss Crump's mind and her pipe dreams, so he talked on about how his life seemed to have folded in on itself, consumed by work and dogged by regret as he saw time slipping away.

"Bird Dog, you sound as trapped as me! Why don't we both just run away together?"

"That sounds nice, Emme, but truth is, I can't think about much else until I get this Mound Builder case resolved." Burdett immediately regretted his words as he saw a cloud sweep over her face.

"Okay, then let's talk and get it over with so we can think about somethin' more pleasant," she said matter-of-factly. "What's the latest?" Though Burdett had been dreading this moment, he decided to come right out with it.

"Today the newspapers are going to report that we found a third body yesterday, this one in Audubon Lake. Her name was Mary Lou Warren." He felt a shiver go through Emme's body.

"Oh, no, not Mary Lou! She was one of Cece's best friends. I met her only once, but she was so nice, and funny too. Why would someone want to kill her?"

"He left another note, talkin' about a lynchin' that happened in Memphis almost forty years ago. Sykes is bent on revenge and is directly threatenin' the whites in East Memphis now. Soon our whole white population is gonna be in a panic. Which means blacks will be too."

"I don't blame 'em!" cried Emme, choking back tears. "*I'm* in a panic! He's pickin' off Cece and her friends, and I could be the next one myself! And he probably knows that I saw him!"

"Emme, it'll be okay. We now know it's Slider Sykes, and he can't stay on the loose for long. Did Cece ever mention him?"

"Certainly not! Why would she have anything to do with him?"

"We found coke in her car." Burdett noticed Emme pausing, thinking, and weighing her next words.

"Then it all starts to make sense. Cece and her friends must have seen somethin', and he didn't want 'em talkin'. Maybe when they were at this man's place, they saw him kill someone else who hasn't turned up yet. Maybe the man cracked and hates white people so much that he's now doin' the thing that will hurt them most, killin' their women." Burdett had to admit that there was a twisted logic in what she said.

"I don't know, Emme, but it's got to be something to do with Cece. She keeps popping up at the center of everything. You knew her; what was she really like?" Emme paused for another moment before speaking.

"Cece could be a ton of fun when she was in the mood, but to be honest, she was really just a spoiled rich girl with an ugly mean streak. I come from nothin', and everything I have is what I've worked for—and believe me, puttin' up with men is work—present company excepted. But Cece? She was given everything on a sterling silver platter and knew that as soon as she was ready to settle down, every guy in town would be linin' up because of her daddy's money. So she was cruel and careless with her friends, me included. What happened to her was terrible, but if anyone deserved it, she did.

"Take Alice Phelps, who was one of my best friends. She was a lovely girl whose only mistake was runnin' with Cece. Then she gets pregnant, and her supposed pal Cece goes out of her way to shun her and force everyone else to do the same. Cece didn't want to be tainted by association, so she destroyed that poor girl, and Alice finally killed herself—and the unborn baby. It was despicable what Cece did, but then guess what she said afterwards. She just waved her hand and said that Alice was too stupid to live. Can you believe it? I could tell you more stories like that, but it just goes to show that if anyone deserved what happened to Cece, it was Cece! I know that sounds terrible, but now *because of her* this man Sykes is after me, and I don't even know why!"

Burdett could feel Emme tensing in anger and moved to defuse the conversation, "Maybe Sykes doesn't know what you saw, but now that the word is out that we can prove he is the Mound Builder, there would be no point in going after you just to shut you up. Too risky. I'm sure he's long gone. We haven't caught Sykes yet, but I expect that we will any minute if he's still around, and then you'll be safe. Until then, I'll keep you safe."

"Thank you, Burdy."

He gave her a long hug, and with that they both dropped the subject, feeling emotionally exhausted from talking about it. Emme curled up tighter against him and held him close, and that's the way they were when Burdett heard a rapping on his back door. Only one person ever came banging on his back door; it had to be Josie.

"Wake up in there, the day awaits us!" Josie shouted. She was already in the kitchen. Burdett bounded out of bed, pulled on his pants, and intercepted Josie before she made it further into the house.

"Whoa, Josie, what's up?"

"What's up is a beautiful day, and you are comin' with us, my friend. I've fixed a righteous Sunday breakfast feast and you're our honored guest." Burdett was thinking fast for an excuse when Josie's eyes suddenly focused over his shoulder with a look of astonishment. "Emme Bryce, is that you?"

Burdett turned and there was Emme, wrapped in a sheet and peeking around the corner. He had another white-out moment, completely at a loss for words.

"Hi, Josie."

"Well, this beats all. Burdett, you sly dog. Welcome back, darlin'. So, I guess that's breakfast for four! Are ya hungry?"

"I'd love to join you if it's okay with Burdett." She looked at Burdett and playfully fluttered her eyes. Irresistible.

"Great, let's do it. What can we bring, Josie?"

"Just bring your appetites and come on over in fifteen minutes. I'm starvin' and the smell of bacon is killin' me. That should give you both time to get some clothes on," she said, raising an eyebrow. With that Josie was gone, screen door slamming behind her, tromping across their adjoining backyards to carry the big news back to Dewey.

Burdett and Emme were left alone, feeling as if a cyclone had just blown through but feeling good to be out in the open, at least with someone.

"Fifteen minutes is actually a lot of time," Emme said with a knowing smile on her face, and stepping up close to Burdett, she let the sheet drop to the floor. As she slowly raked her fingernails down his bare chest and her lips hovered on his, he felt himself shudder uncontrollably with pleasure, and for that one exhilarating moment it was as if nothing else mattered and nowhere else existed. At last he was free.

* * *

A half hour later, they threaded their way across the connected yards past Josie's sculptural menagerie and knocked on Dewey and Josie's rear door. The Taylor house was a compact Craftsman bungalow with dark green shingles and brown trim. Hanging from every eave was an eclectic array of objets d'art and wind chimes that made the house look like a Christmas tree. Dewey answered the door with a big grin on his face.

"Emme, you are a sight for sore eyes. How long has it been? You're lookin' good, girl. Nice to see you." Burdett caught Dewey's wink as Dewey gave Emme a hug, and he knew exactly what his friends were thinking. Their Burdett Project was to find him a mate, and any hint that he had finally found someone would get their unquestioning support.

"Come on in, you two."

The inside of the Taylor household was almost too much to absorb. Everywhere were concert posters or photos of Dewey with music celebrities. And on every surface rested an interesting object that you knew had its own special story. Dewey showed them into his "money mausoleum" where the walls were covered with framed Confederate money of every size and color. Lampshades with Confederate bank bills pasted on them cast an amber light.

"Ninety years ago the money in this room would have made me a rich man in these parts, for a year or two anyway," Dewey said. "My daddy told me to hold on to our Confederate money 'cause the South shall rise again, so I made a hobby of holdin' on to other peoples' Confederate money, which by the way you could buy at a big discount after 1865. Look at this one here; it's my favorite. They say Jeff Davis had this fifty-dollar bill on him when he was arrested. Don't ask me how I got hold of it, but you can bet that every bill here was at one time in the pocket of someone like him."

"What a sad room, Dewey," Emme said. "People scrapin' a livin' and all this wealth come to nothin'. You can feel the sense of loss, not just of what the money represented but of everything they had and the whole life they knew. Left life pretty desolate for a lot of small-time country folks like mine."

"Out with the old, in with the new is what I say, Emme. And let's not forget that there's the colored half of our population that didn't feel so great about things in those days, not that they feel so good about things now. One way or another, every dollar in this room was made on the backs of slaves. Hell, Memphis was actually the center of the slave trade back then. There was a slave market right across the street from where the courthouse is now, run by Nathan Bedford Forrest himself, if you can believe it. They call it this country's original sin, but I got some different thoughts on what the real original sin was. Emme, if you're thinkin' our dead money room is a sad place, let me show you the saddest and lostest of all lost causes."

Dewey led them into the next room which, like Burdett's living room, was lined with glass-fronted cabinets but also tables and open shelves crowded with dusty looking earthen bowls, arrowheads, shell necklaces, and other artifacts. On the walls were detailed maps of the Mississippi River valley, an array of colored pins stuck into them showing the location of potential archeological sites and the digs that he and Burdett had already explored.

"I'm Choctaw and there ain't nothin' left of us. These days, in the name of progress they're knockin' down Indian mounds up and down the Mississippi Valley," Dewey said, looking at a large map. "St. Louis used to be called Mound City 'cause there was so many there, but now those eighty mounds are down to just one."

"As I was sayin' last night, Emme, we've been tryin' to find and save what we can before the bulldozers plow it under or dump trucks haul it away to the landfill," Burdett said.

"Of course, the real damage was done centuries ago when whites passed on to us Europe's biggest gifts to my people—measles and smallpox—and it wiped us out," Dewey said.

"That's awful!" said Emme.

"Some say it was the pigs that DeSoto had with him that went feral, multiplied like rabbits, and passed on the pox. That's where all those Arkansas razorbacks came from, by the way. By the time that French explorer La Salle floated down the Mississippi a century later, we were mostly gone. It destroyed my people and all our traditions. Heck, until recently we thought the mound builders were some other ancient extinct people that came before us, when all along it was just us. Ours was a lost cause that was so lost that no one even remembered it existed," Dewey said, shaking his head, but he was just gaining steam.

"And one of Memphis's founding fathers, Andrew Jackson, made sure of it. He was the worst. He pushed what was left of us out west of the big river all the way to Oklahoma, so there was no one left to tell. You heard of the Trail of Tears? It came right through Memphis, which was the jumping-off spot for the trail west. Jackson Avenue? That actually was the trail itself coming in from the east. Can you believe they named part of the Trail of Tears after that Indian hater? Yeah, original sin is the word for it. They killed most of us and stole the whole damn country. And to Jackson, it was just one big real estate play." Dewey grew silent, reflecting on everything that the room meant to him. "This is a sacred place to me. Maybe someday I'll give all this stuff to a museum if I can find one that'll take it."

"Count me in on that," said Burdett.

"That's right, I got my buddy Burdett to thank for gettin' me into this," Dewey said, punching Burdett on the arm. "Kept me out of trouble when I was a punk and brought me and Josie together to boot. And on the happier side, I do try to look to the future. Of course, the new music is my thing, but I actually believe the South will rise again, and I can tell you the one thing that will make it happen." He paused, waiting for someone to ask what.

"Okay, Dewey, I'll bite, what?" Burdett asked dutifully, already knowing the answer.

"Why, air conditionin', of course! No business is gonna move down here if they have to suffer through the humid Memphis heat. But with AC, all that changes, ya see? Air conditionin' is the future of the new South. Hell, it's what made movie theaters what they are today. Burdett, like I keep tellin' you, get out of the murder business and go into the coolin' business with me." At that moment Josie breezed in, bursting with her usual boundless energy.

"Is he talkin' about air conditionin' again, hon? Enough of that. Let's eat!" They all moved into the dining room where platters of bacon, eggs, grits, and biscuits awaited them. And all through the meal Burdett could not take his eyes off Emme, asking himself again and again how it could be only four days since they reconnected. It was as if they had never been apart.

At last, Emme raised her glass, "I want to make a toast. To this heavenly meal with friends that is a universe away from all our worries and fears, and to Josie and Dewey for bein' the caring friends and neighbors of the nicest guy I know." And as she looked intensely into Burdett's eyes, they all clinked their glasses. Then as if saying to Dewey and Josie that she trusted them completely, Emme leaned over and gave Burdett a long, soft kiss.

"Wow, I'll toast to that," said Burdett.

"Wow is right," Dewey and Josie said together, while Burdett sat there, basking in the glow of it all, and hoping it would never end.

Later when Emme cleared some dishes to the kitchen, Dewey leaned over and whispered excitedly, "Burdett, I know you got a history with Emme, but I take it all back. She's a keeper, man, don't let her get away this time."

"Burdett, she really is sweet," Josie chimed in. "And you can tell she's crazy about you. We're so glad to have had this morning with her."

"I can hear you," Emme said, coming back from the kitchen. "Thank you all for havin' me. I don't get to enjoy the simple pleasures of life that often anymore." With that she kissed them both on the cheek and poked Burdett to go.

Burdett got the message, and truth was, he had begun feeling antsy. Although it was Sunday morning and folks were just finishing up their Sunday services at the many churches scattered through the city, Burdett already was feeling guilty that he'd taken even a few hours away from the search for Slider Sykes just so he could selfishly enjoy the pleasure of Emme's company. Back at his house he dialed into Police Central, and sure enough, all hell had broken loose across the city. He turned to see Emme's face searching his for news.

"I'm sorry, Emme, I gotta go. No news on Sykes and it's gettin' crazy out there. Can you lay low here at my place and stay out of sight for the rest of the day? If anything at all happens, just run back over to Dewey and Josie's. Is that okay?"

"Sure, Burdy, you go get that bastard. I won't be safe until he's behind bars," Emme said. But her bravado seemed forced, and Burdett felt that a scared child lay behind it.

"I'll be back before dark," he said, giving her a lingering last hug, and he left before he could change his mind.

★ ★ ★

The scene at Central was a madhouse. Burdett had grabbed copies of both newspapers en route and saw that indeed his worst fears had been realized. With the news of a third Mound Builder murder—now in the heart of white East Memphis—whites were in terror and the city had become a tinderbox, threatening to explode into racial violence at any moment. The *Sunday Press-Scimitar* had splashed a two-inch headline over Hogue's byline. The prospect of a killer seeking revenge for forty lynchings was blindingly incendiary. People reacted as if World War III had just been declared, Commie threat notwithstanding. At last, the Mound Builder phantom had been made man, with a name and a face: Slider Sykes, black as night. The radio and TV news channels had been posting hourly reports of the latest Sykes sightings, popping up all over the city like pepper on grits. The man seemed to be everywhere and nowhere. Burdett found Eustace busy at his desk fielding phone calls, fresh from church, still dressed in his Sunday best, and emanating a sense of urgency.

"Man, am I glad you're here," Eustace said. "This city's gone wild." The mugshot of Sykes that had been plastered across the front pages had morphed into a spectral menace that included every black man in Memphis, and the department was stretched to the limit running down hysterical reports coming in from all corners of the city. The fact that Sykes had so cleverly avoided the pervasive dragnet simply reenforced the fear that a ghoul was lurking in every shadow, bent on slaughtering Southern womanhood to avenge a century of lynchings. The combustible mixture of fear and hate was erupting on every street corner as blacks and whites alike prepared for the worst, police cars with flashing lights raced up and down the city streets to quell the mounting violence, and the hospital emergency rooms began to fill. Burdett immediately dove into the fray, crisscrossing the city with Eustace to chase leads and hoping that they would get lucky as they constantly kept their eyes peeled for that skulking ghostlike apparition. After twelve hours of false alarms, their exhaustion was rewarded only by the creeping realization that it had been a complete waste of time.

"Detective Vance, I'm not sure we're accomplishing much here," Eustace volunteered at last. "It seems like the same frightened folks are calling in the same terrified reports of the same black man living across the street, walking home from church, or just minding his own business. I'm half surprised that they didn't report me."

"Very funny, but you're right that this is not accomplishing much, and I'm exhausted. Let's call it a day and start fresh tomorrow." Yes, it was time to get a good night's rest, and Burdett knew exactly who he wanted to do it with.

* * *

Burdett arrived back at his bungalow to find the table set for two and a steaming pot of chicken cacciatore on the stove, no doubt courtesy of Josie since he knew he had no food in the house. Emme waltzed into the kitchen with an exaggerated bustle, wearing an apron and playing house with a feather duster. Burdett laughed with relief, grateful again for the respite from the darkness of humanity that filled his days. So she poured him his Old Yannissee neat, hers with a cube, and for the rest of the evening they suspended reality to imagine, what if. Eventually, Emme grew pensive and disappeared toward the bedroom where Burdett found her lying on the bed, still fully clothed but with her shoes kicked off. Easing down beside her, he stroked her hair and traced the line from her neck down her arm.

"Burdett," she said, turning toward him and looking deeply into his eyes. "This has been wonderful. You're probably thinkin' what I'm thinkin', that this could have been our life if we hadn't split up. That was my fault. I'll always remember this day as a glimpse into the life we could have had."

"You've got your whole life ahead of you, Emme," Burdett said. "Feels like maybe this was more a glimpse of the future than the past." And in that instant, their whole future came to him in a singular vision. They stay together, get married, maybe have kids. The haters at the country clubs eventually tire of gossiping about her and move on, and the crowd that the two of them run with, mostly people they meet through Dewey and Josie, don't care anyway. The terror stops once they bag Sykes, and whatever was the deep fear or sense of desperation that she brought with her from Fulton fades away. Maybe Emme's riverboat casino idea takes off. They buy a little ranch house in a safe subdivision out east with a tidy yard and nice neighbors, settle down, join a church, go to PTA meetings at school, have a real life, and grow old together. It suddenly shocked him that for the first time in his life he could imagine his own future too.

"Burdett, ever since we met years ago, I've been wanting to ask you something."

"What's that?"

"What happened to you? There's this cloud that's always been hangin' over you. The rest of us were havin' so much fun today, but you seemed so sad and edgy. It was like you were there but not there. I learned more about you in the last four days than I knew the whole time we were together before. That's partly why I left back then. You're such a mystery. It feels like somethin' happened to you, maybe back when you were little, that just closed you off. Must have been tough to lose your parents so young."

Burdett lay there in silence for a while staring at the ceiling, fighting the tumult. Emme waited quietly, her fingers running gently through his hair as if to say everything would be okay. His mind tumbled back to his days on that Delta mule farm, the happiest time of his life, then he gave an involuntary shiver.

"You really want to know?" he asked. He didn't want to talk about it, but he knew that if they were going to have any chance together, eventually he would have to tell her everything. Might as well be now.

"Remember how I told you that we had that mule breeding operation since before the first war? Back then a mule dealer was at the top of the heap. Pops made real good money, and life was sweet. In fact, life was perfect for a kid like me. My mom died in the '18 flu epidemic. I was so young I never knew her or even missed her. In fact, it turned out that I was adopted and she was not even my real mom. But that's another story, and anyway me and Pops, we were tight. Big Burdett and Little Burd. We had Maxie workin' for us doin' the cookin' and cleanin', and she was like a mother to me. She lived in a little house on the place with her old man Jake and their son Eli. One big happy family.

"And Eli really was like my brother. He was tall and skinny, black as coal, and the funniest guy I ever knew. We were the same age and did everything together—except school, of course. Yeah, bein' a kid growing up on that farm was close to heaven, all freedom once we got our chores done. I can't tell you how many hours we spent shoveling manure, but after finishing chores, our world was as far as we could roam and still make it back by suppertime. We explored miles from home, free ranging, not like city kids today. Our farm was only a half mile inside the levee, so we hiked all over the bottomlands and along the river and creek beds tracking snapping turtles and scaring up cottonmouths. Startin' when we were eight or nine, me and Eli learned how to play guitar together on Pop's old six-string, and we'd hang around with the bluesmen down by the cotton gin learning licks."

"I always loved hearing you play. That's something I really missed about you, Burdett," said Emme. "Can you play something? Please?

"Maybe sometime. Anyway, all that ended with the great flood of '27."

"What happened?"

"It was biblical. In the summer of '26 the rain started across the whole Mississippi watershed from Pennsylvania to Montana and never stopped. By Christmas there was unheard of flooding upstream, and then the spring rains and snow melt up north added to the flood waters. When you have that much flow, it either spreads out or rises up. The Indians understood that. Instead of trying to control the river with levees, they let the flood waters spread and built their own high ground."

"There you go, Burdett, talkin' about those Indian mounds again," Emme said, poking him.

"Well, we thought we knew better, buildin' levees higher and higher, up and down the river, for decades. The trick was to build your levee higher than the levee builders across the river so the floods would top their levee first. Save yourself, flood your neighbor. Nice. Of course, they did it too. Dynamite had the same effect. They called it the levee wars. Each side posted armed guards with orders to shoot to kill anyone rowing from the other side for fear they'd blow their levee. Everyone was out for themselves."

"Sounds terrible. We were on such high ground on the bluff up in Fulton that we never thought about that," Emme said.

"Anyway, that spring the river started risin' fast, faster than ever before. The townsfolk in Greensville scrambled to sandbag their levee higher, and it was a race against time because the water was risin' faster than the sandbags were stackin'. So they emptied the jails and marched the inmates up to the levee top in chains. Then they seized every colored male they could find and pressed 'em at gunpoint into work gangs penned up in the levee camps. Pops told us to stay out of town, so me and Eli were hangin' out on the front porch after breakfast watchin' the rain come down in sheets when the sheriff drove up and asked Eli why he wasn't up on the levee. He was only twelve, but he was tall, and that sheriff just grabbed him and drove off without sayin' another word."

"He could do that?" Emme asked. "That's kidnapping!"

"Exactly. Pops blew up when he learned about it, sayin' Eli was only a child. So he told Jake to stay back at the house and lay low, and we drove up to the levee where the press gangs were working. It was a sight to see, an army of hundreds of black men filling sandbags and desperately moving them in bucket lines to the top of the levee. When we climbed up there looking for Eli, we were the only whites in sight not carrying shotguns, and prisoners in leg irons were everywhere. In every face there was fear and panic. It was a scene straight from Hell." Burdett shuddered at the one memory that he most hated to revisit, but he had to finish now.

"And looking out on the river itself chilled my soul. The water was already licking at the levee top, as dark and menacing as I'd ever seen it, whipped into white caps by the wind. Gusts shivered across the surface in shock waves, and the rain stung when it hit my face. I'd never been so afraid in my life. Pops and I split up and headed in opposite directions to find Eli. I was callin' for him, but you couldn't hear a thing above that howlin' wind." Burdett felt Emme shiver at the thought too.

"Then it happened. There was a rumbling under my feet like an earthquake, and suddenly the whole levee gave way over in the direction where Pops had gone. A hundred men on the levee top instantly washed away. I was screaming for Pops and running toward the levee break, fighting against a stampede of terrified men scrambling the other way. You could see the levee continuing to collapse toward us as the gap widened, like the levee was just evaporating. Suddenly dark hands grabbed me and pulled me in the other direction, and all I can remember was bein' carried on the shoulder of a giant of a man, janglin' in his leg irons and runnin' as though I was light as a feather. He saved me, but just like that, Pops and Eli were gone forever. And I never knew who it was that saved me or if he even survived the flood. He disappeared along with the rest of them."

Burdett had to stop for a moment. Reliving that moment's horror and loss had utterly drained him. His mind tumbled back to imagining what it must have been like for Eli and Pops to be engulfed in that torrent. He initially had fantasized that they had somehow managed to ride the colossal wave to safety and that at any moment he would hear them call his name and his life would begin again. But they were gone forever, and so he came to hope instead that their lives had been extinguished instantly, without experiencing the terror and vain struggle to survive against the unconquerable rage of that wretched river, being twisted in convulsive turbulence, battered by churning debris, gasping for air but inhaling only muddy water. It made him ache. Emme wrapped her arms around him and held him tight.

"Oh, Burdett, I'm so sorry."

"That's not all. Our farm was so close to the levee that the church bells and fire whistles hadn't even started sounding the alarm before that wall of water hit the place. Maxie, Jake, and the livestock never had a chance. The flood consumed everything in its path. The Mounds Landing Crevasse, they called it. The worst levee break in history. For weeks, the water poured through the crevasse, flowing bigger than Niagara Falls, pouring that muddy water, trees, boats, even whole houses into the Delta and filling seven thousand square miles of the Delta ten feet deep. By the time those waters lapped up against the base of the hill country, that river was a hundred miles wide.

"Months later when the water came down, they were still finding bodies of people and animals in trees and everywhere. But they never found Pops or Eli, Maxie, or Jake. The flood washed down into the Yazoo River and then flowed again into the Mississippi downstream at Vicksburg, so they probably got washed out into the Gulf. Who knows what happened to all our livestock. Nothing was left of the farm but the building foundations."

"Burdett," said Emme, squeezing his arm. "I don't know what to say. You lost everything." Burdett didn't really know what to say either. He used to think that the day they died was the worst day of his life. Then they stayed dead. Now he just wanted to push the memory into a dark place so deep that it would never see light again. But that had never worked. He had gone over that day a thousand times in his head, and the truth was that if only he had had the courage to speak up when the sheriff came to grab Eli, everything could have been different. He could have told the sheriff that Eli was only twelve, but he didn't. The sheriff wouldn't have taken Eli, but he did. His father and Eli wouldn't have been on the levee when it collapsed, but they were. If they'd been there at the farm instead when the levee breached, maybe they could have saved Maxie and Jake and outrun the rushing waters in the truck. Then they could have rebuilt after the flood, but they didn't.

"Well, I survived, Emme, and life has a way of moving on. That flame won't ever burn as bright, so best to just keep it turned down low." As he stroked her hair, all he could think was how much he hated that river, even though he had spent almost his entire life within five miles of it, driven by some fatal attraction as if the river was not done with him just yet. Well, he was done with the river. The deadly Mississippi had snatched his world from him, but whoever had saved him that fateful morning had cheated it out of at least one life. It was a debt that remained unpaid, and in his heart, he feared that, like a pact with God or the Devil or both, sooner or later that debt would have to be squared. No, Emme saw it clear enough; there was a dark, empty spot inside him that would never be filled.

Emme was still afraid to stay alone at her place, and Burdett did not want her to leave anyway, so he called off the stakeout telling the crew that she had moved to a friend's house. Burdett suspected that he was hardly fooling anyone, but he was not going to let them document her comings and goings. So she stayed with him again, and they talked into the night about the Mound Builder case, the developing mountain of evidence pointing toward Sykes, and the manhunt that by then was scouring the whole South for him.

"Until you find him, I can't be safe!" Emme said, casting her eyes about the room like a caged animal. "Who knows how he looks now? I wouldn't even see him comin'."

"That's part of the problem, Emme," Burdett said. "Every white person in Memphis who thinks Sykes is out for revenge is thinking that way. We published Sykes's mugshot, but all that white Memphis sees is a black man, and every black man becomes the enemy."

It took Burdett a while to get Emme calmed down enough to fall asleep and even longer to still his own mind, knowing that the next morning he would grudgingly return to a gloomy world of dead bodies, scheming colleagues, missing persons, and a killer on the loose. What was worse, he was in no hurry to sleep because after reliving the horrors of the Mounds Landing Crevasse with Emme, he knew where his mind would take him now, plunging blindly once again into his recurring nightmare and toward the inescapable sound of a thundering Hell. Welcome to my world, Emme, he thought, as inexorable sleep eventually overtook his feverish mind and sent him on his way.

CHAPTER 23

The Truth Will Out, Or Not

Hey, bo-weavil, don't sing the blues no more,
Bo-weavil's here, bo-weavil's everywhere you go/

—*Bo-Weavil Blues*, Ma Rainey, 1924

The next morning Burdett blinked awake early, peeled himself silently away from Emme, and slipped out the back door to face the day. Back at Police Central things had gone from bad to worse. True to form, Chief Donlough had gone into high gear trumpeting breakthroughs in the case, but the press was having a field day and not buying any of it. The manhunt for Sykes had expanded into a nationwide search. Although Sykes had at least two weeks' head start, Burdett's team kept a lookout on his place anyway just in case he snuck back for the cash. After all, that was how they had nabbed Machine Gun Kelly back in the '30s, holed up in a house off South Parkway, not that far from Orange Mound.

The expanded manhunt and national publicity that it garnered had yielded one additional benefit. Eight hundred miles away in sleepy Roanoke, Virginia, police had finally filled in the missing link and identified Jane Doe. Her name was Mimsy Cooper, and she was last seen when she left Roanoke to drive to

Dallas with a stopover in Memphis. No one had heard from her since. She was supposed to be stopping to see a friend from school named Cece.

So all roads led to Cece Quaid and from her to Sykes. Burdett cursed himself for having taken even one minute away from the chase the previous day, thinking that another friend of Quaid's could have been killed in the meantime, and they would not even know it yet. Burdett called a team meeting to focus the investigation on Quaid's girlfriends who, like Emme, were potential next victims. Ricketts was still riding high, taking all the credit for fingering Sykes and going on about how dangerous that darky Sykes was and how he should be shot on sight like a damn mad dog, I tell ya. Burdett sent him and Renfro out to continue the manhunt just to get rid of them and save his ears. Harley and Dugan were tasked to track down every friend of Cece's they could find and ensure that the women were alerted and safely secured. As for the male friends, they would lean on them to flesh out the coke angle and Cece's connections. Finally, he and Eustace were left alone.

"Eustace, are you okay?" Burdett asked, seeing the frown on Eustace's face.

"Somethin' 'bout this Sykes thing don't feel right. Assumin' this is a lynchin' revenge thing, wouldn't it make more sense if the murders were actually random? But they're not. If he's not randomly killin' these girls, then why is he really doin' it? Based on what we found at Sykes's place, he's definitely the Mound Builder, but what does Sykes have against Cece Quaid and her friends? And then he disappears but leaves that pile of money behind? Feels like there's still somethin' we don't know."

"Yeah, Eustace, I've been wonderin' the same thing. There's something we're not seein' here. So here's what I want to do. As you said, there's a benefit to you being able to work the colored side of the equation. Find out who works for the families of Quaid's friends and see what they know. Find out if they ever saw or heard about Sykes. They might talk to you and tell what they've really seen."

"I'm already on it, boss," Eustace said, winking just as Burdett opened his mouth to protest the epithet. And Eustace had his own thoughts on what really could tie this all together. Too early to tip his hand, but he would be pursuing that too.

⋆ ⋆ ⋆

Once Burdett was alone, he launched his own foray into the web of Cece Quaid's connections. Picking up the phone, he dialed the number of Bobby Aiken.

"Hello, Mr. Aiken, this is Detective Vance in Memphis again."

"Go to Hell, Vance, your Chief says I don't have to talk to you."

"Now don't be hangin' up on me, Bobby, or I'll have to come back over to your place again and visit you *and* Mrs. Aiken." Burdett got the emphasis just right, and Aiken grew quiet.

"Whatchu want?" he hissed.

"You're not in trouble, Aiken. But I think you might be able to help us find Cece Quaid's killer. Could you drive into town now to meet with me? I need to show you a few photographs and ask you a few questions. Of course, I'd be happy to come out there to Aiken and meet with you *and your wife* at your convenience."

"No, no, I'll come to you," Aiken said hastily. "It's only a fifty-minute drive."

Two hours later, Aiken was fidgeting across the table from Burdett, his eyes darting around, a trapped animal seeing nowhere to escape. He must have taken shots of whiskey to steel his nerves because the smell hit Burdett in the face every time Aiken spoke in his direction. Aiken viewed photographs of Mimsy Cooper and Mary Lou Warren, and although he claimed he had never met Cooper, he allowed as how he knew Warren in a way that made Burdett suspect he knew her intimately.

"Mary Lou wasn't as flat out wild as Cece. She's one of those slow burners who got white hot when you got her goin'," he said. "It's so sad what happened to her, what happened to all three of those girls."

"Do you know this man?" Burdett asked, showing a mug-shot photo of Sykes.

"Sure, that's Slider. I read how they think he's the Mound Builder, but take it from me, he's harmless. Everyone gets their stuff from him, but I don't think he'd do anything to those girls. It'd be bad for business with the rest of us." Aikens belatedly grasped he had said too much and clammed up. Burdett shook his head at how naïve Aiken was about how the drug world worked. No coke dealer was harmless.

"Don't worry, Bobby, your alibi's rock solid, and we don't care what Sykes was sellin' before he went on the run."

"So, he's really gone, huh? Maybe he's the one what's ended up with that Boss Crump treasure everyone's whispering about."

Burdett abruptly sat up in his seat. "What are you talkin' about?"

"Cece told me all about it. No one knows if it's real or rumor. I think it's bullshit."

"What exactly did Cece say?"

"I don't know. She was goin' on about how it was so hilarious that everyone in town was lookin' for Boss Crump's big stash of cash, but a friend of hers had told her she grabbed the cash in the hours after Crump died. She didn't say which friend, but my guess is it was that Emme Bryce. Everyone knew she was runnin' 'round with Boss Crump, and she's sure clever enough to make the play."

"Do you know Emme Bryce?" Burdett asked, dreading to hear the answer.

"Sure, I met her a couple of times, but I don't really know her. I only heard about her every now and then through Cece."

Burdett's head was reeling about the money. The kaleidoscope had turned again, and everything clicked into place in a new, different, and distressing way. If Emme had the money, she may have been the real target all along. And she had lied to him. Aiken droned on about what a gossip Cece was and the things she had told him about various notables of Memphis, but Burdett was no longer listening. He was imagining the scene in Sykes's drug den, Cece and her friends daintily snorting coke and squealing about Emme and the treasure, ignoring Sykes sitting right there, him taking it all in, a cobra curled up in the corner ready to strike. He must have grasped that to have a clean shot at the money, he had to get rid of them so no one could trace it back to him when he took out Emme. What an evil stroke of genius to invent the Mound Builder's war of revenge to divert attention.

But overarching everything was how Emme had been lying to him all along. Now the crowbar marks on Emme's apartment door made complete sense, and he understood why Emme had been so terrified from the start. Sykes was trying to scare her into grabbing the cash and making a run for it, and when she did, he would strike. So, indeed, he must still be close by, lurking in the shadows, waiting for his chance.

Burdett continued his interview with Aiken, getting a list of every Cece acquaintance and asking what else Aiken knew about Emme, but his mind was numb. Why hadn't Emme told him any of this? If in fact she had Boss Crump's money, she must have known from the start that she was the target. And he had been played by her at every turn. As soon as Aiken left, he called his house to see if she was still there, but there was no answer. He had a very bad feeling. He called her apartment and got no answer there either. He had to find her. In five minutes he was in his car heading toward Emme's place, and ten minutes later he was pounding on her door, suppressing a dreaded fear as to what he might find there.

But she answered the door with a bright smile and a kiss, as if nothing had happened, and for her, nothing had. She looked radiant.

"I'm so glad to see you!" she said, hugging him tight. When he pulled away, she looked at him questioningly.

"Why didn't you tell me about the money?"

"What money?"

"You know, Crump's Stash. You stole it when you heard he was dead. That's why you're so afraid that this killer is after you." The look on Emme's face told him it was all true.

"Burdett, I honestly didn't think it was that big a deal."

"What? How can you say that?"

"It just wasn't that much money. Ed—Mr. Crump—was over here not long before he went into the hospital. He left an envelope with me, sayin' it was cash that he needed to pay someone, and he wanted me to hold it. He didn't say who. When he died, I admit I kept it, but I didn't steal anything since he kind of gave it to me, and no one would be the wiser. What was the harm? I figured it would tide me over 'til I got back on my feet, and anyway he would want me to have it. Here, I've still got most of it." Emme walked over to a small desk and pulled out a fat envelope. Inside was a stack of twenty-dollar bills. "There's about five hundred dollars there, less what I used already for spendin' money."

"But didn't you tell Cece you had Boss Crump's treasure?"

"You're kiddin' me. Is that what you heard? Sure, I told Cece about this envelope. And it sounds just like her to be tellin' people it was that crazy treasure. She always liked to blow things up to make for a good story. If I had that kind of money, do you think I'd still be here in this town?" she laughed, then grew quiet. "I'm really sorry I didn't tell you about this sooner. Is the money somehow connected to her murder?"

"Maybe," said Burdett, "I should keep this as evidence." Putting the envelope in his coat pocket, his mind was racing to catch up to this new information. He was back at square one; the treasure was still only a myth, probably started by Boss Crump himself to check his enemies, but the rumor now had taken a life of its own and maybe was the engine driving everything. In the end, all that mattered was that Sykes really believed that Emme had that cash. He was no less a threat for being a deluded dreamer.

"You've got to get out of here. Grab your clothes. You're going back to my place for as long as it takes."

Chapter 24

When You Come to a Fork in the Road

The jukebox is swingin', and the lights are so bright,
Ain't no stoppin' now, we're gonna set this place alight!
Come on, baby, let's dance till the dawn,
We're gonna keep rockin' the whole night long!

—*Rockin' the Whole Night Long*, Bobby Jones, 1951

Meanwhile, Eustace had been his own kind of busy. During the day, while Vance had been connecting some big dots regarding the murders and Boss Crump's fabled treasure, Eustace had been connecting some dots too. He had not waited to start working the colored side of town as Vance had suggested that morning. In fact, for days he already had been talking to the invisible people: the maids, drivers, bartenders, and workers who filled the interstices of Cece Quaid's wealthy white world, and a different picture had emerged regarding Slider Sykes, Cece Quaid, and the edgy crowd over which she reigned.

Turns out that Cece was the queen bee of the fast lane, and everybody else, including Slider, were simply her worker bees. She was always stirring the pot, demanding loyalty then turning friends against each other, gossiping behind everyone's backs, and always, always partying hard. Coke was her currency and what kept her at the center of the action. She had stepped on scores of toes, which left plenty of sore-footed enemies who wished her ill. And her daddy down on the plantation had no idea just how crazy and toxic his little girl really was.

She was a perfect mark for Sykes, and Eustace had turned his attention there. According to people down on Beale Street, Sykes was only a gimpy loser, sucking up to whites like Cece to get their money but virulently hating them behind their backs. That part fit the Mound Builder profile, but Eustace had a funny feeling about it. Did a loser like Sykes have it in him to kill those girls? Maybe, maybe not. So what was the lynching revenge thing really about? Sykes was only a kid when the last one, George Brooks, was killed. But maybe he was an impressionable kid.

On a hunch, Eustace had returned to the *Press-Scimitar* files on George Brooks and spent his lunch hour carefully perusing the old black-and-white photographs again with a magnifying glass. Then he saw it, a face straight from the mugshot, a younger version of Slider Sykes, wearing a baseball cap and peering over the heads in the crowd. Clearly, he had been intensely aware of the hysteria around Brooks's killing. Had he dredged up that painful experience to put a finger in the eye of white Memphis? His revenge for being drubbed out of pro baseball? It was no doubt a path to pursue.

But there was another path that rang equally true. Sykes was able to operate as the purveyor of illicits to the white Memphis fast crowd without getting taken down by the guys in Vice. The answer was clear enough. He was someone's snitch, giving them the goods on all those wild children of the city's elite, which was handy information that undoubtedly got passed up the food chain. That got him protection, and surprise, surprise, his handler in Vice had been none other than Detective Earl Ricketts, lately of the Special Investigations Unit.

What instantly registered with Eustace was that Ricketts was the one who had originally fingered Sykes, and it had been Ricketts waiting behind Sykes's house to silence him or anyone else who tried to escape. Shoot first and you don't have to ask questions later. Why was that? Almost as if he were eliminating witnesses. Now instead of all roads leading to Sykes, it was like those roads might actually lead to Ricketts, or maybe the two of them were on the same road, working together until one backstabbed the other. The excitement was a jolt of caffeine to Eustace. At long last, his quarry had moved squarely into his sights. He would have to move cautiously now, but fast.

So instead of sharing his information with Burdett and going to look for more black witnesses that morning as Burdett had instructed, Eustace had trailed Ricketts and Renfro in their pursuit of Sykes. Only they were not looking for Sykes at all. Instead, they had posted themselves within view of Emme Bryce's apartment, waiting for something. Eustace did the same, a watcher watching the watchers, and a few hours later they got some action. Bryce arrived in her car wearing yesterday's clothes and scurried inside looking this way and that. Then Vance arrived, stayed a few minutes, and left carrying a suitcase with Bryce in tow.

As they pulled away, Renfro furtively hopped out and hustled down an alley toward the rear of the apartment while Ricketts eased away and followed Vance and Bryce at a distance. Eustace hung back a few beats then trailed the cars until they reached Vance's bungalow, where he saw Ricketts settle in again to watch from a distance as Vance and Bryce entered the house. A few minutes later he saw Vance come out, light a cigarette, casually survey the neighborhood, and drive away. So he settled in himself, clocking Ricketts and waiting to see what would happen next, feeling the heady adrenaline of the apex hunter stalking its prey.

CHAPTER 25

The View of the World from Third Street

Will the circle be unbroken, by and by, Lord, by and by?
There's a better home awaiting in the sky, Lord, in the sky.

—*Can the Circle Be Unbroken (By and By)*,
the Carter Family, 1929

Although Burdett had brought Emme back to his place, he did not leave her there. She was too frightened, and he had to admit, he was too. So, after making a big show of entering through his front door, they crossed over the backyards to Dewey and Josie's, and he left her there in Josie's care with instructions to lock the doors and stay inside until he returned. In her typical can-do style Josie said she was good to go, and to make the point she pulled out Dewey's shotgun, loaded it, and chambered a shell. Crossing over to the back of his own house, Burdett emerged again from his front door and paused on the high front porch in full view to light a cigarette while he perused the streetscape below. Seeing nothing amiss, he hopped back in the Studebaker and eased out of the driveway. It was getting late in the afternoon, and there was someone Burdett needed to talk to before the business day ended.

The emerging connection between the murders and Emme and the hunt for Crump's Stash dominated his thoughts. So he decided to follow the money, and he knew exactly where he had to start. If you want to understand where a man has hidden money, start with his money man. Farrington Barrow, president of United Planters Bank, was banker to Crump and the Machine, and if anyone could sense gaps in the accounting for Boss Crump's fortune, it would be Barrow.

United Planters Bank & Trust Company was a creature of Memphis's history: past, present, and future. It was founded in the years immediately after the Civil War by a band of Memphis merchants who had earned fortunes selling insurance to frightened citizenry during the Union occupation. Since then, United Planters had become a major engine of Memphis's growth, financing everything from the Cotton Exchange to factories to the postwar GI housing boom and, of course, the Crump Machine. The executive offices of the bank were located on the upper floors of the Sterick Building, a white gothic office tower just four blocks from Police Central. At twenty-nine stories, it was the tallest building in Tennessee and dominated the Memphis skyline.

Burdett arrived on the twenty-ninth floor unannounced. He showed his badge to the receptionist, positioned himself with a view of the elevators and stairwells, and said he would wait until Barrow was available. He knew it would be hard for Barrow to slip past him. Farrington Barrow was a well-known figure in town. At six-foot-seven with a booming, barrel-chested voice, you could see and hear him coming from a distance. Burdett watched the clock tick past five and still no Barrow, but then again no one was saying that he had left. At five-thirty the door to the inner office opened, and the man himself came out to greet Burdett with slow-moving self-assurance and an inscrutable smile, seemingly unconcerned that he had kept his visitor waiting more than an hour.

"Ah, Detective Vance," his deep bass voice set to soothe, "so good to see you. Please do come in." A massive hand gripped Burdett's in a surprisingly gentle handshake as he showed the detective into a strikingly modern and airy office populated by contemporary Southern artworks and modern furniture no doubt imported from the finest showrooms in New York City. Late afternoon sunlight was like honey pouring through a bank of windows that wrapped around his corner office with a panoramic view of the Mississippi River, colossal in the foreground and snaking away into the distance across the flat floodplain. Over on the Arkansas side, the river had flooded the bottomlands all the way to the levee four miles distant; the water itself was ablaze with the amber light, and the leaf-bare trees silhouetted against the flood waters looked like tiny black soldiers marching toward the light.

"Spectacular, isn't it, Detective Vance? I have to apologize for my rudeness and for making you wait, but this is why. I needed to pause a moment to thank God for creating such ethereal beauty. But something this glorious must be shared, so here you are."

"Stunning," marveled Burdett. "Apology accepted."

"Step over here for a moment. Looking west you feel as if you're on an island. And as far off as you can see, from the farms hiding behind that levee way off yonder to the cotton brokers scurrying around down there on Front Street, we make it all happen." Looking down from his firmament, Barrow took a deep breath and sighed with satisfaction. "This sight reminds me of a poem that Ed Crump gave me about a man marooned on an island.

I am the monarch of all I survey,
My right there is none to dispute,
From the centre all around to the sea,
I am lord of the fowl and the brute.

"Of course, that was the way that Ed saw things, but from up here, I sometimes feel that I am marooned on an island myself," he said, "and I suspect that you're here to ask me about the fowls and the brutes." He gave a deep chuckle.

"That's about right, Mr. Barrow," Burdett said. "And my guess is that you know exactly why."

"The supposed Crump treasure? Of course! Needless to say, you're not the first to ask about it. I've endured a steady procession of preenin' fowl and bullyin' brutes alike, tryin' to tease out what I know about Ed Crump's finances, and I'm happy to tell you exactly what I told them, which is that I know extraordinarily little."

"A steady procession? Like who?"

"All the usual suspects," Barrow replied with a wave of his hand. "City commissioners, your boss Casper Donlough, a few midlevel future contenders, and a pushy little fellow from your shop."

"Was his name Ricketts?"

"Something like that. I wondered why he came since his boss had already been here. In fact, Detective, I could say the same about you."

"I reckon so, but odd as it seems, I'm not interested in the treasure. I'm only interested in what people will do to get it. So what do you know about Crump's Stash?"

"Hard to say. That kind of cash doesn't get deposited in a bank, so of course *we* would have nothing to do with it," Barrow said emphatically, waving his hands as if to dismiss the whole idea. "But if you're asking for my best-informed *guess*, and I assume that you are, then as a banker I'd have to consider Ed Crump's business model and the city's cash ecosystem. Those are the waters that I swim in. This city breathes in and it breathes out, but the air that it breathes, that sustains its life, is money. Ed had managed to build up a fortune over the years in insurance, real estate, and banking. Never stole personally from the city directly, mind you. He was honest in that way. But his political organization was what made it all work. You could call it his core business. Political machines such as Ed's are year-round cash businesses with steady income from patronage payments and saloon tithes but seasonal expenses, better known as elections. In a properly run operation—Ed's operation certainly was, and I respected him for that—you grow your cash reserves during the off years and then spend them down during election cycles to ensure that the rest of the business continues uninterrupted *ad infinitum.* He had forty-five years to perfect the system. Ed died well before this upcoming election cycle, so my guess is that those reserves had not yet been spent down. If that is in fact the case, then some amount of untraceable cash may be lying about somewhere."

"Any ideas where?" Burdett asked.

Barrow just shrugged. "On the other hand, over the years I've developed my own admittedly unscientific metrics for following the off–balance sheet movement of money in the city. Years when we all knew Ed was spending big on the elections—the U.S. Senate battle with Senator Kefauver in '48, for instance—we could see a different level of personal account activity among our more connected customers. No tainted money coming in, mind you, but certain customers seemed to manage their legal accounts . . . differently." Barrow raised his eyebrows knowingly, but Burdett played innocent and feigned puzzlement.

"My theory was that when they had more off-the-books cash, they used that first and their legal money tended to build up in their accounts. Safe elections, not so much. It's only a rough proxy, but you get the idea. Ed was struggling to keep control the last few years. His hold on the colored voters was slipping. I personally think the Negroes of our fine city were seeing that the crumbs he tossed their way were getting them nowhere. Anyway, more challengers meant more free cash found its way into our customers' pockets, and as a group their accounts showed a corresponding level of inactivity. The money just sat there. So, perhaps the secret war chest was spent down early this time, and that cash is now stashed under the mattresses of the beneficiary political class. You people may only be chasing the echo of something that no longer exists."

"Then why are Machine men like the commissioners and Donlough so convinced that it does?" Burdett asked. "Of all people you'd think they would know."

Barrow shrugged again. "Ed Crump knew that the power of myth can't tolerate the stench of weakness. He could never let on that the coffers were anything less than robust. He fed the rumor of hidden riches at every chance. I heard him myself, many times. Make up a number, the bigger the better. Enough money to crush anyone who stood in his way. Now, in the vacuum that he left, some may think that's the key to the kingdom."

"So you don't believe there's any treasure?"

"I didn't say that. Ed was crafty and never showed all his cards, even to me. I thought I knew where every Crump dollar might be hiding, but then I have to ask myself, how hard would it be over forty-five years to set aside a handful of cash every now and then? Not a reserve to be used, mind you, just money to have, to feel, to gloat over. It would be a comforting thought in your old age, don't you agree? Almost like looking through your old photos and newspaper clippings." To Burdett, the intensity in Barrow's eyes as he said this conjured an image of Barrow himself, closeted somewhere in the wee hours, eagerly fingering his own hidden treasure trove. But he got Barrow's point. Do the math. Bit by bit your little rainy-day fund gets larger and larger, decade after decade, and why would you ever stop if the larger it got, the more power and pleasure you felt?

"So then there *could* be some truth to it?" Burdett asked, feeling increasingly confused.

"Who cares?" Barrow asked. "This bank was here a generation before Ed Crump was born, and it will be here for generations after his death. The whole Crump Machine is only an ebb that will soon be replaced by a flow. That's the history of mankind. Look down yonder. That's Confederate Park there with the Rebel cannons still pretending to defend the city. Their time came and went.

"And see down there in Court Square. It's a tiny green island isolated from the rest of nature by concrete buildings and city streets. I'm sure you've seen the white squirrels in that park. It's a local attraction, even. They saw the first white squirrel there in 1870, the year after this bank was founded. Pretty soon it was all white squirrels, and it's been that way ever since. But just the other day on my way to lunch I saw a black squirrel in there, and I wouldn't be surprised if by the time I die, they're all black or gray or whatever survives and thrives. Everything evolves, Detective Vance. People will forget Boss Crump and this fool's gold. But in the end, when we're all just dust to dust, it's the bank that will survive and thrive.

"Either way, Detective, that's what I know. Every dollar held by the bank has been accounted for, and whatever else is out there in the wild—or not—isn't really our concern. Any more questions?"

"Just one," Burdett said. "Did Crump ever mention anything to you about a riverboat casino project?"

Barrow nodded. "Why, yes, he did. A year or so ago he came here to meet about his plan to sponsor a riverboat casino to beef up downtown tourism. He had partnered with a company, let me see, what was its name, yes, the Riverboat Gamblers Casino Company, which was represented by a very bright young woman named Emmeline . . ."

"Bryce?"

"Yes, that's it. She called herself Emme. She had it all planned out, down to the types of roulette wheels and blackjack tables that would be installed. The plan was to start with one side-wheeler and expand up and down the Mississippi. She was clever about it. Tennessee doesn't allow gambling, but as you know Arkansas does. So her plan was to take advantage of a loophole in the laws regarding the Mississippi River."

"Loophole?"

"The river is a federal waterway, interstate commerce and all that. So as long as the casino was floating in federal waters, it could claim the legal fiction that it was in interstate commerce and enjoying Arkansas's gambling laws, even if it was just moored to a floating pier here at the base of downtown. They planned to put the pier right there," he said as he pointed down to a vacant spot on the waterfront. "It would have made a fortune, and I'll bet that Miss Bryce would have ended up one of the richest people in Memphis. Plus, of course, the bank would have managed the casino's cash accounts."

"Of course. Too bad the old man died before it became a reality," Burdett said.

"Oh, it may still happen, Detective Burdett. Miss Bryce was just in here recently to let me know that the project was still a 'go,' and she was lining up outside backing. My guess is she was talking to interests in Las Vegas or Havana."

"I guess you've got to give her credit for determination," Burdett said, thinking how he had underestimated Emme.

"Determined and smart. And the smartest thing she did was havin' Ed Crump as her mentor."

With that, Barrow warmly shook Burdett's hand and guided him to the door. As Burdett rode the elevator down, he uneasily mulled over the conversation. The recounting of Emme's riverboat casino project was news and cast Emme in a wholly different light. God love her, she was actually on her way to becoming a real player. Good for her. But regarding Crump's Stash he had either learned a lot or learned nothing from the chat with Barrow. The bank president had scoffed at the question of whether the treasure really existed but also showed how it was entirely possible that it did. While he had confirmed that it may have served Crump's interests to perpetuate the myth, the question neither asked nor answered was whether it now served the interests of the bank or of certain bank customers to do the same. Feeling frustrated and confused, Burdett was tempted to disregard the entire conversation. But as he exited the Sterick Building and skirted Court Square on his way back to Police Central, he could not help but try to spot the lone black squirrel that, perhaps, heralded the future in that small corner of the world.

Chapter 26

Connective Tissue

Dark was the night, and cold the ground
On which the Lord was laid;
His sweat like drops of blood ran down;
In agony he prayed.

—*Dark Was the Night, Cold Was the Ground,*
Blind Willie Johnson, 1927

"Okay, Eustace," Burdett said, lighting up a cigarette and rocking back in his desk chair. "I'll tell you what I've learned today, and you do the same." Eustace's mind was spinning, grasping for just the right angle on Ricketts to make his case. But the reality was that the most he had at that point was naked suspicion based on knowing Ricketts for the kind of person he really was. So he just told Vance about the 1938 photo of Sykes and then shut up to hear what Vance had to say, not that he expected to get the whole story of why that woman was holing up in Vance's Duvall Street digs.

Burdett gave him a quick rundown on how the hunt for Crump's cash could be the driving force for Sykes, regardless of whether the treasure actually existed. Cece's exaggerated gossiping about Emme's envelope of cash may have gotten Cece and her friends killed, and Emme may be next on the list, which was why he had hidden her where she would be safe. That was just noise to Eustace, borne out of whatever thing Vance had going with Bryce. He was still certain that the rumors of Crump's pot of gold were only the dying echoes of the crumbling Crump Machine, and it was just like greedy whites to get so hot and bothered over it. Boss Crump was so powerful that everyone wanted to believe there was a fortune that was hidden barely outside of their grasp, a sunken treasure ship in shallow waters, begging to be found. It was too big to not be true.

"So doesn't this give us Sykes's motive?" Burdett continued. "I'm sure it'll make Ricketts and the Chief unhappy that they're now competing with a murderer for the supposed treasure."

Then it hit Eustace like a thunderbolt. The treasure was indeed the connective tissue that he had been missing. At last everything made sense.

"Burdett—Detective Vance—maybe we got this whole thing wrong. Maybe the real killer has been sittin' right under our noses all along." That got Burdett's attention. Then Eustace explained how by doing the Chief's bidding, Ricketts indeed had been searching for Boss Crump's supposed suitcases of cash. But how much cash did it have to be before Ricketts would start thinking he wanted it for himself? Ricketts had known Sykes from before, probably still used him as a snitch to get blackmail material on the high-class whites who crossed the tracks, and he had probably heard from Sykes that Cece Quaid was talking around about her friend Emme Bryce having the treasure. So, before he goes after Emme to take the treasure for himself, he has to frame Sykes and take out Cece, her friends, and probably Sykes too, to eliminate the trail. Given all the reports, maybe Sykes was still lurking in the shadows. But maybe all those Sykes sightings around town were just white hysteria over a menacing black man. If Sykes instead was dead or on the run, that might explain why Ricketts had not even bothered to look for him. Eustace had known for years that Ricketts was a stone-cold killer, but even Vance must know that from the trigger-happy shootout at Sykes's place. Ricketts's twisted mind probably loved the idea of blowing up the whole city with the Mound Builder terror. Eustace reminded Burdett about that photo taken back in '38, how Ricketts was present with his father when Boss Crump announced that the Brooks case had been closed. So he knew all about it even then.

Finally, Eustace told Burdett what he had seen that morning, how Ricketts and Renfro were not interested in solving the Mound Builder case at all, as though they already knew it was really about something else, about the money. Their sights were fixed entirely on Emme Bryce, and that very moment they were staking out Burdett's Duval Street house.

Burdett jumped at that. "What?"

"Listen, with all due respect, I don't know or care what you got goin' with that woman, but she's police business now and it looks like it's the police that are after her."

"Careful, Eustace, you're treading mighty close to the line now."

"So what do you want me to say, boss? That everything's okay and no one'll think twice if she turns up dead in *your* house? Then they'll be askin' where *you* were ten days ago."

Anger swelled in Burdett's head, but he had to shake it out and get a grip. He remembered his promise to the clergy the other night. Just follow the evidence wherever it leads. So he closed his eyes, took a deep breath, and started over, but still he resisted buying that Ricketts was capable of inventing the whole Mound Builder terror.

"Ricketts is the worst, but he's just a pathetic loser sucking up to the Chief," Burdett said, shaking his head. "I already knew the Chief had someone tailing me and Miss Bryce, and since when did Ricketts or Renfro do anything I told 'em to do? I don't like that runt either, Eustace, but how can you leap to the conclusion that he's the killer or that he had that much control over Sykes? He's not smart enough to think up something this diabolical."

* * *

With that, Eustace folded his hand rather than show all of his cards. If he said too much, it would appear to be only a personal vendetta, and he had to admit that there was much truth in that. But he also knew that a colored cop in Memphis could expect no justice if things backfired. He was not yet ready to share everything that he knew regarding Earl Ricketts and his limitless capacity for cruelty, blackmail, and greed. He was patient. Revenge could wait. It already had.

"So now Ricketts knows where Miss Bryce is," Eustace pressed on. "Do you think she's safe, even at your place?"

"Probably safer than ever now that there's a police car staked outside," Burdett said, "But to be even safer, I had her sneak next door to my friends' house. Now let's get on with this damned investigation before another body pops up in Memphis waters."

"Okay, I'll keep workin' the witnesses," Eustace nodded, although he knew that was not going to happen. He planned to keep watching the watchers.

But it was too late for that.

* * *

Before either of them could leave the squad room, Burdett's desk phone started ringing. It was Emme, calling in a panic, her voice choking with fear.

"Burdett, he's been here! Oh, my God, he's been in my apartment and completely destroyed it! Everything!"

"Hold on, Emme," Burdett said, trying to calm her and grasping to understand what she was telling him. "What are you doing at your place? You should be at Dewey and Josie's!"

"I know, I know, and I'm so sorry. I took a quick cab ride back to pick up a few things. Don't be mad at them. I was thinkin' I'd be back safe in their house before they even knew I was gone."

Burdett shared her alarm, realizing that, despite his precautions, events were spinning out of control. Motioning Eustace toward the hallway, he struggled to get a grip on the situation. "Emme, this is serious. Lock the door, get your pistol, and hide in your closet. We'll be there as soon as we can."

He and Eustace bolted for the door, ran out to their unmarked squad car, and drove toward Midtown at breakneck speed. En route Eustace radioed in the emergency and tried to raise Ricketts and Renfro, without response. They arrived at Emme's apartment in minutes that felt like hours, and immediately Burdett's heart sank. Emme's car was gone. Guns drawn, they burst into her apartment and the spectacle of destruction was stunning. It was not simply ransacked. It was utterly, savagely demolished: drawers upended, mattresses and pillows slashed open, walls smashed apart, broken glass everywhere, and no Emme. Then, on the dressing table among her shattered photographs, Burdett spied a single scrap of beer-carton paper, with the handwriting from Hell:

> *This one is for the Big Creek Bottom boys. She got her own mound now and you won't see her never again.*
>
> –The Mound Builder

Looking down, Burdett spotted something dark and shiny on the floor. A single drop of blood. With that, Burdett's mind reeled toward the unimaginable, and the swelling panic exploded into an all-consuming scream inside his head. Then that white-out again, but this time it was white-hot fear crowding out every other thought. He was paralyzed. Sykes had taken her. Peering over Burdett's shoulder at the note, Eustace gave a low whistle.

"Six men were lynched, shot full of holes down in that creek bottom. Accused of burnin' barns. They say the sheriff chained them up in a wagon and wheeled them down into the bottom at night, knowin' who was waitin' there. Of course, no one went to jail for it. Dear God, I hope we're not headed back to that."

⋆ ⋆ ⋆

Burdett seemed to be hearing but not listening, as if his mind were spinning in place. So Eustace stepped away, calmed himself, and tried to focus on priorities. The Mound Builder was only minutes ahead of them and had just seized Bryce. You could almost smell his presence still hovering in the air. But who was it, Sykes—or Ricketts and Renfro? Where were they, and how could this have happened if they were supposedly watching her over on Duvall?

Maybe they were still posted outside Vance's house. Going on automatic, Eustace radioed to Central to get help on the crime scene, put out an all-points bulletin for Bryce's car, and what the heck, the Stooges' squad car too. Then he left Burdett while he quickly canvassed the neighbors in case anyone had seen anything or had noticed what direction Emme's car had headed. No one answered their door until he reached Mrs. Andrews across the street. She was bubbling with information. Oh, of course she knew that sweet girl Emme but hadn't seen her recently, although she said that she had noticed some odd things on the street. For the last couple of weeks, there had been a suspicious black man walking by, several times a day, and then the last two nights there had been a car with two men in it parked on the street across from Emme's house.

"Black man?" Eustace asked and fished a photo of Sykes from his coat pocket. "Was it this man?"

"Oh, gosh, I'm not sure. He was all the way across the street and . . ."

"And the car with the two men in it. The last *two* nights? Are you sure?" Vance had said that he told the Stooges to skip their shifts on the stakeout. Why would they be there last night?

"Oh, yes. It was creepy, them just sitting there in the dark car. Is there something wrong with Emme? Such a lovely girl. Is she in some kind of trouble?"

"We don't know, maybe," Eustace said. "Did you see her leave in the last few minutes?"

"No, Thursday afternoon is my bridge game, so I left before one o'clock and just got back when you two came barreling in."

Eustace handed her his card, "If you see or hear anything, please call me." She looked hard at the card and then at Eustace.

"Oh, my, you're that colored policeman that I read about in the paper. I can't wait to tell my friends that I actually met him—I mean you."

Eustace gave her his practiced sideways smile, thanked her with a nod, and walked away thinking that maybe he would have to get used to being a celebrity of sorts. He hustled back to Emme's apartment and relayed the information to Burdett.

* * *

Burdett had begun to shake off his shock from the mayhem in the apartment and cleared his mind enough to come to grips with what he had just seen and heard. Emme had disappeared only minutes ago and after the ransacking. Slider Sykes must have been here, waiting for her to return. If it was not already too late, they had to find her before he killed her, but how?

To calm his mind, he carefully walked through the apartment, slowly turning full circle in each room and taking in the details of the destruction. That was when it dawned on him that this was not the work of the supposed racial revenge killer that the Mound Builder had made himself out to be. No killer like that would go to this trouble, and anyway, why choose Emme? Why rip apart the mattresses and even the walls?

This had taken hours. Whoever did this had known that he had all the time in the world and had gone through this place as if he were certain something that he wanted was here. And what were Ricketts and Renfro doing here last night after he had called off the stakeout? They could not have been sitting outside last night and missed what was going on inside. Which meant that they weren't outside at all, but inside doing the ransacking themselves. Exactly.

They must have been waiting for the first opportunity to get inside Emme's apartment under the cover of darkness and tear the place apart, and Burdett had played right into their hands by making sure it was empty last night and telling them that they were off the clock. He felt like a chump. The jigsaw puzzle pieces were falling into place faster and faster, but the puzzle picture that was emerging was not a good one.

Those two had been on the hunt for Boss Crump's money all along, and what better place to look than the home of his supposed mistress? Judging from the level of destruction, Cece's rumor mongering about Emme must have convinced them that she actually had it, and they wanted no stone left unturned or mattress left unslashed. This Mound Builder scare was the perfect cover. Sure, it could still be Sykes hunting for the money, and now this tied him to Ricketts and Renfro. Looking over at the Mound Builder's note still sitting on the dressing table, he had to admit to himself that Eustace had been right, it was them from the get-go, probably in league with Sykes.

But then he noticed that something in the apartment was missing. The photograph of Emme and her parents standing in front of the old farmhouse had been on the dressing table but now was nowhere to be seen among the rubble. It was one of her most precious memories. At that moment he knew the next place Ricketts and Renfro would look, the place where they had probably taken Emme to give her the final offer she could not refuse.

CHAPTER 27

The River Always Takes Back Its Own

I was walking down the Levee with my head hanging low,
Looking for my sweet mama but she ain't here no more,
I'm sitting here looking at all of this mud,
And my girl got washed away in that Mississippi flood.

—*Mississippi Heavy Water Blues,*
Barbecue Bob, 1927

Burdett told Eustace they had to go as he bounded from the house running toward the squad car. At that moment Harley and Vinnie pulled up as the first backup to arrive. Burdett shouted to Harley to take charge of the crime scene, waved Eustace toward his car, and they screeched out of the neighborhood headed out Jackson Avenue to Highway 51, the road north to Covington and points beyond. Burdett explained that their destination was Emme's family homestead in the isolated farm hamlet of Fulton nestled behind the bluffs along the Mississippi River.

Eustace could feel the certainty in Burdett's actions, and while he himself had already put the same jigsaw pieces together, he decided to wait for Burdett to speak. Eustace wanted to lead him there, not drive him there. So he tracked their journey north as they left the city and entered the rolling countryside comprising the gentle eastward slope of the bluffs that palisaded upriver from Memphis. That stretch of Highway 51 was mostly populated by gun shops, gas stations, and the juke joints that had once been a spur of the Chitlin Circuit. Now they just looked sadly abandoned. Eustace remembered them well as he watched the scenery and waited for whatever was coming next.

After a few minutes of silence, Burdett spoke, "Eustace, you were right. It feels like it must have been Ricketts and Renfro all along. Ricketts knew Sykes and probably blackmailed him to set up this Mound Builder diversion, maybe even offered him a cut to kill those girls. After what we just saw, it's pretty clear that they've been behind it. But one thing puzzles me. How did you suspect so early that this was about Ricketts? You couldn't have known how his sights were set on Emme."

Eustace let a few signposts fly by before answering. "Because I always knew Ricketts was a stone-cold killer. It was him who killed my brother Caleb, him and his buddy Del DeWitt." He let that sink in for a minute and then said, "And I guess I may as well tell you the rest, that is, if you can listen hard and drive fast at the same time."

And so he told Burdett the whole story of pledged vengeance, how he had manipulated Donlough to get assigned to Burdett just so he could watch Ricketts's every move.

"At first, I was just hoping we could wrap up this Mound Builder case so I could focus on Ricketts, but then the bits and pieces of the case started sticking to Ricketts like flies to flypaper. Ricketts's Vice connection to Sykes and him settin' up the raid on Sykes's house to tag him as the Mound Builder never felt right. My guess is that he promised Sykes a share of Crump's Stash to grab those girls, help put 'em down to cover the trail, and then scare the hell outta white Memphis with those Mound

Builder notes. Given how much Sykes hated whites and loved money, he probably thought it was a hoot. I bet that cash you found at his shack was the down payment, and no doubt Sykes got his final payment too. Ricketts most likely put him in the ground even before the first body surfaced."

★ ★ ★

As Burdett listened, he had to admit that indeed all roads now led to Ricketts, but whatever horrendous things Ricketts and Renfro had done, the stupidity of it all was that it was entirely based on a monumental false assumption, that Emme had Boss Crump's illusory treasure. To Burdett it was only further proof of the twisted effect of greed on the human psyche. Ricketts so wanted to believe that Emme had the money that he was willing to bet the lives of those poor girls, Sykes, and now maybe Emme, on feckless party girl gossip.

He wondered at what point Ricketts and Renfro had ceased being Donlough's tools and decided to act on their own. It must have been weeks ago, around the time that the girls disappeared. Ricketts had been two steps ahead of him ever since—and two steps ahead of Donlough too. Maybe Chief Donlough was not as smart as he thought he was; he had created a monster, and now the monster had a mind of its own.

They blew through Covington's only stoplight and powered west past the state prison in Henning. From Burdett's visit to the Bryce family farm with Emme a decade ago, he knew it was not hard to find. Just follow Route 87 west to the end of the world where it dead-ended on the river bluff at Fulton with a mile-wide, treacherous muddy river below you, lying between you and anyplace else on earth you wanted to go. The road was long and straight, and the rising needle on the speedometer matched the mounting tension in the car. Eustace took out his gun to double-check that it was fully loaded and chambered, and then they began to prepare themselves for what they might find at the old abandoned Bryce homestead.

* * *

The light was fading as dusk settled upon them by the time they turned off the state road onto a nondescript gravel track. It was marked only by a rusty mailbox with the name Bryce painted on it. Grinding gravel, they sped up to the old farmhouse and found Ricketts's car, doors askew, empty. Jumping out, Burdett and Eustace approached the house with guns drawn, but there was only an ominous silence. The front door was ajar, and Eustace carefully creaked it open. In the dim light, he could see a body lying on the floor. Renfro puddled in blood, shot in the head, close range, still warm. Ricketts apparently was not planning to share a dime. Adrenalin pumping, Eustace and Burdett moved through the dark house room by room, dreading at every turn that they would find a woman's body. With a sigh of relief, Burdett found no one, but in the middle of the living room, the rug had been pulled aside and a trapdoor opened to reveal a yawning black chasm; whatever had been there was gone.

Emme's car was nowhere to be seen, so Burdett told Eustace to go to their squad car, radio for backup, and post an all-points bulletin for Emme's car, describing Ricketts as armed and dangerous. He knew they could only head north or east, since the Hatchie River swamp and the vast Mississippi River blocked escape routes to the south and west.

Meanwhile, Burdett had a hunch. They had not seen any cars headed the other direction on Route 87 as they approached Fulton. Unless Ricketts was forcing Emme to take one of the slower backroad gravel tracks, he and Eustace should have spotted her car headed the opposite direction. So, he checked the ramshackle barn and sure enough found Emme's car, hood still warm. The cavernous barn echoed emptiness, but that was the point: something was missing. Where was the skiff that Burdett had seen there years ago, where Emme had spent so much time on the river with her dad? Looking more closely, he could see truck and trailer tracks leading out of the barn. Maybe Ricketts was not heading north or east at all, he thought.

A quick radio inquiry to the Lauderdale County sheriff revealed that indeed there was a nearby boat landing on the big river, Richard's Landing, just a mile away where Highway 87 dead-ended at the river. Bingo.

The darkness to the west was counterbalanced by a full moon rising behind them in the east as Burdett and Eustace quietly drove toward the river, headlights off, until the slope began to fall beneath them as they neared the bluff. They turned off the engine, coasted to a stop, and listened. There were sounds coming from the landing. It was the sputter of an outboard motor idling for a few moments, then it was cut off as if someone had been testing the engine. They paused in the sudden silence, then crept forward under the tree canopy, guns drawn. They soon saw two dark figures, shadowed by the tree canopy but silhouetted against the moonlit river in the distance beyond, moving from a pickup with a boat trailer toward a skiff tied to the floating dock at water's edge. One shadow was carrying two large suitcases which were placed in the skiff. There was a murmur of voices, one trembling with terror. The shadows merged for an instant, then suddenly there was a single flash bang as one shadow splashed into the water.

Burdett raced quickly out of the shadows, almost as if by moving he could somehow reverse time and stop the horror of what had just happened. He sighted his gun on the dark figure climbing into the boat.

"Move a muscle, Ricketts, and you're a dead man."

"Burdett, is that you?" It was Emme's voice. He could not see her face in the darkness, and her voice seemed somehow disembodied, otherworldly. He was dumbfounded by the disconnect, reeling with the enormity of the singular fact of her voice. She was alive. A slot machine arm had just come down in his brain, and his mind whirred frantically recalculating everything that had happened in the last few days. Turning the whole case upside down and rebuilding the evidence backwards, the slot machine locked onto straight sixes; he had hit the jackpot, only it was no jackpot that he had ever wanted. His shoulders involuntarily slumped with the weight of it all, and he had to steady himself for a moment to find his balance.

⋆ ⋆ ⋆

Eustace hung back in the shadows with his gun coldly aimed at Ricketts's head silhouetted against the moonlit river. He steadily increased the pressure on the trigger, ready to put down the bastard at last. Finally, justice for Caleb. Then he heard Emme Bryce's voice calling out Burdett's name. What? It was Bryce, not Ricketts, who had fired the gun. Nothing made sense, but everything made sense.

"Oh, Burdett, thank goodness! He almost killed me!" she said. Eustace stood motionless in the darkness, prepared to shoot her at any second if she made a move. The gun must be still in her hand, he thought. Did Burdett sense the danger? Eustace worried that Burdett's girl-blindness might cause him to hesitate, but he knew that he himself would not, white girl be damned.

"Emme, it's all over," Burdett said. "God help me, I will shoot you myself unless you toss that gun in your hand on the shore." She hesitated for a few beats, and Eustace sensed that she was weighing her best play. Then she seemed to visibly deflate, and she did as she was told.

"Of course, Burdett, it's not my gun anyway. I snatched it away from that awful man Ricketts. You know he even killed his partner back at the farmhouse, and he would've killed me too, as soon as he didn't need me!" Eustace heard the gun clatter on the boat ramp and eased up on his trigger but stayed silent, waiting to see how it played out. She still did not seem to know he was there.

"Burdett, come with me! With all this money, we could have a wonderful life together. London, Paris, anywhere. There's enough money here to start a casino in any city in the world. How about Chicago? Who cares about a dumpy river town like Memphis? Come with me. I love you!" Eustace shook his head in the darkness. He had to give her credit; she didn't miss a beat and she didn't give up. But Eustace suspected that she was talking about a life that Burdett could not remotely imagine.

"Okay, Emme, first why don't you get out of the boat, and let's talk about it," Burdett said. Then Emme collapsed in the boat, weeping.

"Oh, Burdett, this has been such a nightmare. When Ed was near the end, he told me to take these suitcases and hide them. He said that when the time was right he would tell me who to give them to. But he died, and there I was with all this money and treasure. The only place I could think to hide them was up here in the old farmhouse. Daddy had a hidey space under the rug, and it just stayed there. I thought maybe no one knew the money even existed and so I could use it to start my casino. Then it seemed like everyone in town was looking for it, and I was too afraid to say anything. When I mentioned to Cece that I had that little envelope of cash—she knew about me and Ed—she just ran with it, spreadin' all over town that I had Ed's treasure.

"It was all Cece's fault! She couldn't have known that I really had all that money, but she spread the rumor out of pure, wicked spite just to make people hate me even more. That was what Cece was like. She had such a nasty mean streak, and she really liked to kick you when you're down. I truly hated her for that. Of all the phony friends who turned on me, she was the worst. Somehow that horrid little man Ricketts heard her rumors, and the next thing I knew, he started with the threats."

"Wait a minute, Emme, when did this happen?" Eustace could see Burdett visibly stiffen as if he did not want to hear the answer.

"About a month ago. They must have been in it together because around the same time, Cece started askin' all kinds of questions about that Crump's Stash rumor. She even offered to stay quiet about it if I split it with her. I told her she had misunderstood me, but she didn't believe me!" Her disembodied voice was trembling now.

"You mean Ricketts knew Cece?" Eustace heard the interest pick up in Burdett's voice and he could feel his own pulse quicken.

"They connected through that lowlife Slider. Cece liked the white stuff, and he was her connection."

"Ricketts and Sykes were in this together?"

"I honestly don't know, Burdett, but then Cece and the other girls started turning up dead, and that whole Mound Builder ruckus happened. Ricketts told me that I'd end up dead too, if I didn't give him the money."

"What happened to Sykes? He disappeared," Burdett asked.

"Don't you think maybe he hightailed it out of town when those girls started turnin' up dead?"

"So who killed those girls? Ricketts or Sykes?"

"Oh, Burdett, I don't know. They were in it together. Ricketts was behind everything." Burdett paused for a long time and seemed to be mulling over what she had told him. Eustace thought that at last it was clear. It had been Ricketts all along, just as he had suspected.

"So, Emme, Ricketts shot all three of those girls with this little pistol?" Burdett asked, walking over and picking up the gun that Emme had tossed. Even in the darkness, Eustace could see that it was shiny chrome with a white handle.

"Don't you think so?" Emme asked hopefully.

"Then where is that little gun you told me you were carrying with you for protection?" There was a dead silence that spoke volumes, and at that instant the realization exploded in Eustace's brain. There was only one gun. Burdett had already gotten there.

"Emme, it wasn't Ricketts at all. God help us, it was you." Burdett said. His voice was cracking with emotion. "Too many people have died. Why did you do it? Now, get out of the boat!"

Emme finally seemed to break down completely. "Burdett, it all happened so fast," she sobbed. "Ricketts had started to close in on me. He tried to break into my house. I knew I had to disappear, but if I just ran, everyone would know I had Ed's money, and they'd hunt me down 'til the day I died. Then I bumped into Cece shopping that day, and she talked me into joinin' her and Mary Lou and another friend to get high at Slider's place. We were all sittin' in Slider's house tryin' his coke, when Cece got too wired—we were all too wired—and she started in on me again about the money. She was callin' me a gold-diggin' whore and sayin' how everyone in town thought so. I couldn't take it anymore. Somethin' snapped, and I grabbed my gun and shot her. Just like that. It was as if I was walking in a dream. We were all stunned. Then it came to me in a vision. I saw my way out. I had to die but not die.

"I told Slider I'd cut him in if he would help me. So we handcuffed and gagged the other girls. Ed had told me how back when there was a lynchin', the whole city went into a panic over it, so I got the pen and paper and had Slider write out the notes from the Mound Builder about the lynchings Ed had told me about. I guess Slider hated whites somethin' fierce, 'cause he loved the idea. He thought it was fun." Through the darkness, Eustace could almost feel Burdett tremble. She was stone-cold crazy; it was almost as if she was bragging.

"Anyway, we took the two girls and Cece's body in Slider's car over to McKeller Lake. It was like I was in a trance. I shot both of them, and we tied their stockings around their necks with the notes in the bottles. It was Slider's idea to take Mary Lou's body out East to Audubon Lake. He thought it was a big joke and would scare whites even more. And that just left one more note to be found, and one more body—mine—that would never be found, and I would be free forever. That was the note that I left back at my place."

Eustace watched as Burdett took in Emme's tumbling confession, and he knew Burdett must be devastated.

"Wait, where is Sykes in all of this? Did he just take off? Why did he leave behind so much evidence at his place? And a pile of money too?" Burdett asked.

"That was supposed to be the plan. I gave him $10,000, but then he demanded more. I knew that would never stop, and he would blow the whole story. So I made a final deal with him, and let's just say, he's gone for good. I even packed his suitcase for him." She gave a sob that to Eustace was pure theatrics.

"I truly hate myself for what I've done. Cece had been my friend once. But she turned on me and I had to. And him too." In the darkness, her head moved in the direction of where Ricketts's body had disappeared in the muddy waters. ""When I got back to my apartment, it had been ransacked, and I knew it was time to run. So I left the note and took off with the only thing that meant anything to me, the picture of me and my folks. But they must have been watching me. I didn't notice that they followed me up here until I pulled the first suitcase out of the house."

"And the Mound Builder con?"

"God help me, Burdett, but that was all about you. I had to have you on the case. Someone would eventually remember that they saw me with Cece having coffee at Lowenstein's. I had to get to you first to put everything in context and lead you to Slider when the time was right. Everyone knows what a nut you are about that Indian stuff, so I figured it was a cinch that you'd get the case as soon as a body surfaced with one of the notes. Burdett, I was hopin' you still had a thing for me, and then when we were together, I realized that I should have come to you in the first place, before all this happened. Maybe then we would have had a chance. That's probably the saddest part of all this."

"No, Emme, I'm afraid the saddest part is gonna be your final walk to the electric chair." There was a rock-bottom finality in Burdett's voice that was the most forlorn thing that Eustace had ever heard.

"Burdett, I gotta go. I know you won't shoot me now, will you?" And with that she quickly leaned over and gave the outboard motor a pull. It started up immediately and instantly lurched out into the channel. That was when Eustace made his move. He stepped out of the darkness and drew a bead on her.

★ ★ ★

"Eustace, don't shoot!" Burdett cried. "Emme, stop, you'll never make it!" With that Burdett lunged into the water after the boat. The water was icy cold and hit him with a shock. Burdett managed to get one hand on the stern of the skiff, and it immediately pulled him out into the moonlit channel. Emme was leaning back desperately trying to pry off his fingers, when suddenly a huge shadow loomed ahead of them. It was a massive tree moving swiftly downstream like a silent, black locomotive. She did not see it in time. The boat struck the tree at full speed and careened into the air, spewing Emme and the suitcases into the torrent.

In the tumult the boat bucked and struck Burdett's head. He was stunned and sinking fast, slipping into a dream state as the ghosts of his past—Eli, Maxie, Jake, his old man, and a hundred dark souls from the Mounds Landing Crevasse—seemed to clamber from the deep with welcoming arms, wisps of river spirits beckoning him into the depths that been tugging at him for a lifetime of nightmares. As he found himself surrendering to the murky currents that drew him downward, he felt a wonderful peacefulness that had escaped him his whole life. At long last, he would join his loved ones, and it would be over. Then, as if touched by the outstretched hand of God, he felt a hand firmly grasp his and pull him back from the abyss. He broke the surface gasping for air as Eustace dragged him toward the shore. He knew then that he would surely die, but not today.

* * *

When they finally made it to the shallows a furlong downriver from where they had plunged in, Eustace and Burdett stumbled onto the sandy shore and collapsed together shivering with exhaustion. The moon was now so bright that it was like daytime in black-and-white. They looked out onto the mile-wide expanse of the great Mississippi, hoping to see or hear any sign of life, but there was only the dark hiss of the swirling currents.

Eustace lay spent, trying to catch his breath, grateful to God to be alive and feeling as if an enormous burden had been lifted from his heart. Ricketts was gone forever, a victim of his own evil greed. The sense of relief was almost overwhelming. But still, if that was what true revenge was, it was disappointingly hollow. Caleb was still dead for all time, and now Ricketts had escaped the shame and lifetime of penal misery that Eustace had wished for him.

No, he told himself as he shook his head clear, this was better. Events had taken their own strange course. Ricketts had met his unholy match in Emme, and they deserved each other. Now it was over. The racial hysteria, the pervasive fear, the desperate urgency. And Eustace had survived, joyful to be alive, left only to ponder how close he had come to surrendering to his darker self by pulling the trigger to put down a shadow just because he thought it was Ricketts. Without Emme's confession, no one would have believed that she was the killer, and all they would see was yet another black man killing a white woman. God had been looking out for him. Looking out for Burdett too.

★ ★ ★

Meanwhile, Burdett's head was still reeling as he grasped the numbing realization that the soulless river at last had taken everyone that he had ever loved in this life: his father, his best friend Eli, Maxie, Jake, and now Emme. His heart was crushed with self-loathing at his blind eagerness to believe anything Emme had told him. His imagined future had collapsed around him in ashes, a house burned to the ground. That dream of a gentler life with a woman who loved him had become a pitiless joke, a mirage concealing an unimaginable monster. The tyranny of death, the weight of lifelong loss, and a limitless, unutterable grief finally swept over Burdett like an unstoppable wave, and bowing his head, he wept.

Chapter 28

The Letting Go

Was in the spring, one sunny day,
Just when she left me, she's gone to stay.
But now she's gone, and I don't worry
'Cause I'm sittin' on top of the world.

—*Sittin' on Top of the World,*
the Mississippi Sheiks, 1930

Burdett and Eustace stood silently, gazing down at the freshly covered grave and listening to the receding sound of the hearse's tires on gravel, barely audible now as it rumbled away down the dusty farm road on its journey back to town. For a moment Burdett imagined that he once again heard those distant voices echoing up from the old farmhouse, but now there was only desolate silence, save for the sounds of the birds and the breeze rustling in the trees. Unbearably peaceful.

A grove of black locusts topped the rise at the back of the Bryce homestead where the family graveyard was located. Locust blooms filled the air with a sweet perfume that rode across the breeze as a heartening reminder that life still can be a truly beautiful thing. Headstones of three generations of Bryces stood as silent mourners. No one else had attended the burial. Burdett reached out and gently ran his fingers over the words carved into the granite tombstone: Emmeline Ewell Bryce. Casting his gaze out to the picturesque view of wildflowers, green fields, and forests, he wondered why such lovely places were reserved for the saddest and emptiest of life's moments.

"Thanks for coming out here with me today, Eus. I don't think I could've done it alone, and I can't think of anyone else that I'd want here with me, who would really understand without me havin' to explain it."

Eustace put his hand gently on Burdett's shoulder and shook his head. "It's still hard to figure what could bring a person to do what she did."

"Whatever it was, it was always there, only I couldn't see it. For some people, growin' up in the Depression dirt-poor and scratchin' out a hardscrabble life like Emme and her folks, it's as if the need for money is a desperate itch that they can't scratch enough. Gets to where that's the only thing they can think about."

"Maybe they'd seen up close how havin' nothin' can crush a man. But havin' too much can crush him just as bad," Eustace said, looking down at the grave. "Maybe worse 'cause you're always afraid of losin' it."

Burdett slowly nodded his head and let himself fully experience the grief and shame that he still held inside. Maybe it was simply heartache over losing an imaginary person that he thought he loved, not a real person but a black hole that he had filled with his own hopes, demons, and desires. What is the soul of a man or a woman? Only God knew, but someone like Emme was a complete cipher beyond his understanding and probably God's too. Whatever, he knew his grief would take time. As Eustace had said, you can't hurry the letting go. Eus sure hadn't.

The shame that he felt might take even longer to shake. Only Dewey, Josie, and Eustace had any inkling of what really happened between him and Emme, but the fact that he could be so easily fooled shook him to his core. It was as if there was a stranger inside him wanting to break out and willing to grasp at any fever dream to get there. What could he have been thinking? How could he have been so blind? What happens next time? There would forever be a part of himself that he could not trust, and that thought left him as frozen in time as that mastodon pipe sitting on the shelf in his house.

While Burdett stood there pondering the wasted life of Emme Bryce, he also wondered whether the reign of terror that had gripped the city during those tense days would prove to be a defining moment in the path toward a better Memphis. Everyone was relieved that the Mound Builder killings were over and the murderer apprehended—or at least laid to rest—but there was also a palpable sense of reprieve that it had been this particular murderer, and not the one they had feared. Whites and blacks alike breathed a grateful sigh of relief that the Mound Builder's racial vendetta had been only a spectacular hoax, and there was perhaps a new hope that an ugly part of the city's history could finally be left in the past.

The revelation that cute little Emme Bryce was such a cold-blooded killer was wholly beyond people's ability to comprehend, an unhinged aberration that in the end stood alone by itself and meant almost nothing. So the city's matrons, those high-minded keepers of moral rectitude, were vindicated and empowered as their planning for the Cotton Carnival resumed in earnest. Meanwhile, their sometimes-errant husbands no doubt silently rejoiced that they had sagely dodged a bullet by staying away from "that woman" and keeping their eyes on the prize, the struggle over the Crump Machine empire.

And of course, there were new questions about whether Boss Crump's death had been of natural causes in the first place. After all, he died and then coincidentally his supposed mistress—now a known killer—had ended up with his money, so connect the dots. There was discussion in the department about exhuming his body, but Bessie Crump put an end to that talk. Her husband was dead and buried under ten tons of granite monument. An autopsy would accomplish nothing. Conversation closed. It was over.

Easy for them to say, Burdett thought. He still remembered when he returned to his bungalow that sad day, the damp river stench on his clothes as soggy as his spirits. The place had never seemed so quiet and empty. Emme's clothes were draped on his bedroom chair, and her smell lingered on his pillow. There was a searing hurt worse than physical pain, and even curling up with a bottle of Old Yannissee was no help, as he dreaded the new nightmares that were sure to greet him as soon as he closed his eyes. When he awoke the next morning hungover and exhausted from the night's battles, he thought about taking the day off—he surely deserved it—but he knew that the only elixir that would soothe his soul would contain the same three ingredients that had always done the trick: work, work, and work.

So he dove back into the case, tying up loose ends. He and Eustace had fleshed out the timeline of the murders and Emme's planned getaway. Emme had figured it would take a week or two for the bodies to rise to the surface. It did not matter which one popped up first. In the meantime she had moved Cece's car over near the Peabody and planted some of Sykes's coke there. Her phone tip on Sykes had had the expected effect of leading them to Sykes's lair and the evidence she had left there to implicate him. Everyone would think he killed the girls and ran. Ricketts did not know about that, but apparently the phone tip gave him the idea to also finger Sticky Munro as payback.

Emme knew Sykes would never be found because she had "disappeared" him. As suspected, they found Slider's beat-up Bel

Air near Osceola, on the Arkansas side just across the river from Fulton. It was hidden in a dense grove of trees near the town's riverside port. So that was Emme's getaway car if she needed to cross the river to escape westward. She certainly had been a planner. The Bel Air's gas tank was topped, and its trunk was packed with suitcases full of new clothes, Lowenstein's price tags still on them, plus food and water so she could make a clean getaway.

On a hunch, they had brought in a bloodhound, which almost immediately located a shallow grave nearby where Slider Sykes had found his final resting place. Her fifth and sixth victims, Ricketts and Renfro, were given heroes' funerals where nothing was said of the greed that had gotten them killed. A few days later, someone discovered black roses on Ricketts's grave wrapped in an issue of the *Tri-State Guardian*, and the rumor was that it was the sign of a curse that would follow him into whichever Hereafter he was fated to find.

* * *

Eustace could only hope. Curse or prayer, what was the difference? As he stood next to Burdett and kicked a few stray pebbles onto the loose dirt of Emme's grave, he imagined that if indeed divine intention guided Ricketts's path in the afterlife, perhaps ultimate justice finally would be done. It must be. It had to be. At the last moment Fate had cheated him of the catharsis of revenge. Emme's bullet could not be the end of it. So he was okay with Ricketts's escape from rotting in prison for the rest of his life, if instead he burned in Hell for all eternity.

And now he had one last gift to give. Reaching inside his jacket he produced a single dark crimson rose wrapped in newspaper.

"I cut this from our garden just this mornin'," he said as he handed the rose to Burdett. "Maggie says this color is for grief and sorrow, which pretty much says it all. We thought you might like to leave somethin'."

"Thanks, Eustace. Yeah, I would." So Burdett gently laid the rose on Emme's grave and paused for a moment of silence that stretched into minutes.

What Eustace did not say was that he still did not understand how a man as sharp as Burdett could fall for a conniving schemer like Emme Bryce. She was truly evil, but Eustace had to hand it to her, she was good at it. If she had made her getaway even a day earlier, she could have pulled it off. He wondered why she had hung around for so long. Be that as it may, her atonement was now in God's hands, but just to be sure, Eustace bowed his head and said a silent prayer of his own to send her on her way.

Ironically, Emme's demise had become an unexpected blessing for Eustace. His life had changed forever since that fateful moonlit night on the river. He had found his true calling, and he embraced it. The backbiting and open resentment from his colleagues in Homicide had been replaced by a grudging respect, but Eustace had no illusions. He knew it would be a respect that had to be hard won every day, again and again. Except for Burdett. Through the alchemy of shared survival they had forged a new kinship that transcended everything, a brotherhood that was beyond words to describe. He now had a partner in the truest sense.

And from his perch in Homicide, Eustace continued to roll his eyes at the foibles of white Memphis. The murders were solved, but the craziness around Crump's Stash had taken longer to subside. As soon as it leaked that those suitcases of cash had gone into the Mississippi with Emme, a frenzy of treasure hunters began dragging the river for them. Looking out from Confederate Park at the vast flotilla of boats that stretched up and down the river, Eustace was reminded of the photos of the

D-Day armada, and the crowd that gathered to watch the spectacle rivaled the audience for the air show put on by the nearby Naval Air Station to celebrate V-J Day.

Then one fortunate treasure hunter named Wade Wadley got lucky. He snagged a leather suitcase embossed with the Boss's initials, floating in an eddy on the Arkansas side downstream from Fulton. At first, Wadley kept it to himself, but eventually he turned it in to the police hoping to get a reward. And of course, the suitcase went straight to Donlough's office. The call went down to Homicide for Eustace and Burdett to come up lickety-split and see it, and as they entered the Chief's outer office, the sound of Donlough's tirade behind closed doors made Eustace smile. In the inner office the whole cast of characters was assembled—Deputy Chief Ricketts, Marshmallow Miller, and what remained of the Stooges—all cowering from the Chief.

"Hot damn! Shee-it! Fuck Boss Crump! And fuck that Bryce bitch!" Chief Donlough was red-faced and raging. On the floor lay a sodden suitcase slowly leaking brown river water onto the plush carpet. And when Eustace and Burdett examined it, they could see why Wadley was willing to give it up. It stunk of river muck, and there was nothing inside but piles of Crump's sopping press clippings, photos, and keepsakes from his years in power, including a fake jewel-encrusted scepter inscribed "The Real King of the Cotton Carnival."

"Get that fuckin' garbage outta here! I never wanna see it again!" No one else moved, so Burdett and Eustace hastily gathered the suitcase and its contents and beat a retreat back to Homicide to take a closer look.

"It's like this suitcase contained his whole life," Burdett said as he examined a yellowed photo of an old house inscribed "Holly Springs, 1899." "If you ask me, maybe in the end this was the real treasure for Boss Crump. Maybe for Emme too."

"But don't that beat all," Eustace murmured, shaking his head. "Ten people dead and the whole city ready to explode, all for nothin'. It's like I said when you first asked me 'bout Crump's Stash. It was just white peoples' business and nothin' good would come of it."

"Any way you look at it, Eus, it's a tragedy," Burdett said.

★ ★ ★

Burdett admitted to himself that Eustace was right about the lost souls, but there was still a special pang of grief—and guilt—about one particular wasted life. He just wanted to put it all behind him, and he thought his wish might have been granted when the next day the case reached final closure: Emme's body surfaced downstream from Memphis. That put a damper on the treasure hunters. The second suitcase was never recovered—the river's currents made that impossible—so it appeared that Crump's Stash, if it ever existed, would remain entombed forever in that netherworld at the bottom of Old Man River. Oddly enough, Donlough seemed okay with that—just as long as no other players got their hands on it.

Meanwhile, as Harley had predicted, closing the Mound Builder murders had put Burdett back in the good graces of Chief Donlough, at least until Donlough changed his mind. In fact, Donlough was preening over how he had been so right about Emme Bryce all along. And thanks to a series of glowing articles by Winslow Hogue featuring Burdett and Eustace as heroes—amplified from the pages of the *Tri-State Guardian* and the pulpits of the black churches—the city felt a surge of gratitude toward both of them. Donlough managed to ride this by making a big show of waiving department policy and letting Burdett and Eustace accept the $50,000 reward from Palmer Quaid. Burdett then did the smart thing. Taking a page from his

Boss Crump playbook, he gave the Chief the lion's share of the credit, and then from his half he quietly peeled off a thousand as a contribution to Donlough's campaign chest. The Chief was mighty pleased.

"Bird Dog, we gonna make a politician outta you yet!"

Splitting the reward money with Eustace had ruffled a ton of jealous feathers around the department, but thinking black votes, Donlough would have none of it. In any case, Burdett did not care. After all, he knew who the real hero was. He owed Eustace his life, for God's sake. And as he turned away from Emme's grave and slowly walked down the hill to the Studebaker with Eustace at his side, Detective Burdett Vance had no doubt that his newly promoted partner, Detective Eustace Johnson, now a legend in the white and black communities alike, had fully earned his separate and equal share.

⋆ ⋆ ⋆

And Eustace? He was okay with that. After all, white money is still just as green, and as wise Maggie said, justice beats vengeance every time.

EPILOGUE

The tugboat *Cairo Queen* surged against the current as it slowly powered its way upstream just south of Natchez. Perched at the bow of the *Queen*, Milo Tate felt the sun warming his back as he cupped his hands and relit a fat stogie to cap off a tasty meal of canned beef stew and corn bread, courtesy of Captain Billy. A southerly breeze off the stern kept pace with the boat, giving the illusion that the air was still. It was oddly incongruous with the rumble of the engine and the rush of water all around them as the Mississippi streamed by on its twisted path southward toward the Gulf. Milo was feeling toasty. The whole world was feeling A-OK.

The layover in New Orleans had been just the ticket. Girls, music, booze, sleep, repeat. And this time his bankroll had almost held up long enough too. After his cash ran out, he trudged back to the boat only a day early. The way he saw it, he needed the extra day anyway just to shake off that creeping hangover that had started in his head and worked its way down to his toes. And now he was sunning himself like a turtle on a log and thinking that this dry run up to Memphis was a tonic, like being on vacation on a cruise ship. There was supposed to be a barge waiting for them when they arrived, piled high with cotton bales covered with olive drab canvas tarps, bound for downstream ports unknown. But in the meantime, no chores, nice weather, good chow, just lazin' the days away. Milo kept the mood going with whatever crooners he could find on the airwaves. Right now, it was Pat Boone blaring out "Ain't That a Shame" over the Natchez station. Another white man singin' race music for whites. What's the world comin' to?

Leaning over the rail and staring out at the wide river flowing toward him, Milo was thinking back to the dreary day when he had spied that dead girl floating north of Vicksburg. That had been his lucky day. It was big news in New Orleans when the story hit the *Times-Picayune* about a white girl up in Memphis killing other white girls and making it look as if it was a colored guy doing revenge killings. And old Milo himself had found the very first victim. He was a celebrity, and that story had been good for free drinks in every dive he hit from the Irish Channel to the French Quarter. Which is why his cash had held up so long this time.

That was also how he came to be smoking this big fat cigar that he had been nursing since yesterday, trying to make it last. He pulled hard to get it going again as his eyes scanned the current ahead looking for what other surprises the river might yet bring along. He was the hobo who finds a dollar on the sidewalk and keeps scouring the pavement for more, and he could not keep his eyes away from the passing parade of flotsam, just in case his luck held up. It was a way to pass the time and had become a pesky obsession since they had shoved away from the dock in New Orleans. He had gotten pretty good at hooking "whatnot," as he called his junk collection, to the point where Captain Billy said, "No more." But he could not help himself.

Maybe that was why he happened to spot something odd, half submerged, floating toward them. Manmade, like a floating board but with straps. Scampering along the deck toward the stern with his cigar clenched between his teeth, he grabbed a boat hook on the way and snagged the object as it bobbed by in the current, just barely afloat. It was a big leather suitcase, initials E. H. C. embossed on its side, and there was something heavy inside.

ACKNOWLEDGMENTS

There are countless people who deserve thanks for ushering this novel to completion. Let me mention a few. Even a little encouragement at the right time has a flywheel effect when the path forward is daunting and uncertain, and I am especially grateful to those who believed in this book at its nascent stages, including the gentlemen of the BBC and the many others who provided early feedback and encouragement as the story took shape.

I had incisive readings from friends Greg Jordan, Elliot Cafritz, and Jim Oliver, and from my daughter Isabel Selan, a voracious reader who perceptively alerted me to the perils and pitfalls of the manic pixie dream girl. Together, their feedback was infinitely helpful in sharpening the manuscript.

I thank those who make books their life's work and who devoted a portion of that life to this novel: my agent, John Talbot at Talbot Fortune Agency, who has been my trusty river guide sagely steering me through the shifting currents of the publishing world; and my wonderful editor, Marcia Markland at Crooked Lane Books, who made this dream real and made me real in the process, as well as the many other people who edited, designed, typeset, and launched this story.

I am indebted to my daughter Beryl Dann who so skillfully helps me navigate the shoals of the publicist's zeitgeist to get the right eyes on the right book on the right shelf, and to give me time to write. This has been a true gift and a great adventure to share with her.

Lastly and most of all, I am grateful to my wife, Melissa, who from the very first day that I uttered the word "novel" has been unstintingly supportive, saying in thought, word, and deed that she believed in me, and that has made all the difference.